DOUBLE TAKE

Also by Catherine Coulter

THE FBI THRILLERS

Point Blank (2005)

Blowout (2004)

Blindside (2003)

Eleventh Hour (2002)

Hemlock Bay (2001)

Riptide (2000)

The Edge (1999)

The Target (1998)

The Maze (1997)

The Cove (1996)

DOUBLE TAKE

Catherine Coulter

G. P. PUTNAM'S SONS | NEW YORK

G. P. PUTNAM'S SONS
Publishers Since 1838
Published by the Penguin Group
Penguin Group (USA) Inc., 375 Hudson Street, New York, New York 10014, USA • Penguin
Group (Canada), 90 Eglinton Avenue East, Suite 700, Toronto, Ontario M4P 2Y3, Canada
(a division of Pearson Penguin Canada Inc.) • Penguin Books Ltd, 80 Strand, London
WC2R 0RL, England • Penguin Ireland, 25 St Stephen's Green, Dublin 2, Ireland (a division
of Penguin Books Ltd) • Penguin Group (Australia), 250 Camberwell Road, Camberwell,
Victoria 3124, Australia (a division of Pearson Australia Group Pty Ltd) • Penguin Books
India Pvt Ltd, 11 Community Centre, Panchsheel Park, New Delhi–110 017, India • Penguin
Group (NZ), 67 Apollo Drive, Rosedale, North Shore 0745, Auckland, New Zealand (a
division of Pearson New Zealand Ltd) • Penguin Books (South Africa) (Pty) Ltd, 24 Sturdee
Avenue, Rosebank, Johannesburg 2196, South Africa

Penguin Books Ltd, Registered Offices:
80 Strand, London WC2R 0RL, England

Library of Congress Cataloging-in-Publication Data

Coulter, Catherine.
Double take / Catherine Coulter.
p.   cm.
ISBN 978-0-399-15424-9
1. United States. Federal Bureau of Investigation—Fiction.   2. San Francisco (Calif.)—
Fiction.   3. Savich, Dillon (Fictitious character)—Fiction.   4. Sherlock, Lacey (Fictitious
character)—Fiction.   5. Government investigators—Fiction.   I. Title.
PS3553.O843D68   2007   2007009877
813'.54—dc22

Printed in the United States of America
1   3   5   7   9   10   8   6   4   2

Book design by Stephanie Huntwork

This is a work of fiction. Names, characters, places, and incidents either are the product of the
author's imagination or are used fictitiously, and any resemblance to actual persons, living or
dead, businesses, companies, events, or locales is entirely coincidental.

While the author has made every effort to provide accurate telephone numbers and Internet
addresses at the time of publication, neither the publisher nor the author assumes any
responsibility for errors, or for changes that occur after publication. Further, the publisher does
not have any control over and does not assume any responsibility for author or third-party
websites or their content.

To my beautiful sister, Diane,
and her new husband, Larry Horton.
I wish you both overflowing happiness.

~Catherine

DOUBLE TAKE

CHAPTER I

Thursday night

Julia was whistling. She was happy, she realized, actually happy, for the first time in what seemed like forever. The cops had finally given up, the media had gone on to new, more titillating stories to keep their ratings up. And the soulless paparazzi who lurked behind bushes, cars, and trees, one of them even crouched down behind a garbage can, trying to catch her—what?—meeting a lover so they could make a buck selling a photo to the *National Enquirer*? Or maybe writing a murder confession on a tree trunk? They'd moved on after six endless months, focusing their stalking cameras back on movie stars and entertainers who were a lot more interesting than she was. Fact was, it was her husband, Dr. August Ransom, who'd been the magnet for the media, not she. She'd been only a temporary diversion, just the black widow who'd probably gotten away with murdering a very famous man and medium, a man who spoke to dead people.

Free, at last I'm free.

She didn't know how far she'd walked from her home in Pacific Heights, but now she found herself strolling down Pier 39 on the bay, that purest of tourist attractions, with its shops and clever white-faced mimes and resident seals, all just spitting distance from Fisherman's Wharf. She'd stopped at the to-die-for fudge store, and now stood by the railing at the western side of Pier 39, chewing slowly on her precious piece of walnut fudge, watching the dozens of obese seals stretched out on flat wooden barges beside the pier. She heard the sounds of people talking around her, laughing, joking around, arguing, parents threatening or bribing their kids, all of it sounding so normal—it felt wonderful. In April, in San Francisco, it wasn't the April showers that brought the May flowers, it was the lovely webby fog that rolled through the Golden Gate Bridge. The amazing thing was the air even had a special April fog smell—fresh and new and tangy, a bit damp, with a bit of a bite.

She wandered to the end of the pier and looked across the water toward Alcatraz, which was not that far away, really, but the swim could kill you, either the vicious currents or the icy water.

She turned and leaned her elbows on the railing, watching the people hungrily. There weren't that many who wandered down to the very end of the pier. She watched the lights begin to come on. It was cooling down fast, but she didn't feel cold in her funky leather jacket. She'd found the jacket at a garage sale in Boston when she was in college, and it was still her favorite. August had looked both sour and amused when she'd worn that jacket. Because she didn't want to hurt his feelings, she never told him that wearing the jacket made her feel like the young Julia again—buoyant, in both her heart and spirit. But August wasn't here now, and she felt so lighthearted and young in that moment, it was as if she'd float right off the thick wooden planks.

She was unaware of just how much time passed, but suddenly there was more silence than sound around her, and all the lights were on. The few tourists who hadn't returned to their hotels for the night had entered one of the half-dozen nearby restaurants for dinner. She looked down at her watch—nearly seven-thirty. She remembered she had a dinner date at eight at the Fountain Club with Wallace Tammerlane, a name she knew he'd made up when he'd decided to go into the psychic business thirty years before. He'd been a longtime friend of August's, had told her countless times since her husband's death that August had been welcomed into *The Bliss*, that August actually didn't know who'd murdered him, nor did he particularly care. He was now happy, and he would always look out for her.

Julia had accepted his words. After all, Wallace was August's friend, as legitimate as her husband. But she knew August had scoffed at many of those so-called psychic mediums, shaken his head in disgust at their antics, even as he praised their showmanship. What did she believe? Like many people, Julia wanted to believe there were certain special people who could speak to the dead. She believed to her soul that August was one of them, but there were very few like him. She'd seen and met so many of the fakes during her years with August. Even though she'd said nothing, it seemed to her that, according to them, any loved ones who died, no matter the circumstances of their passing, were always blissfully happy in the afterlife, always content and at peace, even reunited with their long-dead pets. But she couldn't help but wonder if August really was happy in *The Bliss,* wonder if he didn't want the person who'd murdered him to pay. Who wouldn't? She did. She'd asked his friends and colleagues in the psychic medium world if they could discover who had killed him, but evidently none of them was possessed of that special gift. This lack of vision was unfortunate, especially for Julia, since the police had fastened their eyes on her and looked nowhere else, at least as far as she could tell.

She didn't know if August had been blessed with that particular gift. TV shows had psychics who could picture murderers, even feel them, see how they killed and who they killed, and who could help track them down. And there were even mediums who, in addition to being psychic, could also speak with the dead. Were any of these people for real? She didn't know.

Who killed you, August, who? And why? That was still the question always in her mind—why?

There was August's lawyer, Zion Leftwitz, who'd called her after her husband's death. August's estate, he'd said on her machine, it was very important, as were her responsibilities to that estate, an estate, she knew now, that wasn't all that substantial.

Obligations, she thought, always there, at least eighty percent of life.

She really didn't want to have dinner with Wallace, didn't want to hear his comforting words, hear yet again that August was at peace. Then she'd inevitably hear about Wallace's latest triumph, perhaps how he'd contacted the mayor's long-dead grandfather. She knew all the way to her boot heels he'd seriously dent her euphoria. And it also meant taking a taxi back home. She had to leave this magic place, she had to hurry.

"Excuse me, ma'am. That's Alcatraz out there, isn't it?"

She turned to see a tall black man, firm-jawed, wearing glasses, a long belted coat, standing close, smiling down at her.

She smiled up at him. "Yes, it is."

"I'm going to visit tomorrow. But tonight—do you know when the next ferry leaves for Sausalito?"

"No, but it's never long between runs. The schedule is on the side of the building over there, not five minutes from Pier 39—" As she turned slightly to point, he smashed his fist into her jaw. The force of the blow knocked her back against the wooden railing. She saw a bright burst of lights before her eyes, then she saw the flash of something silver in his hand, something sharp—dear God, a knife. Why? But words froze in her throat in a thick veil of terror. All her focus was on that silver knifepoint.

She heard a man shout, then heard, "FBI! Stop now, back away from her, or I'll shoot!"

The man with the knife froze an instant, then cursed. He hefted her up and threw her over the railing into the bay. She splashed into the icy water and rolled over the mess of black rocks that stabbed her like stiletto blades. She tried to struggle, but knew in a flicker of consciousness that she wasn't going to escape this, that she was going to fall and fall—was that a seal honking? Was that someone shouting? It didn't matter because everything was going black as her body settled into the jumbled rocks at the bottom of the bay, the water smoothing over her. Her last thought, really more an echo, was that she wouldn't ever get to be happy again.

The weight on her chest was rhythmic and hard, yet somehow separate from her body. Then someone's mouth was against hers, and a huge burst of hot air blasted down her throat, deep, filling her. It felt odd, but then it simply didn't matter. She drifted away.

A man's hard-edged voice shouted in her face—"Don't you let go! Do you hear me? You come back here. Now! I had trouble enough getting you out of the damned bay, not a ladder in sight. Lucky we didn't both drown, so don't you dare let go on me!"

She felt a slap, two, on her cheeks, sharp, stinging, then more hard pressing against her chest, and that brought her closer. The pressure came inside her, hard and harder still, and she felt each and every sharp blow all the way to her backbone.

"Come on back now! Dammit, breathe!"

His mouth was on hers again and his breath was hot again, blessed heat that burrowed deep inside her. She was so cold, freezing, but that hot breath was like a bellows pumping through her. Suddenly, she wanted that heat. She sucked it in madly.

The man's voice, his breath hot on her cheek now, said over and over, "That's it, that's right, come on now, you can do it. Don't give up."

"More," she whispered, not knowing if she'd even spoken aloud. He flipped her onto her stomach and began pounding her back with his fists. When water spewed out of her mouth, he quickly pulled her onto her side. She heaved and gasped, so cold she wanted to scream, but he slapped her back hard again with the heel of his hand and more water gushed out, then slowed to a dribble, snaking down her chin.

She wheezed and shuddered and said, her voice hoarse, "The seals aren't honking anymore."

The sharp slaps against her back stopped. The man said, "Yeah, they've closed down for the day. Hang on now." He rubbed her back rhythmically, and she coughed again, hoarse and loud, and more water dribbled out of her mouth. Where was all that water coming from?

When he couldn't get another drop of water out of her, the man pulled her up to a sitting position and forced her head between her knees. She breathed hard, couldn't seem to stop shuddering.

"Good, that's it, keep sucking in air." He yanked off her wet leather jacket and pulled his heavy sports coat around her.

She hiccupped. "My jacket, my poor jacket. I've had it since I was a sophomore at Boston College."

"It's so tatty it'll have to survive. What's a little water? Hey, I came out of the Crab House and saw that guy clip you on the jaw—and I saw the knife. When I yelled at him, he knew time had run out and he threw you over the railing. He knew I couldn't chase him then, knew I was going right for you, had to get you out of the water. I couldn't even shoot at him—there wasn't time."

"Shoot him? What on earth do you mean?"

Another man's voice came out of the darkness. "Hey, Cheney, can't I leave you alone for a single minute? Where's June? I thought she only came out for a cigarette. I thought you came out to fetch her. What's going on here? Who is this?"

The man sprinted over, squatted beside the two of them, and stared down at her, his expression appalled. "What happened here? Did she try to commit suicide?"

He'd asked the man who'd rescued her, the one called Cheney, but she was alive, thank you very much, and so she answered, "No, a man punched me, but he ran out of time before he could finish me off, so he threw me over the railing. It happened so fast I didn't have time to react at all. He—Cheney—stopped him. He saved me." She paused, giving him a crooked grin. "That's a strange name but I'm used to strange names. Mine's not strange, it's sort of boring, really."

"What is your name?"

"I'm Julia."

Cheney smiled, kept rubbing her back. "It's not all that boring."

The other man stared at her like she was nuts, but she really didn't care. She felt wonderfully tired and slumped back against Cheney's hands. "My jaw feels like someone exploded a bomb inside my face."

"Yeah, I'll bet," Cheney said. "No, no, don't you let go now. Straighten up, you can do it." Cheney lifted her back to a sitting position, pounded her back a couple more times. Thank the good Lord there was nothing left to come up. "That's it, no more water in you. Now get yourself together, Julia. You're going to be all right." He grabbed her arms and shook her. "Time to get a grip here. Come on now!"

She opened her eyes and yelled, "Stop it, you baboon! My head's going to break off my neck."

He stopped shaking her. "Okay, but don't try to fade out again or I'll whack you some more."

She heard a woman's voice. "Cheney? Manny? What's going on here? I finished my cigarette, but neither of you were at the table when I went back inside. Linda said Manny had come to look for you, Cheney. Come on back inside, they just brought our dinner. Hey, what's this?"

Cheney slowly got to his feet, pulling Julia up with him, anchoring her against his side so she wouldn't fall on her face. No, that wasn't going to work. He picked her up in his arms. "Sorry, June. I guess you could say I'm back on duty. You and Manny go back on in and enjoy the cioppino, it's supposed to be the Crab House specialty, the best in San Francisco. This is work, so I've got to attend to it. I'll call you later."

"I'm not work. I'm Julia."

"Yeah, I know."

"What time is it?"

"Nearly eight o'clock."

"Oh dear. I don't think I'm going to be able to make dinner with Wallace."

June said, "What does she mean, she's Julia? You're sopping wet, Cheney. Who is this woman, what—"

Manny said, "Cheney, you want me to call 911?"

"Nah, you go back in and entertain everyone. I'll do it. Sorry, June. I'll call you tomorrow." Cheney hoped the now quiescent woman in his arms wasn't going to freeze to death on him, particularly not after all his hard work, not after he'd bundled her in his wool sports coat.

Manny said, "We've just seen our tax dollars at work. Come on, June. Cheney, thanks for the excitement. Call me tomorrow, let me know what happens."

Cheney nodded to Manny as he pulled out his cell phone and punched in 911. "I need an ambulance at Pier 39—"

His words made sudden sense to her. With all her remaining strength, Julia grabbed his wet collar. "Please, please, not the hospital, please not the paramedics, no doctors, oh God, please, Cheney—"

"Look, Julia, you're—"

"I'll die if you take me to a hospital."

It was the utter certainty in her voice that stopped him cold. He flipped off his cell. "All right, no hospital. What, then? Where do you live?"

He realized she was afraid to tell him.

He saw some tourists standing a few feet away, looking toward them, speaking among themselves. "This is just great. I save your butt and you're scared to tell me where you live. Will you at least tell me your last name, Julia?"

She started to shake her head but it was simply too much trouble. She whispered, "Julia . . . Jones."

"Oh yeah, like I'm going to believe that one. Give me your address or I'm driving you right over to San Francisco General."

She gave him her address. Deadening fear settled inside her, jagged and hard. Her jaw throbbed, and sharp licks of pain suddenly leaped to life in every part of her body. But there was his coat—"I hope I don't ruin your lovely jacket. This is very fine wool."

"Like your leather jacket, it's been through the wars."

Cheney began the long trek back to the entrance of Pier 39, her wet leather jacket over the top of his coat. He shook her every once in a while and said each time, "Don't go to sleep. I mean it."

He thought she said she wasn't stupid, but couldn't be sure.

CHAPTER 3

M ost stores on the pier were closed and dark, and tourists were thin on the ground. A woman with two children in tow asked if he needed assistance.

"No, I've got things under control. Thank you."

"That's nice of her," Julia said, nodding at the woman, who was staring after them. Cheney grunted. He was wet and cold, his feet squishing in his nicely polished leather boots. Her head lolled on his shoulder.

"Wake up!"

"Yeah, okay," but her voice was slurred. "Why isn't your coat wet?"

"I was bright enough to toss it, my gun, my wallet, and my cell on the pier before I jumped in after you."

After ten minutes of hassle with the parking garage attendant, which included trying to get Cheney to go back to Pier 39 to get his ticket validated so he wouldn't have to pay the huge parking fee himself, he navigated over to Lombard, left up Fillmore, then right on Broadway until she said, "It's that one, there, on the left, no lights on." He pulled into the driveway of a mansion—no other way to refer to the incredibly beautiful three-story brick house with tall thick bushes enclosing it on both sides. He could make out ivy climbing the pale brick walls. He parked in the empty triple driveway, a marvel in San Francisco, where trying to find a parking place to pick up your dry cleaning could make a saint go postal. Cheney was sure the views from all the windows were to die for.

"Nice digs," he said.

He'd been talking nonstop to her, no, more *at* her, really, but she'd occasionally murmur an answer so he knew she was hanging on. His car heater had been blasting full force and he wondered why his wet clothes weren't steaming by now. He knew his bringing her home was absurd. Well, if she needed medical help, he knew a doctor who owed him a favor. He'd never forget Dillon Savich telling him at Quantico that it was always smart to have a physician in your debt because you simply never knew when you'd need to call in the marker. Now was probably the time. She was shivering violently, despite his coat, despite the incredible heat from the heater.

"Your purse," he said. "You don't have it."

"I didn't have a purse. My house keys were in my pocket wrapped in a twenty-dollar bill."

He felt inside both pockets of her wet leather jacket and pulled out a crumpled wet Kleenex. "No keys. How am I going to get you inside your house?"

He saw she was trying to figure this out. He waited, then asked her again. "I'm thinking," she said, and she sounded unsure. That worried him and he wondered what Dr. Ben Vrees was doing this fine Thursday evening on his houseboat in Sausalito.

He took her shoulders in his hands and shook her, hard.

"How do I get in, Julia?"

She said, without pause, "There's a key beneath the pansies at the bottom of the second pot by the front door."

"Oh, wow, what a great hiding place," and he rolled his eyes.

"Let's just see you find it," she said, her voice sharp and nasty.

He smiled. She was back with him.

It took him at least three minutes to dig all the way to the bottom of the six-inch pot filled with bright purple pansies to find that damned key, which he then had to wipe on his once-very-nice black wool slacks. He'd pulled them out of the back of his closet for his first date in a good two months. June Canning, a very nice woman, a stockbroker for the Pacific Stock Exchange. He sighed. Oh well, who wanted to spend time between dinner courses outside with a woman who still smoked? And in California?

No alarm sounded when he unlocked the door. Big mistake, he thought. He went back to his Audi, a car that was a bit on the small side for a man his size, sure, but he could park it just about anywhere in the city, even in the narrow alley beside his cleaners. He hauled her out and held her against his side.

Once inside, he found the hall light and flipped it on. He gawked, couldn't help it. He'd never been in such a spectacular house in his life. Truth be told, he'd visited quite a few beautifully restored homes in Pacific Heights over his last four years in San Francisco, but none of them had been on this magnificent scale. But he didn't pause, he simply guided her straight up the wide maple staircase with ornately carved pineapples atop the two newel posts. It wound to a wide landing on the second floor and looked back down into the large entry hall. The ceiling over the entry hall was three stories high, cathedral tall, with an antique gold and crystal chandelier hanging down at least eighteen feet. He wondered how much that sucker weighed, and what you had to do to clean it.

"Which way?"

"To the left."

"Which bedroom is yours? Oh, isn't this a lovely thought—is there a husband lurking around?"

"Not anymore," she said, her voice as flat as the wet hair on her head. "All the way to the end of the hall."

The hallway was wide, its lovely polished maple planks gleaming alongside an antique carpet that ran the hall's full length. He supposed he should have been prepared when he turned on the bedroom light, but he wasn't. He stopped in his tracks for a full second. It was big, bigger than his living room, with impossibly high ceilings and intricately carved hundred-year-old moldings. He saw another door: it wasn't the bathroom, but an immense walk-in closet. The next door did lead into a mammoth bathroom laid with creamy yellow tile with an assortment of colorful Italian country-scene squares set at random on the floor and up the walls. He set her on the closed toilet seat and turned on the shower. Tested it. When it was nice and hot, he turned to see her slumping forward again. He stripped her to her underwear, sensible stuff, no fluff and lace, opened the shower stall door, stopped, and eyed her. If he put her in the shower, she might fall on her face and drown. The fact was, he was cold, too.

He set her down again. "Don't fall over, you got me?"

"No, I won't," and he watched her list to the left until her cheek rested against the toilet paper roll fastened to the side of the long marble counter.

He stripped down to his boxers and undershirt, set his SIG, his cell, and his wallet on the counter, looked at his once-beautiful sports coat in a heap with the old leather jacket and the rest of her clothes on the floor. As he stepped with her into the large shower, Cheney wondered if showering with a just-rescued stranger was in the Quantico manual. He pulled the glass door shut and set her directly under the spray of hot water.

She yelled and tried to pull away from him.

Actually, he felt like yelling right along with her when sharp needles of hot water struck his flesh.

He held her tight until she stopped struggling, then rubbed his hands up and down her arms and her back. She was thin, too thin, but she wasn't small-boned, she wasn't fragile. Was she naturally thin or was it because of something else?

Julia slowly felt herself getting warm, this time from the outside in, and she was getting stronger too. She said against his neck, "I can stand up by myself now, thank you."

He let her go. "How much longer will the hot water last?"

"It's probably getting near the end of its run." She pushed open the door and stepped out, knowing his hand was there to catch her.

He turned off the water and followed her. He looked at her closely and was reassured. She was with him, strong again, and alert. A large bruise was blooming on her jaw, along with many other smaller bruises and abrasions on her arms, ribs, and legs from hitting the rocks in the bay on her way down.

She looked him up and down and smiled. "Thank you for saving me. Nice boxers."

"Thank you. Nice smile." She was there behind her eyes, and he smiled as he added, "You're welcome."

"I'll get some dry clothes for you." She tossed him an oversized towel, took one for herself, and left him in the bathroom.

When he came into her bedroom a few minutes later, she was wearing a thick bathrobe and socks, her head wrapped turban-style in a towel. She held a pile of men's clothing in her hands.

"August was nearly as tall as you," she said as she gave him a clinical look. He was wearing only the big towel, wrapped and knotted around his waist. "He was heavier, particularly around the waist, but you can tighten the belt."

Cheney went back into the bathroom, stared down at his own sodden clothes. Well, everything should dry. But there was no hope for the expensive wool pants, the same ones he'd worn at his graduation from the Academy, two funerals, and tonight, his first date in too long a time.

Instead of boxers, he pulled on jockey shorts, a white T-shirt, and a large dark blue cashmere sweater that felt like sin against his skin. The pants were loose, but he simply pulled his own belt tighter like she'd suggested, and the sweater covered it. The garden-variety dark chinos were long enough. He looked down at his bare feet. A moment later, she called out, "Here are some socks. What size shoe do you wear?"

"Twelve."

"A bit small, sorry."

Her hand passed a pair of Italian loafers through the open door. The leather was so soft he bet he could eat it if he got hungry enough.

When he stepped out of the bathroom, she called out from inside the huge walk-in closet, "Be with you in a moment. Listen, I'm fine, don't worry, all right? I think I'm nearly ready to sweat I'm so warm now. I'm not about to collapse in here."

"Okay." He pulled out his cell and began to dial his SAC, Bert Cartwright, a pompous ass much of the time because he was blessed with a photographic memory for faces and liked to flaunt it, but he stopped. No, this was local police business. He found Frank at home watching a basketball game, his son carping in the background because Frank wouldn't let him borrow his car.

"Hey, Frank, I got a problem for you."

CHAPTER 4

Captain Frank Paulette, SFPD, said, "Gee, thanks a lot, Cheney. Here I was all bored, watching the Warriors kick the crap out of the Lakers, a miracle in the making."

"Which quarter?"

"The second."

"No miracle's going to happen tonight, trust me on this. Listen, Frank, I got a situation here and it's local, not federal. I got an attempted murder for you." And Cheney told him what had happened.

Frank listened, not saying a word, sighed, and raised his eyes to the ceiling. "Why me, Lord? Okay, okay, I know why. I'm a trouble magnet. Wait, don't tell me. You never saw this guy up close?"

"Nope, and there wasn't anything distinctive about him, either. Tall, black, moved fast and smooth, like an athlete. He knew what he was doing, no panic, no hesitation. When I yelled at him that I was FBI and I'd shoot, he made no attempt at all to take me on. He threw her over the railing into the bay and ran."

"Maybe all he had was that knife, no gun. Maybe he was just a mugger, not about to take on a fed, or draw an audience."

"We're not talking an attempted mugging here, Frank. This guy was a pro. Everything he did was professional, even his decision to cut and run. She'll need protection. He's got to assume she survived."

"Okay, I'll buy the guy's a pro. The woman's all right?"

"Yeah. She didn't want to go to the hospital, so I brought her home."

"That's pretty stupid, Cheney. What's her problem?"

"I don't know, but she sounded terrified. She was shivering so badly, I went ahead and brought her home, put her under a hot shower. She's okay."

Another sigh. "What's her name?"

"Ah, well, how about Julia—"

She said quietly, not two feet from him, "My name is Julia Ransom." A slight pause, a deep indrawn breath. "I'm Dr. August Ransom's widow."

Cheney stared at her, dumbfounded. Sodden and hacking up water, she hadn't looked remotely familiar. Of course he recognized her now. The media had been merciless. It hadn't mattered that she'd never been arrested, everyone assumed she was guilty. There were insinuations of police incompetence and collusion, of her sleeping with the chief of police, a happily married Irishman with six children.

"I heard her, Cheney," Frank Paulette said, but he repeated her name aloud, as if he really didn't believe it. "Julia Ransom," he said again. "Well, my boy, you never do things halfway, do you?" Frank fell silent. Cheney heard Frank's wife shouting at him in the background to take out the garbage, heard his son laughing now and the crowd screaming because Kobe Bryant had just scored a three-pointer—no more miracle in the making, at least in this game.

Cheney gave Frank the address, to which Frank said, "I know the damned address. I'll be there in twenty, Cheney. Keep our lady safe. You sure this wasn't a mugger?"

Cheney nearly smiled at the hopefulness in Frank's voice.

"Sorry, Frank. He was out to kill her."

"I'll get a couple of cars over there to keep an eye on her."

"Yeah, okay." Cheney punched off his cell, slipped it into August Ransom's pants pocket.

"The police are coming?"

"Yes. Captain Frank Paulette."

"I thought just about all of them had questioned me, but I don't know him."

"Look, I had no choice. Someone tried to kill you. Frank's a good guy, I've known him for nearly four years, almost as long as I've lived in San Francisco. He won't badger you or treat you like—"

He stalled. She said nothing at all.

He saw she'd spread her leather jacket over the back of an antique chair older than Waterloo, his sports coat on a matching chair beside it.

He said, "I spread out the rest of my wet clothes in the bathroom."

"I'll take care of them. I have a special dry cleaners who'll fix up your sports coat and your slacks. Here's a jacket for you in the meantime."

"Thank you."

She nodded and strode firmly out of the bedroom, wearing old baggy jeans, a red 49ers sweatshirt, and blue Nike running shoes. She'd pulled her damp hair into a ponytail, hair the color of his ancient mahogany desk, dark and rich. She wasn't wearing any makeup. She looked very young.

Cheney walked down the long hallway after her, wearing the dark blue cashmere jacket she'd handed him. She paused a moment after he'd shrugged into it, then slowly nodded. He saw she was tall, with long legs that ate up that endless carpet. He bet she could move in those running shoes of hers.

He could have been enjoying the cioppino with some nice crunchy French bread, but no, Frank was right. Cheney never managed to do anything halfway. *Julia Ransom, Dr. August Ransom's widow.* Well, it would soon cease to be his problem.

She turned at the bottom of the stairs to look up at him. "You look fine in August's clothes. Again, no matter what you think of me—now that you know who I am—thank you for saving me. I'll have your clothes cleaned and sent to you. How do you know a local police officer?"

"I'm a cop too, just not local."

"So you're a tourist cop?"

"Actually, no."

A dark eyebrow remained raised.

She didn't remember? Understandable, he thought, and shrugged. "I'm federal. I'm Special Agent Cheney Stone, FBI, with the San Francisco Field Office."

She stared at him a moment, then threw back her head and

laughed until she almost choked. She knuckled her eyes with her fists, like his teenaged niece.

She said, once she'd caught her breath, "I remember now, you yelled that to the guy who was going to kill me. Oh dear, I've got to call Wallace Tammerlane and tell him I won't make it for our dinner."

He watched her dash to a lovely table set against the corridor wall that held a telephone and a vase of fresh azaleas. He himself called his longtime friend Manny Dolan, told him what was happening, but he didn't tell him Julia's name.

"Damn, Cheney, I think June wanted to jump your bones. She's not a happy camper."

"Keep repeating what a hero I am, okay?"

"Yeah, sure. Have fun with the widow."

When Julia joined him again, she said only, "Wallace wanted to come over, but I told him no. Believe me, you don't want a flamboyant psychic medium interacting with cops. Not a good mix."

"No," Cheney said slowly, "I don't suppose it would be."

CHAPTER 5

Captain Frank Paulette arrived with the two inspectors who'd been the leads on the Dr. August Ransom murder case the previous fall and into the winter—Inspector Rainy Bigger and Inspector Allen Whitten.

The two inspectors nodded at Julia Ransom, saying nothing at all. Cheney saw a flash of contempt on Inspector Rainy Bigger's face, which made him frown, but there was only professional indifference on Inspector Allen Whitten's face. Frank stepped forward and introduced himself to Julia, shook her thin white hand.

Cheney noticed there was no wedding ring on her finger, no jewelry of any kind.

"You're sure you don't want to see a doctor, Mrs. Ransom? That bruise on your jaw looks pretty bad."

She lightly touched her fingertips to her jaw, opened and closed her mouth a couple of times. "It's not broken, only looks bad. Thank you for your concern, Captain Paulette." She looked at Inspectors Whitten and Bigger, weary resignation on her face. "Please come in. This is Agent Cheney Stone."

Both Bigger and Whitten shook his hand. *A fed*, Cheney knew they were thinking, and that meant they wondered whether he enjoyed kicking local cops before breakfast.

Inspector Rainy Bigger gave Julia the once-over, not bothering to mask her dislike. "You're looking particularly well, considering someone smacked you in the face and dumped you into the bay, Mrs. Ransom."

Julia knew Bigger believed she'd killed August and had gotten away with it. She hated how the inspector's hostility made her feel defensive, reduced her to feeling unworthy to be alive. She said, voice clipped, "Thank you. Good genes."

"Or something else altogether," said Inspector Bigger.

Julia said, "Agent Stone, do you think I smacked myself in the jaw, then happily hopped over the railing into the bay for a nice evening swim?"

"No, of course not," Cheney said, and sent Inspector Bigger a *back-off* look.

"No, that isn't what you mean, is it, Inspector Bigger?" Julia said slowly. "You're thinking a falling out among villains, perhaps?"

Inspector Bigger kept her mouth shut, but gave an elaborate shrug.

Cheney was relieved the inspector did have some minimal sense of professionalism.

Inspector Whitten said, "It would appear someone is out to hurt you, Mrs. Ransom."

"I'm thinking the knife put it beyond the 'hurt me' stage, Inspector Whitten," Julia said.

He nodded toward a beautiful Impressionist painting hanging over the Carrara marble fireplace. "That new?"

"You mean did I purchase it with my ill-gotten gains?"

That's exactly what he meant, Cheney realized, but he didn't say anything. He wanted to hear what Julia would say.

Julia said, "August wasn't fond of the Impressionists. I am. I brought it down from my study. It's a Sisley. My husband bought it for me as a wedding present. Do you like it, Inspector Whitten?"

"Well, yes, I do. Bet it cost Dr. Ransom a bundle. So who do you think is after you, ma'am?"

"The man wasn't a mugger or some crazy drug addict. Given how he behaved, what he did—it occurred to me he could be the person who murdered my husband. He would have killed me if it hadn't been for Agent Stone."

"Yeah, Cheney is a hero," Inspector Bigger said.

Frank frowned at both inspectors. Maybe it hadn't been smart to bring them, particularly Inspector Bigger. She was a tangled mess of anger. Why? He'd need to speak to Lieutenant Vincent Delion, who'd be back from vacation in a couple of days, or hell, maybe it was a week before Vincent was back. He said, "It's been six months since your husband was murdered, Mrs. Ransom. Why would your husband's murderer want you dead now? Perhaps you remembered something about him or her? Perhaps you found something that could implicate someone and this person found out?"

"I don't think so, Captain Paulette." But Julia frowned. "I'll have to give that a lot of thought."

Cheney said, "The attempt on your life means something's changed, Julia. Think hard about what's different now, about what could have drawn the murderer out into the open again."

Inspector Bigger said, "You're still big buddies with all the psychics in the Bay Area, aren't you, Mrs. Ransom?"

"I see them occasionally." Like Wallace, tonight for dinner.

"Word is you all hang out together, like a club of sorts."

"What word?" Julia said to Inspector Bigger.

"Bits and pieces, here and there," said Inspector Bigger.

Captain Paulette said, "I haven't heard any word, Inspector. Maybe the real question here is, who stands to gain from your death?"

"No one, Captain Paulette. I have no living relatives. Well, perhaps there are some cousins four times removed, but I don't know who they are. I do have a will. Everything goes to various medical research foundations."

"All right. Now, please, Mrs. Ransom, if you're feeling up to it, tell us exactly what happened."

Julia didn't tell them she'd actually felt happy, that the paparazzi had finally abandoned their various posts in the neighborhood, that she'd felt so alive she'd walked all the way to Fisherman's Wharf, sometimes running for the sheer joy of it, sometimes whistling, saying hi to everyone she met. "I was standing at the railing at the far end of Pier 39, looking toward Alcatraz, watching the fog roll through the Golden Gate. It was getting late. There weren't that many tourists left. The lights were coming on. I realized I had to get home because I had a dinner engagement." She paused, drew in a deep breath. "He was tall, black, nice clothes, smart eyes—you know, like he saw everything and knew what it meant. He wore skinny-rimmed glasses, and he was very polite, asked me about Alcatraz, then about a ferry to Sausalito. I remember he had a nice smile, made me smile back. I told him about the ferry, then turned to show him where to walk to see the schedule. He hit me in the jaw, to daze me, I guess, and then he had a knife in his hand—it was silver, and I saw it had a sharp point, but before he could stab me with it, Agent Stone yelled at him to stop, and so the man hefted me over the wooden railing into the bay." She frowned. "There weren't any seals down there but I swear I heard one of them honking close by before I went under."

"The man only asked about Alcatraz, then the ferry schedule to Sausalito?"

"Yes, Inspector Whitten, that's all. He didn't seem at all threatening. He was well-spoken, over six foot, I'd say, nice-looking, and again, he was very well dressed."

Inspector Bigger marveled aloud, "Only you saw this knife, right? Maybe you didn't really see a knife, Mrs. Ransom, maybe this man was a mugger who nailed you as someone really rich—"

"Rainy—" Inspector Whitten said, warning in his voice. "You said he smiled at you, Mrs. Ransom?"

Cheney saw Julia withdraw, though she hadn't moved at all. But she was stiff all over now, hating this, hating them. She said, voice steady, "Yes, Inspector Whitten, and I smiled back, as I told you. It was impossible not to. He was wearing a Burberry coat, it had that look. Expensive, I'd say. I'm sorry, but I don't remember anything else about him. Then I heard Agent Stone shouting at him."

She watched Frank Paulette write down what she said in a

small notebook. He was left-handed, like she was. He said to Cheney, "How well did you see the guy?"

"I saw his face only once, when he turned around to look at me when I yelled at him. Then he heaved her over the railing and took off. Like I told you, I got the impression he was an athlete, fast, supple. As to his age, he moved young, agile. I didn't even have time to draw my gun. I couldn't go after him because I had to haul out Mrs. Ransom."

"Good timing," Inspector Bigger said.

"Yes, I sure thought so," Julia said, smiling hard at Bigger. "Hey, you think maybe I set the whole thing up to get Agent Stone on my side? Ah, may I ask why I need him on my side? Actually, I didn't think I had a side. Am I missing something here?"

Cheney smiled to himself. There was strength there, he thought, and waited.

Inspector Bigger backed off.

Cheney wondered what had happened between the two women during the investigation into her husband's murder.

Inspector Whitten said to Cheney, to get the attention off his partner, "You got no hint of recognition from this man? Nothing about him was familiar to you?"

Cheney shook his head. "Only that I'd bet the farm the guy's a pro. He was fast and efficient. He didn't alarm her. If I hadn't been outside looking for a friend who was smoking, Mrs. Ransom would be dead. He did exactly what he needed to do to get away, once he realized I was an immediate danger to him. Now the thing is—" He paused a moment. "We know he meant to kill her because he didn't mind that she got a really good look at him. And he knows he very probably failed to kill her. He's also got to know we'll have sketches of him plastered everywhere. He'd be crazy to stay in San Francisco."

Captain Paulette said, "Do you think you got a good enough look at him to help a police artist make up a sketch of him, Mrs. Ransom?"

CHAPTER 6

Yes," Julia said. "I'll never forget his face as long as I live."

"Good," Cheney said. "I got something of a look as well. We'll do it separately, then compare."

Inspector Bigger started to say something, but her brain caught up with her mouth, and she kept quiet.

Captain Paulette pulled out his cell. "I'll see if I can't get Otis over here right now. He lives on Potrero Hill so it shouldn't take him long this time of night. Hey, if I missed the Warrior-Laker game, so can Otis."

"The Warriors are down," Inspector Bigger said. "I was listening to the game on the way over here."

Cheney realized it was only nine o'clock. He said, "Frank, the FBI has a facial recognition program they've modified to allow you to plug in an artist's sketch. We used it a couple months back and caught the perp. We can do it again."

Captain Paulette nodded. "That sounds hopeful, if you're right and this guy is a pro. Yeah, I met the agent who was one of the guiding hands behind it—Dillon Savich. He and his wife, Lacey Sherlock, and another agent, Dane Carver, were here a while ago."

"Yes," Cheney said, nodding, "when Dane's brother was murdered."

"The Script Murders," Inspector Whitten said, leaning forward in his chair. "Lieutenant Delion still talks about it."

Cheney said, "Then you know they aren't into big-footing locals."

"Others in that nice big federal zoo of yours are, Cheney."

"Yeah, well, Frank, what can I tell you. I can speak to Savich personally, see what he can do with the sketch after Mrs. Ransom gives us the guy's face."

Julia remembered the Script murderer who had butchered three people in San Francisco, including a priest. She shuddered to think she was part of that world now. She rose. "While we're waiting for the police artist, I'll make everyone coffee."

When she was out of the room, Inspector Rainy Bigger said, "She's making the coffee? The help goes home at night?"

"Evidently so," Cheney said, and waited to see what else she'd say.

It didn't take her long. She jumped up from her chair and began pacing. "It's obvious one of her confederates decided to knock her off. Ain't that a kick? I guess she must have tried to screw him, or maybe she wanted to stop screwing him."

Captain Paulette said sharply, "That's enough, Inspector Bigger. No charges were ever brought against Mrs. Ransom. You don't have a clue why this guy tried to kill her tonight. None of us do. Yet."

Inspector Bigger looked like she still wanted to spew, but she wasn't stupid. She nodded, looked around the living room. "I'd forgotten what a palace this place is. And now it's all hers. What is she, twenty-eight?"

"Something like that, I'd guess," Captain Paulette said. "Hey, Cheney, why don't you go help Mrs. Ransom?"

Because she doesn't look at me like the enemy, Cheney thought, *Frank thinks she'll talk to me.* And maybe he was right. Cheney didn't say anything, just nodded and walked out into the vast front entrance hall. Which way was the damned kitchen?

He paused, heard a woman's voice, singing low and soft, and walked in that direction. The kitchen was halfway down the back hallway, on the left. Another room the size of his living room, he thought, staring at the array of stainless-steel appliances, with copper pots hanging over a huge center island, and gleaming Italian tiles. Julia was singing to herself, probably trying to keep her fear at bay, as she flipped off the European carafe and poured boiling water into a large glass French press carafe. He wondered if making coffee this way made it taste better.

"I'm here to help," he said, and shoved his hands into August Ransom's pants pockets.

Without looking up, she said, "In the cupboard beside the fridge you'll find some big mugs. I'll get a tray." She paused a moment. "Do you think I should put some cookies on a tray? Something like that?"

He grinned. "I was busy hauling you out of the bay, and I never had dinner. What kind of cookies do you have?"

"Oreos," she said.

"You got a couple dozen?"

"Yep, a brand new bag. Mrs. Filbert says it's the only way she can get me to drink milk."

"Mrs. Filbert?"

Her chin went up. "My cook."

She pulled out a big tray from a drawer beneath the island, a bright beach scene, he saw. As he set out the oversized mugs on the tray, he asked, "Why does Inspector Bigger hate your guts?"

She paused, then walked into the pantry. She reemerged with a big unopened bag of Oreos. He watched her domino the cookies into a circle on a plate and set it on the tray. "You could answer that question yourself, Agent. She believes I murdered my husband. Actually, I think she'd have been singing hallelujahs if I'd drowned tonight or gotten a knife shoved into my throat."

"Yeah, I got that impression too. With her behavior tonight, I doubt you'll have to see her again. Captain Paulette will probably tell her lieutenant she couldn't keep herself professional. The last thing the SFPD needs is your lawyers taking them apart for her behavior toward you."

She shrugged. "Why bother?"

"Yeah, if I were you, I'd rather clip her in the chops."

She looked perfectly serious and clenched her hands. "That would be nice."

He laughed, picked up the tray, and preceded her out of the vast kitchen, their footsteps echoing on the tile.

Ten minutes later Captain Paulette let in the police artist, Danny Otis. "Hey, Captain, do you know the Warriors came this close"—Danny's fingers were nearly touching—"to beating the

Lakers? Well, okay, they fell quite a ways behind after the second quarter, but it wasn't a total wipeout like I expected."

Captain Paulette grunted. "Yeah, right, that's great news. You got your computer? Good, come on in, Danny, let's see what you can get from Mrs. Ransom."

By ten o'clock the Oreos were gone, two pots of coffee were history, and the two sketches Danny got from Julia Ransom and Agent Cheney Stone were done, and surprisingly similar to each other. The detail in Julia's was impressive.

Cheney said, "There are a few differences—but since Mrs. Ransom saw him up close and personal, believe her over me. Do you want me to run with this, Frank? Send it off to Dillon Savich in Washington?"

"Let's make copies first, then yeah, let's see what he can come up with. Okay, guys," he added to the two inspectors, "we'll be able to add this sketch to the APB on this perp. Let's make sure we get it out to the whole Bay Area." He turned to Julia. "Mrs. Ransom, if you think of anything more, call me," and he gave her his card. "I'm having a patrol car sit out in your driveway tonight, all right?"

"Thank you." Julia showed all of them out, then turned to face Cheney, who'd remained standing next to her. "I'll need your address, Agent, so I can return your clothes after they've been cleaned."

He pulled out one of his FBI cards, wrote his address on the back as well as his cell number, and handed it to her. "You're looking a bit on the pale side, Julia. Get yourself to bed. I'll check with you in the morning. Oh yeah, turn on the alarm after I leave." He turned back to her in the open doorway. "Rub Vitamin E on the bruise, it might help."

"Will I see you again, Agent?"

"Oh yes, I'm sure you will, Mrs. Ransom." He nodded to the officers in the patrol car, climbed into his Audi, and drove home to what he once thought was his good-sized Belvedere Street condo, nestled in among town houses and small apartment buildings not a quarter mile above Haight-Ashbury.

CHAPTER 7

MAESTRO, VIRGINIA

Sheriff Dixon Noble took the call from his father-in-law, Chappy Holcombe, at three twenty-five on a Thursday afternoon. It was a moment he knew he'd never forget until he was stretched out dead.

"Dix? Chappy here. I've got to talk to you. This is really important. Can you come out to Tara right now?"

There was something about his voice that kept Dix from telling his autocratic father-in-law whatever it was would have to wait, that he was a working stiff, that the people of Maestro expected their sheriff—"What is it, Chappy?"

All Chappy would say was, "It's about Christie. Hurry, Dix, hurry."

Dix went cold. Christie, his wife, had been gone for well over three years, literally with him one day and gone the next. There had been no word of any kind, not a single lead in all this time. But Chappy wouldn't say anything more over the phone. "Get here, Dix, fast as you can."

He made it to Chappy Holcombe's Tara, a southern mansion

built along the lines of the fictional Tara as described by Margaret Mitchell, in under thirteen minutes. Dix was a mess by the time he pulled into the large circular driveway in front of the house.

Chappy's butler, Bernard, as old as the gnarly pine tree on Lone Tree Hill just outside of Maestro, or one of the sessile oaks in front of Tara, greeted Dix, his bald head shiny in the watery early spring afternoon sunshine. He said, his words spewing out fast, tumbling over one another, "Dix, he's in his study. Hurry, something's bad wrong, but I don't know what it is, just that it's about Christie." Dix hurried after him, not saying a word.

Bernard opened Chappy's study door and stood aside for Dix to enter.

Chappy was so rich he could probably bankroll the state of Virginia single-handedly for at least two days, a man who knew his own power and used it ruthlessly in business and at home, to keep his heir, Tony, and his heir's wife, Cynthia, under his thumb. He was standing by his big antique mahogany desk, looking every inch the tall, lean aristocrat in a beautiful pale blue cashmere turtleneck sweater and black bespoke wool slacks. Dix always felt like a mutt standing next to him. Dix looked closely at his face. Chappy looked haggard, nearly frantic, not a sharp edge in sight, no malice brimming in his eyes, no hint he was a man who could blast a killing verbal blow in a smooth ironic voice. Chappy's pupils were dilated, his face pale with shock.

What was happening here? What had he heard about Christie? Dix's heart pounded hard and fast.

"Chappy." Dix laid his hands on the older man's shoulders, steadying him. "What's wrong? What is this about Christie?"

Chappy shook himself, and Dix saw the effort it took to get himself together. "Jules saw Christie."

"Jules?"

"Yes, you know Christie's godfather—Jules Advere. You've met him over the years, Dix, don't you remember? He's been living in San Francisco for the past year, claimed he wanted a big city with a slower pace. He lives in Sea Cliff, right on the ocean, his house looks toward the Golden Gate Bridge."

"Yes, okay. You say he saw Christie?"

"He called me, said he saw her."

Dix's hands fell away. He took a step back. He stared blindly at his father-in-law, shaking his head back and forth, his brain blank. He had to make himself breathe. He had to get spit in his mouth so he could talk. No, it wasn't possible.

Chappy grabbed Dix's wrist. "You know if anyone else had told me that, I'd have dismissed it out of hand, maybe even belted them, but not Jules. He was there when Christie was born. He knew her all her life. He might be older than I am but he's not senile, Dix, and he's still got the eyesight of an owl. Truth is, I'd trust him with everything but my money."

And that was saying something indeed. Dix had met Jules Advere perhaps a dozen times before Christie had simply up and vanished that long-ago day. He pictured him in his mind the day Jules had flown into Richmond from some weird place like Latvia, a short, older man with a big dark mustache and a good-sized paunch on him that made Chappy razz him endlessly. He'd worked as hard as anyone trying to find Christie, did everything he could to comfort the boys. He'd even hired his own private investigator—but with no luck. No one had had an ounce of luck.

Jules had seen Christie? No, that was impossible. Dix had long ago accepted that Christie was dead, killed by some psychopath and buried in an unmarked grave somewhere, and it had sunk him deep into himself for too long a time, and nearly brought his sons into the pit with him. He thought about his sons, Rob and Rafe, what this news could do to them. He wasn't going to say a word about this to them. Not yet.

He was a cop and he had to take a step back, had to get it together. "Chappy, where did Jules say he'd seen her? In San Francisco? Did he speak to her? Come on now, get your thoughts together and tell me everything."

Chappy slumped down onto a three-hundred-year-old Hepplewhite chair covered with what looked like the original green-and-white-striped brocade. He looked down at his Italian loafers. Dix saw his hands were trembling. Chappy said, "He was attending a fundraiser at one of those big yahoo penthouses on Russian Hill, given by a man supporting a senatorial candidate. Jules said it was this guy's wife—he said there was no doubt in his mind. She was Christie."

"What's this guy's name?"

"Thomas Pallack. I've done business with him. He was here in Maestro once, maybe three and a half years ago, before Christie disappeared. He only stayed a couple of days. I don't think he met Christie, though. He's decades older than even the income tax laws, and he's wealthy, made his money in oil and diversified. Like I said, it's his wife, that's what Jules said—his wife is Christie."

Dix said slowly, patiently, "You know that's impossible, Chappy. You know it."

"I know it, but still, Dix, I'm just not as certain as you are. Yes, yes, I know she'd never have left you willingly. She loved you and the boys more than anything. Hell's bells, she even loved me, even tolerated her brother's idiot wife. But Jules swore it was her. It shook him so much to actually see her he told me he thought he was having a heart attack—searing pain all up his right side and he couldn't breathe. He said he whispered 'Christie' to her and Thomas kneeled down beside him while they were calling 911. He said Pallack leaned close and said, 'My wife's name is Charlotte. Do you understand? Don't forget it.' Jules said Christie looked down at him like a hostess would at someone who was ruining her party, a sort of polite forbearance because the last thing she wanted was for this old buzzard to die on her beautiful oak parquet floor. Admittedly he felt really sick at this point, even admitted he didn't see any recognition in her eyes when she looked at him, and that bothered him because, you see, he knew it was her."

"So you're saying Jules never got to speak to this woman before he collapsed?"

"No, just the one look in the receiving line, and then he was lying on his back staring up at her. The paramedics arrived and whisked him off to the hospital. Turns out he hadn't had a heart attack, but the doctors wondered if he'd suffered some sort of temporary stroke, said it could paralyze your body and make you keel over, that it could happen to an old guy like him. He called me from the hospital a few minutes ago while they were still doing all their infernal tests, said you had to get out to San Francisco, find out what Christie is doing there."

"It's not Christie, Chappy. She's dead. You heard what Jules said, the woman looked at him with no recognition at all."

"Then who the hell is she?"

Dix only shrugged, but all the memories, all the faded pain was back again, almost bowling him over, as it had in those early months after she'd disappeared. *It isn't Christie!*

He said, "We're all supposed to have a twin somewhere on this earth, a thought that should curdle your own blood, Chappy. Evidently Jules met Christie's twin, nothing more, nothing less. It wasn't her, Chappy, it couldn't have been Christie. So you know this guy Thomas Pallack, it's a coincidence, nothing more."

"No, Dix, wait! What if Thomas Pallack's wife is Christie and she's lost her memory or something? She was in some sort of accident or had some sort of mental breakdown? Hell, maybe she escaped something terrifying that made her repress everything."

"Chappy—"

"She might have ended up in San Francisco, met Thomas Pallack by chance, married him for whatever reason, I mean, the guy is older, and—if that's so then naturally she wouldn't recognize Jules. She had to have a name, so she called herself Charlotte. Dix, Jules is *so* certain. You'll go to San Francisco, won't you? Hell, no problem, both of us will go."

Dix didn't pause, simply walked to the door of Chappy's study, and said over his shoulder, "Chappy, I'll tell you what. I'll go to San Francisco, find out what this is all about. I'll meet this Thomas Pallack and his wife. I don't want you to come with me,

Chappy. I need you to stay here, see to the boys." Then he stopped, turned. "Chappy," he said very quietly to Christie's father—not to the man whose soggy morals sometimes drove him nuts, the man who wouldn't lift his foot off his own son's neck—"please don't get your hopes up. It simply can't be Christie. Deep down you know it. You know Christie is dead."

Chappy didn't say a word.

"And don't say anything about this to anyone, all right? Not even to Tony or Cynthia. The last thing I want is for the boys to hear their mother might be alive, have them go through this pain again when I know it simply can't be true."

"You got it, Dix. I won't say anything."

When Dix reached the double front doors, Chappy's white face still stark in his mind, Bernard appeared at his elbow. Dix said, "Make sure you see to Chappy, Bernard. I think he needs a good shot of something. I know Mrs. Goss keeps a bottle of twenty-five-year-old single malt Scotch whisky. What's it called?"

Bernard said with reverence, "Lord of the Isles. She said she gave it to her husband for an anniversary gift, then he up and died the next week. She hoards it. I think it must be about thirty years old now, almost as many years as she's been the house-keeper here!"

Dix nodded. "Maybe she'll break it out this once."

"Doubtful," Bernard said, then blurted out, "Do you think it's Christie, Dix?"

So Bernard had been listening at the door. Dix would have been, too. He looked Bernard straight on, saw the concern in his dark eyes. Bernard had been with Chappy since the two of them were in their twenties. "No, it can't be. It's some sort of mistake. Bernard, like I told Chappy, this has to stay among the three of us. You understand? Not even Mrs. Goss."

Bernard nodded. "Last thing I want is for Rob and Rafe to hear about this."

"That's good," Dix said. "I'll see you again soon, Bernard."

CHAPTER 8

Two hours later, at the dinner table, Dix slipped Brewster, his four-pound white toy poodle, a sliver of chicken breast after he'd stripped off the deep-fried crust. He checked to see that both boys had eaten some of the fresh green beans on their plates, and lied cleanly. "I've got this meeting up in San Francisco that will last a couple of days. The FBI called me today, said they wanted me to talk on a panel about crime scenes. Truth be told, there's still lots of interest about our bizarre murder in Winkel's Cave. That'll be what everyone will want me to talk about."

"Sure is short notice, Dad," Rafe said, frowning down at his crispy chicken leg. Rafe was fourteen, still skinny as a rail, with eyes dark like Dix's. He was going to be a lady-killer, as Chappy told Dix whenever he saw his grandson. Just like Rob. Have you given them The Talk, Dix? Dix rolled his eyes now, remembering how he'd given them both The Talk, though they were as embarrassed as he was. It gave him a headache to think about it. Why wasn't Rafe eating? He was always eating. Dix saw the huge pile of bones on his plate and realized Rafe's tank was full. Dix pointed to the pile of green beans still on his plate, and watched his son pick one up and began chewing on it. "It's not like San Francisco is just across the state or something."

"No, it's a long trip."

"Isn't Ruth coming tomorrow?" Rob asked. "She said she wanted to see me pitch against the Panthers."

Ruth Warnecki, a former Washington, D.C., cop and now an FBI special agent, worked in the Criminal Apprehension Unit at the Hoover Building. He'd known her since he'd saved her life a little more than two months ago. She was smarter than she had a right to be, as obstinate and persistent as he was, and she was endlessly kind. Fact was, he was crazy about her. Thinking about her made him grin at odd moments and sing in the shower, particularly when he pictured her on her back beneath him, her strong legs wrapped tight around him.

So much had happened since he'd found her, so very much, but now Ruth was his; he knew his boys felt the same way, though they also felt guilty about it when they thought of their mother. But they'd allowed Ruth into their lives in a way they had no one else. They laughed with her, worried with her, confided in her.

The four of them had become a solid unit, if not a legal one. Dix had a missing wife, no actual proof of death. If he sought a divorce, he'd have to do it on stated grounds of abandonment. The thought of accusing Christie of abandonment made him sick. No way would he allow that word to come out of his mouth, out of anyone's mouth for that matter, or have it recorded on any document. So what sort of plans could they make? So far it hadn't seemed to matter. He and the boys visited Ruth at her home in Alexandria and she visited them here in Maestro, usually for three-day weekends if she could talk her boss, FBI Unit Chief Dillon Savich, into it, which she usually could. She hadn't spoken recently of reassignment to the Richmond Field Office. Actually, they'd spoken hardly at all about the future. Everything they talked about was short term. He closed his eyes a moment, realized he and Ruth were hovering in a sort of limbo. The future was like a hibernating bear in the corner of the living room, ignored by everyone because it seemed the polite thing to do and, truth be told, it was easier.

He had to call Ruth, see if she still wanted to come out since he wouldn't be here, but he knew she would. She loved his boys, he knew that just as he knew her love wasn't contingent on their future plans. But should he tell her the truth? He had to think about it. He did know she'd never buy the story about an FBI conference, and that would mean another lie altogether. He hated lies, always had. You usually got tangled up in lies, and busted yourself.

Dix said, looking at his eldest son, "I'll bet she'll still want to come see you play, Rob. Thing is, the guy who was going to speak fell over with a heart attack. Yep, I'm their second choice, but on the plus side, I'll get to see a lot of friends I haven't seen in a long time. I want you guys to stick to the rules, you got that?"

Rob was sixteen, nearly as tall as Dix and filling out, growing into manhood. Dix gave him the Eye. Rob took it in and didn't even squirm, just nodded solemnly. He was growing up, Dix thought, and that both depressed him and made him proud. Where had the years gone? "You're in charge, Rob. Don't give him grief, Rafe, okay? If Ruth comes, you guys take good care of her. There's some spinach and sausage lasagna in the freezer. Feed her that, not pizza. She'll probably make up a salad for all of you. And you'll eat it without complaint."

"Sure, Dad," Rob said, and Dix immediately knew Ruth would be surrounded with pizza from the instant she walked into the house, Brewster panting at her heels. He knew she'd laugh and fetch the lasagna out of the freezer, and the boys would get both, and a salad.

Rob said, "Dad, have you seen Ruth's fastball now that I've been working with her?"

Dix nodded. *Ah, Christie, we did good with our boys, and Ruth does well with them too.* Dix had spoken to Christie a lot over the years. His memory of her, the feeling of her presence, would always be with him, easing the bad times and making the good times better. But he knew all the way to his soul that Christie was dead, more than three years dead.

This was an entirely different woman in San Francisco, he had no doubt. But he still had to make the trip, had to make sure, for all of them. If he didn't go he knew Chappy would, and who knew what kind of grief that would cause? And in the back of his mind, a voice softly asked, *If she is Christie, what then?*

Brewster was gnawing on his trouser leg. Dix leaned down and picked up the well-fed furball whose eyes would melt Scrooge's heart, straightened his dark blue collar, and hugged him close.

"Don't you get too excited when you see Ruth, okay, Brewster? She doesn't need you to pee on her again."

The boys laughed. "Brewster loves her leather jacket," Rafe said. "She told me Brewster supports her dry cleaners."

The boys moved on to talking about school. They'd bought his story. Good. The last thing they needed to know was the real reason he was flying to the West Coast.

CHAPTER 9

WASHINGTON, D.C.
THE HOOVER BUILDING

Friday morning

When Special Agent Ruth Warnecki bent down to pull the bottom of her slacks out of her boot she heard Dillon Savich say to his boss, Jimmy Maitland, "Take a gander at this. This sketch is excellent."

"I was thinking maybe it's too good," Maitland said. "Is Cheney sure the witness didn't embellish?"

"Cheney said the reason it's so detailed is that the guy didn't mind showing her his face up close and personal, because he planned to kill her. He ended up throwing her into San Francisco Bay, where she would probably have drowned if Cheney hadn't gotten her out in time."

"Good for Agent Stone," Maitland said, "and a remarkable chunk of good luck for the victim. It was a coincidence, right, Savich? He isn't dating her, is he, or surveilling her, something like that?"

Ruth couldn't help listening in. She knew Cheney. She leaned closer to the door and heard Dillon say, "Nope, I asked him about that. Cheney said he'd never seen her before in his life. The thing about Cheney Stone is he's got great instincts and this karma sort of thing that seems to put him in the right places at critical times. Weirdest thing I've ever heard of. But even without the woo-woo—as an agent, Cheney's good, very good. This Julia is lucky he was there."

Maitland nodded, started pacing in front of Savich's desk. "I've read some of his reports. He's got good recall. Did you know he's got a law degree?"

Savich grinned. "I say thank the Lord he crossed over to the side of the angels."

Maitland grunted, unconsciously flexed an impressive bicep. "Yep, we need him more than the world needs another damned lawyer."

"He started out as a prosecutor, but couldn't accept all the plea bargains they have to make to keep the system from imploding—he couldn't see a whole lot of justice in that, didn't think he was making much of a difference."

Maitland nodded. "You know the SAC out in San Francisco—Bert Cartwright? He's one smart guy, but he bitches about Stone being a hot dog—not covering other people's butts is how I translate that."

"You think?" Savich grinned.

"Of course you and Sherlock are the original hot dogs, if I don't count your dad. Buck Savich drove everyone nuts." Jimmy Maitland paused a moment and Savich knew he was thinking back.

Savich felt the brief dig of loss. He regretted that his dad had never met Sherlock, and had never known Sean. Then he eased away the memory of his larger-than-life father.

Maitland said, "I assume the SFPD has protection on Julia Ransom."

"Yes. When Cheney called he said Captain Frank Paulette was in charge. They're reopening the investigation into Dr. Ransom's murder, but still there's some talk about her being involved since she was their primary suspect six months ago."

"But nothing came of it," Maitland said. "She wasn't arrested."

"No," Savich said, "and now there's an attempt on her life. Interesting, isn't it?"

Who is Julia Ransom? Ruth wondered. *Julia Ransom—her name sounds familiar.* But Ruth couldn't place it. Because she was a cop, and cops were always curious, and, after all, she did know Cheney Stone, Ruth couldn't walk away. Besides, she didn't see much point in walking back to her desk to wait to see Dillon, her brain squirreling around in crazy circles. Eavesdropping was a relief, in fact, from the numbing disbelief that had smacked her in the face at seven-thirty that morning. She'd take it, even temporarily, take anything to distract her, even for a minute, from the weight of Dix's news. No matter what scales you used, the bottom line was that Dix's three-year-gone wife, Christie, was either dead or she wasn't. No possible middle ground. Ruth couldn't help it, she had a horrible premonition about which way the scales were going to tilt.

She heard Dillon say, "I think if this guy is a pro we might catch him, and Cheney says that was the impression he got."

Maitland tapped his fingertip on the image of the man's face in the sketch. "Look at those dead eyes—the sketch artist nailed that. Okay, we've used the facial recognition program now on a good half-dozen sketches—and come up with hits. See what you can do with this."

Ruth knew Dillon was anxious to do just that. "I'll get back to you on this, sir."

Maitland, still strong enough to take on his four grown sons, stretched his back and said, "What a mess this is going to be. The SFPD is going to have to go digging again into all the people Ransom harmed or killed over the years with his free medical advice."

"He didn't give much medical advice," Savich said. "His big rep was as a medium, and that means he communicated with the dead."

Maitland grunted at that. "I remember reading that Edgar Cayce told cancer patients to use peach pits. Now, how about money trails?"

Savich said, "Always lots of them, but to my understanding, the SFPD didn't find anything definitive on the widow.

"August Ransom's estate was short on cash and long on property. His mansion in Pacific Heights must be valued at eight figures, so bottom line is the widow isn't poor."

"Like everyone else, I always thought she killed her old man. What was he, thirty, forty years older than his wife?"

"Something like that. And now someone tries to murder the widow. Maybe she was simply a loose end, or maybe she found out something she shouldn't have. Cheney and the local SFPD will be looking into that."

Maitland gave him a look. "Yeah, yeah, I know. Cheney Stone isn't going to drop this and walk away, and that means you'll involve yourself too. All right, keep me posted, boyo."

"I don't know whether Cheney wants us directly involved yet," Savich said. "But it sure sounds interesting, doesn't it, what with the psychic medium angle? Do you know, Sherlock's read a good deal about psychic mediums."

"Does she believe it's all a con?"

"Whenever I ask her what she thinks, she starts singing the theme to *The Twilight Zone.* I don't think she's taken a stand."

"Has she read any of Dr. Ransom's books?"

"Very likely. I'll ask her."

"I understand they sell well, most of those sorts of books do. Fact is, Ransom was one of the most famous psychic mediums out there."

Savich said slowly, "I wonder if maybe he made a deal with his wife, like Houdini did with his."

"A code, you mean? And only if a medium can tell her the code can he or she be believed?"

Savich nodded slowly. "Something like that. If there really is anything to find out from Julia Ransom, Cheney would be the one to find it. He saved the woman's life. That's got to give him some sort of bond with her. I'm sure that's what the locals will think too."

"I'll speak to the SAC in San Francisco, tell him to give Cheney free rein on this deal if the SFPD wants to involve him. Keep me posted, Savich."

Ruth knew she should back off fast, but her feet were nailed to the linoleum.

Jimmy Maitland nearly ran her over when he came out of Savich's office. He grinned. "Ruth, how's it going? How are Dix and his boys?"

"Ah, good morning, sir. Everyone is fine. I'm driving to Maestro for the weekend to watch Rob pitch in a big game against the hated Panthers of Crescent City."

Maitland shook his head. "Baseball, basketball, football, snowboarding, driving my car—my damned boys littered the landscape with their broken bones. Dix might wish they'd take up a rock band, or something that'd be safer." He waved to Sherlock, who was discussing a bizarre Little Rock, Arkansas, murder case with Dane Carver. He remembered that Dane and Cheney had gone to Loyola Law School. He wondered which one of them had ranked higher in his class.

"Hey, Ruth," Savich called out, "come tell me what you think of this sketch."

CHAPTER 10

R uth knew Dillon was perfectly aware that she'd been eavesdropping, and yet here he was letting her off the hook, even involving her. She looked down at the sketch smoothed out on his desktop. A good-looking black man wearing glasses—he looked focused, like he knew exactly who he was and where he was going in life. She said without hesitation, "He's a pro. And since we've got lots of pros entered in the database, the chances are good we'll get a name. Look at those eyes—this guy is empty to his soul."

"Nah, not empty. Just cold. Hey, you needed something?"

Then Savich looked at her face, really looked, and said, "Close the door."

She closed it.

"Okay, Ruth, sit down."

She sat.

"Because cops can't stand not to know everything that's going on, you were distracted for a couple of minutes listening to that conversation about Cheney Stone and Julia Ransom. But something's going on. Nothing's happened to Dix, has it?"

"Oh no. Well, yes, it has. Dix called me from the Richmond airport. He's on his way to San Francisco." She gave him a desperate look. "It's about his missing wife—Christie. Christie's god-father called Chappy, swore he'd seen her."

A dark eyebrow shot up. He said slowly, "It's not Christie, Ruth. She's long dead. You know it, Dix knows it. But he has to go check this out, you know that too. Now, tell me what her god-father said."

"The godfather's name is Jules Advere. He was positive it was Christie he saw even though he admitted she showed no signs of recognizing him."

And then Ruth repeated the story she heard from Dix, about what happened at the fancy fundraiser at the high-roller's pent-house on Russian Hill in San Francisco.

She felt drained when she finished. Savich studied her face, saw the anxiety in her dark eyes. "San Francisco," he said slowly. "Do you mind if I give my father-in-law a call? Ask him if he knows these people—Charlotte and Thomas Pallack?"

"No, I don't mind. I'm sure Dix wouldn't either."

"Sherlock's dad, Corman Sherlock, is a judge and a native San Franciscan, a rare breed I'm told, and he's into everything local. Also, he's got money, so I wouldn't be surprised if he knows these people socially. Maybe he can solve this problem right away, with-out any fuss."

She said, "I was picturing Dix walking up to this dripping-gold penthouse, ringing the doorbell, this snooty butler telling him that the lady of the house wasn't available. He didn't exactly have a plan except maybe climbing up the side of the house to her bed-room to get a look at her."

Savich leaned back in his chair and crossed his hands over his belly, never taking his eyes off her face. He said slowly, "I agree with Dix. His wife was murdered. What was it, three years ago?"

"More than three years ago now. About this trip to the coast— Dix lied to the boys, asked me to keep a close eye on them this weekend. I gather Chappy will be around as well." Ruth laughed then, ugly and raw, and then she gulped. "Dillon, what if it is Christie?"

Savich rose and came around the desk. She stood up as well. He took her in his arms, hugged her, said against her hair, "It's not. Now, try not to make yourself nuts with this. You can eavesdrop on all my conversations that sound interesting."

"Dillon, call your father-in-law now. Please. If it could be clean and fast—that'd be great, it would be best for Dix, for all of us."

"I hesitate to do this without Dix's permission, Ruth."

"You know he'd want you to, Dillon. Please, for all of us. This is so important, and not only to me."

Savich gave her a long look, checked his Mickey Mouse watch. "It's about seven o'clock on the West Coast." He nodded her to a chair, pulled out his cell, and dialed.

"Sherlock residence."

"Good morning, Isabel. This is Dillon Savich. How are you?"

"Agent Savich! What a pleasure to hear your voice, sir. I'm surely fine, thank you. How's my baby?"

"She's fine, Isabel, keeps me in line."

"How's my baby's baby boy?"

"Sean's the only one who runs right over her."

Isabel laughed. "Good, good. I'll bet he's a perfect little boy. Let me get Judge Sherlock."

Sherlock's father was on the line in an instant. "This is a nice surprise, Savich. Nothing's wrong, I hope."

After reassuring his father-in-law and asking after his mother-in-law, Evelyn, Savich gave him a concise rundown of the players and the very unusual problem. "I know you haven't met Dixon Noble, but he's a good man, Corman, had it really hard since his wife disappeared more than three years ago. He's doing a fine job of raising his two sons. He's a no-nonsense sheriff, sharp, dedicated, tough as a bulldog. You'd like him. So you know this Thomas Pallack and his wife Charlotte?"

"Sure. Thomas has been active in local and national politics for a good ten years now. I think he originally hails from Southern California, one of those fancy beach places, Malibu, if I remember correctly. He was in with the Hollywood set, which, I'd say, has been the ruin of many a good brain. I know he was active in L.A. politics before he got involved on the national level. As I said, he moved up here maybe ten years ago. Maybe there was a falling out, I don't know, or maybe it was simply that he wanted to reheadquarter up here. He made all his money in refineries and oil exploration, but he's diversified now, got his fingers in lots of things, including several software companies in Silicon Valley. He didn't marry until about three years ago—yep, lots of rumors about that, but no, I never thought he was gay.

"I only see him socially, usually at one of his endless stream of fundraisers. Everything's political with Thomas, and I don't want to punch him in the nose in front of his new wife, plus he's up there, nearly seventy, I think. Since he knows I'm not about to back any of the candidates he's pushing, we've had this long-standing agreement—no political harangues and no requests for money from me, except for charities we both support.

"I haven't met his wife, Charlotte. I did hear she was from money, back East, Boston, maybe, but don't quote me. Just an impression. Would you like me to invite them to dinner, Savich? Maybe get to know Charlotte Pallack a bit?"

"Another question first, sir. Does Evelyn know them?"

"I'm not sure. I'll ask her in about five minutes—at the breakfast table."

"Thank you, and please give her my best. I'll have MAX check Charlotte Pallack myself, see if MAX can't find out exactly who she is and what she was doing before she married Thomas Pallack. Oh yes, please keep this confidential. Hey, maybe Dix Noble could dine with you and the Pallacks? Is that possible?"

"Excellent idea. That would put all his questions to rest immediately. I'll call Thomas right now, see if he and Charlotte are free tonight or Saturday night. How's that?"

"I think we'll all owe you. Just a moment—" He asked Ruth, "When is Dix supposed to hit SFO?"

She said, "Around three o'clock this afternoon, their time."

Savich said to Judge Sherlock, "I'll call Dix when he arrives in San Francisco, tell him the plan."

"Why don't you tell him to come on over to the house? He can stay with us. That'll make his presence at the dinner all the more natural. What do you think?"

"Thank you, Corman, great idea, and since Dix is a good friend of ours, it would be very nice for you to put him up."

"Savich, did you hear about this attempted murder of Julia Ransom? Front page, mentions an FBI agent saving her bacon?"

"Well, yeah, some."

"Yeah, you're a damned clam. You running the whole show?"

Savich laughed. "Let me get Sherlock on the line. You two can chat for a minute and she can tell you about Sean's latest computer games—*Pajama Sam* and *Dragon Tales*." He knew Sherlock would tell her father more about Sheriff Dixon Noble of Maestro, Virginia—she'd be excited they would meet. He cupped his hand over his cell and said to Ruth, "I'll be right back."

After he gave Sherlock his cell, he watched her face for a moment as she spoke to her father and heard the familiar warmth in her laugh. When he got back to his office, he said, "Ruth, you know as well as I do that when you've been married to someone, you'd know that person in an instant, no matter how much time has passed, no matter how much the person has changed her appearance. Dix will know tonight. This fast." Savich snapped his fingers. "Right now, Ruth, there's absolutely nothing more to be done. I want you to think about cheering Rob on to pitch a no-hitter against the Panthers, okay?"

She gave a shaky laugh. "Yeah, okay, you're right, but it's hard, Dillon, really hard."

"I can imagine."

"If Rob pitches a no-hitter his brother might run away from home, he'll be so disgusted at all the swaggering." Her shoulders were straighter, Savich saw, as she left his office. She was striding again, long, no-nonsense steps—the Ruth walk—head up, and ready to kick butt.

All of a sudden there was a lot going on in San Francisco, he thought. Funny how many times a particular place became a nexus of things. Savich watched Sherlock walk back toward his office, punching off his cell. He couldn't wait to hear what she had to say about all this. He wondered if she'd admitted to her father that Sean had beaten her at *Pajama Sam*.

SAN FRANCISCO

Friday morning

Evelyn Sherlock said to her husband, "I saw Charlotte Pallack last month at a fashion show at the Hyatt Embarcadero. She's beautiful—no, better than beautiful, she's got style and intelligence and a very interesting face. She was on the standoffish side. Actually, she's always been somewhat reserved since I met her some two years ago.

"I remember Mazie Wallace told me—you know, that nasal voice of hers lowered, but not enough—that Charlotte spent a bundle on clothes Mazie said she wouldn't even want to see off the hanger, but who really knew about her background? Mazie's mean-spirited so I ignored what she said."

"What did that mean—her background? I thought she came from Boston money, something like that."

"I don't have a clue."

"I don't suppose Thomas Pallack was around?"

"Thomas? No, that day it was all women."

Corman said, "I've got to go in about five minutes. Oh, here you are, Isabel. I'm sorry for the short notice, but we're going to have a houseguest tonight and perhaps tomorrow night as well. It will all depend on how the dinner goes tonight. His name is Sheriff Dixon Noble. He's a friend of Savich and Sherlock. And we'll be having dinner for five tonight."

"I hadn't realized you'd already called Thomas," Evelyn said.

"Oh yes. Do you know I didn't even wake him up. He'd already been through the *Wall Street Journal.* All I had to do was intimate that I might be mellowing toward his newest political candidate—what's his name? Whatever, he's running for district attorney." At his wife's laugh, he smiled back at her. "And that did it. He and his wife will be here at seven o'clock."

"That was clever," Evelyn said, saluting him with her coffee cup.

"My roast pork with my special mint sauce, Judge Sherlock?"

"Yes, and apple pie."

Isabel nodded. "We haven't had guests in at least a month. This'll be fun," and she left the dining room, humming and making lists in her head.

Forty-five minutes later Judge Sherlock reached his chambers on the sixteenth floor of one of the ugliest gray buildings in San Francisco, the U.S. Government Federal District Court on Golden Gate Avenue. He dealt with his clerks in record time, closed his door, and booted up his computer. He had twenty-three minutes until he had to be in court. He typed in Julia Ransom's name and began reading. After seeing that morning's newspaper article about the attempt on her life and the involvement of a local FBI agent, he'd bet his newly crowned molar that his son-in-law knew a lot about it. Savich was likely up to his ears in it. The judge was rarely a step ahead of his son-in-law, but this time perhaps he'd dig up something before Savich did with his damned computer, MAX.

D ix landed at SFO right on time. He pulled his single carry-on from the overhead bin and walked out of the airport into a chilly, sunny day. He'd asked a flight attendant about a hotel and had just climbed into a taxi when his cell phone played some New Orleans jazz.

Five minutes later, the taxi was headed to Pacific Heights, where it pulled up some forty minutes later in front of a beautiful three-story Art Deco house with views of the whole bay.

"Nice big money house," the Russian driver said, his accent thick.

Nice big money house indeed, Dix thought. It was like the Tara of San Francisco, only with better views.

A cup of rich Kona coffee in his hand, Dix sat in the formal living room across from Evelyn Sherlock and looked at his watch.

"Yes, it's five o'clock," Evelyn said. "Dix, dear, it occurred to me that you might not have brought a suit. Such a fast, in-and-out trip. Did you?"

He smiled at the beautiful woman who was Sherlock's mother and who didn't look a thing like her. She looked soft and elegant, graceful and smooth, her blond hair in a stylish straight cut that skimmed her jawline. Where had Sherlock gotten her incredible wild red hair?

"Actually, ma'am—"

"Do make that Evelyn."

"Yes, Evelyn. And call me Dix. Well, since this Thomas Pallack is a bigwig, I had the brains to bring a decent suit so I wouldn't embarrass myself. I don't know if it's up to snuff, but—"

Evelyn patted his big hand, so like her son-in-law's, she thought, a firm, strong hand she imagined could pull you out of the deepest mire. "I'll ask Isabel to have a look at it. She'll tell us if it will be appropriate. If it is, she'll press it for you."

Isabel deemed Dix's dark blue wool suit quite lovely for the occasion. His shirt, however, didn't make the cut. He found himself buttoning one of Judge Sherlock's handmade white shirts, slipping on simple gold cuff links, and Windsor-knotting a red and white Italian silk tie. Dix stepped back to study himself in the full-length mirror in his bedroom, a large airy space about the size of his dining room. Then, drawn to the window, he looked out toward the beautiful hillside town of Sausalito, and the Marin Headlands. With all the rain, Evelyn had told him, it was nearly Irish green, but that wouldn't last. Just wait until July, and she'd sighed. His room was filled with English antiques Christie would have loved—Ruth's tastes leaned toward the bright and colorful, the whimsical, like the ceramic rooster sitting on alert just inside her front door. He stilled, stared at himself in the mirror, not seeing anything. Could he do this? How would he face this woman who couldn't be Christie because Christie was dead?

But what if she is Christie?

He realized his hands were sweating, his heart pounding hard in his chest. He couldn't think straight because his brain was leapfrogging around too much. This woman, this Charlotte Pallack, no, she wasn't Christie, but—*What's wrong with you, moron? Christie's dead, long dead. Deal with it.* His brain turned around again and went a different direction. Since this woman couldn't be Christie, maybe she was some long-lost sister? Had Chappy had an affair and not known his lover was pregnant? It went around and around as it had throughout the day. If he'd had his Beretta, he'd have shot himself.

He was terrified of what he wanted, of what he didn't want, of what he'd find out. He admitted he was a basket case, couldn't help it. But he had to get himself together enough to face this woman tonight and he had to be calm and rational and clear-headed. He would know, the instant he saw her, he would know, and then it would be over.

He shook his head at himself in the mirror, brushed his dark hair. He had to get a grip, just face this: *Be the ultimate cool, dude,* as Rafe would say. He continued to stare at himself and slowly nodded in satisfaction. He looked sophisticated, he realized, like a guest should look, a guest polite enough and rich enough to have dinner with society snoots. He had poise, he had confidence, he was ready. He would not fall apart, no matter what happened.

Ten minutes later in the living room, Evelyn Sherlock agreed with his assessment. She patted his sleeve. "If Charlotte isn't your

Christie, she still might try to run away with you," she remarked, rising to straighten his tie, though it didn't need it.

That gave things a different perspective, Dix thought, staring down at her a moment, and marveling again how very different she was from her daughter. Then she tilted her head to the side and said, "I do love a man in French cuffs." He'd seen Sherlock tilt her head in exactly the same way.

"In that case," he said, "I'd rather run away with you."

She sighed, her voice low and throaty, quite sexy really. "Ah, so many elegant cuff links, so little time."

He laughed. "Do you know I think I've worn French cuffs maybe three times in my life?"

Judge Sherlock, calm and aloof, looking like an aristocrat—a lot like a younger Chappy, Dix realized—walked into the living room, kissed his wife's cheek, told her she was gorgeous, and shook hands with Dix. He looked him up and down, examined him the way a father might a son who was bent on impressing a future boss. He nodded. "You'll do just fine, Dix. You'll get through this. Now, you want something to drink?"

"No, thank you, sir—"

"Call me Corman."

Dix nodded. "I don't think my stomach can handle it. Thank you for the loan of the shirt and tie. And the cuff links."

The doorbell chimed and Dix felt his belly fall to his newly polished shoes. If he'd been holding a drink he would have dropped it. Evelyn patted his arm as she said easily, "I do believe the Pallacks are here. Dix, you will be all right. You already know everything that's important to know, and they don't. You'll see immediately if she's your Christie and then it will be over. If she is Christie, naturally, you'll both know it."

Dix supposed that advice fit well, but he stopped thinking altogether when he first saw Charlotte Pallack come into the entry hall. Her smile was Christie's smile, lighting up every corner, her teeth were straight and white, Christie's teeth. Jules Advere was right—it was Christie, down to the pale peach nail polish he liked on her long thin fingers. He swallowed, tried to keep a hold of himself, be the polite stranger being courteous to guests, nothing more. He had to get closer to the woman whose hair was darker than Christie's, but that didn't mean much. She was as tall as Christie, big-boned, but thinner—no, that wasn't important either. He had to look her in the eyes, then he'd know. They had to see each other close.

Judge Sherlock lightly touched Dix's sleeve, drawing him forward. "Dixon, do meet our friends, Thomas and Charlotte Pallack."

CHAPTER 12

Dix stepped forward, hand outstretched, a well-bred, beautifully mannered gentleman. "Mr. Pallack, Mrs. Pallack," he said, his voice smooth and calm as the bay was that evening beneath a half moon and a perfectly clear sky.

He shook Thomas Pallack's hand, then turned to his wife and took another half-step because he couldn't stop himself. He wasn't a foot from her. She smiled at him, gave him her hand. He never looked away from her face. And she never looked away from his.

There was no recognition in her eyes. *She doesn't know me. She isn't Christie.*

But she was Christie's twin, no doubt about that. He could see now why Jules Advere had fallen over from the shock of seeing her.

Her eyes were blue-green, pale, like Christie's, but the shape was subtly different. Her expression was warm and interested, but there wasn't that extra flash Christie had—it didn't matter if she was angry, happy, sad, or brimming with pleasure, a unique joy shone out of Christie's eyes every single day he'd known her. His Christie wasn't behind those eyes. Dix had studied a photo of his wife all the way from Richmond, reminding himself of every detail, the nuance of every feature in every mood. He saw that Charlotte Pallack's nose was a bit thinner than Christie's. Christie had Chappy's nose, and this nose in front of him wasn't it. But it was very close. If he'd seen her from six feet away he might well have fallen over in shock himself. But what if she'd lost her memory, had cosmetic surgery—no, no, that was asinine. She wasn't Christie, she simply wasn't.

He felt immense sadness, felt something breaking inside him, and realized it had been an outlandishly impossible hope that this woman was his long-missing wife.

But no, this woman was a stranger.

"Mr. Noble? Is something wrong?"

Her voice. Damn, it was very nearly Christie's voice. Her fingers tightened around his. He abruptly released her hand, aware that Mr. Pallack, a man older than Chappy, pushing seventy, and on the portly side, his paunch neatly hidden in his beautifully styled suit—this woman's husband—was eyeing him, actually staring at him, eyebrow raised, suddenly suspicious of him now because he'd held his wife's hand too long, was too intense, wasn't—acting normal, Dix supposed. Perhaps he was wondering if this stranger was sexually interested in his younger wife.

Dix quickly stepped back and managed an impersonal smile. *It's over. It isn't Christie.*

He said, "Forgive me for staring, Mrs. Pallack. You remind me of someone I knew very well a long time ago. Like her, you're very beautiful."

That was a perfect thing to say. Thomas Pallack seemed to get his suspicion back under control. It seemed to Dix that he now preened in the face of the younger alpha male who openly admired *his* wife, but he couldn't have her because she was his. As for Charlotte Pallack, she cocked her head to one side and continued to stare up at him, both surprised and pleased with the compliment. She didn't know him, didn't have a clue who or what he was.

It isn't Christie.

Evelyn Sherlock said in a light, social voice, "This twin business—I wish I could find mine. I wonder if she's in a loony bin or perhaps a Mother Superior in an Italian abbey. What do you think, Corman?"

Judge Sherlock laughed, a deep, full-bodied laugh that gave Dix time to regain full control and perspective. "Please, Evelyn, not a Mother Superior, Italian or not, I couldn't handle that. Do you think you'd make the wine at your convent?" He added with a smile to Thomas and Charlotte Pallack, "Do come into the living room. We'll have a drink and some of Isabel's delicious hors d'oeuvres before a dinner that will make us all loosen our belts."

It isn't Christie.

But he found himself walking behind her, studying her walk, comparing it to Christie's. There were subtle differences, but the thing was, it wasn't that different, almost as if she'd observed Christie, copied her—no, he had to get a grip here, he had to cut it off right now. He would go home tomorrow and finally do what he had to do to clear up his marital status. He'd go in front of a judge and actually say the word *abandonment.* Oh God, he didn't know if he could bear that—no, it was time, past time. He would do what he had to do. He would stop living in limbo. It wasn't fair to Ruth. He prayed she would be his Ruth, that he was lucky enough to have found two extraordinary women in his life. Nor was it fair to his boys. They'd all been in limbo for too long.

Dix tried to keep his eyes off Charlotte Pallack during dinner, and succeeded for the most part. It was Charlotte, however, who was sneaking looks at him.

He listened to Thomas Pallack speak, amused at how the man wore his wealth like a royal robe. He knew his own importance, his own power, and best of all, he knew how to hide it enough so that people didn't resent him. He had a lot in common with Chappy, except Chappy was better at it.

Dix accepted a glass of the excellent merlot Judge Sherlock served with dinner. He was pleased he could sip at it and not have his stomach rebel on him. He was still finding it difficult to keep his eyes off Charlotte Pallack—and both she and her husband knew it. Dix knew that if he were Thomas Pallack, he'd want to break the interloper's face. But the fact was the older man appeared to remain fatuously pleased. Trophy wife, Dix supposed, was the unflattering term for Charlotte Pallack.

He looked up from his plate and said, "Mrs. Pallack—"

"Oh, since you're a friend of the Sherlocks, do call me Charlotte."

"Charlotte," he repeated, nodding, knowing a deaf man could hear that extra warmth in her voice. "I can't place your accent. Perhaps it's southern?"

"Why, Mr. Noble, you've a very good ear. I'm from back east originally, then my folks moved to Durham. But I've been in California for many years now. And your accent, it's also got a bit of the South."

He nodded. "I'm from a small town called Maestro, in Virginia. I'm the sheriff there. Do call me Dix."

"Ah, more law enforcement," Thomas Pallack said, and flipped his napkin down beside his plate. "A federal judge and a sheriff." Dix could see that his status had dropped markedly in Mr. Pallack's eyes. He wanted to laugh, but only nodded. "Yes, sir. I am friends with their daughter and son-in-law. As you probably know, both Lacey and her husband Dillon Savich are FBI agents. We worked a local case together a couple of months ago in my town." He took another small sip of the merlot and heard himself add, "Perhaps you know my father-in-law, Mr. Pallack. His name is Chapman Holcombe—everyone calls him Chappy. His main interest is banking, owns Holcombe First Independent. Well, that's not quite accurate—to be closer to the mark, I'd have to say his major interest is making money." And Dix smiled, a man of the world.

Thomas Pallack nodded. "I thought the name of your town sounded familiar. Yes, Chappy and I did business some years ago, very profitably, I might add. However, I haven't been in touch with him, haven't seen him since that time. How's the old curmudgeon doing these days?"

"He's the same as ever. His son Tony runs the banks now, but Chappy hasn't entirely dropped the reins. I doubt he will until he passes."

Judge Sherlock said smoothly, "You said this man was your father-in-law, Dix? Yes, I remember now my daughter Lacey saying you were married to his daughter. I'm sorry, but I don't know her name."

"My wife is dead," Dix said, feeling raw ugly bile in his throat and at the same time admiring Judge Sherlock's chutzpah and his acting ability. "It's been over three years now. Her name was Christie."

"I'm so very sorry," said Charlotte Pallack. "My own father died when I was young."

"Well, Dix," Thomas Pallack said, "you'd best warn Chappy not to bend the law or Judge Sherlock here might send him off to one of our federal gulags."

"Gulags?" Dix asked, eyebrow raised. "I didn't know we'd built any here."

"Our prison system," Thomas said, sitting forward, eyes fierce, "is a disgrace. Our prisoners are in appalling, overcrowded facilities, and the prison administration system is bogged down and incompetent."

"I agree with that," Judge Sherlock said.

Thomas Pallack gunned forward. "The only solution is to release some of the inmates, a furlough system, and then reintegrate them back into society."

Judge Sherlock said, "Don't you know what the recidivism rate is, Thomas? It's higher than the state income tax. I'd say the last thing society needs is to let robbers, murderers, drug dealers, rapists, and assorted other lowlifes back on the streets to wreak havoc." Judge Sherlock paused a brief moment, realizing he couldn't pound Thomas Pallack like he wanted since the man was his guest, dammit. "But you have a point. We need to overhaul the system—and build more prisons."

Thomas Pallack opened his mouth, saw Evelyn giving him a hostess's gimlet eye, and closed it. "Some would agree" was all he said. Dix admired his restraint, but he wondered and questioned: Since Thomas Pallack knew Chappy, had he met Christie, seen her photo in Chappy's library? Hadn't he also at least heard Dix's name? And if he had met Christie, hadn't he noticed how alike his wife and Christie looked?

Evelyn offered Thomas some French green beans with tiny pearl onions and blanched almonds on top. "You, Thomas, know Dix's father-in-law. Such a small world, isn't it?"

Thomas Pallack said, "I remember meeting briefly with Chappy in Maestro—that's the name, right? Then we went on to Richmond to meet with another couple of bankers. I remember asking him why he wasn't in New York. I mean, what's to do in a little one-horse town in western Virginia? Ah, no insult intended, Sheriff Noble."

Dix said easily, "I like the one-horse town very much, sir, even willingly moved my family from big exciting New York to live there."

But Thomas Pallack didn't seem at all interested in that. Between a bite of the French green beans and a dinner roll, he said, "My candidate for district attorney, Corman, Galen Banbridge, is running on a hard-line law-and-order platform. It's possible he might even be interested in more prison construction."

Dix grew still. He looked up at Thomas Pallack, well fed, so very certain of his place in the sun. Who and what was he? He asked, "Does your candidate believe evil should be eliminated from the world, sir?"

"Evil?" Thomas Pallack started to laugh, had the manners to hold it back, but he had his look of contempt down cold. "Evil, did you say? *Evil?* Who in this day and age believes in such medieval nonsense as evil?"

Evelyn clearly pictured Thomas Pallack lying on the floor by her dining room table, his eyes rolled back in his head, with Dix standing over him. Because she was a skilled hostess, she quickly went pre-medieval, to the Queen Hatshepsut Egyptian exhibit currently at the de Young Museum. Thankfully, both Pallacks had visited the exhibit.

Over excellent apple pie and ice cream, Judge Sherlock let Thomas Pallack wax eloquent about his candidate. He did an almost credible job of seeming interested.

Charlotte Pallack flirted with Dix in a lovely discreet way, going so far as to touch her fingers to his sleeve while her husband helped her into her cashmere coat at precisely ten o'clock. Judge Sherlock assured Pallack that he would study the hard-line law-and-order candidate and knew that Pallack probably didn't buy it. Well, he'd shown as much enthusiasm as he could without starting an argument that would have had Evelyn throwing wineglasses at them.

When the front door closed, Evelyn patted Dix's cheek. "She didn't know you and you didn't know her. It's over, Dix, all questions answered. Go to bed now and get some sleep."

CHAPTER 13

At eight o'clock Saturday morning, the Sherlocks sat down with Dix at the breakfast table. They'd already worked out in their downstairs gym and still wore their workout clothes. They looked fit, their faces still shiny with exertion and good health. There was no makeup at all on Evelyn's face. She looked beautiful. Dix took a bite of his sliced grapefruit. "I called Savich and Sherlock last night, told them what happened. And Christie's father, of course." *And Ruth.*

"A difficult call to make," said Judge Sherlock.

"It was very hard." Chappy had been stone silent, and Dix pictured the stark grief in his eyes again, grief that had lessened over the past three years, now brought back to full strength, though he had known, had accepted, that Christie was dead. "I'm sorry, Chappy," he'd said, "sorry for all of us. This woman looked very much like Christie, but she wasn't." So inadequate, but there was simply nothing else to say. Chappy hadn't broken down, and Dix was immensely grateful for that.

He'd called Ruth on her cell so she could have some privacy from the boys. He knew she was trying to keep the immense relief out of her voice. As for himself, he'd tried to keep his voice as flat and steady as he could. As God was his witness, he didn't know what he really felt, at the core of him, where murky questions and even murkier feelings tangled and snarled, and years of memories heaved to the surface to draw him back. He knew only that he'd wanted Christie to be alive—beyond that, he simply didn't know.

Dix watched Judge Sherlock carefully place four slices of crispy turkey bacon on a slice of toast, fold it over, and take a big bite. A BLT without the LT. Corman said, "Savich and Lacey surely knew what happened; they didn't want to bother you until you were ready. Neither was surprised that Charlotte Pallack wasn't your wife."

"They didn't tell me they'd already spoken to you, sir. Actually I can't imagine either of them being surprised it wasn't Christie, being they're cops and have seen too much to believe in happy endings. As have judges."

It wasn't Christie, he thought again, and kept his head down, not wanting them to see the shadow of grief he knew showed on his face. *You don't want to burden folks with your own pain. It isn't fair,* his mother had once told him, and he hadn't ever forgotten it.

"We got it all resolved quickly," Evelyn said matter-of-factly, "and that's what's important now. You didn't have to wait any longer than necessary to know the truth."

He shot her a quick smile. She was exactly right. He'd been able to find out before he'd sunk into the abyss.

"Thank you both for taking me in on such short notice, for getting the Pallacks over here, and, well, for being here for me. I'm in your debt."

Rather than politely declining the offer, Judge Sherlock nodded. "I like a sheriff owing me. Can't hurt, who knows?"

Evelyn laughed. "He never misses a trick, Dix. You've always got to watch him." Something passed between the two of them, something Dix had seen pass between his own parents, something he knew had passed between him and Christie—genuine affection. But there was another face there now—Ruth's face—and he thought again of how very lucky he was. He knew when he got home he would do what he had to do to make it all legal so he and Ruth could get on with their lives. And the boys could settle once again into the normalcy of a family with both a father and a mother. He said to his hosts, "I was expecting the grapefruit to lemon my lips, but it's sweet."

Isabel came into the dining room. "Dix, there's someone for you on the phone. You can take it out here, if you like, in the hallway."

Dix raised an eyebrow. Who knew he was here other than Chappy, Savich, Sherlock, and Ruth, who would have called his cell? He followed Isabel out of the dining room and picked up the phone. "Yes?"

"Mr. Noble? Dix? This is Charlotte Pallack."

He nearly dropped the phone. He would have been less surprised if it had been the IRS. "Good morning, Mrs. Pallack."

"Come now, Dix, do call me Charlotte."

He said nothing, waited. What was all this about?

She said in a rush, "Will you have lunch with me today?"

After he absorbed that, he said carefully, "You and your husband?"

"No, no, only me. We didn't get a chance to talk last evening—my husband always dives right into politics and I, well, I'm from the South, you're now from the South, I wanted you to tell me how everything moves down there now since I've been gone for such a long time. Both my husband and I are very interested in politics back home."

That was one of the thinnest excuses he'd ever heard in his life and he didn't know what to say. Virginia politics? Fact was, he wanted to go home. Even if he caught the ten o'clock flight, Dix would still miss Rob's baseball game, but at least he'd be home. "I have to get home, Mrs.—Charlotte. I have two teenage boys waiting for me, and a baseball game."

She didn't miss a beat. "It's only one lunch, Dix. Like I said, I'd like to have a brief visit with someone from back home, share experiences, you know, stuff only someone who lives there would understand. And of course my husband dines on political scandal and intrigue. As a sheriff you surely know what's going on in Richmond."

She was digging the hole deeper. Why was she doing this? Had she really been coming on to him last night? If so, what in heaven's name did she expect from him today? It sure wasn't a small-town sheriff's perspective on Virginia political malfeasance. Maybe it was something else, maybe there was something she could only tell him in private, without her husband around. He said, "All right. I'm sorry, but I don't know any restaurants in San Francisco."

"Do you like fish?"

At his yes, she said, "How about Port Louis on Lombard

Street. It's not very far from the Sherlocks' house. They have some of the best seafood in San Francisco."

"Okay. Give me the address and tell me how to get there."

A few minutes later, Dix walked back into the dining room. He looked at the Sherlocks. "That was Charlotte Pallack. She wants to have lunch, talk about shared southern experience, Richmond political scandals, whatever." He streaked his hand through his hair. "I'm driving myself nuts, driving you nuts too. I doubt seeing her is one of my best ideas—actually, it might very well be the stupidest thing I've agreed to in a very long time." He frowned. "My gut is doing the salsa, but—what I'm saying is, I think I should meet her, see if maybe there's something she wants to tell me that she couldn't with her husband here."

"At least she had that," Evelyn said, then added when Dix looked blank, "If she hadn't had the very handy southern connection as a hook, I wonder how she would have gotten you to agree."

"What I'm wondering," Judge Sherlock said, slowly rising, "is what it is she has to say to you that she can't say in front of Thomas. It may be much simpler than you think."

Evelyn said. "Charlotte isn't stupid—" She tapped her fingernails on the white tablecloth for a moment, then grinned over at him. "Maybe it's all very straightforward like Corman said— Charlotte simply wants to see you—she fell victim to those French cuffs of Corman's you were wearing last night."

CHAPTER 14

After Dix booked a later flight, he checked in with Ruth with his new arrival time. He knew she was loaded with questions, ready to fire away, but he cut her off. "I don't have any answers now, sweetheart, but I will."

Sweetheart? Ruth felt honey smoothing down the bristles. *Sweetheart?*

Well. She sat back in her chair. "Okay, you got me. Smooth move."

She thought she could see him grinning into his cell.

"Listen, Ruth, the thing is I don't even have the right questions yet. I'll tell you all about it when I get home. Please be patient."

She huffed, sputtered, and laughed. "You're such a damned cop."

But that was only part of it, she thought as she punched off her cell. She was a cop, too, who happened to love him.

Sweetheart. It had a certain ring to it. She was humming until she got back to the interview transcript of a drifter who'd butchered his way through the Northeast. They'd caught up with him when he'd lost his temper in a bar and broken a bottle of Coors over another customer's head.

Dix drove Judge Sherlock's ancient black Chevy K5 Blazer down the hill to Lombard Street.

"At noon there won't be a single parking space within a mile of the restaurant, so don't waste your time looking. Use the parking garage that's in the same block," Isabel had told him. She looked him up and down. "You look tough and dangerous— more macho without those French cuffs."

He laughed. He wore black jeans, short black boots, a white shirt, and a black leather jacket. Usual fare. Tough? Well, okay, that was probably a good thing.

Judge Sherlock shook his hand and gave him a look clear as a neon sign: *Watch your ass with that woman.*

When he saw Charlotte Pallack waiting for him in front of Port Louis, he did another double take, felt the memory of the awful hollowness that had ground him under for so very long. But he got himself together quickly. She wasn't Christie. He prayed he wasn't making a good-sized mistake, giving her the wrong impression, making her think he was coming on to her.

He smiled, and stuck out his hand, forcing her to take it and not jump in for a hug, which he knew in his gut was what she wanted. "Mrs. Pallack."

"No, no, it's Charlotte, please, Dix."

He nodded and they went in. They both ordered the blackened halibut.

"Very New Orleans," he said as he handed the menus back to the red-jacketed waiter.

She only nodded, and immediately launched into questions, not about shared southern experience, not about the two sitting Virginia senators or the governor, but questions about him.

He went answer-lite, keeping things as impersonal as possible. She began asking the same questions again, phrasing them a bit differently. He'd give it to her, she was dogged. When, finally, she wanted to know how his wife had died, he knew Christie was who she really wanted to know about.

He looked into her beautiful eyes, eyes that didn't have Christie behind them. He found himself watching her face closely as he said, "My wife suddenly disappeared over three years ago. She hasn't been found."

He stopped, swallowed, said nothing more.

Their halibut arrived. It was so hot and spicy Dix had to force himself to eat it. It roiled like nasty thoughts in his belly. He picked up a breadstick. It tasted like chalk.

"You don't know what happened to her?"

"No."

"You think she's dead, don't you, Dix? You don't think she could have run away, nothing like that, do you?"

"No. She's dead. Why are you so concerned, Charlotte?"

"I'm interested because it's something that hurt you very much, Dix. I hate that."

Maybe Evelyn was right—maybe she was interested in him. Why? Because it gave her a kick to flex her skills with a man who'd so obviously focused on her last night? She was another man's wife, but evidently, at least on the surface, she had set her sights on him. He'd been an idiot to accept this lunch offer. But the cop part of him was curious. It was time to turn this around.

He asked her, "Do you have any brothers or sisters?"

"A brother."

"Is he your only sibling?"

She paused a moment, then slowly nodded.

He arched a dark brow. So there was something about her brother. He let it go for the moment, and asked, "Where'd you go to school?"

"Boston. I fell in love with a German guy—big, blond, had a brick between his ears—and ran away with him to Munich. That didn't work out at all. My parents were pissed, but at least I didn't marry him."

"Are your folks rich?"

She laughed, nodded for the waiter to pour her more of the smooth dry Chardonnay. She gave him a perfect Gallic shrug. "Rich, poor, what does it matter? Bottom line, one makes choices. One either regrets the choices or doesn't."

"Oh, money matters, all right. Don't forget, I'm a cop. I've seen how many times money matters too much. Why'd you marry a rich man, one old enough to be your father?"

She actually looked like he'd punched her in the stomach. "That—that isn't very kind of you, Dix. Why I married him is really none of your business."

"What do your folks think of your husband?"

"My parents are dead. A long time ago. I've been on my own for a while now."

"How long have you been married?"

"If you must know, three years." Her voice sharpened. "Any more questions, Dix?"

"Yeah, let's cut to it, Charlotte. Why did you invite me to have lunch with you?"

She wouldn't look at him. With her eyes down, she looked so much like Christie he nearly lost his breath. She was wearing a wrap-around silk dress in a pale shade of blue that Christie had favored. It had a deep V-neck, and very long sleeves that fell nearly over her fingers. He saw that her breasts were bigger than Christie's—but that could be simple surgery. What the hell was he thinking?

He wanted to leave. He didn't want to know if she wanted to jump his bones. He never wanted to see this Christie look-alike again in his life. It didn't matter that she probably had some issues with her brother. He didn't care. He wanted to go home. He wanted to hug his boys. He wanted to make love to Ruth and call her sweetheart again. He wanted Brewster to jump on him when he walked through the front door, his tail wagging furiously.

Charlotte leaned forward. "You want to know why I called you? Okay, Sheriff Noble, last night you couldn't stop staring at me. You said I reminded you of someone you knew a while back, someone beautiful. I'm not stupid, I know it had to be your wife Christie. You said your wife's dead, Dix. That means she's gone. For a long time now. So, what's wrong with me?"

So she wanted to amuse herself with him, nothing more than that. He rose, pulled a fifty out of his wallet and laid it next to his plate, realized it wasn't enough, and tossed down two more twenties. "Nothing's wrong with you, Charlotte. You're a beautiful woman and you know it. Now, I've got to get to the airport." He looked one more time at her face, couldn't help himself. He tried to be a cop, dammit, he was a cop, good at seeing what was in a person's mind, but he couldn't get beyond Christie's expression, one he'd seen on her face when she didn't know exactly what to say to get what she wanted.

He forced himself to smile, to step back both physically and emotionally, and gentled his voice. "I have to go home, Charlotte. I have to forget your face, forget how you look so much like her it freezes my heart. Go back to your husband—your choice, your life."

She rose quickly, grabbed his shirtsleeve. "Wait, Dix, wait!" The long dress sleeve fell back. He clearly saw the bracelet around her right wrist, the beautifully faceted diamonds glittering in their small circular settings.

Dix froze. It looked like the bracelet he'd given Christie in Rome on their second honeymoon, on the day of their eighth wedding anniversary, the bracelet she'd worn every single day since that magic drizzling afternoon they'd watched Pietro Magni himself meticulously etch in the words Dix wanted, so pleased with his creation he couldn't stop kissing Christie's hand.

CHAPTER 15

Dix picked up Charlotte's purse and jacket, grabbed her hand, and pulled her out onto the sidewalk into a cacophony of noise, cars, and people thick on Lombard Street during the noon hour. He walked quickly with her close to his side, away from the restaurant, across Lombard, to the parking garage. He pulled her up the stairs to the second level. It was quieter up here, above the din on the street below.

She was trying to pull free of him, panting now. "What's wrong, Dix? What's going on with you? You're frightening me!"

Maybe she was frightened, he wasn't sure. He realized almost any woman would be frantic to get away from a man who'd dragged her into a garage without any people around. He saw questions in her eyes—not Christie's eyes, hers—and something else. Excitement? He didn't release her. He looked down into her face and said very precisely, "Tell me where you got that bracelet."

Charlotte Pallack blinked. She was clearly surprised. "Bracelet? What—oh, this." She shook back the sleeve and rolled her hand back and forth, making the individual diamond circles sparkle and dance. "Why ever do you want to know about this bracelet?"

"Where did you get it, Charlotte?"

"Oh, all right. My husband gave it to me as a wedding present. He said he got it in Paris. Why, for God's sake? Why do you care?"

In that instant Dix the husband became Dix the cop. He smiled at her, released her wrist, stepped back from her, and managed, somehow, to smile. "Sorry about this, Charlotte." He looked down a moment, felt his breathing hitch. He tried to shrug it off, but couldn't quite do it. "Your bracelet—my wife Christie had a bracelet a lot like yours, and it shook me to my feet. She loved that bracelet, always wore it. Seeing it on your wrist—well—"

Her hand was on his forearm and the bracelet winked and glittered. "Oh, Dix, I'm so sorry. I had no idea at all. Well, that's a coincidence, isn't it? Maybe Christie and I are more alike than just our looks. What do you think?"

He said honestly, looking at her again, "I don't know you, Charlotte. I have no idea how alike you and Christie are."

"Dix? Are you okay now? Look, do you want to examine the bracelet?"

It was exactly what he wanted. He had to be careful not to grab it from her. "Yes, please, that would be very kind of you."

He watched her gracefully unfasten the bracelet, watched the glittering pile of diamonds slide through her fingers as she dropped it into his hand.

He knew exactly where to look. He was so afraid of what he'd find his hands were shaking.

He slowly turned the bracelet until he was looking at the underside of the clasp. He knew what should be there: *At Least Forever*. And right below that Pietro Magni's individualized mark, a "p" intertwined with an "m."

He held the bracelet up, examined it closely.

The underside of the clasp was blank. He could see no sign that anything had been scored off. So close, it was so close, so much like Christie's bracelet it made him want to scream because what he'd believed a precious instant ago simply wasn't true. Another chimera, a gossamer veil that hid nothing at all.

In the end this woman wasn't Christie and this diamond bracelet wasn't Christie's either. He hated coincidence, really didn't much believe in it, and now he'd slammed into two that had nearly torn his heart out.

He handed her the bracelet, and she fastened it on her wrist with the ease of long practice.

"I'm sorry, Charlotte, it is very similar, but I see now that it's different. Please forgive me for alarming you."

He gave her his most natural smile, a smile that often made Ruth pause a moment, grab him, and pull him down to her. Ruth had told him to patent that smile.

Not good. He took a step back.

Charlotte reached out and touched his forearm. "I'm so sorry I even wore it, Dix. The last thing I want to do is to cause you pain. This must be very hard for you." She paused a moment, cocked her head to the side, just like Christie did, and said slowly, her eyes on his face, "This is why you're here in San Francisco, isn't it? Someone who knew your wife told you about me and you came to see if I was Christie. We look that much alike?"

He looked down into that beautiful face and had to force himself to think clearly: *This woman isn't Christie. The bracelet she's wearing isn't Christie's bracelet. Let it go. Go home. Forget all of it.*

But she was very smart. She'd figured her way through everything quickly.

"Partly, yes. Someone saw you, believed you were Christie."

"I see. My husband wondered why Corman Sherlock had called him at the last minute when he knew there was little chance the judge would ever have a change of heart about politics." She paused. "Do you know Thomas was pleased as punch that you kept staring at me all evening? He really liked it that a sexy young gun seemed envious of him. So, you are the reason for the dinner last night, Dix? So you could see me?"

"As I said, that was part of the reason. Fact is, I'm a very close friend of Judge Sherlock's daughter and her husband. I'm here to speak at a law enforcement conference. I'll admit it—seeing you nearly drove me to my knees. Talk about an unlikely coincidence, but there you have it. Now it's over.

"You've been very patient with me, Charlotte. Thank you. I have to leave now. I have to go home. Come, I'll walk you to your car. Where are you parked?"

Before he left her beside her silver Lexus on Level One of the same parking garage, she said, "You asked me why I invited you to lunch."

He waited.

"I'm not a young girl, Dix, and the truth is I'm drawn to you. Even though I'm married"—she shrugged—"I'm drawn to you. Thomas is very kind, but—" Always a but, Dix thought, as if that were somehow a valid excuse.

When he didn't say anything, she said, "Will I ever see you again, Dix?"

He thought of all the coincidences, of the two bracelets, and wondered: *Why hadn't her husband had something engraved on the back of the clasp if it was a wedding present?* And then he wondered, *Was it a new clasp? That wouldn't be difficult, simply change out a clasp on a bracelet.*

Something settled in him, it was a decision made, and he felt calm, in control again. He smiled down at her. "Never say never."

CHAPTER 16

SAN FRANCISCO

Early Sunday morning

Julia looked down at her boy, his skin so pale it was nearly translucent. He'd gone easily, simply faded away as she'd held his small hand, and that was a blessing. But he didn't look peaceful, he looked empty and gray.

She watched Dr. Bryer's hand disengage the monitor, the soft flatline hum now silent. Time passed, a lifetime, a moment. He squeezed her arm, trying to comfort her, but didn't. He wanted her to say good-bye and walk out of this sterile cold room and leave Linc.

"He's not here, Julia," Dr. Bryer said. "He's at peace. Come with me now."

Come where?

She saw herself shooting baskets with him down at Skyler Park, saw him doing his favorite hair-raising maneuver in the half-pipe—his back foot smacking the tail of his skateboard against the ground while his front foot pulled the board up high in the air, oh God, too high, then he would pivot, nearly stopping her heart even as his friends shouted "Real tight, Linc, sweet." How very odd, she thought, staring down at him, Linc had never hurt himself riding his skateboard. Yet a skateboard had killed him.

She saw his small intense face as he sketched her and their rental house, waiting until high tide so he could draw the ocean waves nearly kissing the house pilings. She felt his arms around her neck, squeezing until she squeaked, a longtime game between them, not so comfortable anymore because he was stronger every month.

Julia stared at his slack mouth—no more wet kisses on her cheek, welcoming her home. He had his father's smart mouth, always with an answer, but even his father was dead, gone three months now.

Linc was gone too. She had to accept it. But not yet, not yet. She picked up his limp hand as she stood beside the obscenely efficient hospital bed. At least there were no more tubes attached to him. They dangled from quiet machines.

She was more alone than she'd ever been in her life. Please wake up, Linc, please, *but he didn't.*

He would have turned seven in two weeks.

"Mrs. Taylor, come with me now. It's time."

"Thank you, Dr. Bryer, but I would like to stay here with Linc a while longer." She nodded to the older doctor, Scott Lyland, who'd known her all her life. There were tears in his pale eyes. It nearly broke her.

Time passed, a sluggish cold parade of minutes, before she

*heard his deep hypnotic voice, August Ransom's voice, say
next to her ear:*

*"I can tell you what Lincoln is thinking and feeling,
Julia. He misses you, but he's happy, never doubt that. He's
with his grandfather. You know how much he loved Paw-
Paw. And yes, there's his father. Ben loved Linc, Julia, don't
doubt that. I can help you talk with Lincoln, Julia, let me
do that."*

*Then suddenly that compelling smooth voice wasn't talk-
ing anymore, but she heard something, not his voice, but—
she heard something move, whispery, vague with distance, as
elusive as those long-ago feelings that still wouldn't settle. It
wasn't close yet, but it was coming.*
*She heard soft creaks in the oak floor in the corridor, com-
ing closer.*
What corridor?

Julia jerked awake, her breath hitching, disoriented. She realized she'd been dreaming, felt the old pull of the deadening help-
lessness, the emptiness she'd felt when she'd stood beside Linc,
breathing in the nauseating scent of alcohol and disinfectant that
seamed the air itself.

*No, I'm not in Hartford, I'm here in San Francisco, at home, in
bed. It was the dream, the dream again.*

It was a dream she'd had many times over the years, so maybe what she'd heard was simply some new threads woven into the fabric of the dream. Maybe she hadn't really heard anything—

But she heard them again, slow, soft footfalls—Dear God, someone was here in her house, someone was coming toward her bedroom, coming to kill her. Like he killed Linc. No, he didn't kill Linc, that was a stupid accident that shouldn't have happened. But someone killed August and he wanted to kill her too. This time he came to do it right, he'd—

Her terror froze her brain, paralyzed her for a moment. She'd been helpless Thursday night—dear God, only two nights ago—she'd been so surprised by the sudden attack that she'd have died before she understood what was happening. But she wasn't so surprised this time. And she was ready. She'd rehearsed her movements a dozen times in her mind until her body obeyed without her mind coaching her. She scooted to the side of the bed, quietly slid the side table drawer out, and picked up her pistol, its nitron finish glacier cold, and a second magazine. She'd practiced with it yesterday until it felt perfect in her hand, worked with it until her finger knew exactly how much pressure to put on the trigger. Her heart pounded, but the terror transformed itself into a huge hit of adrenaline that made her shake and feel incredibly powerful.

Her SIG P239 couldn't stop a dream that kept running at night in her brain, it couldn't stop a charging rhino, but all she needed from it now was to protect her from a single man. She pulled the covers over a king-sized pillow as she heard another footfall, closer, nearly to her door.

It was very dark in her bedroom; she'd closed the draperies against the bright moonlight. Julia's bare feet made no sound on her run to the opposite side of the bedroom door. Good, she didn't want him to hear her. To make it harder for him, she kneeled down, her back pressed against the wall. And waited. She could hear her own heart, pumping fast, but she held steady, slowed her breathing. Another soft footfall, then nothing. He was here, right outside the door, his ear probably against it, listening for any sound. She pictured what would happen, what she would do.

Was it the same man who'd tried to kill her at Pier 39? The man with his glasses, his Burberry coat, and his lovely smile?

The doorknob turned very slowly. He was coming in to kill her, shoot her in her bed, shoot her dead in her sleep, the bastard. Fierce anger punched up her adrenaline again, enough to make her shake, but it didn't matter. She was ready.

Come on, you creep. I'm not helpless this time. I know my way around in the darkness, and you don't. Come on in, come on in.

The door opened. She saw a gloved hand first, holding a gun.

She eased down to her stomach and held perfectly still as he walked slowly into her bedroom. He moved gracefully, all his attention focused on her bed. She could make out the faint glint of his glasses, the outline of his dark jacket and dark pants.

When he was not more than four feet in front of her, slightly off to her right, he raised his gun. He shot once, twice, two more times into the pillow, the low thumping sounds of a silencer, she realized. He paused, then shot again where her head would have been. He lowered the gun, took a step toward the bed.

"Drop that gun right now or I'll blow your head off."

The man jerked around, fast, and fired at the same moment Julia did. Her bullet smashed into his arm, and he jerked back.

His shot was too high, slamming the wall right where her heart would have been if she'd been standing. He yelled and cursed as he fired again, six more times, the bullets striking the wall above her head. Had she been on her knees, he would have killed her.

But she wasn't, she was flat on her belly.

She fired again, but the shot went wide, into her bedside lamp, smashing it to the floor. He tried to pull the trigger again but his clip was empty. She fired again, heard the bullet strike the wall behind him, and fired two more times as he bolted in a zigzag out of her bedroom. She heard his boots on the long corridor. She hadn't hit him again, dammit.

Julia leaped to her feet and ran after him, fired several more times as he bounded down the stairs. He was moving too fast, dodging from left to right. He suddenly whirled to face her, went into a crouch, paused a moment to aim. No, he wasn't aiming, he was trying to shove in another clip.

She went down on her knees, pulled back behind the railing, shoved a new clip in the SIG and fired again, missed him by inches, but knocked off a chunk of a newel post, sending wood shards flying. Small pieces flew like darts into his face and neck. He grunted in pain, his hand jerking up to cover his face. She continued to fire as she ran down the stairs right at him and he turned and ran. She realized her second clip was nearly empty. She didn't want to run out of bullets. But she couldn't prevent herself from firing one more time. The bullet struck a tile next to his right foot, and she heard him curse. He jerked the front door open as she fired once more, and he was gone. There was no screaming wail. There was no sound at all. He'd disarmed her security system.

She raced across the entry hall, stuck out her hand to grasp the handle. No, don't open the front door, don't give him another chance. He's probably got that new clip in. He could be standing right outside, waiting for her to show herself, grinning as he waited to shoot her. She sucked in deep breaths, felt her heart pumping so loud it hurt. She calmed herself. She was okay.

Her hand closed on the doorknob. She trembled from the rush of adrenaline still shooting through her. No, she had to be smart, she couldn't go after him.

She'd put a bullet in his arm and wood splinters had dug into his face and neck. She'd done good. She hoped he would drop over in her front yard. She wanted desperately to open the front door and look out after him. Wait, how many bullets did she have left in her own clip? Not many, she couldn't have many left.

She cracked the front door open, heard a car start from perhaps half a block away, heard it moving, the sound of the engine dying away.

She ran over to the phone, but she didn't dial 911. She dialed Special Agent Cheney Stone's cell.

CHAPTER 17

Cheney drove from Belvedere Street in Upper Haight-Ashbury to the Ransom mansion on Broadway in just under eight minutes. He cell-phoned Captain Frank Paulette, told him what happened, that he was on his way to Julia Ransom's house.

She was standing just inside the cracked-open front door when he swung into the driveway. He jumped out of his Audi, fanned his SIG around him, examined the shadows. He saw no one, no movement of any kind. He holstered his SIG, held up his hand to keep her back.

When he was nearly to the front door, he said, "You okay?"

"Yes. Don't you remember? I already told you three times I was okay. Come in, come in. I was a fool, an idiot. I could have killed him, but no, I had to tell him not to move and then he turned around—Oh God, Cheney, he moved so fast, but I was down on my stomach on the floor and I did shoot him in the arm. Then he shot at me, fired lots of times but he missed me, he was shooting where he expected me to be and he was too high.

"I shouldn't have told him not to move, all I had to do was

shoot him and keep firing like you told me, but I didn't. Then I shot my lamp. I'm a moron. But I did shoot him in the arm, so that's something. Maybe he'll get blood poisoning, you think?"

Her voice was manic high. When she crashed, he knew it would take her to the mat for hours. She went on talking, repeating herself another two times, while he took in every inch of her. She sounded and looked like a teenager on drugs, nearly incoherent words flying out her mouth. She was wearing a long dark blue sleep shirt with Wonder Woman on the front, gym socks on her feet. Her hair straggled around her face, the bruise just beginning to fade from her jaw.

He placed his fingers lightly over her mouth to shut her up. She talked through his fingers for a moment before she fell silent. When he moved his fingers, she opened her mouth, gave him an insane grin, then managed to close it again, but not before more than a dozen words spilled out.

He said, "The excitement's something, isn't it? You did good, you won. It's okay that you didn't kill the guy. Really, it's okay, you disabled him, maybe."

She took a breath and said, "I guess I didn't shoot him flat out at first because I wanted to know who wanted me dead. Well, maybe I'm rationalizing what I did. I don't remember what I was thinking. But maybe I thought I'm so bright I could take him prisoner and question him. Pound my head against the wall, Cheney, smack me."

"Not yet," Cheney said, smiling. "Keep talking, Julia, only slow down. Okay, so he ran out the front door—"

"I didn't go after him, but I did crack open the front door, and then I heard his car turn over, maybe half a block away. I was hoping he'd be lying dead by the rhododendron bushes, but hey, he's hurt, right? That bullet could have hit an artery in his arm—no, I couldn't be that lucky and besides, where's the blood? When you hit an artery, there's a fountain of blood, right?"

She was speeding up again to manic tempo so Cheney broke in, speaking slowly, his voice loud. "Look over there on the sidewalk. You can see the splatters of blood from here. You didn't get an artery, but you did put a bullet in him. That's enough." He eased the gun from her hand.

"But I should have shot his head off. He got away. He's still out there. Oh, come inside, Agent Stone, come in."

"It's nearly two o'clock in the morning. Make it Cheney."

She started, then laughed. "You're right, this is the second time you've seen me creeped out, only this time you didn't have to get wet." She looked down at the white gym socks on her feet, saw a small hole in the big toe, and grinned. "Can I have my gun back? I'll be careful, I promise. It makes me feel safe, more in control. He would have shot me dead if I hadn't had it."

She was coming down, more herself again, so he gave her back her SIG. She sort of slinked sideways into the living room, fanned her gun toward the shadows.

He didn't smile. "You can put the gun down, Julia. The guy's gone."

"Yeah, okay—" She carefully laid her SIG on top of an antique marquetry table, and turned to see him speaking on his cell. When he punched off, he said, "I called Captain Paulette again, told him I'd arrived. He and his team will be here soon. He'll have his patrol officers out looking for this guy. His officers will start interviewing the neighbors in the morning. It was the same guy, right?"

"Oh yeah, like Thursday night, he didn't even bother trying to hide his face because he planned to kill me. Didn't I already tell you that?"

"Yeah, but tell me again."

"Okay. I couldn't tell all that much when he was in my bedroom because it was really dark, but when he ran out into the corridor, I could see him plain as day. He was wearing his glasses, but not his Burberry. A dark leather jacket. I think he was wearing black boots. I've got to take more shooting lessons, the guy moved so fast. That second time I shot at least two feet wide. I killed my lamp. Then I shot my newel post but that turned out okay. It exploded shards of oak and gouged his face and neck. Got him good, that had to have hurt."

"Well done."

She sighed, and for the first time felt a smack of cold exhaustion.

"Captain Paulette will take care of notifying all the hospitals. Maybe his arm is bad enough that he'll need medical help. Maybe his eyes too. Okay, I want you to start at the beginning all over again."

She sat on one of the brocade sofas next to him, turned to face him. Before she got started, Captain Paulette walked in. "The front door was unlocked," he said.

"Good timing, Frank," Cheney said, and nodded to Julia.

"Hello, Captain Paulette. Okay, I can do this. The thing is, it all happened so fast, but I think I can get it right now."

But for the moment, she couldn't speak. She tugged her sock over the hole in the big toe.

Cheney saw Frank give Julia Ransom the once-over, just as he had. Her eyes were still dilated, confused, and he knew she was trying to adjust to the threat of death suddenly gone. "Okay, Julia, while Captain Paulette contacts hospital ERs and gets his men situated, I want you to lean back, close your eyes, and replay the whole thing in your mind. Take deep breaths, try to think clearly."

"But—"

"You'll think of more details to tell Captain Paulette, you'll see."

Julia heard cars driving up, but no sirens, and that was a relief. Her neighbors still hadn't stopped giving her sideways looks since August's murder six months before.

Cheney saw she was still too wired. He rose, offered her his hand. "Tell you what. While Captain Paulette speaks to the officers, let's make some coffee."

Captain Paulette sent his eyes heavenward. "Thank you, make it strong. Then I want all the pesky details, Mrs. Ransom."

It was 4:00 A.M. when Julia watched the people from the forensic unit pack up their gear and tell Captain Paulette they'd be back to finish digging the bullets out of the walls in the morning. "Lots of flying lead," one of the techs said. "We've already marked several drops of his blood inside the house and outside on the walkway. We've got maybe another couple of hours tomorrow."

Captain Paulette said to her, "I called the cops off your house after it was quiet last night, had them doing drive-bys tonight. Sorry, bad call. You'll have full-time protection again. I should take your gun in but I won't, particularly after I went to so much trouble getting you a permit on Cheney's say-so."

"Thank you, Captain Paulette. I fully plan to keep sleeping with my SIG."

Julia and Cheney watched Captain Paulette detour to a patrol car parked at the curb. She said to Cheney, "Thanks for volunteering to stay. Even with officers right outside, I'm scared down to my bones. I want to say I can take care of myself—I mean, I sure did tonight, didn't I? But, well, still, I appreciate it. Follow me, I'll show you to a guest room."

She paused a moment, eyed him up and down. "I don't think the bougainvillea room is quite in your style. It's too girly-girl. I'll take you to August's room."

It was a large bedroom with a big window that gave onto the bay, with wallpaper that reminded him of the middle of a forest in the deep fall. It was soothing, as mellow as a good massage.

"There should be birds chirping."

"They hibernate with the bears. There are toiletries in the bathroom, even two different bristle strength toothbrushes." She showed him more of her dead husband's clothes and left him to the forest with its magnificent view.

Cheney called after her, "Leave your bedroom door open."

"I'm not about to sleep in my bed tonight. I'll be right down the hall—with the door open. You can count on it. Thanks again for staying, Cheney. I guess I'm a little spooked."

"You're allowed."

She nodded, gave him a tentative smile and walked down the wide corridor away from him. He could tell she was dragging. He hoped she'd be deeply asleep before too long.

As for himself, he was out as soon as he pulled the thick duvet to his chin.

CHAPTER 18

Cheney awoke with a start to the sound of a woman's voice singing an aria from *Madame Butterfly,* one of the few operas he liked. He lay with his eyes closed, and listened. It was a beautiful voice, with good range. He didn't move until she finished.

He cleaned himself up, brushed his teeth with the extra-firm-bristle toothbrush, and went downstairs to the kitchen to see Julia Ransom bending over to pull muffins out of the oven.

He drew in a deep breath. Blueberry, his favorite.

He didn't want to startle her so he waited until she set the pan onto one of the top burners.

"Smells great."

She whirled around, nearly lunged for the gun sitting on the end of the counter. "Oh. Good morning, Cheney. It's still early. I wanted to—"

She was wearing jeans, ballet flats, and a white shirt, her hair in a French braid. And she was wearing lipstick, he saw, a pretty pale peach color, and some makeup to cover her bruise. She wore no jewelry except for small silver hoops in her ears.

He said, "I was sleeping in my forest bed when the most

incredible music began playing in my head. *Madame Butterfly*, right?"

"Yes, it's my favorite. I'm sorry if I woke you up. Sometimes the songs come out of my mouth and I don't realize, that is, usually I'm alone and I guess I didn't think—"

"It's all right, Julia. You have a beautiful voice."

The microwave pinged. "Thank you. Please sit down. I've got breakfast going here."

He looked at his watch. "The forensic team will be back soon."

"I was looking at some of the bullet holes, so much of the beautiful old wood gouged out. They'll get his DNA from the blood, won't they?"

"Yes. Did you study voice? Sing professionally?"

She shook her head as she poured him a cup of coffee, then moved to the stove to scramble some eggs. "Well, for one semester in college I practiced for hours every day, but then—"

"Then what?"

She shrugged. "Then things changed."

He wanted to ask her to explain, but he didn't. Her past could wait.

She was fast. Six minutes later they were eating eggs, blueberry muffins, and crispy bacon, just as he liked it.

Something pressed against his leg and he nearly leaped off the chair. As it was, he sent his fork flying.

"I'm sorry. Hey, Freddy, you scared Cheney. Come here, little prince, and have some turkey bacon."

A large muscular tabby, more white than orange, jumped

lightly onto the chair next to Julia's and begin talking. The desperate meows didn't stop until he had his face in a pile of turkey bacon crumbled on a paper plate. Freddy chewed loudly and he purred even louder. Cheney listened for a moment, then laughed.

"That guy's got an incredible engine."

"Yes, he does. Even when he was a kitten you could hear him from two rooms away." She sighed. "I think I was the only neighbor willing to watch Freddy so Mrs. Minter had no choice but to ask me. Like everyone else, she's not quite sure whether I killed my husband. And now this." She sighed. "I wonder what my neighbors are going to think now?"

Cheney said matter-of-factly, "When the media does a number on someone, it stays done for a good long time. Now that you're the target, the media will jump on that and people will change their minds, your neighbors included. I didn't see Freddy Thursday night or last night."

"Freddy was hiding beneath the sofa in the library. I'm keeping him for a week while Mrs. Minter and her new husband explore the Greek Islands. They're due back pretty soon. It's a good thing Freddy doesn't sleep with me. That creep might have hurt him last night. I sure hope you're right about my neighbors changing their minds about me."

Freddy meowed loudly. She laughed, petted his head, and crumbled up some more bacon. "Freddy did finish out last night with me, though. I woke up this morning and there he was lying flat on my chest. It was tough to breathe."

Freddy suddenly froze. The hair on his back stood straight up and he hissed.

"Get down, Julia!" Cheney shoved her under the table, drew his SIG, and made his way from the kitchen toward the front of the house.

CHAPTER 19

GEORGETOWN, WASHINGTON, D.C.

Sunday

Dix said, "It was her eyes—not quite Christie's—but so close, for a moment I couldn't breathe. I kept wishing I hadn't gone."

Ruth closed one of her hands over his. "You had to go, Dix, you had to see her, you had to be sure. Now you know, and it's over."

"But it isn't over, Ruth, not with that bracelet Charlotte Pallack was wearing. There's no coincidence that great in the universe."

Savich said, "Since you called yesterday, Dix, I've checked out Charlotte Pallack. That's why I asked you guys to come over today and sent the kids off to the movies with Lily and Simon. Dix, did Charlotte tell you she was from money?"

Dix thought back. "Well, not really, but she certainly gave me that impression, sort of like she was the poor little rich girl, rebelling, and so she ran off with a German guy as a young girl, but she didn't marry him, she came back. She said her parents were dead. She's got one brother—there was maybe something there, but I didn't pursue it. I just wanted to leave."

"Okay, here's the deal. Let me say first that it took even MAX a good amount of time to find out much about Charlotte Pallack's past. Seems Thomas Pallack went to great lengths to keep it obscure—or perhaps she did it herself. But MAX was able to start from their marriage license." Savich paused a moment. "We found the girl, Charlotte Caldicott, in the North Carolina Department of Health and Human Services database. She didn't lie about her father, he's dead sure enough, shot by police while he was attempting to rob a liquor store about two months after he'd abandoned his family. Charlotte was five years old.

"Like you said, Dix, she has a brother, younger by four years, David Caldicott. She, her brother, and her mother lived in Durham, true enough, but there wasn't a dime. Her mother, Althea Caldicott, worked two jobs to support her kids, then she died of runaway breast cancer when Charlotte was eleven, David seven. The children were sucked into the foster care system until they were eighteen. Then MAX lost her for a while."

Dix said, "No college?"

Savich shook his head. "It's interesting, though. She did tell the truth when she could. About her brother, David Caldicott— he's now thirty-three and plays the violin for the Atlanta Symphony Orchestra. He was evidently taught as a boy by one of his foster parents, a Maynard Lee Thornton, who played the fiddle like a dream. David had a truckload of talent. Maynard Lee managed to wrangle a violin for him, and was apparently an excellent teacher. Maynard Lee died when David was seventeen.

When David turned eighteen, he took off for Europe, Prague, to be exact, then Paris, then London. According to his bio with the Atlanta Orchestra, he played his violin in clubs, in parks, in cafes, wherever.

"Now I have another unbelievable coincidence for you, Dix, something I'm afraid throws a new light on everything. When David Caldicott got back to the U.S. he applied to and was accepted by your very own favorite music school—Stanislaus."

Dix could only stare at him. "You've got to be kidding me."

Ruth said, "Come on, Dillon, you made that up."

Savich shook his head. "Nope." He drew a deep breath. "Dix, he was in Maestro, at Stanislaus, when Christie disappeared."

Dix nearly fell off his chair. He rose, paced the length of the living room and back again. He felt like a fist was squeezing the life out of his heart. He sucked in a deep breath. He said as he turned to face them, "I mean, really, Savich, this is nuts, some sort of a vicious cosmic joke. The bracelet, Christie's bracelet, it was on Charlotte's wrist. Everything ties together now, but how? Did David realize his sister Charlotte was Christie's twin? Did he murder her? Or was it Charlotte who murdered Christie? But why? Dammit, why?" He slammed his fist against the mantelpiece and winced.

He rubbed his knuckles as he said, "And then there's Thomas Pallack, bloody rich, hooked up through David Caldicott—it had to be—because Thomas knows Chappy, he was in Maestro. But how would David Caldicott meet Pallack? Jesus, Mary, and Joseph, I'm going to shoot myself."

"It's a head slammer, all right," Sherlock said.

"Lots of pieces flying around," Ruth said. "But maybe they'll come together, somehow."

Dix looked from one to the other. "Why, if Charlotte is innocent, if her husband is innocent, if it's all a mad coincidence, why then didn't she simply tell me her brother attended Stanislaus Music School? Like 'Hey, you're from Maestro, Virginia? Gee, my brother attended Stanislaus, and isn't it a small world?' Doesn't that seem like the natural thing to say?"

Savich said, "It's certainly a question to ask her, but a believable answer would be easy, like 'I forgot, it simply didn't occur to me at the time,' or 'It didn't seem important.'" He handed them a bowl of popcorn. "It's well salted just as you like it, Ruth."

"The bracelet, Dix," Sherlock said, "in your gut, how sure are you really that it's Christie's bracelet."

Dix said, "I was very certain when I first saw it, but all I can truthfully say is that it's very similar. She even took it off so I could see it. That doesn't bode well for her guilt, does it? I looked at the back, where I'd had Christie's bracelet engraved, but it was as clean as the day the bracelet was purchased. There was nothing there, no sign of the jeweler's etchings."

Sherlock said, "We've got a guy in forensics who could scrub the queen's name off her crown and no one would know. Platinum is easy."

Dix sat back, folded his arms over his chest. "If it could have been removed leaving no sign, then yes, I'm sure. Maybe if we could get ahold of that bracelet your forensics guy could check it out. But the only way I can see of getting ahold of the bracelet is to steal it."

Ruth said without pause, "I could arrange that. Not you, though, Dix, you don't have enough experience. I'm sure my snitches have some friends on the West Coast who are into breaking and entering."

Savich laughed. "It's true your informant network is top of the line, Ruth, but I'd prefer you didn't contract out a robbery just yet."

Sherlock said thoughtfully, "It's still not a bad idea. If we had that bracelet, we could check out where it was made, and that'd be one unknown down."

Savich said, "Let's hold off a while on that. If there is indeed a connection, I can only imagine what the two Pallacks felt when they walked into the Sherlock's house and saw you, Dix. They had to know they'd been ambushed. At least one of them had to know it was about Christie, probably both."

"Neither of them showed any signs of recognition at all, and believe me, I was watching their faces closely."

Sherlock said, "You know, Dix, I'm wondering why Charlotte called you yesterday morning."

Savich said, "Maybe she and her husband discussed the situation, knew Dix's sudden presence had to be because of Jules Advere, and decided she should try to get some information out of you."

"But the bracelet—" Dix said. "I don't think she knew about it, where it came from, I mean. Or else, why would she wear the thing? It was like waving a red cape in front of a very pissed bull."

Savich said, "I'm thinking you need to come at it from another direction. Maybe you and Ruth should take a trip to Atlanta."

Dix slowly nodded. "Very nice idea."

"But don't strangle David Caldicott yet, all right?"

"Oh boy, this is getting wild very quickly," Ruth said. Her cop's eyes were alight with excitement and anticipation, but they quickly clouded with worry for Dix. She managed to smile at him, patted his arm. "Good. We've got a plan. So, are you all ready for this? Rob pitched five straight innings without a hit yesterday against the Crescent City Panthers."

Dix laughed, letting the tension go for a minute. "He talked nonstop last night until Rafe finally punched him and I had to pull them apart."

Sherlock said, "Do you know that was the first thing Rob talked about with Sean when you guys got here? Now Sean worships him."

Savich looked at his watch. "Lily, Simon, and the boys won't be back from the movies for another half hour at least. I'm betting the boys will talk her and Simon into some ice cream."

"I think it was an action movie," Sherlock said. "They'll come back wired, count on it. I only hope Sean didn't get too excited when the hero got into trouble. At home he starts jumping up and down yelling out advice in his father's voice. Not mine. Go figure."

Ruth said, "Sean will take his cues from what Rob and Rafe do, which is to sit there, eyes glued to the screen, shoveling in buckets of popcorn."

Dix jumped up and began pacing. "Sorry, guys, I can't help it. I need to get more information on David Caldicott before Ruth and I go to Atlanta."

Savich said, "You can sit down, Dix, MAX has already checked him out. There were no red flags, no criminal record, nothing questionable. He's thirty-three, as I said, more a loner than not, he keeps to himself, no wife—presents himself to the world as a talented geek.

"He's played violin with the Atlanta Symphony Orchestra for nearly three years. Word is he's very good."

"Sounds straightforward," Dix said. "But all of you know it isn't, it simply can't be."

Sherlock chewed more popcorn. "Dillon will let you know if anything else pops. Now, what did Thomas Pallack say to Jules Advere when he was lying on the floor?"

Dix didn't have to consult his notebook. "He said, 'My wife's name is Charlotte. Do you understand? Don't forget it.' "

Sherlock hummed. "Seems a mite of an overreaction, doesn't it? Rather than showing concern about Mr. Advere's collapse? Surely that's odd."

Savich said, "To us, sure, but to them? Who knows? Okay, Thomas Pallack and Charlotte Pallack have been married two years and eleven months, not that long a time after Christie disappeared."

"Other than a big-time politico," Dix said, "what else is Thomas Pallack?"

"There's no shortage of information on him. Pallack made a huge fortune in oil—drilling, refining, distributing, had his fingers in every slice of the pipeline pie. Like Chappy told you, he's invested broadly now.

"When he got out of the oil business in the early nineties, he went big into private equities. It wasn't all that risky for him because he knew a whole lot of powerful financial people who probably owed him. He's made several killings in those ventures working with his high-roller cronies. The SEC has wanted to chat with him over the years, but they haven't gotten past his phalanx of lawyers yet. The lawyers plow the IRS under every couple of years too, when they have the gall to audit him.

"Recently he's expressed an interest in an ambassadorship, not to Chad or Slovenia, but a major country in Europe. That may be why he's raised such big bucks on the national political level. On the surface he's like any number of other wealthy individuals looking for a payoff from a sitting president, but there's quite a snag—" Savich gave them a manic grin.

Ruth finally threw popcorn at him. "Talk, boss."

Savich said, "Well, the thing is, Thomas Pallack speaks to his parents."

Sherlock said, "That's a big crime?"

"Well, the thing is—they're long dead, more than thirty years dead."

CHAPTER 20

Everyone stared at Savich.

Dix said slowly, "You're telling me this wealthy old guy believes in spirits? Believes he actually speaks to them?"

Savich nodded. "I was looking into another case for Agent Cheney Stone in San Francisco, and Pallack's name appeared on a client list of a psychic medium who was murdered six months ago. Pallack has been seeing one since his parents' deaths in 1977, every Wednesday and Saturday. I assume he's still doing it. Interesting, isn't it?"

Dix said, "Why would anyone do that?"

Savich said, "Well, that info led to something else about Pallack that could explain a great deal. Pallack's parents were brutally murdered in their Southampton estate on February 17, 1977."

Ruth sat forward, hands on her knees. "Whoa—bad ending. That makes the spirit deal more understandable, I guess."

Dix asked, "Was the murderer caught?"

"Yes, but not by the local cops. It was their forty-one-year-old son, Thomas Pallack, who hired a battalion of investigators to find him. They nailed him when the police finally searched the basement of a neighbor's house. Courtney James is his name; he's in Attica for life. James was a trust-fund baby, lots of old money. After James's parents retired to Italy, he lived alone in the family manse. He was quiet, smart, kept to himself. He managed his father's banks, commuted into New York City every day, regular as clockwork. No one had a bad word to say about him.

"The investigators found the knife he'd used on the Pallacks in the basement. Their dried blood was on it—at least it was their blood type, no DNA then. Rumors began to churn that he'd killed some other people before the Pallacks, that he was a serial murderer, and they were just his latest victims.

"He went to trial and was found guilty despite all the big-bucks lawyers he hired for himself."

Ruth said, "So Courtney James is still alive?"

Savich nodded. "He's nearly eighty now, one of the grand old men of Attica. Since he's got money, he spreads it around to his cellmates, for respect, for loyalty, for protection. No one gives him grief. He even gives the guards and their families Christmas presents."

Ruth said, "How did his lawyers keep him from a death sentence?"

Savich said, "Back then there wasn't a death penalty in New York, so he got two consecutive life sentences."

Dix said, "You said the word got out that he killed other people in addition to the older Pallacks? What happened with that?"

"That was the scuttlebutt, but there were no specifics. Courtney James was tried only for the murder of the Pallacks, but you know what the jurors were thinking about whenever they looked at him."

Ruth said, "Sounds to me like Thomas Pallack may have been the source of the scuttlebutt to make sure James would be found guilty."

Dix said, "I think Pallack would make a great ambassador to France, don't you?"

Ruth laughed. "Yeah. I'd like to find out what Thomas Pallack has to say to Mommy and Daddy every Wednesday and Saturday." She looked over at Dix, saw the sudden draw of pain in his eyes, and knew he was thinking about Christie. She jumped to her feet and headed to the kitchen, calling over her shoulder, "Tea for you, Dillon, and bottled water for the rest of us, okay?"

She was carefully measuring some of Savich's special black tea into an old Georgian pot, pouring the boiling water over the tea leaves, when she felt a hand on her shoulder.

"You're doing good, kiddo. I know this is hard. Be patient, we'll resolve everything, and then you and Dix can get on with your lives."

Without a word, Ruth turned and buried her face against Savich's shoulder, but she didn't weep. She wasn't about to let tears break through the floodgates. She was afraid they'd never stop, and that was the last thing Dix needed. Savich held her until she was together again.

He pressed her back. "You look beautiful, and my tea's nicely steeped. Let's talk about Atlanta, okay?"

Ruth and Savich had no sooner handed out the drinks when

the front door burst open and three kids came tearing in, two of them reeking of teenage testosterone and a sugar high, Sean so excited he was bouncing up and down. Lily and Simon followed behind them, smiling and exhausted.

Savich sent a thank-you to his sister and her husband.

Rob said, "Hey, Dad, *Fatal Vengeance II*—we had to cover Sean's eyes a couple of times, but it was cool."

Rafe said, "Well, not enough blood and guts, but it still wasn't too bad."

"Mama, the popcorn was great and I told the hero just how to cut the bad guys down."

"It was a bad girl, Sean," Rob said. "She was gorgeous but bad to the bone, Dad. She was tough, moved real cool, you know? Just like Ruth."

When the boys finished their blow-by-blow, Sean said with great relish, "Then she got her head blowed off."

Ruth said, "Fourteen large popcorns, Lily?"

"Maybe twenty," Simon said, laughing. "Don't worry, the movie was more action-adventure, not all that much gore."

"Yeah, kind of tame," Rob said and headed toward the bowl of popcorn on the table in front of his father.

Before Dix and Ruth and the boys headed out, Savich said to him, "I'll e-mail you everything I've got. Then you and Ruth can visit David Caldicott in Atlanta."

CHAPTER 21

Sunday morning

Julia held a protesting Freddy close as she wiggled farther toward the wall beneath the kitchen table.

"Don't move, Julia! Keep Freddy quiet if you can."

Cheney, SIG drawn and ready, walked quietly to the closed kitchen door, pressed his cheek to the wood, and listened.

He looked back to see Julia straining to hold Freddy still. Freddy suddenly stiffened in her arms and hissed again.

Cheney went through the maid's quarters to a back door that gave way onto the enclosed garden. He listened, then opened the door onto the overcast morning.

The backyard was large, the back wall lined with huge oak trees. It didn't lead to another backyard, but to an alley. It was filled with flowers nearly ready to bloom, trees and hedges and an ivy-covered fence. He saw no movement. He pressed himself against the wall right outside the closed door and listened.

Nothing.

He walked quietly back into the kitchen, and shook his head

at Julia. She whispered, "Freddy's hissing toward the front of the house now."

Cheney moved quickly toward the front hallway, pulled up, and listened again. He heard the front door rattle, then open. He heard footsteps, heard men speaking, then a woman's voice.

They weren't trying to be quiet. They were coming toward him.

Cheney came out of the kitchen, raised his SIG and said, "All of you, hold it right there."

The woman threw up her hands and shrieked.

One man tumbled over the over, both of them nearly stumbling onto the Italian tiles.

The woman yelled, "Oh God, it's the man who's trying to murder Julia! Mrs. Masters told me all about you the minute we got home. Is my poor Freddy all right? I'm his mother!"

To Cheney's surprise, both men rushed forward, the woman right behind them, swinging her big red purse. He ducked.

Julia yelled, "No, no, don't hurt him. He's an FBI agent!"

SFPD Officers Blanchin and Maxwell burst through the front door after them. Everyone simply froze where they stood. What had taken the cops so long? Cheney wondered. After all, they'd been assigned to watch the house.

Not long after Blanchin and Maxwell withdrew, their guns back in their belts, muttering between them, Julia sitting in the living room, cozy on one of the sofas next to an older man she'd introduced to Cheney as Wallace Tammerlane. Tammerlane was holding her hand, whispering quietly to her. Thankfully, Freddy's mother, still clutching her huge red purse, and Freddy himself had left right after the two officers.

Julia introduced both of the men as psychic mediums. Great, just great. *Psychic mediums,* which meant that in addition to the woo-woo, they also claimed to speak to the dead. More like con artists. The older man, Wallace Tammerlane, looked up, studied Cheney's face and frowned, then said something quietly to the other man, a younger man, about Julia's age. They looked like father and son, both wearing casual designer clothes, shooting him looks to kill.

Cheney had heard of Tammerlane. He'd had a TV show a couple of years back, had written some books, and he lived right here in the city. He evidently wasn't married since he kept easing his tall lanky body closer to Julia's. He looked about fifty, hard to tell since his face was smoother than a streambed rock.

The other man, Bevlin Wagner, Cheney hadn't heard of, which fact he said aloud, with the result that the man looked at him like he was dumber than a turkey and put his thin nose into the air. He was lanky like Tammerlane, who really did look like his father, down to his large dark eyes. But when junior tried to look brooding and intense, he only managed to look like he wanted a drink.

Cheney grinned at him. "You need to practice that in front of a mirror. That's the ticket," to which Bevlin Wagner replied in a voice not quite as deep as Tammerlane's, "You're not in a good place, Agent Stone. I see conflicting shades of black around you." He shook his head and poured himself some coffee from a beautiful silver carafe.

"My dear Julia," Wallace Tammerlane said, voice low, flicking a look toward Cheney, "I was distraught about what happened last night, nearly worried myself into a psychic block. Are you all right, my dear girl?"

"Yes, Wallace, I'm fine, really."

He gave her a longer brooding look. "And this nonsense a few minutes ago, this man waving around a gun."

"He's here to protect me, as are the two police officers who came rushing in."

Tammerlane said, "Let me get rid of Bevlin and this philistine agent fellow, unnecessary, both of them. I'm with you now. I can protect you. We can go over to Cecile's for an espresso. I need to talk to you, take you away from all this. Perhaps August will have something to say."

Cheney said, "If August Ransom is ready to check in, Mr. Tammerlane, perhaps he can tell you who killed him."

Mr. Tammerlane raised dark intense eyes. "It isn't like that, Agent Stone, isn't like that at all. August doesn't concern himself with the past, with what came before—"

"He doesn't care that someone cut his life short? That the same person may be trying to kill his widow?"

Wallace said patiently, "Agent Stone, when a person has crossed over, all his past pains, past insults, all of it ceases to be important. Indeed, all of life's difficulties cease to exist. However, the truth of it is that August doesn't know who killed him. Whoever it was came at him from behind. He told me only that he heard movement behind him, but he didn't have time to turn around. He'd been taking cocaine, a regrettable habit of his, but he said it helped him focus, made him understand things he couldn't have otherwise, and it slowed his reflexes, flattened any fear he might have felt. August felt only a sudden awful sharpness in his throat, then immense cold. That was the end of it, and he crossed over and everything changed. He was in *The After*.

"But he is concerned about Julia. He loves her, has always loved her. He is here for her, not in this room with us, mind you, but close."

"He doesn't know who hired that man to kill me, Wallace?"

"No, my dear, he doesn't know. Those who have crossed over do not become omniscient. They remain themselves."

"But he was a psychic," Cheney said. "Didn't those abilities carry over to *The After*?"

"No, Agent Stone, they did not. He's there, you see, no need for those abilities now."

"Perhaps," Cheney said, his eyebrow arched, "Dr. Ransom could put the word out, ask around with the other spirits, you know. Or maybe he could hang around a bit here, keep an eye on his wife, tell her when evil is closing in on her."

"Evil, Agent Stone? I don't know that I'd call it evil."

"When someone wants to murder another person, what would you call it?"

Wallace shrugged. "Anger, rage, necessity, probably all those things, but not evil. Evil seems to me to be without motive, to exist for its own sake."

Bevlin Wagner surged to his feet, the energy nearly crackling off him. "You said August isn't here, Wallace. Well, I agree with you. He isn't here now, but he *was* before. Then I sensed he had to leave."

Julia jumped to her feet. "He was really here, Bevlin? You're sure?"

"Of course I'm sure. I felt him."

"But why would he leave, Mr. Wagner?"

"Who knows, Agent Stone? There's lots of things for him to do. It isn't all lying around and singing 'Kumbaya.' No, I don't sense Dr. Ransom at all now, and I would like to. I called to him with my mind voice, trying to call him back, but he said nothing at all.

"I do agree with you, though, Agent Stone. If I were August, I'd be here with Julia, not off somewhere counseling some departed soul." He shrugged, stroked his chin with long thin fingers. "But August always went his own path, and dying wouldn't change that."

Cheney wanted to throw up his hands and tell the both of them to go away, but one of them might be Dr. August Ransom's murderer. One of them might have hired the man who tried to kill Julia.

Cheney said, "Do you speak to many dead people, Mr. Tammerlane?"

"Yes, of course. It is a gift, a responsibility, and obligation. I will admit that August fades in and out quickly, that it is difficult for him to maintain a link with me, thus I've gotten only brief images and spurts of his thoughts. I don't know why. Neither does he."

"May I come and speak to you tomorrow, sir?"

Wallace gave him a penetrating look, a very effective look, Cheney imagined, to make you believe he knew things, things that were beyond you, things not necessarily of this world. Cheney knew he had to try to keep an open mind about this, but when push came to shove, he was a lawyer, steeped in skepticism. It was hard-wired in his brain not to accept anything he couldn't see, couldn't manipulate with his hand and his brain.

"Of course, if it could be of assistance to Julia."

"Dr. Ransom was your friend and colleague, was he not?"

"Yes. Poor August and I were close for many years."

"And Julia, how do you see her, sir?"

"She is a dear girl. We were to have dinner Thursday night, but alas—you know what happened, Agent Stone. I will be at home at eleven o'clock. Does that suit you?"

Cheney nodded, turned his attention to the prowling Bevlin Wagner. "Are you related to Mr. Tammerlane?"

"Related? Goodness no. I'm Croatian. Wallace is from Kansas."

He sounded so insulted Cheney wanted to laugh. He cleared his throat. "Would you also be available to chat tomorrow morning, Mr. Wagner?"

He agreed, shooting Julia an intense look. But, Cheney thought, neither man really looked anxious to speak to him. Why was that? Cheney wondered. Because he was FBI? Because one or both of them had murdered August Ransom?

Julia said, "I'll come out with Agent Stone. He'll want to keep me within sight at all times. He's the one who saved me Thursday night, you know."

And it was done. She'd nailed coming with him very efficiently, no fuss at all. Cheney could have told her he actually welcomed her company, and he did want her close, but he liked that smug, triumphant expression on her face. It was better than the empty fear.

"I can still ditch you," he told her when they were finally alone again.

"Nah, you can't get away from me now. Besides, I can tell you all about Wallace and Bevlin." She lowered her voice to a Transylvanian whisper. "Stuff that will make you shudder and turn pale, roll your eyes back in your head, jerk up in your bed in the middle of the night out of a sound sleep, sweating, your heart booming like a native drum. You haven't seen their old interview records yet, have you?"

"No. It's Sunday. Frank said he'd get all the files ready for me tomorrow morning. I'll go over to Bryant Street and look at them before I come here to pick you up. I have this feeling, though, that since you were always their focus, there won't be a lot of in-depth information on any other players."

"Yes, I was their only focus."

"Yes, I realize that. You wanna know something else? Don't you think Tammerlane and Wagner could be related—they look like father and son?"

"I haven't really noticed before, but yes, maybe you're right. They do hang out together quite a bit. Bevlin lives in Sausalito— you're going to love his house. He asked me to marry him a couple of months ago."

"*What?*"

She nodded. "Yep. And dear Wallace asked me for a date at about the same time. I figured that since I'm no beauty, it was because I'm rich. But both of them are quite well off financially, what with the lucrative book deals and their group consultations that bring in something like a thousand bucks an hour. Maybe they would both like to live in this beautiful house with me."

"A thousand bucks an hour? What a racket."

"A racket? Maybe, but—"

"But what?"

"Come on back to August's study. I've got lots and lots of tapes, of August and Wallace, even a few of Bevlin on TV. Also some of Kathryn Golden, another psychic medium. You'll want to speak to her too. Let's see what you think after you've seen them."

"I'm trying to keep an open mind." *Yeah, like I'm going to believe in spirit communication. Not in this lifetime.*

"The mediums—do they see themselves as something like priests—the great connectors between those left behind and those in the beyond?"

"Something like that. *The Beyond* is just one name for the afterlife. August always called it *The Bliss*, Wallace calls it *The After*. I'll give you one of the books August wrote."

"And one each of Tammerlane's and Wagner's."

She nodded. "Yes, and Kathryn Golden too. Come and watch the videos and tell me August isn't for real, Cheney."

CHAPTER 22

ATLANTA, GEORGIA

Monday

David Caldicott lived on Lily Pond Lane in Buckhead. His hundred-year-old wooden house, set back from the road, was funky, no other word for it, with its pale blue and bright yellow paint job, seven bicycles lined up on the deep front porch, and a good dozen glorious old magnolia trees pressing against the house on all sides, making it one glorious fire hazard. Yet the big house fit in nicely with the other well-tended homes on either side. It was the charming one, the one that drew the eye and a smile.

They knew he was home, but had decided not to call him first. This was to be a surprise.

A young girl, nicely tanned, wearing short shorts and a halter top, her hair in a ponytail, opened the door and stared at them. She was chewing gum. She blew a lovely big bubble and popped it, splatting it over her mouth and half her face.

Dix said, "How old are you?"

She gave him a huge grin through the bubble gum, pulled it off her face and suddenly she didn't look like a teenager anymore. "Goodness, I love you, whoever you are. I'm thirty-three. You did think I was really young, right? If not, please lie. My ego needs a boost right now. David's being a real jerk and I'm ready to drop-kick him out the window except it's his damned house." She shrugged. "Come on in. You want to see him, right?"

"Right," Ruth said. "I'm Special Agent Ruth Warnecki, FBI, and this is Sheriff Dixon Noble."

They badged and shielded her as she popped another bubble, looked startled, then shook their hands. "Hey, I'm Whitney Jones. You here to arrest David? Was he smuggling violins from Russia? A stolen Stradivarius maybe?"

"Not that we know of," Ruth said. "No, we need to speak to him about another matter. We'll keep the smuggling in mind, though."

"I know the FBI has this stolen art section, right? He's guilty as sin, I know it. David! Come on down, you've got cops here to speak to you or arrest you, or something."

Ruth laughed, couldn't help herself. "What'd he do, Ms. Jones?"

"He was supposed to cook out steaks with me last night, but he got caught up in a jam session with some of the other musicians in the orchestra, played in this sleazy dive, and forgot."

"A real jerk, all right," Dix said. "You want me to knock some of his teeth loose?"

"Nah, I couldn't French kiss him then. No, I'll get him where it really hurts—he loves sex and that's easy enough to withdraw from his diet. He'll be going cold turkey." She laughed and waved them into a living room filled with an assortment of eclectic furnishings, from a huge overstuffed red velvet brocade Victorian sofa to a heavy, highly ornate, nearly black Spanish chest that looked to be five hundred years old, with every year showing on its highly shined battered surface. Dix supposed David Caldicott used it for a chair since there was a twisted retro hippie table with a chipped lava lamp sitting next to it. Persian carpets covered the banged-up oak floor, many of them so old they were nearly in tatters. Paintings and photos covered most of the walls—highly romanticized pre-Raphaelite copies and dozens of photos, all of them of famous composers and performers going back to daguerreotypes from the nineteenth century, showing men with bushy whiskers, wiry beards, and fanatical eyes.

Sunlight poured through the wide front windows, the only spot where a huge magnolia wasn't pressing in.

She turned when she heard David's voice calling out from the top of the stairs, "Whitney, I'm sorry! Come on, we'll do the steaks tonight after I get home from the performance. Wait!"

"Forget it," she yelled up at him. "I'm outta here, soon-to-be gone. I'm going out with that bank president." She winked toward Ruth and Dix, leaned close to whisper, "That drives him nuts. He still thinks it's a believable threat, even the bank president part. I'll probably marry him, but not until he shapes up first. See you." Whitney Jones sashayed out of the room. They heard her pop her gum just before the front door slammed.

A few minutes later a tall thin man appeared in the living-room doorway, panting, but evidently he hadn't run fast enough to catch Whitney. He was wearing baggy shorts, a ratty light blue T-shirt, and nothing at all on his long narrow feet. He had a lovely big diamond stud in his right ear, about halfway up.

"Was Whitney putting me on? Are you guys really cops or are you selling something? You aren't from a bank, are you? I'd sure like to meet a banker, I need another home improvement loan."

Dix introduced them, told him they weren't here to help him fix up his house, showed David Caldicott their I.D.s. He didn't offer to shake his hand.

Caldicott studied Dix's badge. "Maestro, Virginia? Oh man, this is too much—I went to Stanislaus. You're the sheriff, Dixon Noble?" He grabbed Dix's hand, pumped it, then began to shake his head. He didn't say another word, just suddenly looked afraid, and began to back away. Now that was interesting, Ruth thought, as Dix said calmly, "I understand you attended Stanislaus at the same time my wife, Christie Noble, disappeared, Mr. Caldicott."

"Yes, yes, I did. It was bad, everyone was talking about it, speculating, you know? It was scary. She was gone." He snapped his fingers. "Just like that. I'm sorry, man, did you ever find out what happened to her?"

Ruth saw that Dix had stiffened up, his way of controlling pain, she knew, and so she said, "May we sit down, Mr. Caldicott?"

He turned to Ruth. "Sure, go ahead. Anywhere you like. The chest isn't very comfortable, though. When Whitney and I get married, I plan on inviting her mother to sit there."

They chose the Victorian sofa with the big red cabbage roses.

David Caldicott sat on the floor in front of them and leaned back against the Spanish chest. "Hey, you guys want anything to drink? I think Whitney opened some wine. Oh, sorry, you're cops, you can't drink."

Ruth smiled down at him. "We're fine, Mr. Caldicott. You have a lovely home."

He beamed, relaxed a bit. "Thank you. I bought it three years ago when I moved here. I'm fixing it up myself and decorating it myself. The upstairs is still pretty empty, needs some work, especially the bathrooms, but I'm taking my time, finding exactly the right pieces, the right tile and design, you know?"

Dix said, "Did you know my wife, Mr. Caldicott?"

He nodded and said, "Well, yeah, most of the students knew her or knew who she was. She was awful pretty and really nice. She came to most of the concerts. I know her uncle was Dr. Golden Holcombe, the director of Stanislaus, and a lot of the students tried to kiss up to her, but she'd just laugh and tell them how marvelous they played. I remember after one of my recitals she came up to me and told me how much she'd enjoyed my performance. She even said I was a natural for a symphony orchestra, even spoke about the Atlanta Symphony. I know she was real good friends with Gloria Standard Brichoux—you know, she's that really famous violinist who came down to teach at Stanislaus after she retired from the stage—and her daughter Ginger, who's some kind of lawyer, not a musician—go figure that. Ginger didn't like me much. I don't know why." He stopped and looked hopefully at Dix.

"Were you interviewed at the time of my wife's disappearance?"

"Yes, all the students were. I told the investigator what I told you. I'm really sorry, Sheriff Noble, I mean, she was your wife. You've got kids, right?"

"Right. Now, Mr. Caldicott, I understand you have a sister. She's what, four years older than you?"

"Oh yeah, Char—" His voice dropped off a cliff. He swallowed and looked ready to bolt.

Ruth pinned him with her voice. "Of course you knew that Christie Noble and your sister, Charlotte, looked practically like twins."

"No, well, maybe. They're close in looks, but I never really paid all that much attention. You see, I really never saw that much of Charlotte while I was growing up. We weren't together, hardly ever. I do remember she used to call me a geek when I saw her. Your wife was always very sweet to me, Sheriff Noble. Charlotte's nice to me now."

Neither Dix nor Ruth said anything.

"Yeah, okay, maybe they do look a lot alike, well, maybe a whole lot alike."

"At the time of my wife's disappearance, Mr. Caldicott, you never mentioned this to anyone. Why?"

"Why should I? She's my sister. She wasn't anywhere around at that time." He paused and looked to be concentrating hard. "It's really hard to remember now, Sheriff, how close in looks they were."

Dix pulled a five-by-seven color photo out of his pocket. "Is this your sister, Mr. Caldicott?"

"Well, sure, that's Charlotte."

"Actually, it's my wife, Christie Noble."

David Caldicott began shaking his head back and forth. "Man, no, that's not possible. I swear I never realized—" He gulped, stilled, and Dix could see that he was scared now, and for good reason. What was it?

"Mr. Caldicott, when exactly did your sister marry Mr. Thomas Pallack?"

David Caldicott's head jerked up. "What? Mr. Pallack? You want to know about that old dude?"

"Yes," Ruth said. "When did they marry?"

"About three years ago."

"The date, Mr. Caldicott."

"I don't remember—well, let me see." He jumped to his feet, nearly ran to the fireplace and pulled down a photo album from atop the mantel.

"Here, Charlotte sent this to me." He flipped it open. "They were married on August third, yes, almost three years ago."

Ruth held out her hand, took the photo album from David Caldicott. She thumbed through it. There were only six photos in it. She paused. So this was Charlotte Pallack, Christie's twin, this vibrant beautiful woman standing next to a man twice her age. He was beautifully dressed, but even his Savile Row suit couldn't hide the belly growing there. Still, he looked fit, his color good, his once-black hair receding, and laced with white. No jowls, no bags beneath his eyes—good cosmetic surgery. She thought he looked smart and ruthless, like he could snap his fingers and make a small nation crumble. She said, "Mr. Caldicott, how did your sister meet Mr. Pallack?"

"How should I know, Agent Warnecki? I mean—"

Dix was looking at him as if he was ready to tear his heart out.

He swallowed, retrenched. "My sister has this thing for older guys. Well, not specifically older, but they had to be rich, really rich so she could have anything she wanted. She hated poverty—we were raised in foster homes after our mom died. I was lucky, but Charlotte wasn't, she couldn't fit, I guess, always wanted to get out. Mr. Pallack is very rich, he's powerful, and he adores her. So I guess it's all good with her now." He shrugged, tried a smile. "Old, young—hey, I like Whitney and she looks like jailbait. She still gets carded, and she's over thirty. Now that makes me laugh."

"You were telling us how your sister met Mr. Pallack."

"I'm sorry. I really don't know, just that they got married shortly after they met. That's what Charlotte told me. Love at first sight, she said."

"Did your sister ever visit you at Stanislaus, Mr. Caldicott?"

"No, Agent Warnecki, I don't think she ever did."

He jumped to his feet, waved his hands around a bit. Ruth looked at those hands, the beautiful long thin fingers, the short buffed nails. She wanted to hear him play the violin.

"What's wrong, Mr. Caldicott?" Dix said as he too rose.

"Nothing, really. I have to go grovel, tell Whitney I'll barbecue the steaks tonight." He looked desperate. "She won't let me touch her until she forgives me, that's what she does when she's really pissed at me." He moaned.

Dix said, "Did you ever speak to my wife other than the time she complimented you after a recital?"

"Huh? Oh, yeah, sure. I went into Maestro to buy stuff, like every other student. She'd be around. I remember I saw her once with you. She kissed you and pushed you into the sheriff's office. I remember she was laughing. She was real pretty."

Dix studied his face. Caldicott seemed too young, yet he wasn't more than three or four years younger than Dix himself. He seemed immature somehow, not yet fully adult. Who knew the roads he'd trekked, where they'd led him? He was a musician, evidently a very good one. Maybe that was it. Why not spend the night, go listen to him play? It would give Dix more time to think of another way to approach him.

"The symphony is playing tonight?"

"Yes." He beamed. "I'm playing Rachmaninoff's 1890 Romance for Violin and Piano."

"We would like to hear you perform."

"Oh man, that'd be great. Please do. I really don't have anything else to tell you guys. I hardly ever speak to Charlotte, only the occasional e-mail, and never to Mr. Pallack. Please, I need to go find Whitney before she turns me into a eunuch."

Dix shook his hand. Ruth nodded at him, smiled. "We might be seeing you this evening, Mr. Caldicott."

Damned if his eyes didn't light up. Dix saw the first hint of resemblance between him and Charlotte and between him and Christie. It was the tilt of his eyes, how his smile widened and lightened them.

When Dix pulled out of the Caldicott driveway in the rented Taurus, Ruth said, "I'd wager my knickers he's lying. I just don't know about what and why."

"I don't know," Dix said. "I simply don't know."

Dix and Ruth didn't get to hear David Caldicott play Rachmaninoff's 1890 Romance for Violin and Piano that night. At six o'clock, they got a call from Savich.

CHAPTER 23

SAN FRANCISCO

Monday

It took Cheney twenty minutes to realize that the SFPD believed the two attempts on Julia Ransom's life were evidence of a falling-out between her and her partner in the murder of her husband. He'd talked to the inspectors, read the files Frank had given him early that morning at headquarters. The investigation hadn't been superficial, exactly, but neither had he seen any sign of real dogged grit—the kind of persistence that should have been there in the case of a murdered celebrity. The initial focus was on the widow, and it never wavered. There were several references to an "accomplice," since the cops didn't believe she'd done it herself. Nope, she must have had a man do the deed, though they never found one. They still believed it, only they were smart enough not to come right out and say it to her face. Or to his face.

Cheney knew Julia hadn't killed her husband, hadn't had a partner, it was as simple as that. So while the police were trying to find the man they believed was her cohort and now her enemy, he had to start at the beginning to solve the murder of her husband.

He looked up when she came into August's study, where Cheney was seated at the desk, reviewing copies of the files. "Why were the cops so convinced you killed your husband?"

"Oh, they still are, you know that as well as I do."

"Okay, yes. Why?"

"Because they believed—believe—I was tired of being tied to an old man, yes, a very rich old man, they thought, no matter his fame or the esteem in which he was held. And I wanted his money. There were rumors about a lover, of course, but I'm not telling you anything new, am I? You're reading all about that, aren't you?"

"Yes."

"I have no idea where those particular rumors came from, who started them, or why." She splayed her fingers in front of her. "The tabloids even tossed out names, one of them poor Zion Leftwitz, August's civil attorney, a very unassuming man who starts at his own shadow. And, naturally, most of the psychics in the area—Wallace Tammerlane, Bevlin Wagner, and Soldan Meissen. They didn't mention Kathryn Golden, I suppose because they didn't want to reach that far, and besides, she probably didn't have the strength needed to kill August. For a while they leaned toward Bevlin Wagner simply because in the entire lot of psychics in August's circle, he's the one closest to my age. I have to tell you, Bevlin was bewildered." She actually laughed, hiccupped, and said, "Sorry."

"Bewildered? He wasn't flattered?"

"Oh no. He worshipped August. He would have cut off his hands for August. He looked at me but didn't really see me, all he saw was his god. Well, not until after. As I told you, Bevlin proposed to me. I'm not sure if it was because of a newly discovered passion for me, or whether he wanted to protect August's widow, but I was as nice as could be when I turned him down. I'm glad the police didn't find out about the marriage proposal, otherwise they would probably have homed in on poor Bevlin again."

"I've read there were also rumors August planned to divorce you—another motive."

She nodded. "Yes, I know. Another part of the lover angle—but they didn't find a scintilla of evidence there was a lover. Still, even when they couldn't find anyone to fit the bill, they were still clinging to it when they came to the house Thursday night, and early Sunday morning."

"Did you volunteer to take a lie detector test?"

"No. My lawyer advised me against it, said there was no benefit to me, just risk."

"Maybe your lawyer believed you were guilty too."

She said slowly, "No, I can't accept that. His name is Brian Huff. He and August had been friends for twenty-odd years, and I liked him. He liked me. When I told him I was innocent, he said, 'Of course you are.' I can't imagine his insisting on representing me if he believed I'd killed his friend and client, the man who kept him on a nice fat retainer in case of litigation."

"I've heard of him. He's a very big gun. Okay, would you take a lie detector test now? Get the cops focused on the here and now, and dump the baggage they've been mired in for the last six months?"

"Do you honestly think that would change their minds?"

"They're a cynical bunch, so probably not, but still, it couldn't hurt."

"Then I'll do it."

Cheney sat back in August Ransom's big leather chair, leaned his head back in his hands. "Julia, tell me about your boy."

She looked as if he'd struck her. "The files," she said. "That's in the murder files?"

"Yes, of course. Tell me about him, Julia." He rose and walked to her, took her hand in his. "Please, Julia, it's important I know everything."

She sighed, felt his hand squeeze hers. "It's hard."

"I imagine it is, but you need to let me in, all right? You ready to do that?"

She gave him a long look, saw the concern in his eyes, felt the caring in him, the need—to help her? Yes, she thought, he really did want to help her. "Yes, I suppose you're right. Lincoln— Linc—was his name. He was six years old when one of his friends ran him over on his skateboard and knocked him into the sidewalk. He hit his head, fell into a coma, and never woke up.

"I stayed with him for the three weeks it took him to die."

He frowned a moment, looking down at the files that hadn't included something important. He asked her, "His father was with you?"

"No, his father was dead."

"Dead? What happened, Julia?"

All right, all of it. "Ben Taylor flew one of the Saud family's private jets. Only three months before Linc's accident, terrorists managed to plant a bomb on the plane. The plane exploded over the desert in a ball of flame. Ben, his copilot, two flight attendants, and all six passengers died.

"Dozens of people were apprehended after the murders, but then it sort of faded away, probably because it was distant cousins who were killed and not any of the royal family proper. I think if King Fahd had been on that plane, the Saudis would have joined hands with the U.S. to find bin Laden. King Fahd died shortly thereafter, and Abdallah took over.

"What really surprised me was that a week after Linc's funeral I received a check for half a million dollars delivered by special messenger from King Fahd, along with his regrets and condolences."

"I'm sorry about your husband."

"Thank you. The thing is, Ben was an ex–Army Ranger. I learned too late he wasn't a domestic sort of guy and never would be, even though he did try for a while. He loved flying, and most of all he loved his status as a pilot for the royal family. He loved being in the Middle East, practically lived in Saudi Arabia. He lived like a prince in Riyadh." She stopped, sighed again. "I was disillusioned, of course. I was very close to asking him for a divorce. It wasn't fair to Linc to hardly ever see his father; it wasn't fair to me either. But then, all of a sudden, Ben was dead. And then Linc."

Cheney wanted to comfort her, he really did, but what came

out of his mouth, all matter-of-fact, was "How did you meet August Ransom?"

"I worked for the *Hartford Courant*. I wrote an article about him. When Linc was in the hospital, he came, every single day. When Linc died, he, well, he helped me, comforted me. I came to believe he could really speak to Linc sometimes, believed it to my soul. He spoke to Linc several times after we married. And now August is dead too."

She turned away from Cheney, walked to the dark brown leather sofa, and sat down. She leaned her head back, her hands limp in her lap. "I never asked anyone else to contact Linc for me. I guess I've never believed in any of the rest of them, only August." Julia looked at the empty fireplace grate. "People believed I married August for his money. What with the money from King Fahd, I had no need to marry anyone. I was fine all by myself, and I had a skill. I'd already proved I could support Linc and myself."

"Didn't your husband send you money?"

Her smile was bitter. "Yes, but I put all of it in Linc's college fund. I guess it was some sort of weird point of honor to me. After Linc died, I gave all the money to a children's medical research foundation. I, well, I simply couldn't bear to use it."

After a moment of silence, Julia said, looking away from him, looking at something he couldn't see. "Everyone died. Everyone I ever loved has died."

He didn't think, simply said right out, "I won't die anytime soon, Julia. And you won't either. And we're going to find out why August died, together. Tell me more about your husband—I know he was quite a bit older than you. From reading the inspectors' notes, that was why they believed you wanted out. They believed you wanted a divorce, he wouldn't give you one, so you had him murdered."

"I know."

"Were you his first wife?"

"No. August married for the first time when he was in his late thirties—yes, I know, a late bloomer. His first wife, a musician, died after only a couple of years, of pancreatic cancer. She was only in her twenties, younger than I am now, as a matter of fact. He didn't remarry. When I was interviewing him for my newspaper, we spent a good deal of time together. I liked him; he seemed to really like me as well. I always held back, truth be told, because his big claim to fame was that he was a psychic medium and I simply didn't know if I could buy that—until Linc.

"He didn't demand sex from me, never even seemed interested, maybe not a big surprise since he was so much older. And I was frozen anyway. But I cared deeply about him, and he about me. I admired him, I was loyal to him, faithful to him, although that doesn't make any grand statement about my morals—I was simply never tempted. If someone else had come along before he was murdered, well, that might have made things difficult."

"Are your folks still living, Julia?"

"I suspect you already know most of these answers. Isn't everything in those files?"

"A lot of it, yes, but it's not from your mouth, with your feelings, your own thoughts."

"They died skiing at Vail the year before Linc died. It was a stupid accident, really, and entirely their fault. Both Dad and

Mom loved to ski off-trail, always ignored all the off-limits warn-ings. An avalanche got them in a posted avalanche area. No, Che-ney, I don't have any brothers or sisters, as you most certainly already know."

She looked suddenly beaten down and he hated it. He carefully laid all the files back onto August Ransom's desktop. He started to tell her—he didn't know what—when his cell phone rang.

"Yeah?"

"Cheney, Savich here. Get to a computer, I'm sending you an e-mail with an attachment of the guy we believe tried to kill Julia Ransom. We need you and her to verify. Call back whether it's the guy and I'll tell you about him."

"You got it, Savich," Cheney said. "Let's get on your computer, Julia."

Cheney called up the attachment and stared at the full-color image of the man's face.

"That's him," Julia said immediately. "I'll never forget his face."

Cheney nodded, and used the study's landline to punch in Savich's number.

"That him?" Savich said.

Cheney pressed speakerphone on. "Savich, this is Julia Ransom. Julia, this is Agent Dillon Savich. He ran the sketch through a special FBI facial recognition program, picked this one as the most likely."

Julia said without hesitation, "Yes, that's him, Agent Savich. Please tell me you've caught him."

"Sorry, Mrs. Ransom, we're not the ones to catch him, that's the SFPD. I'll be sending his photo out to Captain Paulette, telling him you've confirmed his identity. The SFPD will have this photo plastered all over the Bay Area in no time. You are certain, Mrs. Ransom?"

"Yes, Agent Savich, I'm very sure."

"What can you tell us about him?" Cheney asked.

"His name is Xavier Makepeace. His mother's Jamaican, his fa-

ther a Brit. He's thirty-seven years old, very successful in his cho-
sen career, which, as you may have already guessed, is assassin.

"I would have to say that as a professional assassin, it wasn't
bright of him to try for you a second time, Mrs. Ransom, since
it turns out your initial police sketch was right on and there was
already an APB out on him. If he moves again at all, this picture
should nail him."

"The problem," Sherlock said, "is that this man's got a good
deal of pride in his work, doesn't accept failure easily. Oh yes, I'm
Agent Sherlock, Dillon's wife. That's Agent Dillon Savich."

"You're married?"

"Yes, we are," Savich said. "Cheney, what have you got?"

"There haven't been any alerts yet from local doctors or hospitals and no sighting of Makepeace as of yet. I agree with Sherlock. This guy may not be ready to give up. Being bested by an
amateur and a woman—that sure wouldn't look good on his ré-
sumé. And Julia actually shot him."

Sherlock said, "Steve in Behavioral Sciences believes what he did
is out of character. He should have left the city by now. He thinks
Makepeace might be taking this personally now, seeing her as his
nemesis, that he's not about to turn tail and head out of town.
He's got to see her die. Sorry you had to hear that, Mrs. Ransom."

"But I shot him," Julia said. "I had to shoot him. Shouldn't he
be as afraid as I am?" She paused a minute, sighed. "Well, isn't that
a stupid thing to say? He's about as afraid of me as he is an ant.
Sorry, I feel like I'm on Mars here. Do you have any idea who
hired him?"

Savich said, "Captain Paulette is the man to keep you posted on that. Maybe if they can catch Makepeace, they can find out." But Savich didn't believe that for a minute and neither did Cheney or Sherlock. Xavier Makepeace was a professional. Even if the cops managed to capture him, he wouldn't talk.

Cheney said, "You said Makepeace's dad is a Brit. Does the son have an English accent?"

Savich said, "We don't know. But he's worked all over the world. He could probably manage whatever accent he wants. And he seems to have no particular loyalties. We think he's worked for the Israelis, for the mullahs, even for MI6 on one occasion. He has no standard M.O.—well, he does prefer to garrote when he can, using wire—but he uses what's expedient to him in the given situation. He's very thorough in his planning, at times even bizarrely complex, and he's been at it for nearly fourteen years. Very few have gotten close to him, and no one close enough to catch him."

Julia said, "August was garroted."

"Yes, we know; soon so will the SFPD," Savich said.

Julia said in a small voice, "He's very scary."

"Yes, he is," Sherlock said matter-of-factly. "But you've got Cheney with you. He's a rottweiler."

Savich said, "Mrs. Ransom—"

"Please, call me Julia."

"Julia, do you remember your husband having a client by the name of Thomas Pallack?"

"Yes, of course. He and Mr. Pallack were together for a very long time, more than ten years, I believe. Why?"

They heard Savich draw a deep breath. "We just might have

some overlap with another case. I think Sherlock and I are going to come over to San Francisco along with a sheriff from Virginia and another FBI agent from Headquarters. A pleasure to speak to you, Mrs. Ransom—Julia. We'll probably see you tomorrow."

When Cheney hung up the phone, he turned to Julia. "Yep, think of me as your rottweiler. Nothing's going to happen to you on my watch. You ready to see Wallace Tammerlane?"

CHAPTER 25

Cheney kept his eyes on the green Camry weaving around in front of him on Lombard Street. When the Camry driver was finally off his cell, Cheney said to Julia, "The videotapes we watched—I swear I wanted to tell you it was all a load of crap, but your husband, he was very good, Julia, very believable. The others too, but August Ransom was the one who really drew me in completely, despite my being the skeptic from hell. How much do you think was excellent performance and how much was real? It was hard for me to tell."

Julia laughed. "I felt the same way before August was with me in the hospital. I remember rolling my eyes when the editor initially gave me the assignment to interview August. I was thinking all he wanted was a lovely positive fluff piece after I found out his wife had used August to contact her dead father and wouldn't stop singing his praises.

"He changed my mind, I'll admit it. I saw him in action, saw how he worked, how he dealt with grieving people, how he eased them into accepting the continual presence of their dead loved ones. He spoke openly to me about how many charlatans there are in the field, that some of them would do anything to earn a buck, and if someone had the talent—the charisma, I guess, the verbal facility, and the ability to make people buy into them—then only God knew many times who was for real and who wasn't. Grieving people, he said, were the most vulnerable people in the world. As I already told you, I still wasn't certain until Linc."

"But you were grieving, deeply."

She nodded.

He turned his Audi off into the Presidio to weave smoothly through the immense former army base, and came to a stop next to the cemetery. He turned to face her. "But you believed he was really in communication with your son?"

"Yes. There is no doubt in my mind at all. Don't you want to go see Wallace?"

"We have time." He wanted to ask her why she had no doubts, but instead, he said, "All right, why don't you tell me what you think of Wallace Tammerlane."

"You already know that both he and Bevlin Wagner are fond of me, that they admired August, that they've grieved at his loss with me. I remember when the police kept pressuring me to give them names of people who could have killed my husband—other than myself, of course—I couldn't say Wallace or Bevlin, I simply couldn't. They're both my friends. But—" She stopped, turned her face away from him.

"It's okay. Take your time."

She took a deep breath, expelled it, and turned back to face him. "The truth is, I've felt so helpless since August's murder, like the police had painted a bull's-eye right between my eyes.

And then this assassin, Makepeace, came after me." She reached out to touch his arm. "Cheney, I want you to know I've decided to keep practicing with my gun so I'll get better. I'm going to keep protecting myself. And you know something? Maybe there'll come a time when I can protect you too, when I can watch your back."

Cheney said slowly, "Not all that many people have ever offered to watch my back. Thank you."

Julia smiled. "You're welcome. So what did you think of the police files on Wallace Tammerlane's interviews?"

"There was only one interview. Not all that much there."

Julia lowered her voice, leaned close to his right ear. "Did you know some people believe Wallace killed his wife back in Spain in the late eighties?"

He could only stare at her. "That's a kicker. You've got to be kidding."

"No, really, it's true. I don't believe it for a minute, of course, but I don't know specifically what happened since it was way before my time."

"There wasn't anything about a murdered wife in the files. Maybe if they'd known about this they would have checked into it. Why didn't you tell them?"

"That's easy. August never believed Wallace was a murderer and neither do I."

"Tell me. Don't edit, Julia." He covered her hand. "Look, Makepeace's two attempts to kill you are obviously tied to Dr. Ransom's murder. I've got to look at everything again, and I need all the information I can get. Don't hold back on me, believing you need to protect anyone, okay?"

She nodded. "August said Wallace and his wife Beatrice lived in Madrid for close to seven years, moved there in the early eighties. Wallace became the psychic to all Spaniards rich and famous, even King Juan Carlos and his prissy crowd, the Spanish A-list. August said Beatrice was a lovely woman, very beautiful in an ethereal blond sort of way, but she was more like Wallace's cipher, his companion shadow, quiet and watchful. He said he'd rarely even seen her speak to another man. She was focused entirely on Wallace.

"In 1988, Wallace took her with him to visit a client in Segovia. She jumped off the Roman aqueduct. It was ruled a suicide even though a witness reported seeing a man with her on the aqueduct. Since no one could find this man, they didn't rule it the Spanish equivalent of death by misadventure, but rather suicide."

"Did Tammerlane have an alibi?"

"No. He'd already left his client."

Cheney shrugged. "Still, it seems suicide is probably exactly what happened. Was there a reason for her to kill herself?"

"August said she was unstable, that Wallace tried to hide the extent of her illness, that he tried to protect her from talk. I guess she finally broke. So, of course the rumor mill started grinding something fierce. When the Spanish media got up to full steam, even King Juan Carlos's name was bandied around. The king wasn't happy about it, needless to say. Wallace left the following week, accompanied his wife's body back to Ohio."

Cheney asked, "Where is August buried?"

"In Connecticut, outside of Hartford. That's where he was born and grew up, where his elderly mother still resides. He wanted to be cremated, he even wrote it in his will, and so I had it done here. His mother hasn't spoken to me since then because she'd wanted to bury him next to his brother and sister, and his father."

Cheney fell silent for a moment. Then he reached out and took her hand again. "Julia, let me say this flat out. I know you didn't kill your husband, so don't ever wonder about that, all right?"

There was that surge of gratitude toward him again. She smiled at him, leaned close—"You wanna guess Wallace Tammerlane's real name?"

"Bernie Swartz?"

"Worse."

He grinned at her vivid face. "I give."

"Actis Hollyrod."

"Come on, Julia. Actis? What kind of a name is that?"

"His parents must have been spaced out on drugs when he was born, don't you think?"

"Something for sure. *Actis.* What a thing to do to a kid."

"Another thing, Cheney. Wallace likes young girls."

"So do a lot of older men. Wait, don't tell me he's a pedophile."

"Oh no, certainly not, but he appears very partial to females who haven't quite yet reached voting age."

"Do you know this for certain? Or are these rumors in the psychic world? Or did his colleagues simply read his mind and see visions of what he was doing?"

She cocked her head to one side, sending her hair falling beside her face. "Do I hear a bit of snark in your tone?"

"I'm trying to be open about all of it. When did Wallace start preferring younger women?"

"I'm not sure. I hope it was after his wife died. August found it funny. He'd say that even though I was way over-the-hill for Wallace, he, August, still appreciated me."

Cheney noticed her eyes then, maybe because of the way she'd angled her head toward him. Her eyes, a quite nice light green, were bright today. He thought of the woman he'd saved the previous week—pale, hunched down, drawn in on herself. She'd changed, and the change had begun when she'd saved herself. She still looked thin, but not fragile, leached-out thin—she looked sleek and strong. She looked ready to vibrate, she was so solidly in the present, focused and involved. Yes, involved, that was it, no longer a victim, no longer helpless.

Cheney realized he liked her, realized he really didn't want her to die by an assassin's hand.

She snapped her fingers under his nose. "Earth to Cheney, you there?"

"Yes. Now, are these all rumors about Wallace's young groupies?"

"Nope. Actually I saw one of his girls coming out of his house. He obviously didn't think anyone was around because he fondled her on the top step. Then he saw me, saw that I'd seen what he was doing, and he looked bilious. When he realized I didn't condemn him or anything, and never made any smart-mouth cracks, he was as he'd always been toward me, kind and charming. Like

I already told you, Wallace asked me out, but before that, he'd call simply to see how I was, to hear the sound of my voice, send me the occasional flowers. I remember telling him once I was far too old for him. He only laughed.

"I only went to dinner with him occasionally since the police were still looking hard at me, probably even had me followed."

"Nah, they don't have the manpower."

"No, really, I just bet they reasoned that since I'd already married one older man, why not another? I could be following a pattern, no?"

"What did Bevlin think of Wallace's wooing you?"

"He's young, he sees Wallace as old. I don't think he was worried, or even cared. The psychic community is small and very incestuous. There aren't many secrets."

"Well, naturally not—they read each other's minds, right?"

"More snark. To be honest, I don't hear much about mind reading, but it would be really scary if some of them could do that."

Cheney turned on the ignition. "Okay, let's go see if we can catch Tammerlane fondling another teenager. Filbert, right?"

"Right, fourth house from the corner on the left."

"A mansion like yours?"

"It's very different from ours—mine. You'll see. How odd. I've never thought of my house as a mansion. It's just my house, where I live, where Freddy sometimes visits and sheds all over the sofas."

He thought of his condo, how it would fit into a third of her downstairs, thought of that big cat hissing, and smiled.

There was a lot of traffic that morning under a steel-gray April sky, and the wind blew sharp and chill. An hour of sun would have been nice, Cheney thought. At that moment, the thick clouds parted and a wide shaft of sun speared through in front of the Audi. A good sign, he hoped.

As Cheney's Audi muscled its way smoothly up the thirty-degree-angled street, he said, "I'll never forget the first time I drove up one of these steep hills—I thought I was going to sail right off the top of the earth. It still gives my old heart a leap."

"Just try it driving a stick."

Cheney said, "A friend of mine, another agent who'd transferred in from Utah, drove a stick, bragged he was the only real man in the office, that it took real skill to do it right, until one day his clutch gave out and he went hurtling backward down into an intersection filled with cars. Thankfully, no one was hurt. No one in our office drives a stick anymore, him included. Do you know your hair looks like my desk?"

She whipped her head around. *"What?* I look like your desk?"

"Your hair—it's the same mahogany color."

"I see. So, do you like your desk? Admire the finish? Polish it every day? Maybe you even like it so much you don't put your feet on it?"

He laughed, felt every care roll off his shoulders for a moment. He hadn't laughed much in too long a time, too much crap at work, too many crooks they couldn't catch up with, too much frustration. But he felt good right then, really good. He said, "Nah, I never put my feet on my desk unless I'm barefoot. I worship my desk, I even have papers under my computer so it won't scratch the finish. I plan to be buried with my desk."

She laughed, lightly touched her fingertips to his hair. "The color of your hair reminds me of a tan-colored Subaru I once owned. Soft and creamy, sort of like a caramel."

He turned onto Filbert Street. "Pay attention. I ain't no caramel. My hair's plain old brown."

He turned right from Filbert, and in the next minute he turned his Audi onto Wallace Tammerlane's wide driveway. "Dear God in heaven, a double garage in San Francisco," Cheney said. "That alone has got to make this place worth big bucks."

"Probably."

"Julia, I know he's your friend, that you care about him, but be watchful—you know his body language, his expressions, okay?"

She gave him a look, then nodded.

As he walked her to the front door of the flamboyant three-story Victorian, he said, "Just jump in when and if you think it's appropriate."

He was including her, really including her. She gave him a blazing smile.

CHAPTER 26

A man dressed entirely in starched black answered the buzzer. He stood squarely in the middle of the doorway. Good grief, a butler?

"Yes? May I help you?"

"I'm Agent Cheney Stone, FBI, and this is Mrs. Julia Ransom. We have an appointment to speak with Mr. Tammerlane."

"I know who Mrs. Ransom is. You're looking well, Mrs. Ransom. Let me say I am relieved that you're looking well. A pleasure to see you. Come in."

"Nice to see you, Ogden."

"I'm very sorry to hear about all this misery, Mrs. Ransom."

They were shown into a Victorian living room, stuffed with hundred-year-old dark Victorian furniture, down to elaborately crocheted antimacassars spread over the backs of the twin sofas and chairs. The walls were covered in dark red silk flocked wallpaper. Doodads, the term Cheney's father used for all the knickknacks his mother displayed in their living room at home, were everywhere—dozens of little carved wooden animals that looked vaguely African, and scores of tiny teacups and saucers, doubtless at least as old as or older than the furniture, covering the shelves of glass cabinets. Cheney didn't see a speck of dust.

Old portraits marched up and down one entire wall, all of them showing nurses and soldiers from what looked to be the Crimean War. There didn't seem to be any family photos or portraits.

"Good morning, Julia, Agent Stone."

Julia turned, let him hug her. "Hello, Wallace. Thank you for seeing us."

Wallace Tammerlane smiled at her. "It's good to see you, Julia. I couldn't very well say no, now could I? I'm worried about you, about this maniac trying to kill you. You do know, don't you, that I had nothing at all to do with these attempts on your life—that I know nothing about them?"

"Of course, Wallace. Agent Stone is now looking again into August's murder, and he needs to speak to everyone."

Wallace nodded. "I will do what I can to help. Agent Stone, I understand why you wish to speak to everyone again about August's murder. But let me say, you may be wasting your time. I don't know anything, nothing at all."

"Thank you for agreeing to see me, Mr. Tammerlane," Cheney said easily. "I'm not here to accuse you of anything."

"I should hope not! Sit down. Julia, would you care for anything to drink?"

She shook her head. They sat. Wallace Tammerlane, however, moved to stand by the ornate fireplace, and leaned against the mantel, his arms crossed over his chest. Cheney couldn't see a single strand of gray in the inky black hair on his head. He wondered if he dyed it. When he'd met the man yesterday he'd thought he was about fifty, but now, he looked to be about a decade older.

He looked tired, but still his dark eyes seemed almost terrifyingly alive and focused. What did those eyes see that he couldn't see? Ghosts? Dead people? Aunt Marge's lost wedding ring?

He was focusing those eyes on Cheney's face, as if memorizing what he saw, and looking deeper. It was a creepy feeling, Cheney thought, and a bit frightening because the man acted as if he knew about hidden things, things burrowed deep inside Cheney that even he didn't know about or remember.

He was dressed all in white this morning, in sharp contrast to his black-clad butler. He had the look of a European aristocrat, lean and long and ineffably bored, except for those eyes.

"What is it you wish to know, Agent Stone?"

"What's your butler's name?"

"My what? Oh, Ogden. His name is Ogden Poe, always compares himself to Edgar. He's always fancied wearing black. I, however, have to pay the cleaning bills."

"Seems to me that keeping white clean would cost much more," Cheney said. "How long has Ogden Poe been in your employ?"

Wallace Tammerlane shrugged. "I don't know, maybe fifteen years. I don't understand that question, Agent Stone. You will appreciate, as Julia already does, that my time isn't my own. I have a client coming in twelve minutes. What can I do for you?"

"Tell me what you thought of Dr. August Ransom."

"He was a great man, a compassionate man. He helped scores of people throughout his life."

"You believe he was a legitimate medium?"

Wallace Tammerlane didn't move a muscle. A faint sneer appeared. "This is an outrage, an insult. How can you ask such a thing? Haven't you assured him of August's integrity, Julia?"

"He's a skeptic, Wallace, as everyone should be. No one should automatically buy what every psychic is selling."

"Listen to me, Agent Stone, skeptic or not, August was one of the greatest psychic mediums of our time. Why, I cannot tell you how many grateful people he's connected to loved ones who've passed over. He was revered by thousands. I admired him, respected him, as did everyone else I know."

"Well, not exactly everyone, Wallace," Julia said. "Someone murdered him, after all, and it wasn't me."

"Of course not, Julia, but I'm convinced, I've always been convinced, that his killer was an outsider, someone jealous of him, someone who took offense at one of his consultations, and this blighted individual held a grudge, wanted revenge."

Cheney said, "Why would a person hold a grudge against him for telling them that their loved one was happy or content, or whatever they are in the ether?"

"You mock what you don't understand, Agent Stone. Not unexpected, I suppose, given who and what you are. August also occasionally helped people who called with an illness."

"You mean he gave them medical advice?"

Wallace Tammerlane nodded.

"I didn't realize Dr. Ransom had a medical degree."

"He didn't," Julia said. "August said that sometimes he could hear a person's voice and visualize what was happening in his body. Then he said he simply knew whether the person was very sick. He'd suggest medicines and treatments, or send the client to a doctor, but he often knew, he said, whether that was right for the patient."

Wallace Tammerlane said, "Yes, that's it exactly. It's the same with me, sometimes."

"So you're saying, Mr. Tammerlane, that he might have missed a diagnosis and this led to his murder, for revenge?"

"Perhaps."

Cheney said, "Did Dr. Ransom ever connect you to any of your dead relatives, Mr. Tammerlane?"

"No, I never asked him to. Truth is, they're a paltry lot, every single one of them except my grandfather. He robbed banks and died in his bed at the age of eighty-three. Why would I want to hear that they're happy? Actually, I don't much care if they're happy or not."

Cheney said, "From what I understand, the psychic line always seems to be that all dead loved ones are at peace and happy, no matter what they did in life."

"Not necessarily," Wallace said. "You have nine minutes, Agent Cheney."

"Do you think your wife Beatrice is at peace now, and happy?"

If he'd shot him in the gut, Wallace Tammerlane couldn't have been more shaken. He lurched forward, nearly falling. "How dare you say anything at all about my wife?"

Julia rose quickly to go to him. "Agent Stone didn't mean it to come out that harshly, Wallace. But he's an FBI agent, and he's got to question you about your wife's death. Surely you understand." Julia touched his arm, to calm him. "I know it came as a shock, but he's only doing his job. Please tell him about Beatrice."

Wallace looked down at her thin white hand. His mouth was tight. "You're saying, Julia, that August told you about that horrible time in Spain and you repeated it to Agent Stone?"

"Yes, of course she told me," Cheney said. "I told her it was critical that she tell me every single thing about all of you. Don't blame her. Now, did August Ransom find proof you'd shoved your wife off that aqueduct in Segovia? Threaten to expose you?"

Wallace shook off Julia's hand, shoved away from the mantelpiece. "I won't listen to this. Julia, how could you?"

"I'm sorry, Wallace. Agent Stone, surely you're not being fair."

Cheney shrugged, looked down at his fingernails.

Wallace shouted, "That's it! I want you to leave now, Agent Stone. Julia, you can stay, but not him. I'm going to call my lawyer, and you can talk to him from now on."

Cheney said, "Tell me, Mr. Tammerlane. As a renowned psychic medium, do you ever speak to your dead wife?"

CHAPTER 27

Wallace Tammerlane was breathing hard and fast; anger reddened his cheeks, nearly reached his eyes. Cheney waited patiently. Finally, Wallace drew in a deep breath. He got himself together. Julia held her breath, watching the man she'd always liked, a man she knew liked her and had honestly admired her husband. She'd never been certain if he was a legitimate psychic or simply a great showman, if he was also a legitimate medium or one of those despicable individuals who claimed to speak to your dead father and tore out your heart. When she'd asked August, he'd evaded her, said only that belief in someone was based on indefinable things, that we each had to decide for ourselves, which meant nothing. She touched his arm again.

Wallace said finally, calmer now, at least on the surface, "No, I do not speak to my wife. I have never tried to speak to Beatrice. She killed herself, that is all. She was an unstable woman, on medications, which she many times forgot to take. Her suicide was the result. It was a horribly painful time for me, Agent Stone."

Cheney nodded. "Your real name is Actis Hollyrod?"

"Yes. My parents were sadistic and insane to name me that. I had my name legally changed when I turned eighteen. I changed it to something more suited to my actual self."

"You knew your actual self at eighteen?"

"Naturally. I knew I had a precious gift from the time I was seven years old, a gift that demanded I use it to help others, to provide healing and comfort to those in grief. I try to provide counsel and hope that will also assist me along my own path to spiritual awareness."

"Mr. Tammerlane, you're speaking of *The Bliss*?"

"No. One must strive for spiritual awareness during the few years allowed us on this earth. *The Bliss* is what is after you pass from this world. I do not use that term. *The Bliss* is one that August adopted many years ago, and many younger mediums have embraced it. I think it sounds pretentious, rather too much like a bit of New Age feel-good nonsense. Sorry, Julia. However, August felt comfortable with it, as do others."

"What do you call it, Mr. Tammerlane?"

"I call it simply *The After*."

"What exactly is *The After*?"

"Simply stated, Agent Stone, it is the continuation of man's after-death destiny, our immersion into the ultimate loving beneficence of a serene and infinite eternity. *The After* is the embodiment of perfection that we will dwell within, Agent Stone."

Simply stated?

Wallace pulled a lovely gold pocket watch out of his white vest, consulted it, tried to keep Cheney from seeing that his hand was shaking. "My client is due in three and a half minutes. My clients are never late."

"Why are your clients never late?"

"Why, Agent Stone? I charge them, naturally. My time is far more valuable than any of theirs, or yours, a common policeman for the federal government. I have a mission in this life and you are interfering with it, for no reason I can ascertain. You come into my house and insult me. You make insinuations about my poor dead Beatrice. I want you to leave."

"Wallace, don't be so angry at Agent Stone. Like you, his mission is to help people."

"You've disappointed me, Julia, disappointed me gravely. I dislike seeing you with him."

"I'm sorry, Wallace," Julia said. "But I'm concerned that the third time this man tries to kill me he just might succeed. And I must find out who killed August."

Cheney said, "I watched several of Dr. Ransom's videos. He said in one of them that he believed that in *The Bliss* there is a sort of caste system—the more worthy the dead person was, the higher the regard everyone already there will have for him."

"Yes, yes, but what does that have to do with his murder?"

"I'm not sure," Cheney said, "but could someone have killed him even believing it would lower his own position in *The After*?"

"August was right. Naturally some people deserve more consideration than others, whether it is here on this earth or in *The After*. There is little justice here, despite the efforts of the FBI or the police or our damnable court system, but in *The After*? It is entirely different there. No one who believed as we do about eternal justice in *The After* could have caused August's violent death. August is basking in the fullness of what his innate goodness grants him in *The After*. Don't you believe he is watching over you, Julia? What do you think he feels when he sees you allowing a stranger to attack one of his dearest friends? Your keeping company with this man does not become the widow of Dr. August Ransom."

Cheney said, "Do you believe in God, Mr. Tammerlane?"

Wallace whirled around as if shot. "What? God? Do I believe in God? What I believe is there is more in heaven and earth than dreamt of in your philosophy."

"So you believe in an eloquent oration of Shakespeare's. What about God?"

"There is always that which is beyond what we are, Agent Stone, what we think we know, what we imagine. There is always what is beyond death, always *The After*. But not some supposedly omniscient, all-powerful personage—God, Zeus, Allah, whatever, take your pick. No. These are man's creations, formalized constructs—man's attempt to explain what he can't begin to understand. Every culture, every civilization has created some deity to comfort them in death, to explain the simple change of the seasons, the rising and setting of the sun, ever since we had words for those things." He flapped his hands at Cheney as if to shoo him away. "I don't like to discuss this with you in any case. Yours is an untutored mind."

He whirled around and walked away from them. He said over his shoulder, "You are incapable of understanding anything of metaphysical importance. You think in provincial paradigms—good and evil, Heaven and Hell, God and the Devil. This is fitting to a man of your station. And I am tired of your insults. Good-bye, Agent Stone, Julia."

Cheney smiled at him. "You're not bad at insults yourself. I really would have liked to know who or what it is who doles out the perks in *The After*. Good day."

They left, passing by a man in his late sixties, huddled in a gorgeous cashmere coat, his face pale, his eyes lost and bewildered, his thick gray hair blowing in the stiff wind.

CHAPTER 28

As he drove his Audi on 19th Avenue toward the Golden Gate Bridge, Cheney asked a silent Julia, "How long were you and your husband married, Julia?"

"Nearly three years. Then he was killed."

Would you have stayed married to that old man?

"How old are you?"

"I'm twenty-nine."

"I had a woman friend who said she was twenty plus nine."

She said nothing, looked straight through the windshield.

"I believe he was in his late sixties, sixty-eight, I think."

"You think? You don't know the age of your own husband?"

"No."

"All right, you're angry with me. Come on out and say it."

She whirled around to face him. "You're a jerk! You were needlessly rude to poor Wallace. You baited him, you sneered at him. I'm surprised you didn't accuse him of molesting teenagers!"

"I thought about it, but couldn't see any payoff."

She smacked his arm with her fist. "Wallace didn't kill August. He didn't kill his wife. Just because you're a skeptic, you don't have to act like an ass."

"All right, so maybe I was a bit over the top. Look, Julia, I'm not only an FBI agent, I'm also a lawyer. I have to see something, feel it, understand it, before I can believe it. And we're pressed for time here—I needed to rile him to see what would happen. I didn't have time to make nice. Do you understand?"

"Be a skeptic, just don't insult my friends."

"I'm thinking it would do you some good to have some different sorts of friends."

"You're right, I do want some more friends. None of them will be cops, that's for sure."

"Hey, maybe you're more interested in Tammerlane than you let on. Are you sure you only think of him as a friend?"

"You're ridiculous, Cheney Stone. You sound jealous. Young men—I'd forgotten about all that testosterone clogging your brain cells."

Cheney wanted to yell back at her, but he reined himself in. "I don't sound jealous, dammit."

"Forget it."

Since it was late morning, traffic wasn't heavy on the bridge. No northbound toll, so Cheney drove right through.

"I won't tell you where Bevlin lives until you promise you won't act like an ass around him."

Cheney sighed. "All right, I'll be more light-handed with Bevlin Wagner."

"You swear?"

"What will you do if I overstep my bounds—or rather *your* bounds?"

"I'll shoot you."

He laughed, couldn't help it, and raised his hand in surrender. "Okay, I'll be very cool with Bevlin."

"Good. Now, take the first exit onto Alexander and stay on it into downtown Sausalito." She paused, looked out the Audi's window. "I wish those blasted clouds would burn off. There's nothing on earth more beautiful than the ocean on one side, the bay on the other, all glistening under a bright sun."

"All chirpy now, are we, since you've got me in a choke hold?"

"Yep. I don't believe in rubbing salt in wounds."

"So you married August when you were twenty-six."

"You're a dog with a meaty bone, aren't you? Yes, that's right. How old are you?"

"Me? I'm nearly thirty plus three, in November."

She laughed, but it wasn't a freewheeling laugh. "Why are you asking me these personal questions?"

"Humor me, please. I'm trying not to be a jerk about it. I just need all the background I can get. You married him because you felt gratitude toward him since he was with you when your son died."

"You just crossed the line," she said.

Cheney drove the beautiful winding road into the town of Sausalito. Due to the heavy winter rains, the Marin Headlands were richly green, nearly an Irish green. By August, unfortunately, the hills would be brown and barren, a perfect setting for Heathcliff.

"So what do you want to tell me about Bevlin Wagner? Other than he wanted you to marry him. Is that his real name?"

"Doesn't sound Croatian, does it? He told me he was from

Split, a city on Croatia's Adriatic coast. Evidently his parents changed their names when they came to the U.S. when he was a young boy. He's never mentioned another name. Bevlin's been on the local psychic scene for about eight years."

"He's also a medium—talks to dead people?"

"That's right."

"So, a psychic medium is your ultimate woo-woo master. Not only can he put on the psychic show—tell fortunes, see a building fall down before it actually does, see a murderer do the deed—he has the additional selling point of talking to dead great-uncle Alfie."

"That's right, and you're being an ass again."

He gave her a crooked smile.

She said, "August told me once that Bevlin had no center yet, that he didn't know quite who he was, or what he was supposed to do with himself. But he was young, there was time for him, he said. August hoped he wouldn't give up on what was in him before he found out what it was and how to use it."

"This guy seemed so intense—if it's for real he's got to be burning himself up from the inside out. On the other hand, when he turned that intense expression of his on me yesterday, I thought he looked like he wanted a drink."

This time a chuckle burst out of her, whole and clean. Good, she wasn't as pissed at him. She cleared her throat. "I shouldn't have done that, really. Maybe Bevlin does drink too much on occasion. I remember a get-together last year. Bevlin was 'intensing' everyone, as I think of it—you know, sitting in a corner pretending to brood and staring everyone down—until I realized he had a fifth of vodka behind him. I saw him turn a couple of times, sort of hunch over, and swig right out of the bottle."

"When his parents came to the United States, where did they live?"

"New Hampshire. Bevlin always likes to say he's from Croatia, first thing when he meets someone new—I think he believes it makes people think of Transylvania and vampires and things that go bump in the night—you know, it makes him sound like he's steeped in otherworldly knowledge."

"Even though Transylvania is in Romania."

"I remember I said something smart-mouthed like that once to August." She frowned.

"What?"

"August didn't like that I'd said it, that I'd poked fun. Take a left at this first light, Cheney. Hey, would you look at all the tourists. They've got to be freezing."

There were a good hundred out-of-towners huddled in jackets on the sidewalks of Sausalito, giving their custom to all the scores of clever tourist shops on either side of the street, ice cream cones and umbrellas in their hands.

"He didn't like it? Why would he care?"

"You've got that bone in your mouth again. August felt I shouldn't mock a man who might have much to offer the world sometime in the future."

Cheney turned up Princess Street and began tacking his way up the hill.

"Do you think Bevlin Wagner has a lot to offer the world in the future, Julia?"

She stared out the window a moment, then slowly shook her head. "I don't know, I really don't. He has written one book on spirituality—*To Watch Your Soul Take Flight*. I have a copy, I'll lend it to you. Read it. It—well, it helped me once."

"All right, I will. But how can you not be a skeptic? I mean, finding lost children, maybe even forecasting disaster, but really, talking to dead people? Give me a break. It sounds absurd."

"Everyone should be a skeptic, but keep an open mind. In the end, though, we all have to make up our own minds, Cheney."

"Why should I really care one way or the other?"

"Because at various times in our lives we have need of something to help us make sense of things—of senseless tragedy, for example. I know that makes us more vulnerable to those who would deceive us—you bet it does. But if you've never felt ground under with despair or grief, if you've never been forced to focus inward rather than at your outward daily routine in the world, then I don't think you should judge them or what they do because that inner eye of yours is closed to it, as they'd say."

"Inner eye?"

"That's their word for it. They speak of it as a door deep in our minds that cracks open occasionally, usually when we have need of spiritual comfort. Of course you can't prove it with any sort of science or critical argument."

"Is your inner eye open now?"

"No. That's Bevlin's house up there, perched right over the cliff."

CHAPTER 29

Cheney parked the Audi on the narrow curb at the base of a dozen steps that led upward to an eagle's-nest house.

They walked up the thick old wooden steps to Wagner's house, skinny trees and brush pressing in on either side—it felt like a small wilderness, dense and wild.

The front door was ajar and so they walked into a small, dimly lit entrance hall. Cheney called out, "Is anyone here?"

"A moment," a man's shout came from upstairs. "Go into the living room, on the right."

The small front room was all windows that looked toward the bay—the tip of Belvedere, Angel Island, even Alcatraz was in view. Beanbags, all of them bright red, were scattered throughout the room, some in small groupings, some alone. The walls were bare, no bookshelves, no photos, nothing but those dozen or so bright red beanbags.

In less than a minute, Bevlin Wagner walked into the living room, wearing only a thick white towel knotted below his waist.

"Hi, Bevlin," Julia said, evidently finding nothing strange in this.

He walked up to her, leaned down, and kissed her mouth, then straightened to study her face. "You look beautiful, Julia. I was so worried about you yesterday, you were so pale, so frightened."

She nodded. "I'm fine now. Thank you for taking the time to speak to Agent Stone."

"No problem." Bevlin, the towel loosening a bit around his waist, nearly mesmerizing Cheney, said, "Agent Stone. I'm pleased you're keeping Julia safe."

When in psychic Rome, Cheney thought, and shook the man's hand. He wanted to tug on the towel just to see what he'd do. Bevlin Wagner was dead white, and his burning dark eyes and long black hair made for a compelling contrast. He had very little body hair.

"I was in the shower, didn't want to keep you waiting."

"You're always in the shower, Bevlin," Julia said. "Go put some clothes on. We'll be right here when you get back. I promise I won't let this dangerous FBI agent search the beanbags."

Those soul-probing dark eyes hit Cheney's face square on. "I didn't have time to wash my hair," Bevlin said.

"It looks clean enough, don't worry," Julia said. "Get dressed."

Bevlin left the room, whistling *Bolero,* if Cheney wasn't mistaken.

"He does this exhibitionist thing often?"

"Oh yes. It's sort of his trademark. I don't know why, since he isn't all that remarkable a specimen."

"Has he ever lost the towel?"

"Yes. He paraded out with his towel once when I arrived before August did. The towel hooked on a doorknob and whipped right off. I looked him straight in the face and told him I knew a really good personal trainer."

"He wasn't insulted?"

"Didn't seem to be. He said personal trainers were too hairy except for the women, and they scared him."

Cheney laughed. "What's the deal with all these red beanbags? How long has he been doing this?"

"Ever since I've known him, and I don't have a clue."

Bevlin Wagner came back into the room, wearing old gray sweats, his long narrow feet bare. "Agent Stone, I know you're here to question me about the attempts on Julia's life."

Cheney said, "Yes, I appreciate your time. Mainly, I'd like to ask you about Dr. August Ransom's murder. There seems to be little doubt that the attempts on Julia's life and his murder are connected."

"I don't know anything about any of it, I'm afraid." He looked over at Julia and blessed her with his sweeping intense look. "If only I did know something—are the two really related? Okay, maybe, maybe. Wallace and I wondered about that, of course. I must tell you this, Agent Stone, when August visited me last night, he told me he really doesn't like you, that you might be dangerous, and I should be careful not to anger you. He's displeased about your being with Julia. He didn't say so, but I'd wager he'd be much happier if she were with me."

Julia said, "Bevlin, there is no earthly—or unearthly—reason for August to be concerned about Agent Stone. He's trying to find out who garroted him, after all. Despite what Wallace says, I think August would want his murderer brought to justice."

Cheney said, "Bevlin, what you said, it is what August thinks, not what you think, is that right?"

Bevlin walked to the huge front window. "Of course it's what August thinks." He paused. "The fog's finally lifting. I have three clients today. The first one a batty old doll who wants to give all her money to a nice-looking young man who says he'll set up a trust for her. There's a big commission for him, naturally. God knows what's in the fine print." He shuddered.

Julia asked, "What is your role in it?"

"I've already approached her husband, so to speak. His name was Ralph, owned a large piece of Sausalito at one time. He asked me to call his son, try to keep her from losing every dime he earned. Said those dimes had been too hard to come by to hand them over to a smarmy, good-looking crook. Ralph said he heard she's not going to be joining him for a number of years yet, so she'll need all the money he left her. I called the son a little while ago." He shrugged again. "He was foaming at the mouth. Maybe some good will come out of it, we'll see. Hey, Agent Stone, maybe you could go pop this crook."

Cheney found himself drawn in, believing for a moment that this very strange man had indeed spoken to Ralph, a very dead person.

He couldn't help himself, whatever Julia thought. "Did you really dial up the dead husband, Mr. Wagner, give him the lowdown?"

"Ralph? Well, not really," Bevlin said. "It was one of my guides who tugged on me, told me to talk to this old geezer, he needed to know what was going on."

"Guide?"

"Yes, my guide. I am speaking English, not Croatian, Agent Stone. All of us have guides, all of us. But some of us are too unaware to even recognize that they're there. I happen to have a good dozen of them, all for different matters, you see. One knows finance, one speaks beautiful Hindi, one has perfect pitch, is very proud of that and is often telling me what he's listening to at the moment, and the key that's being played—but he's not much use, as you can imagine. There's this one guide, all he can talk about is Egypt, about all the time he spent in the library at Alexandria.

"My best guide is a real schmoozer, can chat up those who have passed over, tell me what's in their hearts."

"Do your guides have names?"

Bevlin frowned. "Do you know," he said slowly, bending those dark eyes on Cheney's face, "I've never thought to ask and they've never offered. They're all very individual, really. I never had need of names to speak with them."

Julia said, "Bevlin, you said yesterday you knew August had been there, but he'd had to leave. But you spoke to him last night?"

"Of course."

Cheney asked, "When you spoke to him, was it through a guide?"

"Ah, August is different. He isn't like other people who've passed. He already knew how things work, how to get through to me."

"I've never heard about guides before," Cheney said. "I mean, are they dead people who volunteer for this duty?"

"That's a novel thought, Agent Stone. They're simply—there,"

Bevlin said. "Simply there, like when I first realized I could see things other kids couldn't, a guide told me what was happening. He's still with me. Sometimes he wakes me up when I oversleep and a client's coming."

Cheney said, "Can you talk to one right now?"

Bevlin Wagner eased down into a big red beanbag and closed his eyes. He sat perfectly still.

Cheney felt like he'd wandered into Disneyland Croatia.

Bevlin's eyes slowly opened. They looked dreamy and vague. Odd how that could change so quickly. "I spoke to my first guide. He told me I had the gift but I have to continue to grow before I can truly become what I was meant to be. He said I had to work on being more grounded, and listen to those who know more than I do. He knows I can reach my potential, and he's doing his best to help me."

"But why did he come to you specifically and not someone else?"

Bevlin cocked his head at Cheney. "This might take a while. Please go into the kitchen, have some coffee. I made it this morning."

Then he closed his eyes. For a moment, Cheney was convinced he'd stopped breathing. He took a step forward.

"No, it's okay," Julia said. "Let's go to the kitchen. You really don't want to try his coffee. He has bottled water."

"Yeah, sure." Still, Cheney kept looking back over his shoulder at the man sitting as still as a tree stump on a red beanbag.

CHAPTER 30

The kitchen was down the hall to the right. It was small and filled with light, a round scoopout at the end holding a small table and two chairs, done in country French.

Cheney said thoughtfully, "He said he had a financial guide. Wouldn't that mean he knew how to play the stock market? I wonder why Bevlin isn't living in a mansion."

Julia opened the refrigerator and pulled out two bottles of water, handed one to him. "August used to say that everyone would believe in psychics if one of them won the lottery. Who knows? I certainly don't. Look out back, no yard to speak of, it just goes straight up to the next house. I think there are two more houses above this one. This place isn't bad, if you ask me."

"He is very weird, Julia."

"Different, Cheney. He's merely different."

"Well, then, look at this situation. There's this guy out there sitting on a red beanbag, looking dead, and he's talking to a spirit guide. Do you think I'm dangerous?"

"Yes."

He spewed out some water. His left eyebrow shot up.

"Like recognizes like. You see, I've discovered I'm dangerous too." Her voice sounded low and mean. At this point in time, he thought, she was right. She said, "Thing is, I'm wondering why August would tell Bevlin you were dangerous. I think you're right, Bevlin might be projecting his own feelings a little."

Cheney grinned, clicked his water bottle against hers. "There you go. Maybe Bevlin's guide doesn't like me, or maybe he or she is lying."

Julia downed the rest of her water and grabbed another bottle from the fridge. "Let's go see if Bevlin has connected with his guide."

They walked back to the living room. Bevlin Wagner was lying on the floor, flat on his back, his arms crossed over his chest, his eyes still closed.

"All he needs is a white lily," Cheney said. "Or maybe black, I'm not sure just yet."

"No, not lilies, I'm allergic to lilies." Bevlin opened his eyes, sat up, and wrapped his arms around his knees. "My guide said one day it seemed he simply woke up and there I was, this scrawny little kid who spoke to his parents and wondered why they didn't realize they'd already had that particular conversation."

"Déjà vu?"

"Yep. When I was little, I never thought about it, it was simply the way things were. It happened with friends sometimes too. I already knew what everyone was going to say."

"So your guide was what—asleep—until you came along?"

Bevlin shrugged, came gracefully up to his feet. "More like he was simply there, maybe not fully aware of who he was, or what he was intended to do."

Julia tossed him a bottle of water. He snagged it out of the air, opened it, tilted it back, and drank the entire thing straight down.

"This sort of thing would make me thirsty too," Julia said to Cheney.

When he was finished with the bottle, Bevlin arced it toward the single wastebasket in the far corner of the room. It banked off the wall and fell neatly in, gave a small bounce, and settled.

Cheney said, "So you have no thought at all about who killed Dr. Ransom?"

"Of course I asked him when he warned me about you. I've also asked my other guides. Neither he nor any of the others seem to know. That, or none of them wants to tell me. I'm not sure which. Maybe they don't think it's my business, maybe they don't think I can handle it. August didn't see who it was, he told me that, just as he told Wallace." Bevlin shuddered. "He said it all happened really fast, but he still felt the horror of it, knowing he was going to die, and there was nothing he could do about it. He said he didn't feel all that much pain, a blessing, he supposed, thanks to the gift of cocaine."

Julia said, "I wasn't aware August used cocaine until the police found a stash locked in one of his desk drawers and the medical examiner found cocaine in his system. I thought I could always tell if someone was high on drugs, but he kept it a secret from me, and he did it well."

"All his close friends knew he used cocaine," Bevlin said. "It never occurred to me to mention it to you. In any case, he said he sort of let go and then he was on the other side and he realized his knees wouldn't ever hurt him again. That pleased him."

Cheney said, "Bevlin, I've been wondering why your guides don't make you filthy rich."

He scratched his armpit. "The thing is, the guides don't know everything. When I was young I wanted to bet on a horse whose name was Second Sight—I asked my guide and he said he had no clue which horse would win, but he didn't like the name. Too cutesy, he said. Funny thing—Second Sight won. My guide made himself scarce for a while after that."

Cheney said, "You knew Dr. Ransom for what? Seven, eight years?"

"Yes, something like that. He was a great man. I'm hoping he'll help me focus, help me see more than I've seen before."

Cheney said, "You mean he'll be another guide?"

"Hmm, I hadn't thought of it like that. Perhaps so."

"Who do you think killed him? Not what the guides think, what do you think?"

Bevlin said matter-of-factly, "If you asked me to pick someone in the profession, I'd vote for Soldan Meissen. He's a real fruitcake, has all these silly affectations. I hear he's into dressing Far East now, wears silk robes and smokes a hookah, plucky bugger. The man is disturbed, and he's greedy. Julia knows his history.

"You can forget Wallace. He's harmless. As for Kathryn Golden, I call her a TV whore. She sure hates that, gives me the evil eye. She's a very good TV whore, in fact. Her name was Betty Ann Cruther. She changed it about twelve years ago. It's no secret, she tells anyone who asks. It's odd though, no one ever asks. I wonder why Kathryn picked Golden—why such a ridiculous color?"

"Ask a guide," Cheney said.

"Good one, Agent Stone. I will tolerate your company so long as you are of use to Julia."

Julia said, "You didn't say if you thought Kathryn could have killed August."

"Nah, Kathryn wouldn't ever hurt August. She was in love with him."

"I didn't know that," Julia said. "Surely you're wrong about that, Bevlin."

"No, I'm not. Why would you know? No one would ever say anything about it to you. Fact is, babe, devious old Kathryn wanted August for years. They go back fifteen years at least. I don't know if he ever slept with her, none of my business. Of course August wouldn't say anything about it. He liked Kathryn and he wanted you to feel at ease around her.

"She once got drunk with me and Wallace. I think Soldan was there, looking down his nose at the three of us, and she prattled on about how she and August were kindred spirits.

"I'll tell you, the more big-name clients she latches on to, the more it goes to her head. She's a bit like Soldan, who's turned into an even bigger ass since he got his skinny little foot on TV. Thinks he's better than all of us now."

"Well, Soldan is richer, Bevlin. So is Kathryn. Actually, so is Wallace. He's got a butler, for heaven's sake."

"Ogden has always been with Wallace, even when he was poor. I just hope Wallace pays him more now that he's raking in the money."

Cheney said, "On the other hand, Julia, Bevlin is much younger than the rest of them. Give him time."

"Thank you, Agent Stone, but the truth's the truth. I can take it. Did you know that Kathryn's latest book sold forty thousand more copies than mine? Mine was better, but hers hit the public pulse just right. I suppose I'm a bit jealous, and my guides really frown on that."

Cheney said, "Is Kathryn Golden a legitimate medium?"

Bevlin shrugged.

"How about Soldan Meissen? He's all over TV."

"I forced myself to watch Soldan—sounds like a magician's silly name, doesn't it—The Great Soldan—anyway, I watched him once on an afternoon talk show. He did this cold reading on the studio audience. That means he's never met any of them before. He did the usual shtick—you know, 'I feel a W, yes, a W, a W, or an F, that's it, it's either a W or an F—and the month of June, that's important, real important to someone.'

"He spoke fast, that's real important to keep the potential marks moving with you. He was smooth, and sure enough, someone shouted, 'Yes, yes, I was married in June, June the nineteenth, and George almost made it to June, died May twenty-seventh.' There's always someone married in June, right? So Soldan moves to the stand right in front of her and leans close. 'Yes, it is George, I can see that now. Perhaps we can talk to him.' And blah blah blah. He was good, impressed the hell out of most people in that audience. He moved so quickly it was hard to tell he didn't have all that many hits. I mean an F and a W—and the woman yells it's really a G for George, not remotely close, but no one notices. You see, if you're fast enough, charming enough, and silky smooth, it doesn't matter what you're selling." He shrugged again.

"All it takes is one person to connect to what you're throwing out there and you've got your hook in. That's what Soldan's best at."

Cheney said, "That's called a cold reading?"

"Yeah, as opposed to a hot reading, which is fraud, you know, getting information about people without their knowledge before the fact."

"So," Cheney said, wanting to sit down but not about to fling himself onto one of those beanbags, "this Soldan is a con artist?"

"Maybe."

"And Kathryn Golden?"

"She's good-looking, you know, and uses that well. But I can tell you for sure she's a psychic. I've seen her fall into a vision and I know it was for real. She told Wallace once that he'd left his jockey shorts in Violet's backpack. She was this young woman Wallace was seeing at the time. I thought Wallace would belt her, especially since he didn't know if he really had left his shorts there. And Kathryn's about the best I've seen at reading people, especially those who don't realize what she's doing."

Julia said, "But you think she made that up, you know, to tease Wallace?"

"Hey," Bevlin said, "in this business you can say you spoke to Oswald and who's to say otherwise? You can look at a photo of Sonny Bono, claim he's singing all over heaven wearing bell bottoms, that he hated being a politician but he really loved skiing and just look where that got him. Or you can say that when John Jr. hit the water, his mom Jackie was first in line to welcome him into the light, whatever. Again, if all you're interested in is entertaining, or getting an emotional response, there's little to stop you. Who's to say you're making it up?"

Anyone with half a functioning brain, Cheney thought. He was feeling the mire creeping up to his knees. Time to refocus. "You think Kathryn might have murdered Dr. Ransom because he refused to leave Julia for her?"

"Nah, Kathryn wouldn't ever be into that sort of thing. Also, she knew August really loved Julia, so there would never be a question of his leaving her for any other woman."

He smiled at Julia. "No, August wouldn't have left you even if the famous Madame Zorastre from nineteenth-century Prague had come back and offered herself. August really admired Madame Z, as we refer to her. I never heard him say that about any other psychic. Hey, he's probably met her by now, don't you think?"

"Why not?" Cheney said.

Suddenly Bevlin walked away from them and over to the big front window. He looked down. "I thought so," he said over his shoulder. "My fuzzy old doll's here and I've got to convince her that her husband wants her to listen to what his son has to say about this trust scam. Please find out who killed August, Agent Stone, and keep Julia safe."

Cheney and Julia passed the fuzzy old doll on the stairs going back down to the street. She paused, a little bird of a woman dressed in frilly pale blue. She looked them both up and down, and slowly nodded. "I can see that Mr. Wagner has helped you. You're wonderfully attuned to each other. How lovely to be young and want to bundle all the time. Now it's going to be my turn. Mr. Wagner will be so pleased for me—I'm going to marry my sweet young man." And up the stairs she went, her step light, her pink scalp showing through her fluffy white hair.

"Oh dear," Julia said. "This isn't going to make Bevlin's day."

"Or Ralph's. I feel like I've fallen down the rabbit hole. Bundling? Didn't that go out in the eighteenth century?"

"No, it never does."

CHAPTER 31

Xavier Makepeace stood at the window of his hotel room in downtown Palo Alto and sneered down at the people scurrying about like pointless lemmings, none of them going anywhere, none of them worth anything. He imagined picking up his Kalashnikov and mowing a wide swath down the middle of that unending noisy herd, thirty rounds so fast it made your teeth sting. It would put all those useless cretins right out of their misery.

His Kalashnikov, his favorite assault rifle, was cheap and simple, and it never let him down. He always spoke its full name, liked the way it flowed on his tongue when he whispered it aloud, not the ridiculously shortened AK-47. Too bad he'd had to leave it tucked it away in his home in Montego Bay. But still, he enjoyed thinking about how it would feel to spray bullets from his open window—he could almost hear the screams, suck in the smell of terror, and the odor of gunshots and death. It always revved him like nothing else.

Nothing revved him at all right now. He turned away from the window.

He thought back to the years before he'd gotten his Kalashnikov, the years of his youth when he'd gathered young Jamaican men around him with bribes of the very best, the most potent ganja, their spiritual aid and, it seemed to him, their only escape. He'd believed he could lead them to do almost anything at all, and what he wanted was to rob the pasty-faced Brits, break their wills, send them scurrying back to that cold, benighted island of theirs. He thought he'd convinced some of the young men to put their future in his hands, to rebel against all the Brits' stupid laws and tedious education, their bloody imperialist history and foppish speech, the greedy thieves. His father included. His father, who'd been sent to what he thought a dismal little island as a civil servant to improve the locals' lot. Yeah, like he had cared whether that was going to happen.

Xavier had realized before his father had that the young men hadn't wanted to be improved. They wanted to spend their days sprawled in the shade, wallowing in the numbing bliss of their ganja. They stayed polite to his father and had backed away from Xavier, like he was crazy and they might catch it.

Xavier thought of his father's endless rules and regulations, that supercilious way he looked down his nose at those he considered his inferiors, and that included anyone who hadn't attended Sandhurst.

And yet his father had lowered himself to bed a local, and Xavier was the result. The old man eventually sent him to England for an education he said would rival the prime minister's. Xavier had hated the relentless cold, the bone-numbing damp, and the rain, always the rain, snaking down his neck, making him so miserable he'd wished he'd die.

And how he'd hated the Brits. At school they rigorously caned

their rebellious young to make them strong, and he was no ex-
ception. He'd heard them say more times than he could stomach
that it was for his own good. He thought he might bomb Sandhurst out of existence one of these days. It was something pro-
foundly pleasant to look forward to.

Xavier realized he'd clenched his hands so tightly they were
cramping. How could that old bastard still twist him up?

Bad memories, he thought, that's all. His old man was well
and truly gone, ever since Xavier had squeezed three neat shots
into his chest on a sodden black night in Belfast, years and years
ago. His father was there to negotiate with those hate-filled
blighter Irish, and ended up sprawled on the street between his
two dead bodyguards. Xavier had watched the life fade out of his
pale icy eyes, filled first with disbelief, and then final awareness.
He leaned down and told his father that a lowly Siberian peas-
ant had invented the Kalashnikov and what did he think of being
shot with that? His father hadn't answered, he'd died instead.

Xavier had stood over that sodden bloody mess of tweeds, a
still-furled umbrella lying next to him. He hadn't told those dark-
eyed men in Belfast that he'd have been happy to kill his old man
for free. His father had fetched ten thousand pounds, and he'd
enjoyed that money, along with his inheritance. At least, he'd
thought, the Irish were trying to rid themselves of the bloody
English, and he'd done his part. For a price.

Incredible weapon, the Kalashnikov. He'd once thought the
M16 was the god of all assault rifles until he'd been with a group
of Palestinians on a raid in the desert and the damned thing had
jammed, victim of a blizzard of blowing sand. Why, he'd asked

their leader, did they use weapons that didn't work in this hell on earth? But the Arab had only shrugged, said there would always be hardships for those who tried to carry out Allah's wishes. Xavier found their hard-wired hatred of the Israelis insane—as if the Israelis hadn't lived side by side with them over thousands of years as they'd fought and lost to a host of invaders. He knew deep hatred like that knotted you up, made you an easy target rather than a fluid shadow, unseen by your enemy because you moved too fast and sure. Hatred made you stupid. The Palestinians had looked at him when he'd said that, then away, quickly, and he'd known in that moment that without their hatred, they'd have nothing at all, their lives would be pointless, like that paltry stream of humanity parading below his hotel window. It was then he'd eschewed all contact with groups of any kind. He was by himself now, depended only on himself and answered only to himself. He was the perfect assassin, swift and silent and deadly, terminating his targets without flaw, without fuss.

Until now.

He felt rage rising in his throat, a sour peppery taste, and wanted to choke on it.

A stupid little woman, an amateur who should have died in San Francisco Bay, a lovely deep knife thrust through her heart, had shot him, maimed him. Of course he couldn't have factored in an FBI agent that first time, couldn't have predicted he'd be there at that precise moment. What a bit of luck for that walking-dead bitch. Well, that hadn't been because of any flaw in planning on his part.

But when she'd shot him on Saturday night—there had been

no *deus ex machina*, unexpected and unforeseen, to rescue her. He closed his eyes, still couldn't believe what he had let happen. The dozen small cuts on his face and neck were a constant reminder, and he could still feel the shock of pain when he'd tweezed out each splinter. The bullet had only hit the fleshy part of his arm and thankfully gone through. He'd been able to tend to it himself.

She could have killed you. Why hadn't she? Why had she bleated out a warning? He was there to kill her, for God's sake. She was a wimpy amateur, thank God, paralyzed by fear even when it came down to saving herself. *She could have shot you in the middle of your back when you were facing her bed. You were lucky, lucky, lucky—*

His hands fisted again. How he wished he had his Kalashnikov. He could walk right up to her front door, and when she opened it, he'd pump twenty rounds into her, all in her face, shredding bone and flesh, splatting blood and brains all over the acres of marble, rich wood, and the paintings marching up the walls. And anyone else with her. Then he could walk back out of that posh death house, whistling, and leave this foggy cold city.

But what he had was his Škorpion VZ 61, thirty years old and no longer made. It was his mentor's in a guerrilla force in southern Africa, until he'd been shot in a raid, and Xavier had uncurled his fingers and taken it. His Škorpion was small, light, and easily concealed, and it was fitted with an efficient silencer.

He swallowed three more Aleve.

He'd had two chances at her, two solid chances, and she was still alive. His employer wasn't happy, but no matter. He was not going to slink away now, no matter what orders or stupid rants he heard. This wasn't acceptable. He'd never failed and he wasn't about to fail now, to turn tail and run. He sat down at the stingy little desk, picked up the cheap ballpoint provided by the hotel, and drew a piece of hotel stationery from the drawer. He would get her this time. He began to write out a list of what he would need.

CHAPTER 32

EAST BAY

Monday afternoon

About the only time Cheney used his portable GPS was when he had to cross over from the known into what he called Middle Earth, namely drive over the Bay Bridge to that place others called the East Bay, with its overflowing cities, tangle of overpasses, and signs that pointed to more highways and still more signs. Oakland, Hayward, and a dozen other cities, most of them growing, spreading over the barren hills, out until it was Palm Springs hot in the summer.

"I see you aren't comfortable driving in the East Bay," Julia said as she watched him punch in the address in Livermore.

"Drives me nuts. I got lost every time I had to drive over here until I got this." He pointed with great affection to his GPS. He loved the soothing female voice telling him to turn left in two tenths of a mile, and then that comforting pinging sound as he went into the turn. "Okay, let's make this our last interview today.

The traffic's already getting bad. It'll be rush-hour gridlock by the time we drive back to San Francisco."

Julia nodded. "You did okay with Bevlin. Can I trust you not to fly into sarcasm mode with Kathryn Golden?"

"I'm reformed," he said, and crossed his heart. "I'm sympathetic and sensitive. I promise."

"Yeah, right."

After a few minutes, Julia shifted in her seat to face him. "What are you thinking about, Cheney?"

"That cold reading deal Bevlin Wagner described. Why, if the dead person is standing right beside the medium, doesn't he simply tell the medium his name, tell him who he's there to see? Doesn't he remember his name? Are the dead playing some sort of weird game? Sorry, Julia, but it doesn't make much sense to me. It sounds to me like they're simply fishing, trying to hook in some poor schmuck who's grieving and desperate to know that his loved one who died still, somehow, exists, and is somehow sentient."

Julia said, "Oh, the psychic field is full of charlatans, wannabes, and shysters, all right. I watched a tape of a woman medium—she really had some poor young man going, telling him his mother was right there beside him and that she wanted him to stop his grieving, that he had to depend on himself now, that she knew her passing had frozen him in place and he needed to move on. She wanted him to know she loved him as much now as she had before she'd passed. The medium realized she'd got something obviously wrong because the young man didn't respond, and so she quickly switched in midstream in a different direction. She suggested he hadn't gotten along with his mother, and when he responded and nodded, she knew she had him. She kept talking, hinting around what his mother was like—that she always spoke her mind, that she was always telling those around her what to do—and soon she had the young man nodding some more. She used the guy's guilt to get to him, and by the end of it, he was crying and clutching the medium's hand, and I thought, how low do you have to be to perpetrate such a lie on a vulnerable person? And all for money, I guess, for a name, for self-aggrandizement.

"I'll tell you, Cheney, August hated those *slicks*—that's what he called the so-called psychic mediums on TV. All you have to do is read the long release forms every TV show attendee has to sign to know there's something seriously amiss with the whole thing. They basically make you swear you won't say a single word to anyone about what happens during the show for as long as you live. You probably have to swear to keep quiet even after you're dead."

Cheney cut his eyes to her. "There are release forms?"

"Yes, isn't that something? The producers and the psychics want to cover themselves since a person could tell the media after the show is aired how thoroughly the show was edited, how the psychic was bumbling around.

"August called it the Barnum philosophy at work—give people what they want. If they're hurting, be the compassionate expert who will take away the hurt. It's the grieving people who make it all work. They'll overlook the most egregious blunders— or misses as they're called—and still believe that beloved dead Uncle Albert is there, at the medium's elbow, watching over them, telling them he's happy as a clam himself, and even happier they're doing well and they're not to worry about him."

Cheney said, "And Uncle Albert didn't even bother to tell the medium his name? It boggles the mind what people can be led to believe."

Julia nodded. "It takes a lot of talent to be able to run the ultimate scam—convincing the marks they're talking to dead people. Sometimes mediums justify it by saying they're helping people get through their grief, helping them by using their own brand of counseling. But August never believed in anything based on a lie. If those people want to be grief counselors, they should be up front about it."

Cheney said slowly, "I don't understand, Julia. Didn't August Ransom claim he spoke to dead people?"

"Yes."

"Did the dead at least give him their names?"

"I can't say, since his consultations were always private, and he never spoke to me about them, or to anyone else."

"But you believe he spoke to the dead? Communicated with them, passed on messages to those grieving left behind?"

"He told me he'd spoken to Lincoln, and I believed him."

She sounded so certain, so settled in her belief. He eyed her. He didn't know what to think. He decided to leave what she'd said alone. She'd evidently bought into everything her husband had told her. He wasn't going to make her defend him.

A horn sounded, and he focused on the road again. He finally saw the exit sign to Livermore. "I want to hear more about all this, but first, we've got about five minutes for you to tell me about Kathryn Golden."

She said, "I think Bevlin's wrong about Kathryn being in love with August. She's too—together, I guess is the right word, too focused on what she is, to love someone like that. And besides, if she wanted him, why would she kill him? Why not me? That doesn't make any sense."

"Maybe when she approached him one last time and he turned her down, she was enraged, made plans to get even."

"She always has lovely fingernails. I can't see her doing anything to endanger them, much less garroting him. Okay, that was a bit snippy, but the fact remains no way does she have the strength to garrote anyone."

"Okay, you're probably right. So she could have hired someone. I'm getting the picture here that you simply never considered her any sort of threat, that you might even like her."

"I suppose I do like her, and you're right, I never saw her as a threat of any kind. August loved me, I knew that. He never gave me cause to doubt it."

Cheney chewed that over for a moment, then asked, "Do you think she's really psychic? Like August was?"

"August used to say that many people who thought they were psychic simply overflowed with intuition. With those people he really believed did have psychic gifts, he said he pictured two big beakers—one to measure their actual psychic ability, the other to measure their ambition for material gain. He saw their beakers filled accordingly when he made a decision about them. He said

Kathryn's psychic beaker was more than half full, but her ambition beaker flowed nearly to the top. So she stepped over the line sometimes. But he said she was so smooth and charismatic, such an expert at reading people, she could make anyone believe she was communicating with their dead Saint Bernard."

When Cheney pulled onto Raleigh Drive, a street that speared up a barren hill where the houses were large and set wide apart, he paused a moment, looking around. "The psychic medium business appears to be good to Ms. Golden."

"She's practically a regular on daytime TV, you know, some of the talk shows. She even had her own show for a couple of years. She's written a couple of books and both did fairly well, as Bevlin told you. I read *The Soul's Search*. It was actually good. The fact is, Cheney, though I've never disliked her, I have gotten the impression she thinks I'm an opportunist, that I married August mainly for his money. I suppose she thinks August was taken in, dazzled by my youth and beauty."

"Do I hear a whiff of sarcasm?"

"Well, yes. Youth and beauty, give me a break."

Cheney looked at her high cheekbones, the bruise fading, her creamy white skin, and her pale green eyes, ever so slightly tilted at the corners, her mouth with its light coating of pale peach lipstick. He wondered if Kathryn Golden had a point.

Julia was saying, "I don't know of any scandals in her past, nothing like that. She's always been a little aloof to me. She did love August, though not, I don't think, in the physical sense. She admired him as much as everyone did."

She added as they pulled into the driveway, "I don't like it that we didn't call her, to tell her we were coming."

"We know she's at home, that's enough," Cheney said as they walked up the flagstone path to the front door. There were flowers everywhere, in beds lining the walk, in flower boxes, and hanging in baskets from thick black chains, in wild spills and vibrant colors, scenting the dry air with jasmine and violet. "We might learn something by catching her off guard. It's an old trick. Hey, the door's open, just like Bevlin's. What's with psychics?"

Julia shoved the door open, called out, "Ms. Golden? Kathryn? It's Julia Ransom."

There was no answer.

Cheney called out this time.

Still no answer.

They walked into a windowless entrance hall, the marble tile such a dark green they looked almost black in the dim light. "Suck in some air," Julia said.

Cheney sniffed. "It's vanilla, too much vanilla."

"It's her trademark scent."

Kathryn Golden appeared in the living-room doorway, framed and posing. She looked around forty-five and was dressed beautifully in a full-skirted long-sleeved black dress, her black hair in a stylish chignon. She wore open-toed three-inch heels and diamond studs in her ears. She looked ready to tango. TV appearance?

She arched an eyebrow. "Julia, whatever are you doing here? And who is this man?"

"This is Special Agent Cheney Stone, Kathryn. May we speak with you?"

"I've been watching the news. I hope you're being careful. Yes, now I recognize you, Agent Stone. You saved Julia's life."

Julia nodded. "Yes, he did. Agent Stone is continuing to keep me safe."

They followed Kathryn Golden into the immense living room that stretched, Cheney saw, the entire length of the house. It was long and narrow, with thick burgundy drapes closed over the wall-to-wall windows set at both ends. The floors were darkly varnished, bare of rugs. He looked over at a huge dark-veined golden marble fireplace on the opposite wall that looked like it had never been used.

The room was starkly elegant, like a museum, until you realized all the furniture groupings in the long room were black woven rattan. The extreme contrast in styles wasn't tacky, but rather oddly charming. There had to be a story behind this. Then he noticed the modern art covering one of the stark white walls, dark violent paintings, some of them of mouths that seemed to be screaming at him. It gave him the willies to look at them.

Suddenly Kathryn Golden stopped in her tracks, and didn't move, didn't even seem to breathe.

CHAPTER 33

Ms. Golden? Are you all right?"

"Please be quiet. I'm having a vision. You and Julia—back away. Go sit down."

Julia didn't seem at all alarmed or find this particularly strange. She shushed him, pointed him to one of the long rattan sofas.

He watched Kathryn Golden kick off her high heels, sink to the floor, and assume the lotus position facing the fireplace, her black skirts billowing out around her. He guessed she knew better than to wear a tight skirt. He saw she had a nice French pedicure and perfect fingernails.

He opened his mouth but Julia shushed him again.

They sat silently as Kathryn Golden threw her head back, clenched her hands on her thighs and began to weave, left to right, right to left, and started to keen, an eerie sound that was vaguely ridiculous but nevertheless raised gooseflesh on his arms.

She began moving in a wide circle now. He heard her breathing heavily. He felt like arresting her for fraud, or maybe for trying to scare an officer of the law.

The weaving lessened, the keening became low, almost a whisper. Then, suddenly, it was over. She snapped awake, came to her feet in a single graceful motion and smoothed her skirts back down. She slipped her heels back onto her feet.

She sat down opposite them, crossed her legs, and stared at Julia. "My vision was about you, Julia. In it, I was you—I felt young and limber, like I could leap into a tree if I wanted to. It felt so very good. Then I saw a man and I knew he was watching me—rather you. I saw deep cold blackness at his center, saw the virulent purple flashes of his narcissism and his pride in himself and his work.

"He's the one who wants to kill you, Julia. That first time at Pier 39 you were nothing to him, only a job to carry out. He didn't hate you, nothing like that. But he does now." She stopped because her breathing had kicked up. She closed her eyes a moment, then slowly opened them, blinking.

Julia said matter-of-factly, "He was all over the news, Kathryn, his picture, the fact that he's probably a hired killer, the works."

"Always the little skeptic," Kathryn said, pleating her skirt with long thin fingers. "August said you often refused to believe anything anybody said, except for him, of course.

"What I told you is the truth, Julia, and it's deeper than the news. I saw what's inside him, what he's about. He's very dangerous and very smart, but he's barely human anymore. He's empty and cold. He wants to kill you, wants it to his very core."

"The cops didn't release his name to the media," Cheney said. "Did you see in your vision what it is, Ms. Golden?"

"I am not a performing seal, Agent Stone."

Proof enough, Cheney thought. "Did you happen to see where he is, ma'am? We need to bring him down before he can take another shot at Julia. Can you help us find this monster?"

She drew in a very deep breath, let it out slowly. Her dark golden-green eyes, witch's eyes, never left his face. Maybe that was where she'd gotten her last name.

"I think he has an author's name, isn't that odd? Usually, of course, people don't think about their own names, but I got this flash—he happened to look at a book and he felt at one with it. An author's name, is this close?"

Damn. "Yes, it's close."

"Good. Now as to where he is. Again, he wasn't thinking about where he is. But he's watching me—well, he's watching Julia, and he's planning. I could feel chaotic energy roaring through him, the feeling he could outrun anyone, fight anyone, kill anyone who tried to stop him. But you know? I think he has bad eyes, though. You know already he wears glasses. He thought, only a moment, that maybe he'd get laser surgery, but he's afraid to, his vision is too important to him."

She turned to Julia. "If I'm pulled into another vision about him, perhaps it will be to where he's staying and I'll see it. I don't want him to kill you. To lose poor August and to then lose you six months later—it would be too much. But I don't understand. Why would anyone go to all this trouble to kill you? Fact is, if he knows why, he doesn't care enough to even think about it in passing. You're a challenge to him now, maybe the biggest challenge he's ever faced from his prey. You're his entire focus now."

Julia said, "Who do you think killed August, Kathryn?"

"My opinion?"

"Yes, as a person, not a psychic."

Kathryn said, "I don't know, but you should talk to Soldan

Meissen." The same one Bevlin named, Cheney thought. "He was so jealous of August," she continued, "it was eating him up. Perhaps it was something as simple as his wanting some of August's big-name clients. I heard he netted one of August's very rich longtime clients, Thomas Pallack."

Julia said, "I did know that. But I haven't spoken to any of August's clients in a very long time now. Thomas Pallack was with August for more than ten years."

"Few of them wanted to speak to you because they believed you were guilty and they didn't want to be involved in any of that. I'll wager whoever it was behind August's death wanted you to be blamed, Julia, and so you were, but you survived the investigation. I think the person who hired this killer is afraid of you, afraid you'll find something out, or you've already found out something that points to him, and that's why he or she wants you dead."

She paused, sighed. "At least you have August's journals, you've seen firsthand how he changed lines, just as he changed yours. You've experienced through his own writing exactly what he was." She sighed again. "How I wish I could read August's journals. Perhaps you'd let me see them, Julia—"

"I didn't know August kept journals, Kathryn. I've never seen them."

Cheney said, "Did you ever actually see Dr. Ransom's journals?"

Kathryn nodded. "One evening, maybe eight months ago, I was dropping off some papers. August was in his study and he was writing when I came in. Unfortunately he was holding his notebook at such an angle I was unable to make out the words. I remember he told me it was the only record of his life that meant anything, all the rest was just empty words."

She rose. "I have a meeting with a producer in twenty minutes. Agent Stone, you have a rich crimson aura, beautiful, really, vibrant and powerful as a rushing waterfall. I've never seen a policeman with an aura like that."

What to say to that?

"Oh yes, and there's something else—you hurt him, Julia. The man was thinking he needed more Aleve for the cuts on his face and neck. His arm must not hurt very much, at least he didn't think of it when he thought of the Aleve."

All over the news, Cheney thought, except for the painkiller. The Aleve was a nice touch. Suspects giving alibis knew that specifics added verisimilitude. Evidently it was the same with psychics.

"I felt his anger like a furnace blast, Julia. Then he was aware his feet hurt and it distracted him for a moment. They're new David Smith boots, and they'd rubbed blisters on his heels. That first time at Pier 39, he ran all out, not good in new shoes."

"You weave in some fine detail, Ms. Golden."

Julia frowned at Cheney and said quickly, "Kathryn, did you get any clue whether he was the one who killed August?"

"No, there was nothing about August." Kathryn rose, looked from one to the other, and said, "Are you lovers yet?"

"No," Cheney said as he rose slowly. He stared into her golden-green witch eyes.

"You will be. Funny how I never pictured you with a policeman, Julia. On the other hand, I never pictured you with August either. He was so much older than you, from such a very different generation, but it didn't seem to matter to him. He felt a bond with you, something special that held him firmly to you. I often wondered what it was.

"Let me add that August was special to me as well. Dear God, how I miss him, every single day. Do you know I haven't been able to speak to him? I don't know if it's my own grief that keeps us apart, but I suppose that's possible."

Cheney said, "When the man was thinking about Julia, did you get any sense about when he was going to come after her again?"

She shook her head. "He's so angry, so enraged she's still alive, so bewildered that he failed, really, and that he's got to try again soon. I felt urgency riding him, but nothing specific."

Julia said, "You saw him staring at you—at me. Did it happen recently?"

"I don't know, but it would make sense, wouldn't it? I don't think I've ever had a retro-vision before. But he didn't think about the time or the day."

"Kathryn, do you see anything else at all that might help us?"

Kathryn Golden shook her head.

"I don't want to die, Kathryn."

"No. I'm sure August doesn't want you to join him just yet either. You're much too young."

Cheney said, "Don't tell me Dr. Ransom is sitting here with us, hovering over Julia, all concerned?"

"If he is, I don't know. I told you, Agent Stone, I haven't been able to contact August. I simply knew him well enough to know what he would think.

"I have to say, Agent Stone, that your aura isn't all that rich anymore. There's unpleasantness ripping through it. Now, if you will both excuse me, the producer is here."

"I don't hear anything, ma'am," Cheney said.

The front doorbell rang.

CHAPTER 34

Late Monday afternoon

Dix slowly rose when he saw Charlotte Pallack coming toward him, weaving in and out of clusters of happy-hour young professionals at the Ugly Duck on Post Street. Odd, but he didn't see Christie this time, not for even a brief moment. He saw a woman he didn't know at all, a woman who had lied to him, a woman who'd been wearing Christie's bracelet. He saw immediately she wasn't wearing it now.

He let her come to him, smiling at her as he waited. When she reached him, she rose up on her tiptoes and kissed him on his mouth.

Dix tightened his hands about her upper arms and slowly eased her back. She looked up at him, excitement in her eyes, or perhaps it was satisfaction. "Do you remember what you said to me when you left me on Saturday?"

"Never say never."

He saw the flare of triumph in her eyes; she couldn't hide it. She said, "Such a memorable line, Dix. Ah, but I knew you'd come back. I'm so pleased to see you again."

She kissed him again, lightly touched her fingertips to his cheeks. "You have a five o'clock shadow."

"I'm sorry about that but I just got in."

She arched a brow at him. "It's only been two days, Dix."

"It seems longer," he said, "much longer." He looked up at the waiter, all in black with a white bow tie, and asked him, "What have you got on tap?"

He ordered a Budweiser for himself and a white wine for Charlotte.

"Two days," she said again. "I must admit you did surprise me. You really called me from SFO?"

He nodded. "The moment I got outside the United terminal, yes."

"Are you staying with the Sherlocks again?"

"They very graciously invited me back." He gave her what he hoped was a sexy look. "Mrs. Sherlock said I'm welcome because I'm tall, dark, and dangerous. I must add that Judge Sherlock laughed."

She laughed as well, took the glass of wine from the waiter, and clicked her glass against his. "To getting to know new friends better, much better."

He cocked an eyebrow at her. "How about to the beginning of something that just might be very interesting indeed."

"Hear, hear," she said. "Was your flight okay?"

"As much as any flight can be nowadays."

"What about your sons? You're leaving them again so soon." Did she sound suspicious?

He touched his fingertips to the back of her hand, gently

smoothing them over her skin. "I told them I had more law enforcement consults out here. Since they're all caught up with end-of-school finals and proms, it really doesn't bother them that I'm not there all the time." A lie, he thought, a big honking lie. If his boys had heard, they'd have laughed and pounded on him.

"Are you here to seduce me, Dix?"

Was that excitement in her voice?

"We'll see, won't we? You know, I heard about your brother, Charlotte, the one who plays the violin with the Atlanta Symphony Orchestra and attended Stanislaus Music School in my town."

She blinked, rapidly, and then she nodded slowly, as if coming to a decision. She sipped her wine. "Is that why you came back to see me?"

"I did wonder why you'd lied about something so obvious, something that did indeed give us a very real connection."

"Very well, I should have told you. Given how much I look like your missing wife, it would make sense for you to do all sorts of checking on me. You want the truth, Dix? His name is David Caldicott, as you know—that's my maiden name—and the fact is we haven't spoken to each other for a very long time. We had a falling out years ago, over money, of course. I loaned him some and he never paid it back. It was he who kissed me off, then headed to Europe. I've seen him only once since he came back. The meeting didn't go well. And no, he still hasn't paid me back.

"I heard he attended Stanislaus. I've heard of it, of course, but to be honest, I never connected it to you."

"My wife knew your brother. Isn't that a small world?"

"Incredibly small."

"She liked to go to the concerts and recitals at Stanislaus. She really appreciated your brother's talent and told him so."

"Since you checked David and me out, can you tell me how he's doing now?"

"He's doing well, though I wonder why he wouldn't call you after he'd met my wife to tell you how much you two look alike."

She drank a bit more wine. "Do you know, I'd like some peanuts."

Dix had decided to give her three minutes to think. He wondered what would come out of her mouth. He called the waiter over for a brief discussion of mixed nuts. When the nuts arrived, Dix watched her pick an almond from the bowl and slowly chew it. When she swallowed, she asked him, "Did you speak to David?"

Did he hear wariness in her voice? "No, I merely read his bio and found out he was your brother. That made me remember that Christie mentioned him."

"So, you haven't given it up, this idea there's some connection between your wife and me? David never called me, not once. So you see, there's nothing important you need to know about David at all. He's just a musician and something of a flake. I wish him well. So I'm hoping we can put it behind us now. Tell me, Dix, how long are you planning to stay here this time?"

"That depends," he said slowly, his eyes on her face, then only on her mouth. She licked her bottom lip and he stared at her tongue stroking over her wet mouth, and he smiled, with what he hoped looked like the promise of hot sweaty sex. Light color flushed her cheeks. Good.

"When you make up your mind, Dix, call me. Right now, my husband is expecting me."

He frowned as he looked down at his watch. "I promised Mrs. Sherlock I would be there for dinner too. I'm sorry you have to leave so soon, Charlotte." He clasped her hands between his. "But I had to see you, and I didn't seem to have a choice."

"I'm glad you called me."

He ran his fingers over her hands, her wrists. "I see you're not wearing the bracelet."

"I thought about it, but I didn't want to give you cause for any distress, so I left it in my jewelry box. Perhaps we can get together again tomorrow, maybe for the afternoon. What do you think?"

"Do you have a specific restaurant in mind?"

"No, not a restaurant, Dix. I was thinking I'd like someplace more private, like the Hyatt Regency at the Embarcadero. I'm like a little girl when I ride up in those glass elevators. What do you say?"

He wondered cynically if the Hyatt rented rooms for the afternoon, since that's what she was intimating. "That sounds interesting. Can I call you?"

"Absolutely. Use my cell. I'd really like that."

He rose, then walked around the table to help her out of her chair. They stood in the middle of the busy restaurant, simply looking at each other. Slowly, Dix lowered his head and kissed her. He felt no pleasure as she slid her tongue over his lower lip, only determination.

CHAPTER 35

SAN FRANCISCO

Monday night

Ruth lay on her back, gulping in air, hoping her heart wouldn't burst right out of her chest. She was sweaty, she was grinning like a loon, and she felt incredible.

She laughed at the wonder she felt. "My, I do think you gave your all, Dix."

Dix wondered how she could even string words together, amusing words, at that. His all? That was the truth, he was nearly dead.

He managed a grunt. "Maybe you were closing in on yours as well."

"I did try my pitiful best. You know, when I compare you to all the others, I have to say you're flying really high, right up there near the top."

He didn't know where his laughter came from after everything that happened that day, but it burst out of his mouth. He hugged her to him, kissed her ear. "Do you know this is the same bed I slept in Friday night? It feels much better with you in it. The Sherlocks are good people, letting all of us invade them after they just got rid of me two days ago."

"Do you think we were quiet enough?" Ruth whispered against his ear as her palm flattened over his belly.

"Since I put my hand over your mouth, I don't think anyone heard us. Stop moving your fingers, Ruth, I'm nearly dead here. Wait, my heart just kicked back in, I can feel it, thank God. Do you want me to rise up and fly high again?"

Ruth grinned in the soft dim light thrown off by the lamp on the bedside table. "I remember how dear Lance could rise up and fly, anywhere at all, even in the shower. Goodness, now that I think about it, Lance could even sing."

"How old was Lance?"

"I do believe he turned eighteen during our acquaintance. I thought about giving him a car for a graduation present, but he was such a rowdy lad he might have gotten hauled in by the cops for speeding, so I decided on a watch instead."

"That means I'm going to have to lock Rob up in about a year and a half. No girl in Maestro will be safe."

"Oh dear, Rob and Rafe are nearly that age—that certainly changes one's perspective on things. Now that I think about it, Lance was twenty-one, maybe even twenty-two. Maybe it was a graduation present from college."

Even as he grinned, realizing how really good he felt at this moment, reality climbed up on his chest and stared him in the eye.

"Stop it, Dix, come back here. Life is always out there, but neither of us have to face it every moment. Come back." She took his hand, brought it down to his chest, and pressed her hand down over his. "It's the strangest thing," she said. "I can feel your heart through your hand.

"Another strange thing," she continued. "Every day of the week you get up in the morning, chow down your peanut butter toast, navigate to the Hoover building hoping you won't kill any of the idiots on the Beltway, and you arrive at your job, which is to hunt down murderers and various other sorts of psychopaths. Everything's all nice and normal and expected, and then something weird happens, something that knocks you off your pins, something like this deal we're in right now, and suddenly we're not in Kansas anymore.

"But you know something? No matter what smacks me in the head, I know I won't have to deal with it by myself any longer. You'll always be there for me. It makes the world exceedingly nice, Dix."

He came up onto his side, leaned over her, and riffled his fingers through her dark hair, all wild about her head, a beautiful contrast to her white skin, and those dark eyes that seemed to see all the way to his soul.

She touched her fingers to his cheek and heaved out a soft sigh. "I love you."

She loved him? This incredible woman actually loved him? "You've never said that before," he said.

"Now was the time," she said simply. He was basking in what

she'd said when she added, "On the other hand, I also love football, and thank the good Lord there's only four more months to wait."

He turned his hand palm up and twined his fingers with hers. "Now you're doing your Ruth thing—mixing the utterly serious with a joke. What would you think," he went on as he leaned up to nuzzle her jaw, "of getting married before football season starts? That way we'll have a good week for me to fly high and sing arias to you in the shower before we're yelling our heads off in front of the tube for the Redskins. And you know what would be really good about that?"

"Great sex whenever I want it?"

"That too. Better yet, it would mean no more questions, no more doubts, no more putting things off—"

"Just you and me and a big bed and a bigger—?"

"You gonna finish that thought?"

"And a bigger heart, Dix. I'm so glad I staggered into your woods. I would love to marry you. You and the boys are the center of my life now."

He leaned down to press his forehead against hers. He felt the goodness in her, the bone-deep honor, and the strength. "Have you ever considered that maybe tracking down killers and psychopaths isn't all that normal and expected?"

She kissed him, stroked her hand through his hair. "Nah. What I can't understand is milking a cow or taking apart a smoking motherboard."

He grinned, fell onto his back, felt her hand move to lie flat on his belly again. He lay quietly, finally heard her breathing even into sleep. No wonder. Both of them were tired to the bone, what with the long flight from Richmond, then dropping her off here at the Sherlocks' because of his decision to see Charlotte as soon as possible. He'd tried to get some information out of her, anything at all they could use about her and her husband, but she had cut it short. He had no idea if she really wanted to see him again, or was pretending. When he'd told Ruth he might have to play-act at seducing her, she'd merely nodded, and said in that no-nonsense way of hers, "It's your call, Dix."

After he'd left Charlotte, he'd stood by his rental car a moment and felt cold to his soul. He knew something wasn't right about Charlotte. He knew too that something really bad was out there that concerned Christie, waiting for him to find it.

Savich and Sherlock, with Sean and his nanny Graciella, had arrived a little after six o'clock, welcomed by all, especially Sherlock's parents. Isabel called out over their heads that she'd made her baby's favorite sausage enchiladas.

Sean had yelled "Yes!" until told by his mother that she was Isabel's baby, not him. Sean had looked puzzled a good long time about that.

Of course, there'd been more discussions, more plans made over a big pot of coffee—until all of them, in their pajamas and their jet lag—were shooed off to bed by Mrs. Sherlock.

And now, as Dix lay in the sinful big bed, Ruth's head on his shoulder, he thought of the endless string of lies he'd told the boys, and felt the knife of guilt twist in his gut. And if that wasn't enough, he realized he hadn't told Ruth he loved her. What a moron he was. What was a marriage proposal without at least some mention of love? He was an idiot. He'd tell her first thing in the morning when she awoke, warm and soft with sleep.

His last thought before he fell asleep, his face against Ruth's hair, was about Christie. *I'm going to find out what happened to you, Christie. I'm going to find you justice. And then I'm going to let Ruth share my heart with you.*

CHAPTER 36

Cheney stood at the front window of his condo, leaning to his left so he could manage a glimpse of his partial view of the Golden Gate. Julia was asleep on his sofa, sprawled on her back. He was glad she'd wanted to come home with him, away from the media, the crime scene tape, the neighbors, and maybe another visit from Makepeace. Suddenly she said clearly, in an anguished voice, "Linc, oh Jesus, no! Linc!"

She began to sob, deep wrenching sobs, and she wept, saying over and over, "Linc, oh no, please Linc. Don't leave me. No!"

He gathered her up, rocked her. "Julia, wake up. You're okay, it was a nightmare. Come on, wake up."

She did immediately, staring up at him in the dim moonlight coming through the front window.

"You had a nightmare. You're okay now."

It took her a moment to gain control. "Thank you, Cheney. I guess with all the stress, those nightmares are slipping right in."

He wondered how often she dreamed of Linc, but now wasn't the time to ask. "You want some warm milk or something?"

She managed a grin. "No, I want to go back to sleep. Why aren't you in bed?"

"I'm too hyped up, I guess. I'll go sack out soon now."

"You're afraid he'll come here, aren't you?"

"My address wouldn't be all that hard to find out. Thanks to Captain Paulette, there's a squad car down the block keeping an eye on the place. It wouldn't be Xavier's best move to try it. Actually, it'd be nuts."

"He is nuts." She shivered. Without thought, he pulled her close again, felt her hair against his face.

She said against his neck, "Can you believe Kathryn wondered if we were lovers? I haven't even known you a week."

He was silent, thinking she didn't sound at all angry or alarmed, perhaps only surprised, maybe even curious. She was wearing one of his white undershirts, and it was falling off her shoulder.

Julia said, "You didn't believe anything she said, did you?"

He was aware that she smelled of something soft and flowery. "Fact is, she could have heard or deduced most of it and guessed the rest. Pretty commonsense stuff, all dressed up with purple prose—that's what I thought when she said it. 'His core was black, his pride was purple'—and the bit about his aching feet, come on, give me a break."

"When you say it, away from her drama and atmosphere, it does sound like some ridiculous tale a good storyteller could spin."

Cheney said, "She's some showman. I suppose that's her greatest skill."

"But she did say she thought he had an author's name."

He frowned. "Yes, she did say that."

She yawned. "You're still dressed."

"Yes."

He leaned down and pulled her blanket over her. "Go back to sleep, Julia."

Sean Savich's eyes popped open. Something didn't smell right. That was it, he wasn't in his own bed or in his own room. He was someplace else, someplace scary. He knew a monster was hiding in the closet. The monster could see his bed, could see him. He was sure the door was slowly pushing open and he nearly stopped breathing. Even though Graciella had showed him there were only clothes and shoes in the closet, he knew she didn't understand, didn't know what he knew. This wasn't his closet, so he knew Graciella couldn't see the monster; it hid itself until she closed the door. And then it waited a long time before it slowly oozed out from its hiding place in the closet wall and tasted his clothes, getting his scent. The monster was coming out of the closet now, and it was bad.

Even though Graciella was sleeping in a twin bed not ten feet away from him, it wasn't enough. No way could she save him in this strange place. Sean's heart pounded. He watched the closet door as he slithered out of the narrow twin bed, slipped through the bedroom door, and ran as fast as he could down the hallway. It was strange, he didn't know where to run since he didn't know where he was. A huge black shadow barred his way. He sobbed and closed his eyes as he ran through the shadow. He was heaving when he eased inside the first closed door. He saw two people sleeping in a big bed. He raced to the bed and climbed up to burrow between them. Something wasn't quite right, but he didn't care because they were big and he was too afraid of what was lurking in the hall. He was safe now. Sean pressed closer. They wouldn't let anything hurt him. Everything was all right.

At seven o'clock in the morning, Dix was jerked awake by the sudden jab of an elbow in his neck.

"He's still asleep," Ruth whispered.

Dix slowly lowered the little boy's arm and turned slowly to his side to face Ruth. Sean was between them.

Dix whispered, "Nightmare, I guess. Did he wake you up when he came in?"

At that moment, they heard Sean's name shouted from outside the door. It was Sherlock, and she sounded scared to her toes.

Ruth slipped out of bed, pulled on the robe she'd tossed over the end of the bed, and opened the door. "Sherlock, it's okay. Sean came to sleep with us in the middle of the night. He's okay."

Sherlock rushed into the bedroom, as if she couldn't believe what Ruth had told her was the truth, and skidded to a stop. She shook her head, relief pouring off her. "Oh, Sean." Graciella came running into the room on her heels, her face pale as the moon.

Sherlock saw her little boy in Dix's arms, dead to the world, and sucked in a deep breath. "All right, then. It's okay." She turned to give her husband a blazing smile. "Dillon, we're in here."

Dix said, "Nightmare, strange house, and we're the first bedroom next to Sean's. He landed here. There was no problem."

Sean yawned, raised his head, looked at Dix and smiled. "Hi,

Uncle Dix," he said. "Where's my mom?" And he turned to look at the other side of the bed, stretched out his small hand, and frowned. "Where's Mama?"

"Well, that's a fine thing for him to think, isn't it?" Sherlock said.

Savich laughed. "Hey, Champ, you ready for some Cheerios?"

Dix got another elbow in the neck when Sean dashed out of bed to get scooped up by his father. He saw Savich whisper against Sean's cheek, "Hey, you're at your grandparents' house, in San Francisco. Do you remember that?"

Sean reared back in his father's arms, studied his face a moment, and said, "Cool. I can play with Grandpa and Grandma."

Dix said, "I remember when Rob would wake up with a nightmare and come running. Rafe usually came running in right behind him, didn't want to be left out. That kid could make up scarier tales than Rob, who'd actually had the nightmare."

Ruth said as she punched him lightly on his bare shoulder, "The boys are in good hands, Dix, stop worrying about them. Mrs. Goss and Chappy will spoil them rotten. Tony and Cynthia will take them to NASCAR, and all of them will be in Rob's cheering section at the ball game tomorrow. And by the time we get back to Maestro, Brewster will rule at Tara."

Dix realized he still hadn't told Ruth he loved her.

CHAPTER 37

Tuesday morning

The reason Cheney kept checking his rearview mirror was because of Kathryn Golden's phone call at six-thirty that morning.

"I had another vision, Agent Stone. It was him, the man who wants to kill Julia. He's been to Pacific Heights, he managed to break into Julia's house, I saw him, and then he came out again because she wasn't there, and he was angry. He knows about you, Agent Stone, I think he's found out where you live. He doesn't know if Julia's there, but he's coming. He's in a car, driving. He looks calm, but he isn't, not really—it's like a layer of snow covering up a fire. He's coming. Please be careful."

And he'd thanked her, hung up, and sneered. Another safe guess on her part. The only thing that had surprised him about her "vision" yesterday was her guess about the assassin's name. Maybe she knew someone in the SFPD and that person had leaked it to her. Yeah, that was possible, even Julia had mentioned that. And now she'd called him to tell him something else equally obvious. It wasn't such a stretch to realize he was keeping Julia safe at his place. Of course Makepeace was out there. But on the road? Could be. He sneered again.

But as he negotiated the heavy morning city traffic, he kept chewing on it, and checked his rearview mirror more often than he would have if Kathryn Golden hadn't called with her damned vision.

Julia sat quietly beside him, a lot calmer than he was, even though he'd told her about Kathryn Golden's call. She'd said only, "It can't hurt to listen."

Now he worried that Makepeace had come around and seen the cops guarding his condo and decided to wait for them to leave. Maybe he was now following them. He thought about calling Frank Paulette, asking for backup. But what would he tell him? A whacked-out psychic had a vision?

He looked back again. The San Francisco morning rush-hour traffic was thick, but he didn't see anyone acting suspicious, no one moving up through the tangle of cars to get closer. Maybe he was hanging back, biding his time.

Cheney was freaking himself out. He had to calm down. He wasn't about to scare Julia any more than she had to be. He looked over at her. She was still quiet, starting at nothing in particular that he could see. What was she thinking?

He checked the rearview mirror again.

Julia said, "Do you see him?"

"No, I don't. The chances are he's nowhere close."

"If Kathryn's right and he's already been to my house, maybe it would be safe to go home for at least a shower and some clothes. Maybe we call Soldan Meissen after that?"

She still sounded more calm than he felt. He said, "First I'd like to introduce you to some FBI friends of mine who just got into town last night—"

He had subconsciously registered a white Dodge Charger and now his brain zeroed in on it. The Charger was moving up, not going all that fast, not all that obvious. But the Charger was passing a black Ford SUV, weaving easily back and forth in the lanes on Geary, efficient and smooth, as if out for an easy drive. Cheney couldn't see the driver, couldn't even tell how many people were in the car, but he knew it was Makepeace, felt it in his gut. *So you're coming for us, are you? You want to get this show on the road? Fine by me, you crazy mother.*

The Charger was only four cars back now.

Cheney turned to her. "Julia, I want you to hold on, okay?"

"What? Oh, he's here? Kathryn was right?"

"Whatever. Yes, I think Xavier is behind us, coming up now. He must really be pissed to come after you in full daylight, in damned rush hour, in the middle of San Francisco. I want to get out of all this traffic. If he starts firing we have to be able to move out fast. I'd just as soon avoid any civilians getting hurt too."

She looked back. "The white Dodge Charger?"

"Yep."

"He's three cars back. Where are we going?"

"Hold on," he said again, whipped the Audi around a station

wagon, and floored the gas. She was thrown back, felt her seat belt tighten against her chest. Oddly, she wasn't scared, not particularly, more excited really, and wasn't that screwed up? She grabbed the chicken strap, jerked around to look back—

A bullet exploded the back window, spewing spears of glass everywhere, embedding itself in the back of Julia's seat.

"Get down, all the way! Keep your head covered," Cheney yelled.

Julia popped her seat belt and squeezed down as far as she could into the small space in front of the passenger seat.

Cheney tossed her his cell. "Punch four—it's Captain Paulette's personal number."

Another bullet came through the jagged-edged mess of glass and slammed again into the back of the passenger seat. With no glass window to slow it down, the bullet tore through and drilled into the Audi's glove compartment, not an inch above Julia's bowed head. He nearly stroked out. "Try to scrunch down more! Lower!"

Cheney looked in the rearview and finally saw Makepeace, in his sunglasses. It would take some time before they heard any cop sirens, before the sound of approaching cops might force Makepeace to peel away. What could he do in the meantime? The truth was, he really didn't want Makepeace to peel away. He wanted to bring him down, but first he had to protect Julia, he had— He said aloud, "The thing is, Julia, I know San Francisco very well and Xavier Makepeace doesn't."

He pressed down on the gas again and soon the Audi's

speedometer passed seventy miles an hour in the middle of San Francisco. The hit of it all was more powerful than a Turkish double espresso.

And then he knew exactly what he was going to do.

"Julia, tell Captain Paulette we're heading west to Ocean Beach, just south of Cliff House."

The chances were good no one would be on the beach this early in the morning. It was cold and windy and the air was thick with mist. It would be foggy out near the ocean. And that meant a long stretch of empty beach.

Julia said, "Captain Paulette, this is Julia Ransom. I'm with Cheney and we're in a bit of trouble here—" and he listened to her tell Frank exactly where they were, and where Cheney was headed.

He saw her punch off the cell and lay it calmly on the floor next to him. He gave her a quick smile. "Hang in there, this might get a bit hairy, okay? Keep down."

She heard another bullet strike metal, then the sound of a distant siren.

Cheney cursed but didn't slow.

Julia said, "The cops can't ignore two maniacs speeding through the city. If there are enough of them, they might box him in."

Dream on, he thought, but said, "Might happen, but it's not what I want. Now, we've got to make it to the beach. I'll try to keep this guy off us, Julia."

Cheney jerked to the left across Geary onto 29th Avenue amid blaring horns, ripe curses, and the sound of screeching tires. He dodged and swerved, cannoning his way through the Richmond District, with its narrow streets, funneled by cars parked bumper to bumper along the curb on both sides. He looked back, grinned at the white Charger speeding after him. "Oh yeah, nearly there now, nearly there, stay with me," his mantra now, she thought, and when she heard him say it again, she laughed.

"Hang in, Julia."

"No problem. Can I come up now?"

Cheney looked back to see the Charger cut off by a screaming Chevy driver, then saw Makepeace back up and swerve around the parked cars on 29th. He'd gained most of a block on him. "No, stay down. He's still there. That's right, you putz, don't give up on us yet. Come on, come to papa."

There were more sirens now, and they were closer.

Makepeace fired twice. One bullet tore off the passenger-side mirror, sending it crashing against the side of a parked car; the other grazed the rear bumper of a Miata backing out of a driveway.

Cheney flew across Fulton and into Golden Gate Park, saw a huge Lexus nearly on him. He slammed on the brakes and jerked the wheel to the right at the same time. He thought he felt the heat of that big monster as it roared past, massive enough to smash his Audi and kill both of them. He caught a glimpse of a woman's white face, the terror in her eyes, before he took an insane fast left turn on John F. Kennedy Drive, nearly shearing off the front fender of a parked station wagon.

There weren't many cars in the park, thank God, but he had to slow some for a dozen or so bicyclists and a long tail of runners. He laid on the horn, giving them time to scatter, which they did. They jetted past the bison paddock, and took a fast right. It was a straight shot now. Julia eased up into her seat. She saw the Queen Wilhelmina Tulip Garden and the Dutch Windmill on her right, saw the looming red light, and managed to hold back a scream as Cheney drove straight through the light onto the Great Highway.

CHAPTER 38

Horns blared, brakes screeched, and rubber burned as he swerved and dodged the two-way traffic.

Cheney yelled, "Did I ever tell you I learned to drive in a four-by-four on the beach?"

He was smiling as he ripped across the Great Highway onto the long concrete parking lot, thankfully empty of cars and people, just as he'd hoped. The parking lot ran along the storm wall that rose above the beach a good six feet. Julia saw the storm wall looming diagonally up in front of them. She didn't consider the narrow openings for beach steps until—her heart nearly stopped when they went airborne.

"I won't kill us! Hang on!" Incredibly, he was laughing with something like joy as they flew, and, truth be told, she felt a tickle of joyous terror in the air herself.

The Audi landed hard on sand, still damp from high tide, slamming them against their seat belts, snapping their jaws together. Cheney whipped the Audi hard left, and the car flew forward along the beach wall. "I used to race dune buggies on the beaches in South Carolina, mainly Hilton Head. Come on, you maniac, come on, you can get me. Hot damn, he just went flying through." He hit the steering wheel with his fist and yelled, "Gotcha!"

"What do you mean? You wanted him to come after you?"

"Oh yeah. This sweet little Audi A4 has all-wheel drive. He doesn't."

Julia looked back to see the Charger hit the beach hard some forty yards behind them, kicking up sand and water like a rooster tail. "He looks like he's having a problem getting traction. No, wait, okay, he's turning toward us. He's coming, Cheney."

Cheney was grinning again. She wondered whether, if she weren't in the car, he'd have flipped the Audi back around to face the oncoming Charger, maybe gunned the engine a couple of times in challenge, and headed straight at Makepeace like a knight in battle.

But he couldn't take the offense because he had to protect her. Another bullet struck, close to the back tire. In that instant Julia remembered her SIG was in her purse. Sweet Mary and Joseph, where was her purse?

She didn't have time to find it. Cheney gunned the Audi toward the long storm wall. She'd sat on that wall many times with her legs dangling, watching the waves and the honking seals. Now it seemed a terrifying monolith waiting to crush both of them. She saw another beach access in the concrete wall, a dozen concrete stairs climbing up. As they closed on it, the Audi never faltered, never lost its traction. It took the stairs like a bullet and sped through the opening. Julia could have licked the concrete wall on either side. She was pumped. She yelled out a shout of wild exultant terror.

Cheney slammed on the brakes and turned the wheel at the same time. They screeched to a one-eighty. He threw the Audi into park, yelled for her to keep down, and jumped out the door hunched over, his SIG drawn.

But she didn't get down, no way would she hide now. She stared, fascinated, as the Charger tried to pull out of a lunatic slide and gain some traction and speed toward those stairs, spewing sand. She saw the instant Makepeace realized the Charger wouldn't make it up the stairs. He threw the car into reverse, bumped hard and fast back down the concrete stairs and lurched back onto the beach.

Cheney ran toward the wall, firing at him, emptying his clip. He reached into his jacket pocket, pulled out another clip, and fired again. The Charger's windshield shattered, then the rear window, sending out shards of glass.

Makepeace jumped from the Charger and crouched behind the driver's side door, firing back short bursts. Cheney threw himself down behind the concrete wall.

Julia eased out of the Audi, and looked over the top of her open door. Makepeace was twenty yards away. He looked as calm as a judge, his face expressionless behind his dark sunglasses.

She spotted her purse on the floor of the backseat. She grabbed her SIG and kneeled down on the concrete, keeping the door between her and Makepeace. She saw Cheney was pinned, and she fired her gun as she waved wildly at Makepeace.

He fired back at her in one smooth motion. She flattened herself on the concrete parking lot, her heart pounding in her ears, the sound of the bullets so close they deafened her for an instant. He continued to fire at her, emptying his clip. It gave Cheney his chance. He ran forward, nearly bent double, firing steadily. The Charger's door window shattered, Makepeace's arm jerked, and his pistol went flying to the sand.

Makepeace looked toward Cheney once, back at Julia, and leaped into the Charger, gunning the engine. But the Charger couldn't find traction in the sand. Cheney kept firing as he ran down the stairs toward the car. A bullet ricocheted off the hubcap of the left rear tire. Cheney emptied the second clip trying to hit the tires, but they were spinning madly, kicking up blinding sand, the car jerking and heaving, fishtailing again in the sand.

He patted his pockets, but he knew he was out of bullets. Makepeace stopped trying to gun the car, and the Charger finally gained some traction. He headed back down the beach away from them.

Cheney stood there, his gun down at his side, staring after the car. "Well, damn," he said as Julia came up to stand beside him.

"You shot him. I saw him jerk. Did you see him drop his gun?"

Cheney whirled around, grabbed her arms and shook her. "Are you all right?"

"Yes, yes, I'm okay."

He shook her again. "What were you doing? You shot at him, and waved! Made yourself a target! Are you nuts?"

"Most definitely. If you hadn't been so set on shooting him, maybe you could have shot out his tires?"

"I tried. I got a hubcap."

"Yes, you did. Too bad we didn't stop him."

Cheney let her go when his relief finally passed his anger. Still, he frowned back at her before he walked over to pick up Make-peace's pistol, and stared at it. He'd seen only one like it before in his career—in a weapon collection owned by a former FBI as-sistant director. He ran his hand over the gun. "Would you look at this—a Škorpion VZ 61. This is a Czech-made machine pis-tol that hasn't been manufactured since the seventies. I wonder where he got it, and why he's not using a more efficient weapon. How did he get this thing into the country?" He shaded his eyes and looked down the beach. Makepeace was gone.

The sirens were blaring so loud it hurt their ears. They walked back up the beach access steps just as half a dozen police cars piled into the parking lot. The lead car screamed to a stop not six feet from them. Two officers jumped out, using the car doors for shields and aiming their weapons over the tops of the doors.

"Police! Drop your weapons now!"

Cheney didn't hesitate. He dropped his SIG and Makepeace's pistol to the concrete. "There, no guns. Don't shoot us! I'm rais-ing my hands over my head, nice and slow."

The first officer's gun continued to point right at Cheney's chest. "Don't either of you move! I said drop the gun, lady, drop it!"

Julia dropped her SIG. "Sorry," she yelled back.

"Don't move!"

"No, we won't," Cheney said.

They stood like a frozen tableau for an eternity—at least a minute—while the cops spilled out of black-and-whites and a couple of unmarkeds all around them. Cheney prayed no one would get rattled and start firing, when he heard a blessedly familiar voice. Captain Paulette yelled, "Don't shoot them, Gibbs, they're the good guys." Cheney watched Frank climb out of his car, look south as he spoke on his cell—doubtless he was sending cars after Makepeace's Charger. Frank punched off his cell, yelled out, "Hey, Cheney, my men tell me you were doing some wild-assed driving."

Cheney yelled back, "I may have wounded him, his gun arm, but he's still driving, a white Charger. His car's all shot up so you can hardly miss it." Cheney leaned down and picked up the two pistols. "Look at this sucker, Frank."

Frank took the pistol. "Ain't this something—long time no see. A terrorist's wet dream, this pistol, way back when, particularly in Africa. It's Czech—and surprise, surprise, the cartridge is American design."

"Maybe we can trace it," Cheney said.

"I doubt that, compadre, but we can try."

Cheney picked up Julia's SIG from the ground, handed it to her. "Hey," he said to her, "we made it."

"I think," Julia said slowly, looking out over the pewter water, "that I just might let you teach me beach racing sometime."

He laughed.

A patrol car skidded up. The officer yelled, "Captain, we found the car. The guy took off on foot, or maybe wired a car on the street. We ran the VIN already. The Charger was stolen out of a garage in Daly City last night. The owner sure isn't going to be happy when he sees his ride."

CHAPTER 39

CALIFORNIA STREET

Tuesday afternoon

Savich saw a flash of irritation on Thomas Pallack's face as he turned from his window on the thirty-sixth floor of the Malden-Pallack building on California Street and looked at the two men and two women who stood in his office doorway. Then he saw a look of unease, perhaps fear, but it was gone quickly. Savich recognized the formidable intelligence, the suspicion in Pallack's eyes, and thought, *Dix, if you'd come, he would have called security in a heartbeat and removed us all.*

Thomas Pallack looked at each of them in turn, assessing them, Savich thought, for what sort of threat they posed to him. He stood motionless now, no expression on his face, and fingered the business card Savich had given to his assistant. When he waved to his assistant standing in the open doorway, she nodded and let herself out of the office, after a quick searching look at her boss.

Pallack said, "The view would be splendid if the fog weren't

lying so thick over the city and the Marin Headlands, there"—
he pointed—"behind the Golden Gate."

They all dutifully stared out the huge window. Only one of the
Golden Gate Bridge's suspension towers peaked above the fog.

"The fog usually burns off by noon," he continued, "but not
today, unfortunately. Mrs. Potts tells me all three of you are FBI
agents and for some reason I don't understand, you, my dear
Julia, have come with them.

"Let me say both Charlotte and I are distressed at all your
trouble. It has all been an immense shock to us, as well—we are
very sorry."

"Thank you, Mr. Pallack," Julia said.

He inclined his head to her, nodding. "Perhaps that is why
you're here with the agents? They're protecting you from this
maniac?"

"That's certainly true, Mr. Pallack."

"You used to call me Thomas."

"Yes, Thomas, I will."

He said, "I see from your card that you're Special Agent Dillon Savich. I hope you are all here to tell me you've caught the
people responsible for all this."

Savich said, "Not as yet."

"A pity. Do these agents have names?"

Savich introduced Sherlock and Cheney, each of them flash-
ing their shields. He motioned them to sit in the stiff modern
chairs facing his desk.

"Now you may tell me what I can do for you."

Savich said, "As part of protecting Mrs. Ransom and investigating her difficulties, Mr. Pallack, we are reviewing Dr. August Ransom's murder. We believe the two may be related. We would appreciate any assistance you're able to provide us."

Thomas Pallack gave them a slight bow of his head.

Savich said, "We understand you were a client of Dr. Ransom's for many years."

Thomas Pallack nodded, sat back in the very comfortable-looking leather chair behind his very modern desk, all glass and polished steel, and folded his hands on his belly. He'd eased considerably, Savich saw, felt back in control of his universe, and that was what Savich wanted. Pallack said, his voice expansive and smooth with confidence, "Surely you must know the SFPD interviewed me after August's murder, along with his other clients. They would have all those records. Unfortunately I wasn't of much help, nor were any of his other clients, as I understand. So, I don't know how I can help you now."

"You are obviously a very intelligent, very successful man, Mr. Pallack. Perhaps over the intervening months you've recalled or wondered about some details that could assist us? How long were you with Dr. Ransom?"

"Over ten years when he died."

"You were pleased with his efforts on your part?"

"Yes, of course, or I wouldn't have stayed with him that long. August, as you know, was able to engage my dear parents for me in dialogue, pass along to me what they were saying and feeling, their advice and counsel on business problems, for example. My father was an incredible businessman, and I value his opinions. Our sessions were deeply meaningful to me."

Cheney sat forward, picked it up. "Do you find Soldan Meissen as helpful as Dr. Ransom, sir?"

Thomas Pallack turned thoughtful, perhaps a pose, Cheney didn't know, but he watched the man carefully. Pallack fiddled with an expensive pen, tapped it against an onyx paperweight, buying himself thinking time, Cheney thought. He saw Sherlock was watching Pallack as intently as he was.

In point of fact, Sherlock had formed a picture of Thomas Pallack in her mind in the preceding days and she realized now she wasn't that far off, except for his eyes. They weren't the eyes of a megalomaniac or a political ideologue, they were dark gray turbulent eyes, a brooding poet's eyes maybe, or a killer's eyes. She didn't know which. She shook her head at herself. No, Thomas Pallack was an extraordinarily successful businessman, very rich, still in full control of his empire at nearly seventy, accustomed to using his power. It was possible he was nothing more than he appeared—a man with one clearly insane obsession, but many people had obsessions or fixations of some kind. He'd communicated with his murdered parents for many decades now, but he was still able to run an empire. And there was something about him that drew you, that made you want to listen to him, hear what he had to say.

The silence stretched on for a moment. No one attempted to break it. Thomas said finally, "You asked me about Soldan Meissen, Agent Stone." He frowned, shook his head. "I doubt this means anything, but there is a lot at stake so let me be completely honest. There is something about Soldan that sometimes shakes my confidence. I can't tell you what, exactly, only that I am never quite as satisfied at the end of our sessions as I was with August. Soldan is quite legitimate, I know that. He has proved many times that he can contact my parents. They speak through him to me, and yes, I recognize their words and expressions, their sly wit, their endearments. Soldan isn't a fraud, if that's what you're after."

"Then what is the problem, sir? Do you think he isn't telling you everything your parents wish him to?" Sherlock asked.

Pallack shrugged. "Come now, three FBI agents, and you're actually taking this seriously? You're considering that one can really talk to the dead?"

Savich's face and voice were both expressionless. "We're not really asking about that, but about your perceptions of him."

"That's an improvement over the not-so-subtle ridicule of those fatuous boneheads at the SFPD. They didn't for a minute believe August was the honest-to-God real deal. I don't think they had anything but contempt for him or any of his friends and colleagues. They wouldn't have cared all that much that he was killed except that he was famous and had high-powered connections. The media spurred them on since they found the psychic angle all very sexy, and so the cops had to go through the motions."

Julia said, "They seemed to care enough when they had the handcuffs all ready to snap on my wrists."

Thomas Pallack looked at her. "They focused on you, Julia, for the simple reason that they could understand the motive you might have—a beautiful young woman married to a very successful, very rich older man. They had no grasp whatever of who and what August really was about, how he couldn't help making some enemies among the living when he communicated with the dead. So they aimed at you. The black widow, yes, the fools could understand that because they'd seen it immortalized by Hollywood, and accepted it to be true. Ridiculous of course to anyone who knew you, knew August, knew what was vital and honest in him, but there you have it.

"I am very sorry it has required attempts on your life to force the police to revisit August's murder to find a tie-in. And not simply local law enforcement, even the FBI. Actually, I don't understand how you are involved. Shouldn't this be strictly a local matter?"

Savich said easily, "We were asked to bring in a fresh eye, Mr. Pallack. This is what the Criminal Apprehension Unit at the FBI is designed to do. We come in only at the request of the local police."

Sherlock said, "We understand you asked Kathryn Golden to contact your parents, but she was unable to."

"She told me she got nothing but static during her attempts. Very odd, she told me, that something like that rarely happened to her."

"And so you sought out Soldan, or did he come to you?" Savich asked.

"He offered his services to me, as I recall."

Julia said, "And yet you don't feel complete satisfaction with Soldan, that is what you said."

"That's right, Julia. Sometimes I feel we're speaking of issues my parents and I discussed some time ago, a sense of déjà vu, if you will, as if we're not making much progress. It's frustrating, but there you have it.

"Now, I have answered your questions. You will answer mine. Why are you so interested in my sessions with mediums?"

Savich said, smooth as the dark India tea Isabel had made him for breakfast, "As a successful businessman, you would never consider information gathering a waste of time. It's what you do, it's what we do. Do you have any idea who killed Dr. Ransom?"

CHAPTER 40

Do you know," Thomas Pallack said slowly, still fiddling with his pen, "the inspectors from the SFPD never even asked me that outright. I've thought about it over the months, Charlotte and I have discussed it. Would any of his colleagues kill him? Were they jealous of him because of his success, or perhaps his wealth? Yes, probably, but that is commonplace in the world—it doesn't seem a likely motive for murder. From what I hear, many of his colleagues worshipped him.

"I've come to believe it had to be one of his many clients, past or present, perhaps someone he inadvertently harmed with information he passed on to them, or someone he enraged at something he told them."

Cheney said, "Evidently there were a couple of dozen people Dr. Ransom was seeing at the time of his death. The SFPD concluded that none of them seemed likely. You included, sir."

Thomas Pallack shrugged. "Well, it certainly wasn't you, Julia. The idea that you married August for his money is ludicrous. I mean, even if you'd wanted to, there is no way August would have been unaware of your intentions. But you know"—he cocked his head at her—"I suppose it was natural for them to wonder why you did marry him."

"Perhaps you can ask Soldan," she said.

"Perhaps I can," he said.

Cheney asked, "You saw Soldan Meissen last night, Mr. Pallack?"

"Yes. Normally my visits are on Wednesdays and Saturdays. However, because of an unavoidable commitment on Wednesday, I had to see Soldan last night. I assume you already know my regular schedule."

Cheney nodded. "And you were left feeling dissatisfied again last evening?"

"Agent Stone, my parents weren't very talkative last night. I was disappointed, but this sometimes happens. They appeared to have a lot on their minds, their focus seemed scattered. They weren't interested in discussing my problems."

Julia said, "What do your parents think of Charlotte?"

That was a conversation stopper, Savich thought.

"My wife?"

"Yes, what do they think of her, Thomas? I'm simply interested because, like August and me, Charlotte is much younger than you. Does this disturb your parents?"

"They have no problem at all with Charlotte. My mother thinks she's beautiful. As a matter of fact, she is always telling me Charlotte is well-meaning, a positive influence on me."

Since Julia had brought up Charlotte, maybe it was time—maybe—and so Savich said, "Mr. Pallack, speaking of your wife, when did you last speak to your brother-in-law, David Caldicott?"

To everyone's surprise, Thomas Pallack shoved back from his desk, bounded to his feet. He was quick for his age. "What is this about, Agent Savich?"

Surely this show of temper was over the top. Savich said easily, "It simply came to mind, sir. I gather you are aware your brother-in-law failed to show up for the symphony performance last night. His girlfriend has reported him missing."

Pallack sucked in lots of air, seemed to calm a bit. He sat back down. But there was deep suspicion in his eyes and in his voice. "Very well, if you must know, I spoke to David last week, I believe. He was fine, he was happy with his girlfriend, he was pleased to be playing with the Atlanta Symphony. Why is this at all to the point? So he missed a single performance? Perhaps he was ill. David isn't missing, that's nonsense."

Savich said, "Fact remains, no one's seen him since yesterday."

Pallack laughed. "I admit, missing a performance is unlike him, but these things happen. Let me tell you, David probably took off for New Orleans and is at this moment jamming in some smoky hole with some of his grotty musician friends. He's done this before, gone away for up to a week. He forgets everything. He's not missing. This is absurd."

Cheney asked, "Has he ever disappeared on one of his unplanned jaunts since he joined the Atlanta symphony?"

Pallack shrugged. "I can see this alarms you. I will ask Charlotte what she knows about this, if anything. I doubt she even knows anyone is looking for him. Of what concern is this to the FBI?"

Savich said, "The FBI interviewed David Caldicott in connection with another case, Mr. Pallack. The agents who interviewed him felt he was holding something back, and then he up and disappeared. It seems logical that his disappearance may be related, don't you agree?"

"I fail to see how, Agent Savich."

"Bear with me, sir. Tell us, do you know Chappy Holcombe?"

"Naturally I know Chappy Holcombe. Again, you are journeying far afield, Agent Savich. What does Chappy have to do with any of this?"

"You have visited Maestro, Virginia? To visit Chappy?"

"Yes, once, quite a while ago. On business. Why?"

"Was this when your brother-in-law was studying at Stanislaus Music School?"

"Perhaps, but I didn't know David Caldicott until right before I married Charlotte. He came out here to meet me. So what? Listen, Agent Savich, I've had about enough of this." Thomas Pallack rose slowly and leaned over, his palms flat on his desk. It was an excellent intimidation pose, Sherlock thought. "You will tell me what is behind these intrusive questions or I will call my lawyer. Trust me on this, you do not want me to call my lawyer."

"You have the same lawyer as Dr. Ransom, don't you?" Cheney asked. "Zion Leftwitz?"

"He's one of my corporate lawyers. Simon Bellows is my civil lawyer." He reached for his phone.

Savich looked over at Sherlock, who appeared thoughtful, then she slowly nodded to him. "Very well, Mr. Pallack," Savich said. "Let me bottom-line this. You are married to a woman who greatly resembles another woman who disappeared from Maestro, Virginia, over three years ago. They look so similar they could be twins. Her name is Christie Noble. She's Chappy Holcombe's daughter. Perhaps you met her when you saw Chappy?"

"My Charlotte resembles this Christie? So what? Listen, I seem to recall Chappy had a daughter, but no, I never met her. You said she disappeared?"

Sherlock said, "You are acquainted with my parents, I believe, Mr. Pallack."

"Yes, it is my pleasure."

Cheney said, "You met Christie's husband, Chappy's son-in-law—Sheriff Dix Noble—when you dined at the Sherlocks last Friday night."

Thomas Pallack became very still, his eyes darkening to become completely opaque, with malice, Sherlock thought. She never looked away from him as he said, "I remember the dinner and I remember the sheriff. Ah, I see now, that is why he stared at my wife throughout the evening. He believed she was his wife?"

Sherlock nodded. "Yes, but only for a moment. He realized quickly enough your wife wasn't Christie. As Agent Savich said, she was Chappy Holcombe's daughter. You said you never met her?"

"That's right. Tell me, how did this sheriff know about Charlotte?"

"Do you remember a fundraiser you gave two, three weeks ago, Mr. Pallack?" Savich said. "One of your guests met your wife, and collapsed."

"Why yes, Jules Advere. I felt very badly for him. But we dealt with it. I haven't spoken to him but I understand he's fine now. So what?"

"Yes, he's feeling better. Do you remember leaning over him. Mr. Pallack, speaking to him?" Sherlock paused a moment, then said quickly, deliberately, "You said to him, your exact words, I believe—'My wife's name is Charlotte. Do you understand? Don't forget it.' Now wasn't that a strange thing to say, Mr. Pallack? It sounds remarkably like a threat to me. Could you please tell us why that made you so angry? Why you reacted that way to a guest who'd collapsed at your feet?"

Pallack erupted, roared to his feet, and slammed his fist on his desktop. "Dammit, you're way out of line here. I have no recollection of anything like that occurring, none at all. Who the hell do you think you are to—" He stared hard at Sherlock. "I see now, it's your father talking here. He told you about this and put his own unique spin on it, but—"

Sherlock said, "Our connection is to Chappy Holcombe. Jules Advere and Chappy go back a long way, as you must know. He called Chappy from the hospital, and since Sheriff Noble is Christie Holcombe's husband, he flew to San Francisco to check it out. It so happens that Sheriff Noble is a friend of ours, and we hooked him up with my parents. None of this comes from my father."

Savich said, "What Sheriff Noble found very odd was that when he told you he was from Maestro, you didn't mention that your brother-in-law attended Stanislaus. Your wife didn't say a word about it either. Help us make sense of this, Mr. Pallack."

Thomas Pallack was flushed now, his eyes hot and dangerous. A man this angry, Sherlock thought, could shove a stiletto into your heart. He said, "I wondered how Corman and Evelyn could possibly know a hick sheriff from some bumfuck place in the South—so the dinner invitation was for the benefit of the sheriff, was it?"

"I couldn't say," Sherlock said. "But why didn't you or Charlotte say anything, Mr. Pallack? It seems to me it would have been perfectly natural for your wife to jump right in when Sheriff Noble said he was from Maestro—goodness, her brother attended Stanislaus, seems she'd have remarked on what a small world it is, what a coincidence, and immediately engaged him in lively discussion."

"Evidently my wife didn't care to, if indeed he did say where he was from. Listen, the fact is, this Sheriff Noble was no one important, and he meant nothing to me or to my wife. He was simply a body at the dinner table to whom one was civil, nothing more."

Pallack didn't know his wife had met with Dix twice now since the dinner? Of course he might simply be pretending not to know. She said, "Mr. Pallack, after Jules Advere collapsed at your house, you had to know he would call Chappy. He was Christie's godfather, after all. You had to know there would be follow-up."

"I tell you I didn't even know who this Christie was!"

Sherlock sat forward, pinned him, her voice very quiet. "Were you frightened, Mr. Pallack? Were you cursing the vagaries of fate? You knew something would happen, realized someone would come. Did you watch your phone, waiting for it to ring?"

"I am frightened of nothing, Agent Sherlock, I have no reason to be. Now, I've been patient. I've cooperated, answered all your questions. I have nothing more to say. If you wish to continue with this insane inquiry, you will speak to my lawyer. I want all of you out of here now."

"Good day, Mr. Pallack," Cheney said as he ushered Julia out of the office after the others. He said to Mrs. Potts, who hovered protectively outside the big man's corner office, "We never got to see the fog burn off."

Her hands were on her hips and there was fire in her eyes. "No, you didn't," she said, "and I doubt you'll ever be here again to witness it."

CHAPTER 41

Savich was about to turn the ignition in his father-in-law's big black BMW when Sherlock's cell phone burst into "The Sound of Music."

"Sherlock here. *What?* You've got to be kidding me!"

Savich turned to face her. Both Cheney and Julia sat forward in the backseat, all eyes on Sherlock.

When she punched off her cell a few minutes later, she said, "Well, that was Ruth. She said the local news just reported the car chase and shooting through the park and on the beach, and that a psychic had warned Cheney and Julia that she'd seen it all in a vision, and this same psychic was helping the police now."

"But she didn't, she's not," Cheney said. "I mean it wasn't exactly like that."

"Get a grip, Cheney," Julia said, "we're talking the media here."

Cheney said, "Please don't tell me the media identified the psychic."

Sherlock said, "Unfortunately they did. They showed Kathryn Golden's picture."

"But how did they know? We didn't tell a soul!"

Cheney said, "You didn't, Julia, but I told Frank Paulette all about her, about how her call early this morning had gotten us moving out of my condo. There were lots of cops around in that parking lot at the beach who, I suppose, could have overheard. Or it was a reporter who pried it out of one of the cops who thought it was all a big joke, who knows?"

Sherlock said, "Ruth said the reporter mentioned a source at the SFPD."

Julia pounded Cheney's arm. "Oh no, Cheney, he'll go after Kathryn, you know he will."

Cheney quickly dialed Kathryn Golden's phone. One, two rings, then, "Hello?"

"Ms. Golden? This is Agent Stone. Listen to me now. The media gave out your name on the news. I want you to leave your house right now, do you understand? Pick up your car keys and go get in your car. Drive to the police station, all right? Do you understand me?"

"Yes, yes, I understand."

"Go, now! Leave your phone on. I want to be able to hear you."

He heard her breathing, heard her footsteps as she ran through her house, heard her say, "Where are those damned car keys?"

He heard her breathing hitch, then the blessed rattle of a key ring, her feet pounding loud. She said, "I'm nearly out, leaving now. *Oh God!*"

He heard the front door bang open, heard her scream. There was the sound of scuffling, and a thud, then there was nothing at all, only the silence of the open line.

"Oh God, he's got her. But how could Makepeace have gotten to Livermore so fast?"

Savich said, "He was hiding nearby, that's how. But why would he choose Livermore as his base?"

"I don't know why, but he got her, just that fast," said Cheney, snapping his fingers.

Sherlock said. "Julia, call the Livermore Police Department, tell them to get over to Kathryn's house. I'm calling Dix and Ruth, she said they both wanted in on this."

While Savich gunned Judge Sherlock's BMW, he imagined Dix driving his father-in-law's old black Chevy Blazer like a madman, Ruth giving him directions as best she could. Cheney called Captain Paulette.

"First David Caldicott disappeared, and now Kathryn's taken," Sherlock said. "I surely do hate this."

Cheney said into his cell, "It isn't good, Frank. I called her, told her to get out, told her to leave the phone line open. I heard him take her."

"Yeah, Cheney, the wife told me how the damned media bleated it all out. I've got some calls to make, then I'm on my way out there. Damnation, I'm going to kick some major butt about the leak. Let's hope you're wrong, but of course you're not."

Since Savich didn't have a siren and he didn't want to get stopped by the Oakland cops, he kept the Beemer right at the speed limit.

Julia grabbed Cheney's arm. "You know he's killed her, Cheney, you know it, the moment he burst through her front door."

"Not necessarily, I didn't hear a gunshot."

"But you have his gun! He could have strangled her or stabbed her or hit her on the head."

"No, I didn't hear anything like that." A lie, but it wouldn't help her to hear about the thud. "Hang in there, Julia, we don't know, simply don't."

Sherlock turned in the front seat to face them. "What should we know about Kathryn Golden?"

"Sorry, let me give you guys some quick background." And he did. "—and when she called me this morning, she told me she'd had another vision, that Makepeace was coming in a car. I rolled my eyes, I'll admit it, but it made me look in my rearview every other second, and I spotted him.

"I would have sworn most everything from the so-called vision she treated us to yesterday, any of us could have known or guessed—and for the rest, she probably had a source inside the SFPD."

"What do you think, Julia?"

"Kathryn's always bragged about all the insiders she knows. A cop too? Why not?"

"Savich, you've got maybe twelve more minutes," Cheney said. He paused, looked down at his cell and punched in Kathryn Golden's number. A man answered on the first ring. "Is this you, Agent Stone? A little late, aren't you? Too late. Oh yes, tell the bitch you'll be too late for her too. I'm coming for her," and he punched off.

"Makepeace answered," Cheney said. "I don't know Golden's status. I heard a bit of an English accent this time, which means he wasn't trying to hide it."

Sherlock said, "Or he's rattled and he couldn't control it."

Savich looked at Julia's face in his rearview mirror and pushed the Beemer to eighty miles per hour. They streamed around cars and drivers' startled faces. He grinned. "Okay then, let the cops chase us to the psychic's house if they want."

They pulled into Kathryn Golden's driveway behind three local cop cars, Dix and Ruth right behind them.

"Julia, stay in the—"

"Don't even think it, Cheney Stone."

Captain Paulette, siren blaring, screeched to a stop at the curb. He waved at the cops spilling out of the house. "Stay back, guys," Frank said over his shoulder as he jogged up to the Livermore police, and showed his badge. He was back in a moment.

"The front door was open, nobody home. The local cops want to know what's going on. When their lieutenant gets here, I'll have to tell him. I told them it's a kidnapping, or a murder. They're calling in their forensic people to dust for prints, and that's fine. Damn, you know, you guys are sure keeping me pumped."

"I'd like to go inside," Savich said. Frank ran interference for them, and when Lieutenant Draper drove up three minutes later, Frank filled him in. Draper sent some of the cops who had come out of the house to spread out and question all the neighbors. There was no clue to what Makepeace was driving.

When Savich stepped into the entrance hall, there was a dead, queasy silence, a layer of fear in the air.

Sherlock said beside him, "You can feel how empty the house is."

Savich nodded, and thought, *And the fear, your fear, that fear is still here. But he didn't kill you here, in the house. He took you.*

"I wondered how he got here so fast, as I'm sure all of you have as well," Frank said, "and so I checked and guess what—Ruth, you heard the second special media report, my wife did too. The first one was over an hour before."

Cheney said, "So that makes him as much as an hour away. He could have killed her right here, but he took her. What does that tell us?"

Dix said, "Maybe he was afraid the cops would drive up any second, so he got in and got out fast, taking her with him."

Julia said, "Maybe he took her because the news said she was working with the police to help find him. They talked about her vision—maybe he believes she really did see him driving after Cheney and me."

Savich said, "If he does believe she's psychic, then he'd want to take her out of the mix."

Dix thought about that for a moment, then shrugged. "Okay, I can buy that. Why not?"

Julia said, "I agree. It would make sense from his point of view. Maybe he thinks she knows where to find me."

Savich breathed in the dead heavy air again. He felt Kathryn, felt her fear, her terror, and he felt something else, something cold and deadly.

Dix said, "Fact is, we really have no idea why he grabbed her so quickly."

Savich said, "No, we don't. Captain Paulette, we'll go back to San Francisco. You'll let us know if the police find any witnesses, all right?"

When they'd stepped outside Kathryn Golden's house into

the late afternoon heat, Julia's cell phone rang. She stepped away. "Wallace? Yes, I know, but have you heard about Kathryn being kidnapped? No, no, unfortunately the police have no idea where she is. What—? There are six of us in all. Yes, three are FBI agents and one is a sheriff. Really, Wallace, what—"

She listened, then slowly punched off, and said, "That was Wallace Tammerlane." To Dix and Ruth, she added, "He's a psychic medium, one of August's best friends. The thing is, he's asked that all of us come to his house, as soon as we can get there. He said it's urgent."

Cheney said, "But what does he want?"

"He didn't tell me, only said it was about Kathryn and it's urgent."

Ruth looked from one face to the next. "We don't have much of a choice, do we? So, let's go see the psychic."

Dix said, "Why do I think I'm about to take a bus to never-never land?"

CHAPTER 42

When all of them arrived at Wallace Tamerlane's beautiful Victorian an hour and ten minutes later, Wallace's black-garbed butler, Ogden Poe, greeted them at the door and ushered them into the living room. Wallace and Bevlin were seated in chairs facing each other in front of a roaring fire.

"What are you doing here, Bevlin?" Julia asked.

Bevlin shrugged. "Wallace wanted me to come over. It's better with more people, you know."

What was better, Sherlock wondered, but she knew a showman when she saw one and was willing to wait. "Some digs," she said to Julia as she stepped into the living room. "Look at all those little teacups and saucers. I've seen similar ones in the Victoria and Albert Museum in London. And all the old photos of the Crimean War, I wonder where those come from?"

Bevlin said to Sherlock as he rose, "I don't like Victorian fuss. I like space and views."

"You're a hippie philistine," Wallace said. "Red beanbags— just saying it makes me shudder."

"Those red beanbags represent small vibrant areas of being," Bevlin said, whatever that meant, Cheney thought.

"All of this is very interesting," Julia said, aware that the three FBI agents and Sheriff Dix Noble were getting more impatient with each passing minute, "but we have more important things to do. Wallace, since you demanded that all of us come, let me make the introductions."

Wallace shook hands with the three FBI agents, pausing briefly in front of each of them. To Sherlock, he said, "Sometimes people look at you and smile, and don't see your substance. That's always a very bad mistake to make, isn't it?"

"Yes," Sherlock said, "one would think it is."

He turned to Ruth, looked at her closely, then slowly nodded. "You are extraordinarily good at your job, Agent Warnecki. You see so very much, don't you?"

"We all see too much sometimes, don't you think?" Ruth said.

When he reached Dix, he became very still. Finally, he said, "I see a nearly desperate man, Sheriff Noble, about what I don't know, but it's clear to me that you're frustrated and angry."

"You think?" Dix said. "You're a whiz at reading people, aren't you?"

"Yes, I am. Sheriff Noble, you're here, in a psychic's house, plainly, because you can't see any other options. I would say you are perhaps the most determined of all your colleagues to discount anything I may say or do. I ask you to be patient."

Dix looked at him, stony-faced.

Wallace lightly laid a hand on Dix's shoulder. "In the end, you will do what needs to be done, I imagine," he said, and stepped back. And that made Dix think of Charlotte—he'd forgotten to call her.

Wallace smiled at Julia, who stood very close to Cheney. "The two of you," he said, and shook his head. "Life continually surprises me."

When Wallace's eyes rested on Savich, he slowly nodded, but said nothing. He finally said, "I asked Bevlin to come over as well. As I told Julia, the more people here, the better for our efforts."

"What efforts?" Cheney asked. "Come on, Wallace, enough dancing around. Tell us why you wanted us to come."

"Very well. Both Bevlin and I are very concerned about Kathryn. Since you don't know what this madman has done with her, we decided that a séance, of sorts, might help us locate her.

"I wanted all of you here because I need all of your strength, your focus, your concentration. I can assure you, I am very serious. I cannot guarantee success, that is, I cannot guarantee you that I will connect to Kathryn, but I am going to try.

"Before you arrived, Bevlin and I spoke about Kathryn's vision—actually, I feared it would make the assassin hotfoot it right to her."

"I did too," Bevlin said.

Dix was still staring at them as stony-faced as before.

Sherlock said, "So I gather you believe her visions are authentic?"

"Oh yes," Wallace said. "Well, for the most part. Sometimes Kathryn embroiders, and why not? Clients love detail, all the emotional stuff she dredges up, it pulls them in deeper. She says that the trappings, you know, the background, the stuff surrounding the dead person in her visions, aren't usually very clear.

It's like there are filmy draperies blowing over everything but the person. But one thing I'm sure of—if she said she saw this guy, then she saw him. Do you agree, Bevlin?"

"I know Kathryn's a really good performer, knows how to cuddle right up to her clients. She senses very quickly what they need and want, and colors in her lovely pictures once they give her the clues she needs. But there've been times I've had the feeling she is seeing beyond what's there, really seeing."

Wallace said, "The fact is, though—and I can see all of you are thinking it—anyone could have called up Agent Stone this morning, told him to beware the assassin, to watch for his car because the assassin was after him. It seems nothing more than common sense."

Ruth held up her hand. "You said we're here to help you conduct a séance, Mr. Tammerlane, that you want to try to contact Kathryn Golden."

"Yes, that's right."

Bevlin said, "The only problem we see is that if Kathryn is really scared, it might freeze her up, prevent our communicating with her. Then Wallace probably couldn't reach her. On the other hand, and we must face this, she could already be dead. Then it would indeed be a séance."

"Well, you're a medium, aren't you?" Dix said. "That should make things easier all around."

Savich said, his eyes on Wallace Tammerlane's elegant, aesthetic face, "No, she's alive, no doubt at all in my mind."

Wallace Tammerlane frowned at him, a dark brow arched. "Then I hope to connect to her. This isn't a shot in the dark. A couple of years ago Kathryn and I experimented on sending each other messages telepathically. We wrote down what we believed we'd received from each other. We had quite a few hits. We were both pretty amazed." Wallace looked closely at Savich. "When I look at you, Agent Savich, I see a man who has, in his turn, seen a few things in his young life. Do you believe in psychics, Agent?"

Savich said easily, smiling, "I don't know that I believe in psychics or mediums, Mr. Tammerlane. However, I do believe that fear, that love, can sometimes come through to us, loud and clear."

"Ah," Wallace said slowly, staring at the big man he thought might be more powerful, perhaps even more dangerous than the man they were chasing, "so you've dealt with ghosts."

Savich continued to smile. "I'm willing to have you give it a try, Mr. Tammerlane. All of us want you to try to find Ms. Golden. We will all do as you say."

"All right. Good. Ogden!"

Ogden Poe glided into the living room, silent, an eyebrow raised.

"Dim the overhead, Ogden, you know I can't work in this bright light. And pull the drapes tight. The rest of you, I must have utter quiet. See to the arrangements, Ogden."

When the drapes were pulled, the lights dimmed, Ogden moved two sofas together. He motioned for them to sit close.

Wallace Tammerlane walked back to the huge wing chair facing the fireplace, turned its back to them and sat down. His voice floated over them. "I want all of you to hold hands, to connect your collective energy, to direct it toward me."

Soon there was complete silence. Wallace began to hum. It sounded soft on the silent air, rose and fell, but was always there. Embers crackled in the fireplace.

Wallace said aloud, his voice deep and smooth, "Kathryn, are you there? Let me know if you can hear me. I know you must be afraid."

A log cracked and fell apart, sparks flying upward. Shadows formed fantastic shapes on the walls. There was no sound. All of them settled in during the long moment of silence, and their hands remained clasped. Then Wallace said, "I'm thinking about you, Kathryn, trying to see you. Can you hear me, hear my mind? You must tell me where you are. You've done it before with me, do it now."

More silence.

In those long moments, Savich felt the soft warm air settle over him, enfolding him like a blanket. He felt Sherlock's hand in his, as soft and warm as the air, and he concentrated on Kathryn Golden, pictured the photo of her he'd seen on her dresser. A handsome woman, an intelligent face, eyes that saw, perhaps, things other people's eyes didn't. He remembered Samantha Barrister, long dead, yet he'd seen her, spoken to her, that long-ago night in the Poconos. But unlike Samantha Barrister, Kathryn Golden was alive. He wasn't sure how he knew this, but he knew.

Was it possible for Kathryn Golden's mind to connect to Wallace Tammerlane's?

Kathryn was smart, he knew she was smart, knew she was so frightened that her fear was eating deep. Savich stilled, and felt a ripple of awareness touch his mind, veer away, circle back again. It was very gradual, this awareness sifting like a shadow through his mind. No, not a shadow now. Savich felt a sudden ferocious fear—frantic and violent. It burrowed into him, paralyzing and chaotic. Then he perceived that whatever it was touching him had begun to change. The fear softened, the cacophony waned, and then there were jagged lines. He saw them clearly, like the static on an old TV. Savich forced himself to focus again, to smooth away the jagged lines. They began to slow and lighten until they finally faded into nothing. Savich saw it clearly now, a movement, not from the corner of his eyes, but straight in front of his face. It was a pale and vague image, rippling in soft colors, then it slowly sharpened, and he saw her clearly even though she was in a dark place. A woman, her hair straggling around her face, her clothes ripped, her feet bare, tied to a chair, a gag in her mouth. He saw her head jerk up. It was Kathryn Golden. She was alert now, her every sense focused on him. *Oh God, who are you? I feel you. He's left me, but not for long. Help me. Dillon? Is that your name? Help me.*

Savich focused on her face, the ugly bruise on her jaw where Makepeace had struck her. Without even wondering what he was doing, he thought, *I will, stay calm.*

Oh, thank God you're there. Dillon—

Then it was as if someone yanked a plug out of the wall. She was gone. His mind was empty of her. Had he imagined it? Had he experienced some kind of waking dream? No, he had not.

Wallace Tammerlane stood up a minute later and faced them. "I'm sorry, I don't think I got through to her. There wasn't any answer."

Ogden turned up the lights.

"Maybe," Savich said, rising slowly, "the line was busy."

When at last they were ready to leave, Savich shook Wallace Tammerlane's hand, then Bevlin Wagner's. "Thank you for your efforts. We have to be leaving now. If Kathryn makes contact with you, or you happen to find out anything that could help us, please call my cell." He gave each of them his card.

Cheney turned at the front door. "Do either of you keep journals?"

"Of course," Tammerlane said, and Bevlin nodded. "All of us do."

Savich heard everyone else murmur their good-byes, Bevlin assuring them it was okay, that they'd find Kathryn, that Wallace would keep trying.

When Julia and Cheney piled into the backseat, Julia asked, "What do you want me to do, Dillon?"

"First, I want you and Cheney to have that visit you were planning with Soldan Meissen. He's somewhere in the middle of this, he must be. Then I want both of you to come to the Sherlocks' house. You're both going to be guests there, along with the rest of us."

CHAPTER 43

There was a stark white half-moon shining directly down on Cheney's borrowed wheels, an older dark blue Audi, on temporary loan from the dealership while his own Audi was getting patched up from its beach run that morning.

It had all happened twelve hours ago. Amazing. He turned to Julia. "You hanging in there?"

"It's been a wild day, that's for sure."

"What did you think of Tammerlane's séance?"

"Well, I suppose it didn't work, did it? We're no closer to finding Kathryn. Do you think she'd dead, Cheney?"

He thought about that for a moment, then said, "No, the fact is, I don't. However, I'm still not certain why Makepeace took her."

"How about he believed she could have some visions for him, about where I am. What do you think?"

He laughed. "Yeah, right."

But Julia wasn't so sure. She'd lived in the world of psychics for three years, and sometimes she still wasn't at all certain what was and what wasn't real.

"I hope I can keep focused. Soldan Meissen's got to be at the center of this thing, along with Pallack, and now he's Pallack's medium."

She nodded. "I think you'll find Soldan interesting. He's, well, he's even more different. You'll see."

"None of the others we've spoken to have much respect for him."

"True. However, given Thomas Pallack's experience—I mean he was with August and also with the famous medium Linz Knowler before him—I can't see how Soldan could con him. He'd be very hard to scam."

"I remember seeing Soldan on TV maybe three months ago on one of those Hollywood entertainment shows. He was standing in a gloomy cemetery, naturally after dark, with manufactured fog creeping up to his knees. He was wearing jeans and three-inch stack-heeled boots to make him look more formidable, I guess—tough sell, let me tell you, because Soldan is really quite puny-looking. He was standing next to an oohing and aahing fluffy blonde who was handing him eight-by-ten photos of famous dead people. He told the camera what these folks were doing, how they felt about what their famous living relatives were up to. The blonde seemed to be impressed.

"August always said Soldan couldn't carry it off in front of a camera, that anyone seeing him would believe he was a gold-plated fraud. He'd say Soldan gave psychics a bad name."

Cheney pulled into Soldan Meissen's big circular driveway, stopped in front of the front door, cut the engine, and looked around. "Another big spread. I guess the psychic business is thriving."

Julia said, "Oh yes. Atherton is one of the biggest hubs of conspicuous consumption in the Bay Area. Soldan used to have a Spanish-style hacienda, then moved two blocks and went Oriental."

Cheney looked at the long, single-story house, solid windows all along the front, bonsai trees thick on the ground, crowding close to the house. "Is the guy married? Any children hanging around?"

"I don't know about kids, though there may be a former wife. A couple of months ago I heard a woman moved in, but I don't know anything about her. I sure hope he's here, Cheney. It's late. Maybe this time we should have called."

"Nah, a surprise visit you never know what's gonna pop. Look, there are some lights on at the end of the house."

They walked along a flagstone path lined with Japanese-garden-style bushes and flowers. There was a double front door lacquered glossy black with shiny gold dragon's-head doorknobs, flanked by a pair of huge Asian stone statues, too dark to tell any detail. Cheney pressed his finger against a dragon's snout and heard the bell chime some creepy music from that old Bela Lugosi film *Son of Frankenstein.*

"Maybe the guy's a warlock too."

There was no answer for perhaps a minute, then came the sound of mules flapping up and down on tile. The door was opened by a woman wearing a very low cut frothy peach peignoir that floated around her ankles. She looked, Cheney realized, with those prodigious breasts framed by silk and feathers, like a saloon girl from a western movie, a little over the hill, a little too much makeup, but authentic enough, at least TV authentic.

Cheney said, "Hello. This is Julia and I'm Cheney. We're here to see Soldan. Is he available?"

"You look familiar," the woman said to Julia. "You don't, sir. It's after nine o'clock. At night. What do you want? Soldan is tired. We don't see uninvited visitors. Besides, I don't like the look of either of you." She stared at Julia. "Yeah, you do look familiar. Is there a reason I don't like you?"

Cheney smiled at the woman; she looked like she could shoot them both, then blow the smoke off the end of her six-shooter and toss back a shot of straight whisky. "We're harmless. Actually, maybe you have met Julia. She's Julia Ransom, Dr. August Ransom's widow. And I am Cheney Stone, FBI. We won't take up much of Soldan's time. And who are you?"

"You're sounding all chummy, aren't you now? I'm thinking you're the best-looking paid federal assassin I've ever seen. Fact is, you probably make use of being gorgeous, don't you, makes it easier for you to flimflam innocent women like me."

"Nah," Cheney said. "They don't pay me that much."

"A federal assassin making jokes—you're smart too, but really not that funny."

"Who are you?" Julia asked.

"I'm Sol's mother. Okay, okay, you got me. Obviously I'm far too young and beautiful to be his mother. I'm Sol's sister—

younger sister. Hey, I bet if I don't let you in, you'll pull a gun and force your way in. Isn't that what you secret fed enforcers do?"

"Yeah, that's exactly what we do," and Cheney showed her his SIG on the clip at his waist.

For the first time, Cheney saw a flash of genuine alarm in her eyes, though it was hard to tell since she was wearing so much eyeliner. She held out her hands in front of her, to ward him off. "Don't you dare! All right, come in, I'll warn Sol." She gave Julia a dismissive look. "Shame on you, plastering your plain face all over the TV news." And she sashayed away, clip-clopping on the three-inch peach satin mules.

Cheney said, "Look how that silky thing floats around her as she walks. If she weren't so scary, it'd be sexy. Is she really his younger sister?"

"Why not? Don't you know? After all, you're the federal hired gun."

They walked down a wide long hallway that ran the full length of the house. The front was all glass windows, with a series of open rooms to their left, and a line of translucent shoji screens covered in rice paper that slid shut to provide privacy. The screens were all at half-mast now. He could see into the rooms, decorated with Asian statuary, from small naked bronze boys to three-foot stone gods. A huge gong that looked to be as ancient as the goddess sitting next to it was hunkered down in the middle of the largest room.

Eastern mysticism to add to the mix? Truth be told, Cheney didn't think anything much could surprise him after the trio of psychics he'd already met.

He was wrong.

Soldan Meissen sat in the middle of a half dozen huge silk pillows piled in front of a low, elaborately carved, red lacquered table, smoking a hookah. Smoke wreathed his bald head and fogged his rimless round glasses. He was slight, and looked swallowed up in a crimson silk robe belted at his meager waist with a wide black silk cummerbund. One narrow bare foot stuck out from the bottom of the robe. Ugly toes, Cheney thought, gnarly and bent. He realized he had seen him a couple of times on TV, but not like a little pasha in full costume. Why wasn't he wearing a fez to complete the presentation?

The man observed them in silence for a moment through a veil of lacy smoke, then said in a lovely deep voice, "Why did you bring these people into the house, Ancilla? You know I do not deal with clients after eight o'clock at night. It is now well after nine o'clock. Who are they?"

"They forced their way in, Sol. One of them is a federal agent, at least that's what he said. This person standing beside him is Julia Ransom."

The rheumy eyes turned toward Julia. A slight smile unseamed his tight mouth. He carefully set down the end of the tube connected to the detailed Oriental glass hookah, its cooling water bubbling and frothing. He took off his glasses and cleaned them on the sleeve of his silk robe. "Ah, you are my sainted August's beautiful widow, yes, I recognize you now, Mrs. Ransom. Forgive me. We met once, several years ago at one of August's soirees. Your aura was murky with grief and I believed that odd since you'd so recently married August. But then I came to understand.

Still, I was glad August didn't see auras. It would have distressed him to know the depths of your pain. Ah, do call me Soldan and I'll call you Julia. Sit down, both of you, take your ease."

They made themselves as comfortable as they could on the silk cushions. Cheney could feel Julia had tightened, probably because she was thinking about her son, but she said nothing.

"I would have thought your aura would once again be chaotic from what I heard on the news today, but it's not. The reporter said you were with an FBI agent in a mad car chase all the way to the beach. But you survived. I'm pleased about that. Oh, I see. The little drama was well staged even though I only saw the back of you when you climbed into a police car. I myself found it very effective. If there are people who believe you murdered August, that incident will turn the tide. You looked quite heroic."

"You don't think I killed August, do you, Mr. Meissen?"

CHAPTER 44

Soldan Meissen drew deeply on his pipe, then carefully laid it down again. He frowned at his toes and tucked his feet beneath his silk robe. He built the tension around him with superb skill. He said, "To kill a man such as August Ransom would require, I believe, a phenomenal degree of enmity, the result, I would think, of a steadily building rage. I see no signs of such a rage in your aura."

Julia only smiled. "What you saw on TV today was not staged. The man who chased us was the same one who tried to kill me on Thursday and Saturday night. His name is Xavier Makepeace."

"Hmm," Soldan said, holding the tube between his long thin fingers again and sucking in deeply. He whispered, his eyes now closed, "Did this man also kill my poor August?"

"It's possible," Cheney said. He waited until Soldan opened his eyes, then showed him his shield, and offered his hand, but Soldan ignored it. He drew again on his hookah.

Ancilla said to Cheney, "I'll bet you were the one who couldn't abide August, or at least your fed bosses couldn't, and you murdered the poor man. Or had your partners do it. That's why he's trying to kill you, no honor among assassins."

"That's a pretty good theory," Cheney said, cocking his head at her.

Julia said, "No, Agent Stone didn't kill my husband."

"Hah, so you say. But you're consorting with a federal assassin, aren't you? Who can believe you?"

"Neither you nor your sister are what I expected, sir," Cheney said, looking around at the violent, eye-crossing array of colors and exotic fabrics that filled the smallish room, mixing in with the gently outward floating hashish smoke from the hookah. There was no furniture, no books, no attempt to instill confidence that this man could speak to the dead. Huge silk pillows, and fabrics, not much else. Soldan Meissen reminded him of an emaciated long-ago pasha in Istanbul, quite at home at the Topkapi Palace. But Cheney doubted he'd have much interest in a harem.

Soldan ignored Cheney, stared at his bare toes again, and frowned. "I must have a pedicure, Ancilla. Make a note of it."

"Yes, Sol," Ancilla said, pulled a pen and small pad from her bosom and wrote on it.

"She is not my sister. She is my assistant."

"But I look like his younger sister," Ancilla said and fluffed her long hair.

"Do you like the table? It's Japanese, you know. I acquired it recently from one of those automobile moguls in Tokyo. Isn't it exquisite? I had it lacquered crimson. It was a very dark blue before, clashed with my spirit, dimmed my connection to *The Beyond.*"

"*The Beyond*?" Cheney said, eyebrow arched.

"That can hardly surprise you, Agent Stone. Yes, that is what I call it. *The Beyond.*" He offered Julia his hookah pipe. "Would you like to try some of my delicious Asian delight?"

Julia shook her head. "Not this evening. I fear it might disrupt my aura."

"What would you say if I were to arrest you for doing drugs, Soldan?"

"You are an assassin, not a vice cop. You are also not very amusing."

"He tried to be funny with me too, Sol," Ancilla said. "But I told him he wasn't."

Cheney said suddenly, without preamble, "I understand that after Dr. Ransom was murdered you became the medium for Mr. Thomas Pallack."

Soldan inclined his head, puffing contentedly. He looked toward Ancilla. "What is the day today?"

"It's still Tuesday, Sol, very late on Tuesday, I might add."

"How strange, I won't see him tomorrow night, Wednesday night. Yes, every Wednesday and Saturday I am with Thomas. Only he had to break our session for tomorrow night. I saw him last evening at his lovely home on Russian Hill from six o'clock to eight o'clock in the evening. I did not return home until nine o'clock, very late for me."

Cheney said, "Did you kill Dr. Ransom to gain control of his rich clients, Soldan?"

"It doesn't sound like something I'd do, does it, my dear Ancilla?"

"No, Soldan. You loved Dr. Ransom. You thought he was practically a god. If he had asked you to kill this federal assassin you would have done it gladly."

"Probably so," Soldan said and sucked in deeply.

"From Dr. Ransom's bank records, Thomas Pallack paid him a great deal over the past ten-plus years."

"Oh yes, I would imagine so. He provides excellent reimbursement to me as well." He puffed again.

"Did you make contact with Mr. Pallack's parents, Soldan?" Julia asked.

"Naturally. Vincent and Margaret Pallack are quite gregarious, always pleased to speak to their son, though Mrs. Pallack did tell me tonight that she believed her poor Thomas was, sadly, looking his age. She even mentioned the age spots on the backs of his hands. She said she didn't trust his wife Charlotte, told me to tell him to be careful of her. She was surely too young for him and what did he think he was up to?"

"Did you pass this along to Mr. Pallack?" Cheney asked.

"Only a bit of it so Thomas would know that he was indeed in contact with his parents. Evidently Mrs. Pallack was always a possessive mother. That didn't change when she died.

"Her sniping is a mother-in-law's jealousy, nothing more. I myself am very fond of Charlotte. She's done Thomas a world of good, keeps his spirits bolstered, laughs when she's supposed to, and is of immense assistance to him in all his political fundraisers. Thomas's mother was simply being bitchy, not at all uncommon amongst the departed, you know. Some of the dead are like that—mad and vengeful. So is Margaret Pallack, on occasion. I'm relieved she hasn't terrorized anyone. She would be very good at it."

Cheney asked, "Do you stop aging once you die, Soldan?"

"Oh yes. Thomas looks older than his parents now. He's quite a bit older than they were when they were killed. This disturbs them, naturally. They don't want him to die. For two reasons: They don't want to have to spend eternity with a son who looks older than they do, and they'll lose their only strong connection to this world since there are no other relatives here who would even think to call them, much less want to."

Cheney said, "You make it sound like picking up a video phone and punching in the right numbers."

Soldan merely puffed away.

Cheney was frowning. "Soldan, you mentioned the dead terrorizing the living. But that's the movies. Do you think a dead person can really physically affect a living person? In other words, if Margaret Pallack wanted Charlotte Pallack out of the way, could she make it happen?"

"You'd need to be a federal assassin for that," Ancilla said, and sneered at him.

"Usually," Soldan said, "once a person crosses into *The Beyond*, they lose their corporeal being, with all its advantages and disadvantages."

"Disadvantages?" Cheney asked.

"Liver disease, for example," Soldan said. "That is why I indulge only in my Asian delight. The liver is a sensitive organ. It does not deal well even with the finest vodka."

Cheney said, "So not all the dead lose their ability to assume a corporeal form?"

"Yes, they do, only—this is difficult but I'll try to explain it simply enough for you, Agent Stone. Some of the dead appear to be able to tap into a source of energy—it's black, this energy, and it's frightening. I have no idea where it comes from, no one does. I myself have never tried to connect with any of the spirits who wallow in it, and I don't ever want to. They scare me. I don't know what it is they want. Do they truly terrorize people like you see in the movies? Maybe it's all a myth. I don't know."

Cheney asked, "Have you spoken to August since he was murdered?"

Soldan said, "August roams, endlessly. He's a nomad in *The Beyond*. I suspect he will calm down within the next decade or so. A violent ending, it shocks the psyche, you see."

CHAPTER 45

D id you ask him who he thought might have killed him?" Cheney asked.

"What an interesting question, Agent Stone. No, I did not put that question to him precisely like that, but it was obvious he didn't know. He did mention to me that before his murder he was trying to locate a new cocaine dealer since the one he had was becoming unreliable."

"Why has Thomas Pallack wanted to speak to his dead parents for so many years?"

"How very odd," Soldan said after a long pause, eyes wide open now, sucking in his Asian delight. "When I look at you through my delicious smoke, the two of you appear to merge. It's a lovely aura that envelops the both of you. Your aura, Agent Stone—I see clashes of purples and reds that show a formidable intelligence at the service of sheer determined meanness, a violence deeply controlled, beautifully controlled, yes, and channeled.

"Julia's aura—right now it roils like dark clouds in the sky, with pulses of fear, so many unanswered questions. But there is hot excitement where you merge. She dampens your anger, you lessen her fear. It is quite remarkable."

Cheney said, "That's very interesting, Soldan. I can see you're good at what you do. But answer my question, please. Why the obsession with his parents? It would seem to me they'd have nothing left to talk about."

Soldan merely frowned at Cheney and continued puffing.

"Soldan," Julia said, sitting back on her heels, "we're thinking that the same person who killed my husband is trying to kill me. What Ancilla said about an accomplice trying to kill me, that simply isn't true. You know I would never have harmed August. Neither would Agent Stone."

"No, of course you wouldn't have, but you didn't love him, Julia. What you felt was immense gratitude toward him, not a passionate, full-bodied love, the sort of love a young woman would heap on a man who'd caught her heart, no, you cannot say that, not with any honesty. But gratitude, you overflowed with gratitude since August joined you to your dead son, provided you comfort in your time of need."

Julia, Cheney saw, looked shell-shocked. She nearly tipped off the huge silk pillow. Then she stared straight ahead, as if unable to move. She said finally, "I know August didn't tell you about Linc. He wouldn't. It would be a betrayal of me. How do you know Linc died? How do you know August was there with me?"

Soldan Meissen gave an elaborate shrug. The crimson robe nearly fell off one thin shoulder. "I know many things, my dear. August didn't tell me, not exactly. I am telepathic, something August accepted, though it frustrated him that he was unable to channel that power within himself."

"Or you did a bit of Googling," Cheney said, eyebrow arched.

Ancilla gave Cheney a dirty look.

Julia said, "Did August ever try to connect with you telepathically, Soldan?"

Soldan nodded, gave a dainty cough behind a narrow hand that sported three plain gold bands on his fingers. "Yes, of course, but he couldn't connect to me. As I said, he didn't have that particular ability. It was all by chance that I happened to wander into his mind when he was thinking about your boy. I removed myself immediately. I never said anything about it to him. Agent Stone, I would not stoop to Googling to find out a person's secrets. I am psychic, nothing less than that, I assure you."

Cheney said, "And did it come to you that Kathryn Golden was abducted today?"

"No, it did not, I regret to say. Perhaps if it had I could have done something. I did, however, see the special report on television. My poor Kathryn—all beautiful breasts and a lovely mind, two exceptional attributes in a psychic," Soldan said. "Ancilla, I know you dislike Kathryn, but there is no reason for you to. Please bring me a cup of oolong. My Asian delight makes my throat dry."

Ancilla, a huff in every step, left the room, her mules slapping on the tiles.

"I don't suppose you had anything to do with Kathryn's abduction?" Cheney asked him.

Soldan said nothing, merely frowned after Ancilla. "I told her to wear soft-soled shoes. I dislike the noise, but she said her footwear was none of my business. Can you imagine that?"

"Why don't you zap her with a single bloody thought?" Cheney asked.

"When I become God perhaps I will be more inclined to smite down those who deserve it," Soldan said, and even gave Cheney a full-bodied smile, showing a gold molar. "I am thinking that when this occurs, Agent Stone, your torments will begin."

Julia said, "Soldan, when did you last see Kathryn Golden? You've known her for a long time, haven't you?"

"Certainly, but it's been some time since we've seen each other. The three of them—since August was killed, they formed this precious little clique—Bevlin, Wallace, and Kathryn. Too good for me, the frauds. The report on the television said she was possibly abducted by this man, Makepeace, the man who wants to kill you, my dear Julia. I can't imagine why he'd want that lovely albatross around his neck. What on earth good would Kathryn Golden be to anyone?"

"Maybe Makepeace wants his own psychic," Cheney said.

"Ha, Agent Stone."

Julia said, "Do you know, Soldan, it seems that all four of you, even the three you seem to dislike so much, you all adored August. Why is that?"

"How can you ask that, Julia? You knew his powers firsthand. You saw how he brought comfort and enlightenment to so many disillusioned souls floundering in pain. He simply radiated goodness and peace."

Cheney asked, "Did you ever see or read Dr. Ransom's journals?"

"Oh no, that wouldn't ever do," Soldan said, and puffed.

"Kathryn also mentioned August's journals," Julia said, frowning, "but I never saw them, never even knew about them. I certainly never found them when I was going through August's things."

"Such a pity. Ah, my oolong. I trust it has only one Splenda in it?"

"Of course, Sol."

"Thank you, Ancilla."

He carefully set his hookah pipe on a small dish and sipped his tea. Then he took two more sips and sighed in pleasure. He looked at them. "I have told you as much as I can. I have been as honest with you as I can. I will ask you to leave now. I must have my rest."

Ancilla was standing in the doorway, tapping one mule.

Cheney said as he rose, "Thank you for seeing us. Would you be willing to tell me your real name?"

"My name is only the slightest modification of the actual name my beloved parents bestowed on me at my birth."

"What was that name, sir?"

But Soldan Meissen only waved his hookah at them. Cheney gave him a small salute, took Julia's arm and followed Ancilla out of the pasha's chamber.

CHAPTER 46

Tuesday night

Today has been one of the strangest days in my life," Julia said. She yawned, stretched, and leaned against the wall of the Sherlocks' upstairs hallway, her head resting just below a painting of a young girl repairing a fishing net.

"And one of the longest," Cheney said, resting his hand against the wall beside her head.

Her eyes suddenly brightened, and she leaned close, whispered against his ear, "You want to know what would actually have been more fun, if I hadn't been so terrified—car racing on the beach."

He laughed. "Don't forget that, it's even better in a dune buggy."

"You got him away from us, Cheney, that was a really good plan you had." She sighed. "I only wish I'd been a better shot."

"No, I was the one who should have nailed him." He lightly trailed his fingers down her cheek. "Anyone else I know would have been scared stupid, but you were enjoying yourself."

"Are you seeing me as some kind of maniac like you?"

"I'm thinking a maniac is a good thing in some settings. Actually, though, what I'm seeing right now, right in front of me, is a very beautiful woman."

She gave him a brilliant smile, both exhaustion and excitement clear in her eyes, at least to him. Now wasn't the time. He stepped back. She said, "Is that an example of a maniac talking?"

Cheney shook his head. "No, that's the plain truth." He streaked his hand through his hair, making it stand on end.

She laughed and smoothed it down, her hand resting a moment on his cheek. "Cheney—"

"You know, I was thinking Wallace sure read Dix right this evening. His frustration is building fast."

"Poor man, I can't say I blame him. The not knowing if his wife was alive or dead for over three years, I can't imagine going through that. And he still doesn't know where she is. You'll find out, Cheney, I know you will."

He could do nothing but stare down at her, and marvel at the utter certainty in her voice. He said, "That deal with Wallace—I have to say we got what I expected. Exactly nothing."

She nodded. "But you know what I found fascinating? It was the way Wallace looked at Dillon—with acceptance, only it wasn't really that, maybe some sort of recognition, no, that sounds absurd. I don't know." She gave a big yawn, clapped her hands over her mouth, and said through her fingers, "I'm sorry. Long, long day."

He took her hands, looked at the length of her. "It's time for you to get some sleep. Me too."

He dropped her hands, opened the guest room door, and

pushed her inside. "Nice room," he said, looking around at the pale yellow walls and the white bedspread, and started to close the door.

"Hey, wait, don't go just yet," she said, holding the door open, but then she stalled. What was she to say? *I've known you for all of five days and I want to jump you?* She managed a smile. "So much has happened to me since Thursday night, it's really set me to thinking about my life and what I was going to do with it.

"When I met Sean Savich, I saw Linc in him and I wanted to cry, and forget about the past and the future both. I was sucked right back into that black hole of grief. But then that adorable little boy took my hand, told me he beat his mama at computer games, and he began explaining the strategies of a game called *Pajama Sam.* And I laughed, couldn't help myself, and I climbed right back out of that hole." She paused a moment. "Do you know he told me his dad was giving him a skateboard for his next birthday? He said his dad had been a champ a way long time ago, and he was going to give him lessons. I wanted to yell at him never to get near a skateboard, but then I realized, perhaps for the first time, that what happened to Linc . . . it had been a stupid accident, tragic and heartbreaking, but no one's fault, and it was over, not forgotten, never forgotten, but over, no one to blame, certainly not the skateboard Linc loved so much."

"So what did you say to Sean?"

"I told him when I came back east, I wanted to drop by and take a few skateboard turns with him and his dad. I told him I had a few moves that might astonish him. He told me that would be cool, and he high-fived me."

He slowly drew her into his arms and held her, his hand against the back of her head, and pressed her lightly against his shoulder. "He's a great kid. I'll bet Linc was a great kid too. Did Linc look like you, Julia?"

She pulled back and he saw the sheen of tears in her eyes. Then she swallowed and smiled. "Nope, Linc looked just like his father."

"I think I heard Sherlock say the same thing about Sean."

She shook her head. "I'm sorry, Cheney, for getting sentimental on you—"

"No, no, shush, it's okay." He hooked her hair behind her ears and cupped her face in his palms. "There's so much going on here, Julia, so much we still have no clue about. I hate not being in control and I know you feel the same. But everything will be resolved, you'll see. Now, we're both very tired. Do you think you can sleep?"

"Oh yes, but I'd probably sleep better if—well, never mind that. If you find you can't sleep on your monk's cot down in the Sherlocks' gym, you can always lift some weights. You're such a puny little guy, after all."

He laughed. "Mrs. Sherlock told me the cot wasn't too bad, she'd slept there once when she was so mad at her husband even three guest rooms away was too close to him. Don't worry, Julia— Makepeace has no clue where you are. Even Frank Paulette doesn't know, which means no leaks through the SFPD."

"I'm not worried, at least not right this minute. Cheney—it's odd, isn't it? Look where we are on a Tuesday night, all that's happened, how we met all of five days ago."

"Nights," he said, "it was five nights ago." And Cheney couldn't help himself. He leaned down and kissed her mouth, felt warmth and acceptance, and a leap of excitement that could have easily brought him down. He had to leave her but he didn't want to. This was really bad timing. He pulled back, touched his fingertips to her nose, smoothed her eyebrows, and wanted to ask her to tell him all her secrets. But now wasn't the time, dammit. "Good night, Julia."

Julia felt suddenly so alive she could jump right out of her skin, and here he was saying good night to her? Five days—who cared if they'd met an hour ago? "Oh my. Well, good night, Cheney."

"Don't worry, Julia."

He stood, unmoving in the hallway, until she closed her bedroom door. Earlier, Wallace Tammerlane had looked at the two of them and said something about life continually amazing him. Wallace didn't know a single blessed thing about amazement.

Cheney walked slowly down to the gym, eyed the narrow cot, and sighed. It would be a long night, even if there were only a short number of hours left in it.

In the next guest room down the hall, Dix was lying on his back, his arms crossed beneath his head, staring up at the shadowed ceiling, trying to ground himself, to order his squirreling thoughts, but it was difficult. They'd only arrived in San Francisco yesterday, and between then and now they'd done nothing but work and talk and talk. He supposed he'd agreed with Savich that he shouldn't see Thomas Pallack, but he'd wanted to. He'd wanted to take that old man's wrinkled neck in his hands and squeeze until he told the truth.

He still didn't know a single thing. Bless Sherlock for recording their interview with Thomas Pallack. He'd played it twice. He wanted to face Pallack down, he wanted to find that damned bracelet. What he wanted, dammit, was the truth. What he wanted was to find Christie.

But all he could do was lie there, stewing, his problem-solving ability dead in the water.

He liked Julia Ransom, didn't want Makepeace to kill her. He wondered what had happened to the kidnapped psychic, but his brain just kept neon-flashing Charlotte and Thomas Pallack, and he wanted to *know* so badly he didn't think he could stand it. Maybe he should force himself to finally call Charlotte, maybe make a date to meet at the Hyatt, although in his gut, he knew he wouldn't find out anything useful. Charlotte was way too smart. The only thing he'd get from her was more syrup-sweet lies. It was very possible too she was using him to gain information just as he was her.

Ruth came up on her elbow beside him. "I miss the boys and Brewster."

"I do too."

"We'll find out everything soon, Dix, have some faith. You know patience is one of a cop's main virtues, so stop making yourself crazy. I know all this is complicated and Julia Ransom is now in the mix with this Makepeace character, but we'll find out about Christie. Keep the faith."

He brought Ruth against him, momentarily distracted with

her warm breath on his neck. "It's hard," he said. "Now my mind jumped to David Caldicott. I know if he left willingly it was because he was involved in Christie's disappearance and our visit scared him badly."

"So you think he took off, maybe left the country?"

"Or he didn't leave willingly," Dix said. "He told someone that you and I had been to see him. You know it had to be Pallack, there's simply no one else. And Pallack panicked? About what?"

"David's been missing only a day and a half. You spoke to the Atlanta detective who's on the case."

"Yeah, the cops blew off Whitney Jones's pleas for help yesterday, stating the party line—a day hadn't even passed, and did they have a fight, was there another guy, another girl? But then, bless her heart, Whitney was bright enough to tell them about David meeting with the FBI."

Ruth grinned down at him. "That sure woke them up, and a very good thing. You know they're digging to locate him since the FBI is involved, for whatever reason. What did you tell the detective?"

"A bit of the truth, enough to whet his curiosity."

Ruth said, "Well, if they can't find him, I know we will, Dix."

He chewed on his misery for a moment, then Ruth said, "What did you think of our séance this evening?"

What he'd felt had been stark moments of anger—at being there wasting his time, having to deal with what he couldn't explain, couldn't see, didn't want to begin to accept, but he said only, with some contempt in his voice, "I was too tense even to be entertained by Tammerlane's show. It was a waste of time. On the other hand, I finally got to meet a couple of crackpot psychics." He added, "They were interesting characters, I'll have to admit that."

"So you think it was all B.S.?"

"No," he said, "that's oversimplifying it. But all the discussion about telepathy, Wallace Tammerlane sitting over there, humming, for God's sake, trying to communicate to another psychic, and all of us sitting on the sofas, holding hands like a bunch of dummies, with the light dimmed." He sighed. "All so Tammerlane could reach Kathryn Golden with his mind."

And he snorted his disgust. Ruth was so charmed she kissed him. She raised her head, touched a fingertip to his mouth, and said, "You certainly have a way of cutting right to the heart of things, don't you? Haven't you told me how you sometimes felt Christie close by and you told her things about what was happening with you and the boys?"

"That's nothing more than my subconscious self trying to find some comfort."

"Yeah, maybe you're right. Go to sleep, Dix." She kissed him again, settled back against his side, her head on his shoulder, and about thirty seconds later she was down for the count herself.

In the last room down the hall, Savich quirked an eyebrow at Sherlock over Sean's head. He was snuggled between them, his toy Porsche Carrera tucked against his chest, snoring lightly. "I like the bright red," Savich said, sighing. He could still see his own beloved Porsche exploding in a raging ball of flame in the midst of utter chaos that black night at the Bon-homie Club, leaving nothing to salvage but a single shiny hub-cap that had rolled down the sidewalk. The hubcap was hanging on the wall in his garage.

Sherlock said, "It's been what, three months? I'm thinking you've mourned your Porsche long enough. Maybe it's time for you to graduate from driving my Volvo. My Volvo feels your pain, and it lowers her self-esteem when you compare her to the Porsche, and find her so lacking. I heard one of the agents say driving the Volvo was going to break your spirit."

Savich very nearly shuddered whenever he had to drive the stalwart Volvo. He fondly recalled the sheer power of his Porsche, its temper when another car got too close, its spurt of insane speed when he needed it. He sighed. "It always seems like we're up to our ears in something—like now. Here we are in San Fran-cisco dealing with psychics and assassins."

"We'll get through it, we always do. Hey, maybe by this weekend."

"That might not be so crazy. Things are coming together fast now."

"I know, they are." Sherlock kissed him, then leaned over to kiss the back of Sean's small head. "He's got so much black hair, just like yours." Beautiful smooth shiny hair, not a single twisty curl or kinky wave, not like hers. "He's out," she whispered, and settled in. "I'll take him back in a moment."

"After his nightmare last night, I'm thinking maybe he should stay with us tonight. It's the strange-house-and-bed syndrome, no one his age does all that well with it."

"Did my mom tell you that after she and Graciella took Sean to the zoo, they hit the crooked block of Lombard Street? Sean was so excited he wanted her to drive it three times."

"Graciella told me. Your dad is taking him down to the courthouse tomorrow, introducing him to some of the clerks, interns, and judges. He even promised him he'd show him a crook or two—I think he meant a defense lawyer, but I'm not sure."

She smiled as she reached out to touch his face. "Are you still freaked out about what happened at Tammerlane's?"

"No. Sweetheart, I don't want any of the others to know about what happened, okay?"

"Nor should they," Sherlock said, and yawned. "I can't begin to imagine what Director Mueller would say if he heard you'd cell-phoned a kidnapped psychic without the cell phone."

Despite the strange bed and all the excitement, all three were soon asleep, Savich the last to fall.

Toward morning he dreamed of Kathryn Golden. She was alone again, in a closet, bound to a chair, her hair hanging over her face. She seemed to be asleep. He wanted to speak to her, but somehow no words came from his mouth or into his mind. She never stirred. He came abruptly awake, his heart pounding. What had that been about? He looked at the digital clock next to the bed. It was nearly five o'clock.

He knew there'd be no more sleep. He quietly left the bed, tucking in the covers around Sean's neck, lightly touching Sherlock's shoulder. She was smiling in her sleep. He looked down at the two most important people in his life and felt overwhelming gratitude.

He pulled on his pants, picked up MAX, and headed down-stairs to the Sherlock gym. He drew up short, seeing Cheney sleeping on the narrow cot, sprawled on his back, arms and legs over the sides of the bed, deeply asleep. No way was he going to wake him. He went to his father-in-law's study, and set to work. He wanted to know more about the Pallacks' murder in 1977 and all about the man who'd butchered them, Courtney James. He frankly didn't think he'd find anything useful, but who knew what might pop up?

CHAPTER 47

SHERLOCK HOUSE

Wednesday morning

Savich handed Sean a piece of his freshly baked croissant, which he'd smeared with a big dollop of strawberry jam. Sean grinned up at Isabel and said, "My mama says you make the best croxants in the known world."

"Yes, indeed I do," Isabel said and ruffled the little boy's dark hair. "You look just like your daddy and that's a fine thing. He's so handsome one of the neighbor women said she wanted to take over my job for a while so she could get close to him, maybe steal him away from my little Lacey."

"Who's little Lacey?"

"That's your mama, sweetie."

Sean shook his head. "No, Isabel, Mama's name is Sherlock. Everybody calls her Sherlock, except me, and I call her Mama."

Ruth frowned as she stifled a yawn. "I didn't even know her name was Lacey. Well, how about that, speak of the sweetie and Sean's mama. Dix, meet Lacey."

Dix looked up from his cereal bowl. He looked tired, his eyes dark with shadows. "Hi, Lacey. No, that doesn't feel right—it's got to be Sherlock."

"Or Mama," Sean said.

Sherlock was wearing her usual FBI uniform of black pants, white blouse, short black boots, her SIG clipped to her belt. Her curly hair shone brightly in the morning sunlight flooding through the kitchen windows, thick and red as Isabel's lipstick. Her blue eyes were as bright—a soft summer blue. She kissed Sean's cheek, nipped her husband's earlobe.

Ruth said, "Hey, where are Cheney and Julia?"

Isabel said, looking down at the fork in her hand, "Julia told me she had to talk to Cheney, so she went down to the gym. I took down a big plate of croissants and a pot of coffee a half hour ago and from the sound of it, they were having a nice full-bodied, loud, ah"—Isabel shot Sean a look—"discussion."

"What are they fighting about?" Sean wanted to know.

"Well, nothing really, Sean," Isabel said. "It's more a discussion, like I said."

"A full-bodied discussion," Ruth said.

Isabel cleared her throat. "Maybe they're going to work out a bit."

Dix smiled into his orange juice.

Sean said, "When Mama's mad at Papa, she jumps on him."

"Ah, well, yes, sometimes," Sherlock said. She grinned at her husband and poured herself some tea from her mother's prized Edwardian teapot.

Sean said, "Julia told me about her little boy. She said he died."

"I didn't know that," his father said.

"Do you think Julia and Cheney are working out with Grandpa and Grandma?"

Isabel poured Dix and Ruth more coffee. "Could be, Sean, but first I think they wanted to be alone for a little while, you know, talk things over."

"The discussion," Sean said. "But, Isabel, I don't understand. What—"

"Oh my, Sean, I believe some toast just popped up." And Isabel escaped to the other side of the kitchen.

Sean said to Dix, "Rob and Rafe told me how their mama, Christie, died a long time ago, Uncle Dix," and he slipped his hand into his mother's.

Dix said, tightening all over, "Yes, she did, Sean."

"I don't want my mama to die and leave me."

"She won't," Dix said. "That's a promise from a big bad sheriff, okay?"

Sean nodded.

Dix rose. "That reminds me. I need to speak to my sons, see what they're up to and hope they're telling me the truth."

"Say hello for me," Ruth called after him. She added, "Hey, Sean, I hear you're going to go check out the courthouse with your granddad this morning."

Cheney and Julia appeared in the kitchen doorway. They looked well-rested, and relaxed, and Julia's eyes were shining.

Nothing like full-bodied discussions to jump-start a person's day, Ruth thought.

Cheney's cell phone rang, and he turned away.

When Cheney walked back into the kitchen, he took a quick look at Sean, and said, "That was Makepeace. He told me where Kathryn Golden is. He told me to come get the worthless idiot, she's of no use to him at all. She's at the Mariner Hotel in Palo Alto, Room 415."

"It's obviously a trap," Savich said.

"Yes, but it doesn't matter," Julia said. "We have to go get her. Let me get my jacket, Cheney."

Savich said, "Wait. Neither of you is going anywhere. You know very well that Makepeace is probably waiting there with a scoped rifle. No, you're staying right here." Savich went into command mode. "Ruth, Dix, you guys head down to Palo Alto. Sherlock and I will follow once I've made some calls and gotten as much protection as I can."

Ten minutes later, Dix and Ruth were on 280 South headed to Palo Alto.

In the Sherlock home entrance hall, not a foot from the front door, Julia stood toe-to-toe with Cheney. "I'm not staying all snug and hidden in the Sherlocks' damned gym. I'm coming with you and Sherlock and Dillon."

"No, you're not, Julia. And don't even think about comparing yourself to Sherlock. You're a woman like she is, I'll go along with that, but she's a professional, and she's trained to kick butt. It would be incredibly stupid for you to show up at that hotel. He's after you, he wants to kill you. I'm not about to take the chance. Forget it."

"He's after you too, Cheney," Savich said mildly. "I would be if you'd stuck your nose in my business as many times as you have and beaten me. No, both of you are staying right here. Captain Paulette just pulled up. You two tell him what's going on. I've got phone calls to make."

Cheney and Julia continued to argue. "He's down in Palo Alto, waiting for us to show."

"For all you know, he's off trying to kill the mayor."

"Don't be cute. Look, Julia, if I have to tie you down, I will."

"Or the two of you could pay a nice visit to the gym downstairs again," Sherlock said.

Savich said, "Listen, when we've gotten Kathryn Golden back, all of us need to meet at Julia's house. We need to find August Ransom's journals. Just be patient. Sherlock, we're outta here."

A minute later, they were on the road in the judge's black Beemer.

Frank said to Cheney, "If they get the psychic safe and everyone's back up here, I'll get everything ready to go—I'm thinking a couple of undercover cops, no SWAT, that's overkill, what with Makepeace in Palo Alto."

"You know the available resources better than I do," Cheney said.

Forty minutes later, Savich dialed Dix's phone from the car. "You there yet?"

"Yeah, we just drove up."

"Okay, you're going to meet a Lieutenant Ramirez of the Palo Alto PD. I told him a good bit, but not all of it."

Dix said, "It's obvious Ramirez has already set things up here. He's got plainclothes cops searching around the hotel. We were talking—what if Makepeace is setting a trap in some other way?"

A bomb, Savich thought, Dix meant a bomb. He said slowly, "Makepeace would have to have contacts to purchase explosives, if that's what you're thinking. It could be anything. Tell Ramirez to be very careful."

"All right. The doorman's looking nervous. He knows something's going on. Can't anybody keep a lid on things?"

"You know that's impossible. You keep your eyes open, Dix."

Savich heard Dix speaking, and then Ruth said something to the valet.

Dix said, "Okay, we're walking into the lobby. There's Ramirez, trying to look like he's waiting for his damned luggage or something. He might as well be wearing a sign around his neck that says *Hey, I'm a cop.* I've got to go, Savich. I'll call you as soon as we've got Golden."

Savich didn't even bother to question himself about it. He simply thought, *Kathryn, Dix Noble and Ruth Warnecki are on their way up to your room with the local Palo Alto police. You'll be fine.*

Savich was disgusted with himself. Why had he believed for a single instant that she'd heard him?

He pictured Makepeace jumping out of the elevator at them, mowing them down, and dialed Dix's cell again. He couldn't help it, he had to talk to him again. He pressed harder on the accelerator. The Beemer shot forward. They were still about a half hour away.

Dix said, "Savich, stop your worrying. We're being very careful, everyone is. No sign yet of Makepeace. We're going into the room now." Savich heard a door open.

"We're in the room. Kathryn Golden's in the middle of the room, tied to a chair. She's gagged. Let me get to her, just a second—"

"Dix—"

Savich heard a loud explosion.

He frantically dialed Dix's cell again.

There was no answer.

He dialed Ruth's cell.

He got voice mail.

Kathryn!

There was no answer.

CHAPTER 48

Afrightened young voice answered on the tenth ring at the Mariner Hotel. "I'm sorry, but I can't talk to you. There's been an explosion, someone tried to blow up the hotel. I've got—"

"Don't hang up! I'm the FBI. What's your name?"

"I'm Melissa Granby, sir—Agent Sir."

"Take a deep breath, Melissa. That's good. Now, tell me what's going on."

"A couple of seconds ago this guy—he said his name was Makepeace—he called us, said a bomb was going off in the hotel in Room 415. Then there was this loud explosion, and everyone's screaming, guests are running down the stairs, it's crazy—"

"Stay with me here, Melissa, slow down. You're doing fine. Are there any police there?"

"Police? Yes, I see a uniformed guy running toward the stairs."

"This is critical. Stop him. Now."

Bless her young heart, he heard the yells, the running, the panic in the background, then he heard her shouting above them all for the officer to stop.

A few seconds later, a man's impatient voice came on the line.

"Who the hell is this? You better really be FBI and not some dumb-ass reporter."

"Yes, I'm FBI, Agent Dillon Savich. I'm in on the operation with Lieutenant Ramirez. Please go straight up to Room 415, then call my cell and tell me what's going on." Savich gave him the cell number. "What's your name?"

"Officer Clooney."

"Officer Clooney, please hurry."

There was nothing more Savich could do except speed, which he did. He felt Sherlock's hand close around his. She said, "I've got our I.D. ready to shove in a cop's face if we're stopped."

Savich let the Beemer ease up to ninety. He slammed his fist against the steering wheel. "I was afraid of a bomb, but there wasn't time—damnation, I should have gotten bomb squads there straight off, bomb-spotting equipment—"

"Yeah, yeah, maybe we'd have had them in a couple of hours, which we didn't have. Stop beating up on yourself. Concentrate on getting us there safely."

"You're right. But Dix and Ruth—Kathryn Golden—"

"Be quiet, Dillon. Dad's Beemer needs you."

Savich eased the speedometer to one hundred. Thank heaven traffic was fairly light.

Sherlock said, "So Makepeace calls in the bomb himself, even identifies himself, tells everyone the room number, and blows it right away. Why? Are you making any sense of this?"

Savich said, "Maybe he told them the room number because he wanted people to find Kathryn right away, wanted everyone focusing on her, on the explosion, getting tied up in all the chaos.

Meanwhile he's hoping to see Cheney or Julia, betting everyone will haul butt down to Palo Alto. Or, maybe hoping we'll leave Cheney and Julia in San Francisco."

Sherlock said, "Problem here, Dillon. Makepeace is down in Palo Alto setting off a bomb, he as good as asked Cheney to come on down and let him try to kill him again. Does he think we're that stupid? Wouldn't he be able to figure out that Julia's safe in my folks' house in San Francisco, with Cheney protecting her?"

At that moment, Savich's cell played "Born to Be Wild." "Is that you, Officer Clooney?"

"Yes, sir. It's bad, Agent Savich. Here's Sheriff Noble."

Thank God. "Dix, are you okay? Ruth? You got Kathryn Golden?"

Dix stood in the midst of the rubble, swiping his hand over his eyes to clear away the dust, holding his arm. "Ruth and I are both okay, well, nearly. Kathryn Golden's in bad shape, Savich. There's lots of blood, and she's unconscious. Ruth's stanching the blood from a wound on her leg. Lieutenant Ramirez's face is bloody, mine too. Two of his men are slightly wounded.

"The room's a mess, lots of smoke, lots of alarms, but maybe more noise than real damage. He probably used about half an ounce of Semtex, or some equivalent. But why not more? What I'm not getting here is why this little boom when he could have blasted the whole hotel to hell and gone, and us too? Why didn't he?"

"Dix, hold on a second. Was the bomb detonated after you untied Kathryn and she stood up?"

"I'd say so, yes, wait. That's right, it didn't blow right away.

Actually, she'd stepped away from the chair, three, four steps, then bang."

"So he's close by, using binoculars to see into the room, which means he blew the charge exactly when he wanted to. He probably connected the bomb to his cell phone. Get the cops to canvass the buildings across the street, he'd have to be able to look into the room. Are the drapes open?"

"Yeah."

Savich heard Dix speaking to Ramirez, heard Ramirez talking to his officers. Then Dix was back. "Okay, done. And we've closed what was left of the drapes."

Savich said, "I'm thinking he could be across the street, or— am I an idiot or what? You said it yourself, Dix, it doesn't make sense. Quick, check around the hotel room—up at the ceiling line—see if there are any digicams pointed at you, or a cell phone—that'd be the easiest way."

Dix said, "You think he's got two cell phones and he's been watching the hotel room ever since he left? That would mean Makepeace doesn't have to be across the street, Savich, he doesn't even have to be in Palo Alto. He could be in frigging Oregon."

"Yeah, he could. If Makepeace blew the bomb exactly when he wanted, that would mean he didn't want to kill Kathryn Golden or any of the hotel people or cops who found her when he sent them up to her room."

Dix said, "Okay, he sees us drive up and that spurs him to move. He calls the hotel and lays the bomb threat on them. Let me see if I can find— Hey, wait a second, just get away from me! No—not now—"

There was what sounded like a scuffle, then someone fumbling with the phone. Ruth, a bit out of breath, said, "A couple of paramedics grabbed Dix to wrap a pressure bandage around his arm to stop the bleeding. Okay, I'm going to look for a camera of some kind. Hang on." Not ten seconds later, she was back on the line. "You nailed it, Dillon. There was a cell phone fastened into the folds of the draperies, the camera aimed right at Kathryn's chair. When I picked it up, spoke, the line was dead. But Makepeace has been watching us—or listening to us. Why would he wait for us to move away from the chair before he blew it? Why would he care if any of us was killed?"

Savich said, "Maybe he only murders for a purpose. Maybe mass murder isn't his style. Maybe he knows killing all of you would have brought every law enforcement agency in the world down on him."

Ruth said, "Or maybe he was hoping Cheney would be the one trying to free Kathryn, and he would have blasted the bomb right away. They're carrying Kathryn Golden out right now. She's unconscious."

"Sounds like you and Dix need to get to the hospital too, see to his wounds. You promise me you're okay, Ruth?"

"I'd better be. Dix looks like he wants to start a brawl. We'll call you from the hospital, Dillon, let you know everyone's status."

Savich heard Dix yelling at someone in the background. He pulled off at the next exit. "It's back we go to the city," he said. "Even though I can't tell you for certain where Makepeace is, I want to get over to Julia's house and find those journals. They're at the center of this thing, Sherlock. I think we'll find some answers when we find those journals."

"Are you going to let Julia come with us?"

"It's a tough call, but you know, Julia knows every nook and cranny in her own house. We need her. Captain Paulette will provide enough people to keep Makepeace away, if he so happens to show up there."

"From your mouth to God's ear," Sherlock said.

CHAPTER 49

At two o'clock that afternoon, Julia, with Savich, Sherlock, and Cheney close behind her, unlocked the front door of her house and stepped in. The large entryway was filled with shadows, empty and silent.

She shuddered. "It seems like I've been gone years rather than days," Julia said. "It's like a stranger's house."

Cheney took her hand. "We don't want to stay here any longer than necessary, Julia." He frowned at Savich, who raised his hand.

"Listen, Cheney, we've already discussed this into the ground. We've got to find those journals. Both you and Julia said Kathryn Golden put extraordinary emphasis on them. Julia knows this house, knows all its hiding places. They've got to be here, so let's get busy. The sooner we find those journals, the sooner we're out of here. Julia, you said you already searched your husband's study, but we'll start there."

"I didn't really search everywhere, simply gathered all his things up."

"Okay, then you and Cheney go to the study. Cheney knows more about hiding places than a drug dealer. Sherlock and I will start here in the living room."

When they were alone, Savich walked to the front windows

and pulled back the thick draperies. He saw a man across the street dressed in an aloha shirt, trimming a neighbor's bushes. Another man was mowing a yard. Both were undercover cops.

He joined Sherlock in front of the painting over the mantel. "So that's Dr. August Ransom," he said. "His eyes are dark and intense, just like Wallace Tammerlane and Bevlin Wagner." Were they a necessity, he wondered, for the psychic package? He glanced into a mirror on the wall beside the fireplace, and his own dark intense eyes stared back at him.

"Let's get to work."

There weren't any wall safes behind paintings, there weren't any safes behind the books that filled the single bookshelf against one wall. Sherlock checked the floorboards—no hollow sounds, nothing under the carpet.

"Well, I say we do the kitchen next," she said. "I vote for the Sub-Zero freezer."

Julia and Cheney walked into the living room, Cheney shaking his head. "Nothing. We even moved his big desk aside to check the floorboards. Zilch, nada."

Julia said, "I'm thinking I should check August's bedroom next. I did only a quick clean-out. He worked in there as well." She turned to leave the living room when in that moment there was a very slight creaking of an oak plank overhead.

They all stared upward. Cheney already had his SIG pulled. Savich placed his finger on his lips. "Julia, how would he get in the house without any of the cops outside seeing him?"

She looked perfectly blank, then, "I remember. There are some ancient fire stairs hanging from outside the attic window, bolted to the side of the house. They're mostly covered with vines and bushes because August thought they were an eyesore, wanted them hidden."

Cheney said, lowering his voice, "We're not going to take any chances with Julia. She and I are going to hunker down in the kitchen pantry; it's probably the safest place in the house. We'll be as quiet as we can."

Savich said, "I don't care what happens, keep Julia safe. Sherlock, you're with me."

Once Cheney and Julia had disappeared, Savich and Sherlock walked to the foot of the grand staircase, and stood quietly, listening.

There was not a whisper of a sound.

"Maybe it was only a creak from an old house," Sherlock whispered.

"Possible." He motioned her to the other side of the stairs, opposite the door to the living room, beneath the staircase.

Sherlock dropped to her knees, keeping a clear view up the stairs to the second-floor landing. She didn't have much patience. It drove her nuts to hold herself still and not run up the stairs, listening to her own heartbeat, the thump of her pulse in her throat, wanting to scratch an itch, but not daring to move. They waited, until her feet were numb and her stomach was growling. She looked at Dillon, still motionless as a shadow on a still night.

Like her, he was partially hidden behind a newel post, the one Julia's bullet had blown apart on Saturday night.

Savich was thinking of his father, a man who'd marveled at this ability in his son because he, Buck Savich, had been a live wire, never still, always on the move. Savich looked over at Sherlock. He could practically see wild waves of energy jumping off her. He knew she was well-trained, an excellent shot, and blessed with great reflexes, but he couldn't help feeling the familiar punch of fear in his gut whenever she was in danger. He doubted it would ever fade. What amazed and pleased him was that she felt the same way about him.

Why wasn't there another sound? Maybe because there was nothing there. But he didn't believe that for a second. He'd wager Makepeace was standing still as a rock, like they were, listening as intently as they were. He had to know they were in the house. Did he also know about the cops outside? Probably. Ah, but he couldn't be sure they were on to him. He had to come out of the corridor and onto the second-floor landing. He had to make a move, it only made sense. Surely he was waiting for Julia to come upstairs. Did he have any idea why they were here? Savich bet he knew exactly why they were here—how, he didn't know, but Makepeace knew.

One eternal minute passed, then another. It seemed like a decade. Makepeace had to know something was wrong by now. It had been too long since anyone had made any noise. Then Savich knew why. "Down, Sherlock!"

An explosion rocked the house. Smoke and flames shot at them from the upstairs, debris spewing onto the landing and stairs from the corridor to the left. Smoke billowed down the stairs, blanketing them. This wasn't for show—not like at the Mariner, mostly smoke and noise—this was a huge blast, meant to destroy, meant to kill. There was another explosion more distant, from the corridor to the right, probably from Julia's bedroom at the end of the hall. Her bedroom was right over the kitchen.

Plaster fell in large chunks from the ceiling, walls heaved and bowed. Savich grabbed Sherlock's hand and together they ran through the billowing black smoke gushing all around them. They heard the huge house shudder, the sound of collapsing ceilings and walls and the crackling of flames, gaining purchase now, spreading fast. Heat swooped down from the second floor, swallowing the air.

The kitchen ceiling was crashing down in big chunks, the beams still holding, but now in flames. Black smoke was filling the room.

They saw Cheney and Julia running toward the back door, wet dish towels pressed against their faces, Cheney trying to keep Julia behind him.

"We've got to cover them!" Savich shouted and raced toward them.

Cheney and Julia burst out of the screened door, and were running, bent over, toward the flower-covered brick patio, when a bullet struck Cheney in the chest and knocked him back against the house. He lurched sideways, managed to grab Julia and flatten her against the house, twisting to slam his body against hers.

Another bullet struck him in the center of the back. They heard him grunt, but he still pressed hard against Julia, covering her as best he could.

Outside, Savich peeled to the right, Sherlock to the left, separating themselves as targets, trying to get Makepeace between them, firing steadily toward the back of the property, the only place where Makepeace could have found cover.

"Get down!" Savich yelled as Cheney began to turn, his gun in his hand.

"No, Cheney, stay with Julia! Get down!" Savich shouted again, still firing. He saw Cheney and Julia sliding down the wall onto the patio, between two big ceramic flowerpots that provided them some cover. A bullet struck one of the pots, shattering it, spewing dirt, primroses, and shards of ceramic into the air.

Flames and smoke billowed out of the upstairs windows and through the open back door. Chunks of burning wood crashed down onto the patio behind them. Savich and Sherlock emptied their clips into the lower branches of the oak tree at the back of the property, and slammed in new clips. Savich raised his hand after a moment. They were both on their knees, hidden behind thick wooden trellises, covered with wisteria.

Everything was quiet again.

Savich listened. Above the crackling flames, he heard cops shouting, a couple of guns firing, and sirens wailing in the distance. His breath was pumping out. It burned from breathing in smoke.

Sherlock said, "Captain Paulette's officers must have gotten around the back."

"Yes," Savich said, scanning the trees. "I think Makepeace is gone, cut his losses."

They slowly rose, still fanning the area, searching for the slightest movement. It was hard to see clearly through the thickening black smoke pouring out of the blazing house, blanketing the backyard.

"I don't know if we hit him," Sherlock said.

The heat and smoke pressed them hard now, pushing them back, coughing and wheezing, gasping for air. They heard the shouts of cops coming around the sides of the house, tasted the acrid smoke snaking down their throats, and knew they had to get out of there.

Savich prayed the cops had shot Makepeace.

The roof over Julia's bedroom crashed down into the kitchen with a muffled roar just as the fire trucks pulled up out front.

CHAPTER 50

Sweat was pouring off their smoke-blackened faces. Savich and Sherlock went down on their knees beside Cheney as he yelled up at Julia. "Stop hovering and patting me, I'm okay, I'm fine."

"Hold still, macho. He shot you twice because you had to play the damned hero—"

Cheney looked up at her filthy face, her hair straggling out of her ponytail band, and her red bloodshot eyes. He knew there was smoke in her lungs and that worried him. He saw wild fear in her eyes, lightly touched his fingertips to her mouth, and said, "You sure look pretty."

"*What?* Have you totally lost your mind?"

Sherlock laughed, couldn't help herself. "Enough with the compliments. Come on, you guys, we've got to get out of here."

But Julia was holding him, her breathing hitching now. He grabbed her hands. "Listen, Julia, I'm okay. I'm wearing a Kevlar vest. No bullets inside me. Just hurts a bit, that's all."

"Yeah, well, I'm wearing one of those vests too, so why did you shove me against the wall and climb all over me?"

"I serve and protect, ma'am."

She was sputtering, she was so frazzled. And trying not to smile.

Savich looked up when Frank Paulette came down on his haunches beside Cheney. "Hey, boy, you're looking a little green around the gills. Got hit on the Kevlar, did you? You're going to have some big-time bruises and some sore ribs, but there's nothing like Kevlar to keep you alive. How about we get our butts out of here right this second?"

Savich pulled Cheney up to his shoulder in a firefighter's carry and ran around the side of the house, the rest of them protecting Julia as best they could.

They ran across the front lawn and stopped at the curb, still huddled together, covering each other. When Savich eased Cheney off his shoulder and onto the ground, Cheney decided that, Kevlar vest or not, it felt like he'd been kicked in the chest by a pissed-off Pamplona bull. Cheney looked up at Frank, who'd just pocketed his cell. "Tell me your people got him, that's all I want to hear. I'll stand up and dance if you tell me that."

"Not yet, but he can't get far. We've got cops on the ground, fanning out, we'll get him. Savich said they laid down thick fire. Maybe they got him."

A beam from a gable at one end of the house exploded and crashed, raining down hot fireworks.

"Captain!"

Frank slewed his head around. "You got him, Booker?"

"He didn't steal a car, Captain, he stole himself a motorcycle, hid it in some bushes beside one of the neighbors' driveways, a few doors down. Charlie saw him roaring out, fired at him, and now half a dozen cops are after him. It won't be long."

"Did he look wounded to you, Booker?"

"Charlie said the guy was hunched down, had his helmet on, so they couldn't tell. I don't know how Makepeace got past Salter and James, Captain, but they never saw a thing until the whole place blew."

Cheney said, "Okay, you really can stop patting me, Julia, I'm okay."

"Hold still for a minute, boy." Frank unbuttoned Cheney's shirt, pulled the Velcro straps open on the Kevlar vest. He lightly touched his fingertips where the bullet had flattened in the material high on Cheney's chest. Then he peeled off the vest, turned Cheney on his side, and looked at his back. "Oscar-winning bruises, Cheney. If you hadn't been in front of her, Julia here might not be so happy right now."

They stood watching half a dozen powerful arcs of water pound onto the flaming roof. Cheney saw that Julia's face was blank as she stared at her burning house. He saw her hands clench into fists at her sides as she watched the flames leap out of her bedroom windows.

He took her hands, smoothed out her fists, kissed her black palms. "Listen to me, you're all right, and that's all that matters. We made it."

Soon all of Julia's neighbors spilled out of their houses, staring at the fire in horror and fascination, some of them wetting down their own gardens and roofs with hoses, some of them huddled together in small groups. Several came over to Julia, bringing blankets and coffee, but mostly everyone just stood around and watched.

The fire chief, Lucky Mulroney, headed their way ten minutes later. "Good news, Mrs. Ransom. We've got the fire under control. It looks like maybe half of your house may be structurally intact, but the inspectors won't be certain until they've gone over it carefully." He looked back. "A bomb—quite a thing. I hate to see one of our beautiful old houses burn."

"Yes," Julia said, not looking away from August's house. "He was trying to kill me, Chief Mulroney, but he didn't. This is the third time—" She was interrupted by a TV van screeching to a stop some ten feet away. A man shoved the side panel open and jumped out, a camera on his shoulder, panning until he saw Julia, then he shouted as he zeroed right in. There was probably a microphone as well, she thought. She smiled toward the camera, and waved her black fist in the air. "Did you hear that, you loser? You missed me!"

Then Mulroney threatened to turn one of the hoses on the van if they didn't back off. Frank had some of his men form a perimeter.

Sherlock said, "I'm wondering how Makepeace knew Julia would come out the back of the house."

Savich said. "He was playing the odds, though the fact is, he couldn't be sure."

Frank said, "Or it could mean there was someone with him— Makepeace was in the back and his partner in the front, but where? I had lots of guys spread out in front."

Cheney said, "You might never find where Makepeace was

hiding with so many people tromping around all over the place."

"We'll keep looking. Maybe the guy smoked, left a butt."

Sherlock said, "We heard footsteps upstairs, Frank, not all that long before it blew. So Makepeace had to be in the house."

She continued after a moment, "Maybe that's why he didn't go for a head shot on you, Cheney, he had to move too fast to get out of there and wanted to be sure he hit you. Then Julia would have been in the open."

Cheney rubbed his chest. "He got me straight on in the chest and in the center of my back, both fine shots."

Frank said, "Does anyone have a clue who this partner of his could be, if there was someone? The guy out here to watch the front?"

Savich shrugged. "Could be the person who hired Makepeace to kill Julia, or he could have hired some local talent. The thing is, though, we've never heard of Makepeace working with a partner."

Savich's cell rang. He listened, then punched off. He looked at them. "That was Dix. Kathryn Golden's still heavily sedated. They don't expect her to make much sense for a while yet. They've got her at Stanford, a cop on her door."

A police officer came running up. "We found the motorcycle, Captain, but Makepeace was long gone. That's the bad, here's the good." The officer grinned big. "We got us a witness, an old guy who was walking to the little park right across the street from his house on Brinkley with his seven-year-old great-granddaughter. He said a man plowed his motorcycle real fast right into a mess of thick bushes on the far side of the park, didn't even try to stop. Then the guy jumped off. In the next minute this small blue car pulled up and he got inside. Car took off. The old guy said he doesn't know about cars, so had no clue as to its make, didn't see anything else. Our people are canvassing the neighborhood. Someone else had to see something."

Savich said, "Officer, wait a moment. Cheney, you and Julia should go back to the Sherlocks' house. Sherlock and I will go speak to this witness."

Sherlock heard Julia say, "I'm so relieved Freddy went home on Sunday."

Savich arched an eyebrow. "Freddy?"

Cheney was laughing. "The neighbor's cat."

As they walked away, they heard reporters yelling out questions to them from twenty yards away.

CHAPTER 51

About a half mile from Julia's house, on Brinkley Street, Savich and Sherlock found the old man standing on his narrow front porch in front of a 1940s cottage, leaning on a cane. He told them first thing that he'd stashed his great-granddaughter safely inside the house. "A wild thing it was," he said, shaking his head, "happened real fast. My name's Tuck Wilson."

Savich introduced himself and Sherlock, pulled out their shields. The old man stuck out his hand. Savich automatically started to shake it, then realized both he and Sherlock were black and filthy. He smiled at the old man. "I don't want to dirty you up."

"I appreciate that. So you both were in that fire in the big Ransom place," Mr. Wilson said and motioned toward the door. "It's all over the news. You want to come in and clean up?"

Sherlock smiled. "No thank you, Mr. Wilson. We need to ask you some more questions about the man on the motorcycle."

"Call me Tuck, everybody does except for my little great-granddaughter. She calls me Friar, smart-mouthed little punk."

Tuck Wilson waved them toward a wooden swing, but they shook their heads.

"—after the man drove his motorcycle right into the bushes, what exactly did he do?"

"Like I told the other officer, the guy jumped right off—he seemed real familiar with a motorcycle, smooth—okay, he turned and looked up the street. Not more than a minute passed before this blue car drove up, he jumped in the passenger seat, and they took off."

A whole minute, Savich thought, and smiled. "Please tell us what the motorcycle guy looked like, Mr. Wilson."

Tuck waved his cane toward the bushes. "He was more tall than not, a black guy, and he moved real fast and he was strong and graceful-like. He had on an old banged-up black leather jacket, I could see the nicks in the leather even with my old eyes. He had on some boots, not cowboy boots, but black boots like a biker would wear. He was wearing a helmet. When he first jumped off the motorcycle, he pulled it off. He was wearing glasses, isn't that a kick? He saw me, I know he must have, saw Alice too, but he didn't make any sort of move on us. No, he just concentrated on the street, and watched for the car."

"Excellent, Tuck," Savich said. "Okay, think back now. You see the blue car drive up. You see the driver. Tell us about him."

"Hmmm, now that's a bit more difficult, it all happened real fast. It was a man, young like the first—" Tuck broke off, laughed. "You gotta understand, anyone who isn't on the shady side of sixty-five looks young to me. Alice said they were both old, but she's seven years old."

"Middle-aged, maybe?"

"He just wasn't getting on like me."

"The driver, was he bald? Glasses? What was he wearing?"

"No, he wasn't bald, I'm sure about that. I couldn't tell you exactly how much hair he had on his head, only that I could see some. The color? I couldn't tell, really couldn't, sorry. I remember thinking it was weird how his fingers kept tapping on the steering wheel while the motorcycle guy climbed into the car. Then he started yelling."

"Could you hear what he was yelling about?" Savich asked.

" 'Hurry,' that's what he yelled, yelled it twice, and then he cussed and stomped on the gas. Now that I think about it, that car really took off fast. So it probably wasn't an everyday sort of car, probably a fancy one, German, maybe, sounded real sweet and smooth."

"Friar, you didn't tell them the guy driving the car was mad, real mad."

Savich and Sherlock looked down at a little girl who'd slipped out the front door and was peering around at them from behind her great-grandfather's waist. "You're Alice, right?"

Alice stared up at Sherlock. "I bet your hair's real beautiful, ma'am, but not right now. It looks like you need to wash it. Oh, I'm Alice Douggan and this is one of my ancestors, Friar. That's what he calls himself."

Sherlock smiled between the two of them. "Is it all right, Tuck, if we speak to Alice?"

"Sure, no problem. Alice, stop hiding behind me. Come out here. You stand straight and tall, get those shoulders back and you tell them what you saw. Don't add in all sorts of little details from that imagination of yours or else they might arrest you. They're federal agents."

Alice walked around Tuck, stood front and center. She cocked her head to one side, studied them straight on. Not at all shy, this cute little fairy. "You sure are dirty. My mama would skin me alive if I ever got as dirty as you are. You were in that big fire, right?"

"That's right," Savich said, and went down on his knees so he was eye level with the little girl. "I sure like your freckles. I wish my wife had some to go with her red hair, but I guess when she came down the line, the good Lord shook his head at her. When our little boy asked for some, he shook his head at him too."

"I don't like them. The kids make fun of me, call me speckle face."

"Wait until you're twenty-one and smiling real big. All the guys will line up to talk to you. And I want you to remember what I told you."

The little girl smiled back at him. Can't help it, Sherlock thought, content to let Dillon take over. "Alice, you said the man driving the car was mad?"

"Oh boy, was he ever. He was yelling and cussing something fierce at the motorcycle guy, worse than Friar ever does. My mama would have cleaned his mouth out with her organic barley soap. It tastes worse than oatmeal."

"You didn't hear any of his words other than the curses?"

Alice shook her head. "He had real long legs, and he looked like he could twist the head off a snake."

"Who?"

"The black dude, the one wearing glasses. When he opened the car door, he cussed a blue streak right back at the man who was driving, called him a dickhead."

"Alice—"

"I'm sorry, Friar, but that's what he called the man—dickhead. He said, 'Shut up, dickhead, and drive.' "

"Okay, let's move on. The man driving, Alice. What did he look like?"

"He was old, but not as old as Friar. There aren't many people that old. He was wearing this really neat ring and he was banging it against the steering wheel. I'd like to have a ring like that. I could wear it on a leather band around my neck, like my friends do at school."

Savich said, "Tell us about the ring, Alice."

"He wore it on his marriage finger, but it wasn't a wedding ring, it was this big silver band thing with a black square sitting on top of it, all flat, with a lump in the middle. Just like Friar's. I noticed it because the sun hit it just right, like a light sword, and made it glow."

"That sounds like a Mason's ring to me," Tuck said. "You really saw that, Alice? You're not making that up?"

"I saw it, Friar, I really saw it."

Tuck said to Savich, "Thing is, I've got a Mason's ring, she's seen it a million times. No, I'm not wearing it today, my arthritis is kicking up."

"Yes, it was a lot like yours, Friar, I promise."

"Well," Sherlock said five minutes later as she climbed into the passenger side of her dad's Beemer, "do you think she made up the Masonic ring?"

"We might as well go with it, or at least with a ring on the guy's wedding finger that maybe looks a bit different." He smiled. "Cute kid. That hair of hers was so blond it was nearly white. Now, we know the guy with the ring had some hair, but we don't know what color. And he was old or he was young, depending on whether you are seven or eighty."

Sherlock said, "If Makepeace was cursing back at the guy who was driving and yelling at him, then it doesn't seem likely the driver was the one who imported him to kill Julia. He sounds more like a local Makepeace hired to help him today. I'm thinking what happened was more than the guy bargained for, got him really scared."

Savich said. "We'll see what the canvassing officers have come up with."

Sherlock gave him a big smile and ran a finger down her face. "So, I guess Alice was right, and it's time to go play in the shower?"

Savich grinned, showing white teeth, just about the only white showing in his face. He covered her filthy hand with his, pressing her palm hard against his leg. "This was too close, Sherlock."

"Yeah, yeah, that's what you always say." She leaned over and kissed him, saw he was still thinking of what could have happened. "I like having you around, Dillon. If you hadn't yelled for me to hit the deck right before the bomb exploded, I might have gotten whacked by some flying stairpost. But we're all right, Julia and Cheney are all right, the cops are all right. Hey, I wonder if my underwear's black."

"I'll let you know," Savich said, and released a pent-up breath.

When he pulled into the Sherlocks' driveway, he saw Ruth standing in the open front door, waving at them.

"What now?" Savich asked the rhododendron bushes, and followed Sherlock to the house.

CHAPTER 52

Savich and Sherlock got off the elevator at Stanford Hospital and headed toward the ICU. A police officer sitting in a chair in the unit outside Golden's door eyed them up and down as they approached, then slowly nodded and rose, even before they had their shields out.

"Officer—Lazarus, I'm Agent Savich," Savich said and shook his hand. "This is Agent Sherlock. Anything happening we should know about?"

"No, sir, everything's calm now. But before—everyone thought she was dying. The doctors and nurses, they really moved fast."

Savich's heart sped up again, remembering how he'd felt when Ruth had told them Kathryn Golden's heart had failed. But she was okay now, thank the good Lord.

"The neurologist is with Ms. Golden. I heard him assuring everyone she was stable now. Lieutenant Ramirez and one of his detectives left about five minutes ago. He didn't look very happy, what with her still unconscious."

"Any problem with the media?" Sherlock asked.

Officer Lazarus gave her a manic grin. "Yeah, I've booted out three or four of the varmints since I've been here. They're sure having a good time, what with the bomb exploding at the Mariner, and Ms. Golden being a psychic and all, it means they have more to report about than the hike in our parking meter rates. Hope you find the guy who did this."

When Savich quietly opened the door, he saw an older man wearing a white coat, his shoulders a bit stooped, his stethoscope pressed against Kathryn Golden's chest. After he jotted something in her chart, he looked up at them and frowned.

"You just came from the Mariner?"

"How can you tell?" Sherlock asked him, giving him her sunny smile. "We scrubbed up pretty good before we came."

"It must be the eau de smoke you're wearing. Lieutenant Ramirez isn't here. Who are you? What do you want? Why did the officer let you in?"

Both Savich and Sherlock held up their shields, introduced themselves.

"Hmm—FBI. I never met any FBI agents before. I'm Dr. Saint." He looked closely at Sherlock. His shoulders straightened. "You and I are both blessed and cursed with our names, aren't we?"

A kindred spirit, Sherlock thought. Like her, he'd undoubtedly heard it all. She said, "My dad leans toward calling it blessed— he's a federal judge in San Francisco, likes the looks of abject terror he gets from defense attorneys and their clients. Actually, we missed out on the Mariner business. We were in another fire up in San Francisco. Please forgive the smoke perfume."

"You were at that house fire in Pacific Heights? Really? I just heard about it—some big mansion was bombed, right?" At Savich's nod, he shook his head. "Too much crazy stuff going on around here. Hey, you mean those two fires were connected?"

"It's a little too soon to tell you that yet," Sherlock said. "How's Ms. Golden?"

Dr. Saint bent over her, lightly touched his fingertips to her temple. "As you can see, she's been better. We had quite a scare with her heart rhythm and blood pressure a little while ago, and moved her into the unit here. That could have been from blunt-force trauma or head injury, but it seems to be under control now. The primary concern is that she's never been fully alert, and we're simply not sure why. The CT and even the MRI were normal, no hemorrhages, no edema. As for the rest, she's got some bruises, some contusions, and a nasty cut on her leg that Dr. Ring sutured up. Her vitals are stable now. She's not in a coma, but in a sort of a twilight state, partly from the drugs we had to give her. Now we just have to wait because she doesn't seem quite ready to come back to us. She's been through quite an ordeal."

"Yes," Savich said, looking down at her, "she has. You're sure her heart is all right now?"

Dr. Saint nodded. "Never any guarantees in life or in medicine, but I doubt it will happen again, not at this point."

Kathryn Golden's face was pale as the fog that had hung outside the Sherlocks' windows that morning, except for the faint bluish bruises. Both of her arms lay straight at her sides, IV lines tethered to both wrists. Still, she didn't look as bad as Savich had thought she would, which was a relief. He would have recognized her anywhere, since he'd seen her so clearly last night. He said, "We'd like to sit here with Ms. Golden for a while if that's all right with you, Dr. Saint."

"I don't see why not. It's your time, and she isn't going anywhere. Sometimes the sound of a voice can actually help, so if you want, talk to her. If there's any change we need to worry about, we'll see it on the monitors." He shook their hands and left, smiling and nodding to Sherlock. Savich looked from his wife to Dr. Saint's retreating back, eyebrow raised.

"What can I say?" Sherlock said as she walked to the single chair by the window. "You combine the smell of smoke with my name and I become irresistible."

Savich was smiling as he sat at the side of Kathryn Golden's bed. He leaned close, picked up her hand, and lightly rubbed his fingers over her skin. Too dry, he thought.

He focused on her and began speaking. "I'm here, Kathryn. I hope you can feel that I'm here, feel my hand holding yours. You're going to be fine, there's nothing to worry about. You scared the doctors for a little while, but you're okay now. It's time for you to wake up. I'd like to meet the person I've been thinking about so much lately."

There was no response, but Savich continued, telling her what had happened at the Mariner Hotel. He spoke to her for perhaps five minutes, then paused, and looked over at Sherlock. She simply nodded at him and so he turned back. "Let me tell you about my little boy, Sean. He's with his grandfather today. My father-in-law is a San Francisco native and a federal judge. They're over at the courthouse, way up on the nineteenth floor. Can you imagine the fun he's having—the center of every adult's attention.

This morning he said he wanted to watch his granddad punch out a criminal."

There was still no response.

"Kathryn, do you know Thomas Pallack? I understand he was a client of Dr. Ransom's for many years, in fact right up to the time of Dr. Ransom's murder."

"Yes, I know him."

Savich smiled down into her eyes, still vague with drugs, but she was finally awake. He nodded to Sherlock as he lightly squeezed Kathryn's hand. "Hello. I'm Dillon Savich."

"I would know you anywhere. Hello. I'm Kathryn."

"Do you want me to fetch the doctor?"

"No, please, not yet. Let me get my wits about me."

"It's a pleasure to meet you at last. The doctor said you've got stitches in your leg, some bruises, and a concussion, but you'll be okay. And that's my wife Sherlock over by the window."

Kathryn nodded to Sherlock, and turned back to him. "I'm glad I'm not going to leave this earth just yet. You asked me about Thomas Pallack. Yes, I know him."

"Then you know his wife, Charlotte Pallack?"

"Charlotte Pallack—I've met her, but I really don't know her well at all. All I do know is that I don't like her. No, it's more than that. Whenever I see her, I always see this strange aura about her, constantly shifting and changing. Sort of like a chameleon, like she's someone, then she's someone else. There's something about her that leaves me with a nasty feeling. I can't get a handle on it."

"Did you know her brother plays the violin with the Atlanta Symphony?"

"I—well, maybe, that sounds familiar. Maybe I heard Thomas say something about him."

"It seems he's gone missing. No one's seen him, including his girlfriend, for over two days now. Do you have any thoughts about that?"

Kathryn Golden focused her eyes on Savich's face. Her eyes weren't dark and intense like her colleagues'—like his—but a golden-green, a witch's eyes, Savich thought, and had to smile at himself. She whispered, "I need to think about it."

"You're tired. I was really just talking to you to make sure you were all right."

She clutched his fingers. "No, please don't go."

"All right, here, take a sip of water."

She drank for a very long time.

"That's good. Thank you." She looked up at him, studied his face. "I tried to picture you in my mind by the sound of your voice, all deep and dark as a lava stone. I wasn't that far off. I could see you, but you weren't clear. Was I clear to you?"

He nodded.

She tried to raise her hand to touch him, but the IV lines didn't allow it. He wrapped his fingers around hers and squeezed them again.

"Do you need to rest?"

"No, no. Thank you for waking me up. I was busy scaring my-self to death. That man—with the author's name—Makepeace, you called him. He was very frightening."

Savich felt her pulse speed up and backed off. "Yes, he is. Take a moment, Kathryn, relax, all right?"

She was silent a moment. She closed her eyes and breathed in deeply. He felt her pulse slow.

"How do you feel?"

"Sort of foggy, I guess, kind of dull and heavy-feeling. No pain to speak of."

Savich looked up to see Dr. Saint come into the room. He blinked when he saw that Kathryn was awake, one of her hands in Savich's.

"Well," Dr. Saint said, leaning over Kathryn, checking her eyes and studying her face. He eased his stethoscope to her heart, listened. He slowly straightened. "How long have you been awake, Ms. Golden?"

"Five minutes, something like that," she said. "Thank you for taking care of me. You're Dr. Saint, right?"

"Yes," he said. He studied her another moment, then announced, "You're awake and you appear to be fine, Ms. Golden. I'm thinking I should spend more time in the nurse's lounge concentrating on stealing Fig Newtons out of Nurse Joliett's locker without getting caught. It seems to work miracles."

"Do you know, I think I'd like a Fig Newton," Kathryn said.

Dr. Saint didn't have a problem with that either, and luckily, Nurse Joliett didn't mind sharing. "You don't need both those IV lines anymore. We'll free you from the one in your left wrist. You might find it easier to chow down on those Newtons." Dr. Saint stood by her bed, fiddling with his handheld, an eyebrow arched at the two of them. "I don't suppose you're going to tell me you're surprised Ms. Golden here suddenly woke up and wants to munch?"

"I suppose it was simply time for her to rejoin us," Savich said easily. "I think I'd like a Fig Newton too."

Dr. Saint started to tell Savich they really should leave now so his patient could rest, but something told him maybe he shouldn't meddle. Sounding a bit ruffled, he said, "I understand you're a psychic, Ms. Golden."

She was chewing happily on a Fig Newton, and nodded at him. "That's how I met Agent Savich last night, at a séance, actually."

"Oh? Last night? I thought you'd been kidnapped yesterday afternoon. How—"

Savich raised his hand. "Be satisfied with your miracle, Dr. Saint."

Dr. Saint looked from one to the other of them, but he didn't say anything more. "All right then, I'll leave you to it. Please, Agent Savich, if she tires, let her rest." Before he left, he gave Sherlock another long look. Sherlock smiled, and waved him away.

Savich said, "Trust me on this, Kathryn. Makepeace won't ever get near you again."

She gave him a very long look, swallowed the rest of her Fig Newton, and nodded. "If you're up to it, a few more questions." At her nod, he continued. "I'd like you to back up, Kathryn, and tell me everything you remember that happened. Begin when Makepeace came into your house."

He saw her shudder, and didn't blame her. "I hate to think about it, not because I was so terrified, but because I was helpless. I've always hated being helpless.

"He hit me on the head with the butt of a gun. When I woke

up, I was tied to a chair in a closet, his clothes all around me. I had no idea where I was but I knew it had to be that man trying to kill Julia. But I couldn't figure out how he even knew who I was. Did he follow Julia and Cheney to my house?"

"No. As Cheney was trying to tell you, the media had you on TV special reports for a couple of hours, announced that you were assisting the police, how your 'vision' had helped save Cheney's life."

"Maybe we could hire him to attack the media instead of me."

Savich grinned. "What happened?"

"I felt you then, and I managed to form a blurry picture of you in my mind. We'd only begun speaking when Makepeace opened the closet door and dragged me out. He let me go to the bathroom, and he let me eat a slice of toast, said it was left over and he didn't have a dog. He frightened me. I could feel the frustration and rage pouring off him. But you know, he was whistling the whole time.

"He asked me where Julia was. I told him I had no idea, how could I? And he said since I was a psychic, since I was helping the police, even had a vision for Cheney Stone and Julia Ransom, why then, I could tell him where they were now, couldn't I? He wanted a vision from me. And that was why he took me in the first place."

Savich said, "Maybe, but I think that his big motive was to get you out of the game. And he had a use for you with that bomb."

"Yes, that makes sense. Well, I told him I couldn't simply do a vision on command. He hit me a couple of times, then he forced me back into the closet. He didn't let me out until this morning. I tried and tried to contact you, Dillon, but there was just nothing.

"When he brought me out of that hideous closet this morning, he asked me again to tell him where Julia was. I told him I saw her at her house in Pacific Heights, with Cheney guarding her. He seemed pleased. He grinned at me, patted my face, and left, whistling.

"It took me a moment to realize he hadn't locked me back in the closet. I tried and tried to get loose, but he'd tied me too tight. And I tried again to reach you, Dillon, but you weren't there.

"Then the police came running in and the bomb exploded."

Savich pulled Makepeace's photo out of his pocket. "This the man?"

"Oh yes, that's Makepeace."

"He didn't say anything at all before he left you?"

"No, nothing."

"Did he receive any phone calls?"

"Yes, one, but I couldn't hear what he said."

"It doesn't matter. I know he was getting ready for his big production."

"I'm sorry I can't be of more help."

Remarkably, she gave him a big smile. "Then I woke up to see your face. Thank you for helping me back."

Kathryn looked up to see Sherlock smiling down at her. She said, "Do you know, I think Fig Newtons are about the best thing in the world?"

CHAPTER 53

Xavier Makepeace watched Johnny Booth twitch. The man never stopped twitching; it was like there was a battery inside him you couldn't turn off. Johnny flexed and unflexed his fingers, banged his fist yet again on the steering wheel. He hadn't stopped twitching, cursing, or banging his fist and yakking about how they were going to get caught for sure and it was all his fault. "You screwed up, dude, you screwed everything to hell and gone. You can fly right off to Zanzibar, but I don't even have a passport. What am I going to do? I knew I shouldn't have listened to you, shouldn't have listened to Zannie—she's always saying you're some kind of international modern i-con—whatever the hell that means. She's probably got the hots for you."

For at least the third time, his voice calm and soothing, Xavier Makepeace recited the same words. He hated to repeat himself, particularly to someone he considered a moron. "How would the cops get you, Johnny? We got away clean, you told me yourself. No one saw you at the Ransom house, no one saw us driving off after you picked me up. Isn't that what you said?"

"Yeah, yeah, but that don't matter. Thing is, like I told you, there was that old guy—"

"You said he was an ancient old coot and the little girl with him couldn't have been more than five. So what?"

"He was staring real hard at me, and that little gal, she looked sharp as my pa's stiletto. I tell you, dude, they both saw me and studied me, yeah, that's it. Maybe the old guy got my license plate. Besides, there were lots of people out. Somebody else could have seen me, somebody I didn't notice. My pa used to say you have to watch every bump in the road, they was always hiding close by to trip you up. Yeah, the old guy could have described me to the cops and you can bet one of the vice cops will recognize who I am. Cops ain't so stupid as you think they are. If you wasn't wearing the Kevlar, you'd by lying on your back not breathing. They nearly nailed you this time, didn't they?"

He had to shut this moron up soon or his head would explode. And maybe Johnny was right, maybe the old guy described him well enough for an I.D. Well, it didn't matter one way or the other, did it?

Makepeace said, with infinite patience, "But they didn't, did they? And they won't get you either, Johnny. Stop your worrying." But the moron was right, they'd very nearly nailed him. Put four bullets in his Kevlar, three of the four kill shots. That made him even angrier than Johnny did.

"Take the Pacifica exit, Johnny, I want to stop for a while downtown. There's a nice crab restaurant there, you'll like it."

"What's with your accent, dude? You've changed it all of a sudden. You're starting to sound like some weird-ass Brit. Hey, I don't want to go to Pacifica, I don't live anywhere near Pacifica." Makepeace stared him down and Johnny started cursing again and banging the steering wheel, calling himself names now, but he took the exit.

Makepeace said, "You can take a cab home, Johnny. With all the money I gave you for this failed job, you can call a limo to take you home. Take a right here. I want to go down to the beach."

"Beach? You nuts, dude? *The beach?* Listen, I want a bonus for my health scare, man, I nearly seized up with an attack. It was only a burglary, you said, practically a setup. You owe me a bonus."

"Turn, Johnny."

Johnny turned onto the narrow beach road that wound back on itself across a low sloping hill down to the wood-strewn brown sand beach. There was a small parking area off to the right, with several walking trails feeding off it. "Pull in here, Johnny. I want to commune with nature."

"Was that some sort of lame-ass joke? Well, I'm not laughing, am I? Forget nature. You gonna give me a bonus? You know I deserve one after what you pulled."

"Yes, you're right, I can surely afford to take care of your worries. Trust me."

There were no other cars in the small parking lot. Johnny cut the engine and sat back, rubbed his hands over his face. "Hey, I'm sorry I got so freaked out. I wasn't expecting the crazy trouble we ran into. I mean, there were cops all over that neighborhood. Like they were waiting for us. They were waiting for you, weren't they? How'd they know you was coming?"

I'd hoped they'd be there, that's what made it interesting. He smiled.

He rubbed his hand over his shoulder where one of the agents had shot him, nearly missed his Kevlar vest and hit his neck. That was close. He pictured a big dark guy, and a woman, red hair, lots of wild red hair. He'd find out who they were. He'd taken out the other agent, Stone, a clean shot to the heart, a clean shot to the back—unless he was wearing Kevlar as well. With that guy's streak of luck, and that was surely all it was, Makepeace imagined that he was.

"I didn't know you was going to blow up that house, you never said a word about blowing up no house. Hey, just look out at the ocean. Ain't it beautiful? Clear as a bell—I never understood why they say that. How's a bell so clear?"

"A church bell, Johnny."

"Whatever."

"Yeah, look at it, Johnny," Makepeace said, and pulled out a length of silver wire.

CHAPTER 54

Wednesday evening

Cheney said, "No, Julia, you're not going anywhere, forget it. You're only safe here at the Sherlocks' house. No one knows where you are."

"Cheney, listen to me. My house is a smoldering ruin. I don't know what if anything can be salvaged. I've got to deal with the insurance people, with the clean-up people, with the arson investigators from the fire department. And I don't have any clothes to wear." She looked down at the pair of turquoise blue sweats she was wearing, courtesy of Evelyn Sherlock. The legs ended two inches above her ankles.

Cheney had to admit she looked faintly ridiculous.

Ruth said, "Don't worry, Julia. I'll get you some clothes tomorrow. Cheney's right. You need to stay close."

Savich walked into the living room, his cell in his hand. He looked at each of them, then asked Sherlock, "You remember how little Alice described a ring on the getaway driver's marriage finger? And Tuck said she was describing a Masonic ring?"

"Yes, why?"

"The Pacifica police found it on the finger of a dead man who had been garroted and left in a small dark-blue Ford at a beach parking lot outside of Pacifica. The cops picked up on it and called Frank right away. The Ford was all souped up, the detective told Frank—probably the getaway car.

"The guy," Dix said, "who was he?" He lightly scratched the flesh around the stitches in his arm.

"They identified him as Johnny Booth, not an upstanding citizen, as you'd expect. Two felony counts on him for armed robbery and pimping, served a total of nine years in San Quentin. He was once booked for killing a liquor store clerk, but got off. Vice thought he'd left California because of the three-strikes law."

Sherlock said, "Makepeace doesn't like loose ends, does he?"

"Maybe he's just cheap," Ruth said. "Didn't want to pay the guy his fee."

Cheney's cell phone rang. He nodded, and walked out of the living room. When he came back, he looked shell-shocked. He said, "Makepeace has been busier than we thought. That was Frank again. He just heard from the police in Atherton that Soldan is dead. He was found lying back on the silk pillows in that exotic room of his wearing his red silk robe, a deep gash in his throat where he'd been garroted. Frank said he'd been smoking his hookah and reading Mark Twain's *Innocents Abroad*. He'd been dead only about an hour, the ME said. Ancilla, his assistant, found him when she got home from an AA meeting.

"Evidently the murderer slipped behind him, looped the wire around his neck, and that was it. Since he'd been smoking all evening, according to Ancilla, it couldn't have been very hard to sneak up on him.

"But once Makepeace had the wire around his neck, Soldan did fight. The ME says it looks like there's skin under Soldan's fingernails, probably from Makepeace."

Ruth said, "Makepeace has got to be a mess—bullet wounds, a scraped face from that newel post exploding, and Meissen's fingernails—and the guy's still going."

Julia said, "He's got a powerful need."

Sherlock said, "I wonder why he didn't clean Soldan's hands once he'd killed him. He's a professional and professionals wouldn't leave hard evidence like that."

Dix raised his head. "Who cares? Makepeace certainly doesn't. We still don't have him and we don't have Pallack." He rose and walked to the front windows and said over his shoulder, "What we've got is nothing—no evidence, no witnesses, not a single one of Dr. Ransom's journals that we all hoped would give us the reasons and the motives—" He faced the windows again. "It has to be Pallack, all of you know it."

"Yes, I agree," Ruth said. "I wonder why he had Makepeace kill Meissen."

Savich said, "For some reason Meissen was a danger to him. Don't forget, both Ransom and Meissen were his own personal mediums. He's in the center of all of this, Dix is right about that. We'll get there, Dix, be patient." But Savich could tell his words were falling on deaf ears.

"Hey," Ruth said, "maybe it was Meissen who hired Makepeace to kill August Ransom."

Cheney said, "Only if he wanted his clients. Sounds nuts to me, but we're talking woo-woo here so who knows?"

There was a tense silence because no one knew what to do next, when suddenly Savich stood and announced he and Sherlock would be leaving for New York on the red-eye.

They drove to SFO in under twenty minutes and made it to the gate with five minutes to spare.

CHAPTER 55

ATTICA, NEW YORK

Thursday

Big Sonny Moldavo of the New York Field Office met Savich and Sherlock at their gate when they deplaned at JFK and escorted them to the black Bell FBI helicopter waiting to take them to Attica. "Bobby's your pilot, hell of a wild man. He was a helicopter pilot in Desert Storm, buzzed the Republican Guard whenever he got bored, but, hey, don't worry, he'll get you there." When Big Sonny left them in the wild man's hands, Bobby spit a good six feet, stretched, and gave them a lazy grin. "You guys must be real important to get such fancy treatment. Okay, Attica's between Rochester and Buffalo—it won't take too long. Climb aboard and buckle up." In the next minute they'd lifted off and were soon looking down at a beautiful clear day over lower Manhattan.

Sherlock took a drink of water, and handed the bottle to Savich. He drank deeply, wiped his mouth with the back of his hand.

She looked down. They'd already passed over Manhattan and the suburbs. They were flying over flatlands now, broken with pine and oak forests. Occasional small towns dotted the countryside. She pointed down to a red barn, glittering in the morning sunlight.

Savich nodded. "This whole business—even though we know it's Pallack, there's no way we could talk a judge into granting us a warrant to search his penthouse or his office."

She drummed her fingertips on her leg. "I know, but you've got to remember we only arrived in San Francisco two nights ago—amazing, given all that's happened. Why are we going to see Courtney James now, Dillon?"

"I had MAX look him up the other morning. He was a neighbor of the Pallacks so he knew all of them, Thomas Pallack, and his parents. For years. And I realized he must know Thomas Pallack better than anyone else living. If anyone can fill in the blanks, I figure it's James.

"Then we hit all the excitement with Makepeace and I had to put him on my mental back burner.

"But the thing is, even though it's only been two days we've been on this, I'm worried about Dix. He's so frustrated he looks ready to burst out of his skin. I have this hope, Sherlock," and he raised her hand to kiss her fingers, "that since we're stopped dead in our tracks in San Francisco that maybe, just maybe, Courtney James will have something to say that will break up the roadblock."

"What could he tell us? All his knowledge, his memories of the Pallacks, is thirty years old."

Savich sighed. "I know, I know."

"But you're hopeful."

He kissed her, said against her mouth, "Yep, I'm hopeful. We'll see."

Sherlock hoped so too, although she couldn't imagine what Courtney James would tell them that would be of any use. She yawned. Even though both of them were good sleepers on planes, the last few days had wiped them both out. It had to come to an end soon, she thought, it simply had to. She leaned her head back, closed her eyes, the sound of the helicopter blade rumbling through her head, and imagined the three of them playing on the beach in Aruba.

An hour later Bobby set them down on the rippled asphalt helipad at Tomlinson Field, the small airport outside Attica, and waved them to a nondescript beige Ford Escort parked at the edge of the tarmac. He gave them both a sharp salute and a lazy smile, said he was glad neither of them had been big yakkers, and in the next breath added, "Hey, maybe we can have some more fun on our return trip."

"Can't wait," Savich said. "I was just thinking the ride over was smooth as my treadmill."

Sherlock said, "Yeah, I especially liked how my stomach heaved up to my ears when you banked halfway over to set us down."

Bobby smiled. "I'll have to do something about that, won't I? I wouldn't want you two big shots to be bored on the way back to the big bad city."

The sun had disappeared behind darkening clouds thirty minutes before, and was still a no-show in western New York. The wind kicked up occasional gusts that dusted up the dirt beside the road. The trees, they saw, were greening up nicely with the spring rains. The land was flat, cows thick in pastures, and Alexander Road was light on traffic. Savich drove past the Attican Motel, thinking he'd like to turn in, pull the shades down in a room, and sleep with Sherlock until Monday. Coming east on the red-eye wiped you out.

Two guards and an administrator escorted them to the hospital, a basic three-story red brick building, like most of the other buildings in the vast correctional facility. There they met Warden Daniel Rafferty, who adjusted his thick glasses to closely check their I.D.s even though they'd already been checked twice, and shook their hands. "Courtney was having problems breathing during the night so we brought him here to check him out. He's had some heart problems for years now, but never anything life-threatening. Still, we like to be careful. He's on the third floor. This way."

Sherlock whispered behind her hand when the warden was a goodly distance ahead of them, "We're met by the warden himself, who refers to our mass murderer as Courtney? It sounds like they've given him such fine care he might fund a new building if he's ever paroled."

Warden Rafferty laughed, turned, and grinned at her. "The acoustics in the hospital are truly phenomenal. You're right, of course. Courtney James is in a class by himself. Do you think he's really a mass murderer?" The warden shrugged. "He's here for life, so what does it matter? Fact is, I like the old guy. I've never been able to see him committing any random murders because some odd voice told him to do it. Come this way."

Savich and Sherlock followed the warden through two sets of secure doors, both manned by guards who dropped their looks of hard-eyed intimidation when Sherlock nodded and smiled at them.

Warden Rafferty ran into a doctor coming out of Courtney James's room, which was private, he remarked, because none of the other prisoners wanted to crowd in on the old man's space. "The doc here will tell you that even the meanest thugs, the most vicious psychopaths, make way for Courtney. They defer to him in the food line, walk with him nice and slow during exercise so he won't be alone. He has the money to get them most anything they want, legally or otherwise—you know, cigarettes, candy, CDs, and the like—but he also treats them with respect. He even gives me a rather tasty fruitcake for Christmas every year made by monks somewhere in Oregon, and he has a crate of Krispy Kremes flown in for the inmates and guards."

Dr. Burgess, stoop-shouldered and rumpled, looked at the agents with old, tired eyes, then he turned to Warden Rafferty. "He has a fruitcake sent to me every Christmas too. Courtney's doing fine. I took him off the oxygen. I think he overdid it with the big poker game last night and he's just tuckered out."

Sherlock raised an eyebrow.

Warden Rafferty laughed. "They all have a deck of cards. They've developed a sophisticated code to tap against the walls of their cells to communicate—a call, raise, a fold. Evidently,

Black Tooth Moses was winning big, especially from Courtney, and didn't want to stop. Since Courtney wouldn't ever want to disappoint him, he kept going until he collapsed. Scared the crap out of all the inmates, Black Moses the most. And the guards, needless to say." His mouth kicked up a bit. "Yep, they like the old guy and those Krispy Kremes, glazed, still warm to the touch and nearly as fresh."

They walked into the small white-walled room with its three hospital beds, two of them empty. There was one utilitarian chair in the corner and a single window that looked out onto one of the yards. They followed Warden Rafferty to the bedside.

They'd seen photos of Courtney James from the time of his arrest in 1977 to when he was pronounced guilty by the jury in 1979. But nearly thirty years had passed. None of the photos re-sembled the old man they saw now.

"Courtney?"

Vivid blue eyes stared first at the warden, then took in Sher-lock and Savich. He grinned. "What's this? You bring me a pretty girl? My, would you look at those beautiful blue eyes, sort of like mine. Hmm, could I be her granddaddy, you think?"

"I don't think so, Courtney."

"Then I'm on my way out, Warden?"

"Nah, you're a fixture. She's not just a pretty girl, she's an FBI agent. Her name's Sherlock. This is Agent Savich. They're here to speak to you. You feeling up to it?"

"Of course I'll speak to this pretty girl. I haven't seen a pretty girl in thirty years, and I haven't seen such beautiful hair in all my life. My mama dyed her hair red, but you could tell, you know? But your hair, Agent Sherlock—you married, sweet girl?"

Sherlock leaned down to his thin, sharp cheekboned face with its pale, amazingly unlined skin. A sick old man, she thought. Interesting how it blurred the reality of what he'd done. "You've got to be careful, Mr. James. Agent Savich is my husband."

Courtney James said, "Nah, he can't be jealous of me, I'm just an old man on his way out. Maybe I should try to look pitiful—put those oxygen clips back in my nose. Big fellow, isn't he? Looks like he eats nails for breakfast."

"Not me," Savich said, "I eat Cheerios along with my little boy."

"Ain't that a kick now?" His smart old eyes went from one to the other and back again. "You want to talk to me? About what? You reopening the case? You want to get me out of here?"

"That would be nice," Savich said, "but I don't think it's going to happen."

"Well, Agent, the thing is, I can't tell you where any of those bodies are buried since I never killed those folk they thought I did. I killed the Pallacks, true enough, and the good Lord knows I'm sorry I got caught. Fact is, they deserved it. They were a pair of shits, especially her. She was worse than both her husband and her son." He sighed deeply. "Can I touch your hair, Agent Sherlock? That's quite a name you've got there."

"Thank you, Mr. James." Sherlock didn't pull away from the old man when he raised his thin veined hand to smooth her thick hair.

Warden Rafferty was moving from one foot to the other, doubtless wondering why they were playing around like this, but he kept quiet, something Savich appreciated.

Savich said, "Okay, Mr. James, you've flirted enough with my wife. You back off now or I'll have to hurt you."

The old man grinned wide again, showing white teeth that looked like his own. "You're a lucky boy," he said. "Okay, you're here to ask me questions. Obviously something's happened. What's up?"

Savich said, "I want you to tell us all you remember about the Pallacks. The parents and their son Thomas. You said Mrs. Pallack was the worst, worse than her son and her husband. Tell us what you mean."

Courtney James looked over at the blank white wall. "It was a long time ago, but you know, some things are like photographs, they stay in your brain forever. I can still see the look on her face when I stabbed her the first time. Okay, let me get back on track here. Margaret Pallack was the prettiest woman I'd ever seen, and she knew it. She was almost sixty, Pallack sixty-five when I killed them, but you know what? She was still a beauty, tall and slim— she stayed fit, had her own gym in her house and exercised every day—and she had beautiful dark hair that curved around her jaw. A stranger would have thought she wasn't a day over forty. And did she ever know it, and use it."

"Why would you kill a woman you so obviously admired?"

"Well, now, pretty girl, since you ask, the thing is, she slept with me. I never admitted that to the cops, prurient little bastards, never told them anything, really, since they'd already made up their minds that I was this demon psychopath, that I'd butchered everything that moved. But I don't care now that you know. The truth is, I had loads of provocation, a whole bulging truckload.

"I think that whole serial killer nonsense was Thomas's doing. Thomas Pallack was a chip off the old block, his mama's old block, always tied to his mama's leash, was Thomas. I remember that the prosecutor kept trying to sneak in references to 'other crimes' and 'other people,' that sort of thing, but they didn't have any proof of that.

"Yeah, I'll bet it was Thomas. The snooty little creep always hated me. I'd see him staring at his mother, then over at me, and he looked vicious, like he knew. You know something else? He looked jealous. I used to wonder if he'd have tried to frame me for killing his parents even if I hadn't done it. But the thing is, his folks, they really asked for it like I said, they really did." He stopped talking for some time, just stared blankly at the white wall in front of him.

Finally, Savich said, "Mr. James, you're speaking very freely to us, and we appreciate that."

"And why shouldn't I, Agent Savich? I'm nearly eighty years old. How much longer can I last in the warden's lovely country home? Like I already told you, I spent years with everyone believing I was a serial killer, that I heard voices from the devil, nonsense like that. I remember having to deny it even to the shrinks in here, but no one wanted to hear it.

"Now, here are two federal agents who are finally ready to hear what really happened. You are, aren't you?"

"Yes, Mr. James, we came a long way to find out what really happened."

"Ah, you're such a pretty little girl. I hate for you to hear all this, even though all the blood is dry now, but it isn't pleasant—"

"I'm pretty tough, Mr. James. It's my job to be."

He looked at her with his bright blue eyes, intelligent eyes, assessing her. Then he gave her a sweet smile, and Sherlock had to remind herself that he was a murderer.

He said, "I'll tell you anything you want to know."

"Good," Savich said. "Please include me in that too, Mr. James. May we record this?"

The old man slowly nodded. He said, "Her name was Margaret. I called her Maggie May. I remember I used to sing 'Maggie May' when we were in bed. That was before I killed her."

CHAPTER 56

Why?" Sherlock asked him when he went silent again.

"Because she was older, I suppose, like the Maggie May in that old Rod Stewart song. I was her young man even though I was middle-aged then, ten years older than that loser son of hers. Yep, I slept with her, you know, and no one ever really knew about it. I kept our secret, let her keep her reputation even in death."

Savich said, "You never told her son Thomas?"

"Yes, but not until later. He suspected, but he didn't know for sure."

"You said you thought Thomas was jealous of you."

"Oh yeah, I think Thomas felt some things for his mama a son shouldn't feel. I think he could have settled in quite naturally with all the other sicko perverts on somebody's couch. What he didn't realize back then, maybe he still doesn't, is what a conniving bitch his precious mother was."

"What do you mean?" Sherlock asked. "What happened?"

He gave her another sweet smile. "After she'd slept with me maybe three months, she told me one afternoon when I'd slipped into her house and found her in the kitchen—her husband was off playing golf—that her son told her I buggered little boys for money, stuff like that. She said Thomas told her I'd made a pass at him. It wasn't nice what she said to me, and she didn't shut up. Then her husband came in through the back door into the kitchen and she looked like she'd swallowed her tongue. I remember as clear as day how I stood up and smiled at him, not a nice smile like I give you, Agent Sherlock, but a real mean smile. I told him flat out I was sleeping with his sweet-assed wife because he was old and bony, but hey, she was sexy and hot, and a pretty good lay, even if she was a gold-plated bitch.

"The old man threw his golf clubs at me, can you imagine? Landed six feet short, of course, since he was such a bloody wuss. I laughed at him and he came at me in a rage. I remember her screaming. I picked up one of those fancy knives she was using and stuck it in his neck. All that blood." He paused a moment, and they saw a flash of pleasure. "Blood everywhere and she wouldn't stop screaming, so I stuck the knife in her chest. Do you know she only made this little squeaking sound, that was all? Then I stabbed her a whole bunch of times. I don't remember how many, I just kept going, in and out, in and out.

"They were dead, lying on that huge kitchen floor, bleeding all over the white tiles. It was a mess, I'll tell you.

"There was no one around. It was a Sunday, you see, and the hired staff had the day off. I stood there, looking down at them, and thought about what I was going to do. I'm not stupid, so I cleaned up really good, took the knife, and left. Since the Pallacks' house was only two doors away from mine, I could go through the backyards and not be seen by anyone.

"I thought I was home free there for a good long while, but I knew Thomas was eyeing me, like he knew I'd done it, but he couldn't prove anything. I'll have to give him credit though, Thomas came after me with all the money he had. He hired half a dozen investigators. It was only me he wanted, even though he pretended he was checking out all the neighbors. I think they wire-tapped my phones, talked to all my relatives, even got ahold of my credit card reports.

"One day I came home early and found the police in my basement and I knew I was in deep trouble. Thomas must have helped them get a search warrant. My lawyer told me the cops found medieval torture instruments in the basement and there was dried blood on them."

Savich nodded.

The old man shook his head. "But it wasn't my stuff, it was my dad's. He was a real history nut, loved that old stuff, anything the inquisitors used, he had to have it. Everyone knew about his torture chamber, as he liked to call it—he was an eccentric. There wasn't any blood until Thomas got some and smeared it on some of my father's equipment. My old man was harmless."

"They found the knife behind the radiator," Sherlock said.

"Ha! I wouldn't be that big a fool. That was another knife. Thomas must have gotten some blood the same type as his parents' and rubbed it on the knife—no DNA back then, so it was easy. Then he planted it for the cops to find."

"What did you do with the knife you used?"

"I dropped it in the Lansky River five miles away from my house. But what could I do? Nothing, that's what.

"It was all over for me anyway, and I knew it. How can you fight being framed for a bunch of murders nobody committed at all?"

Sherlock said, "When did you tell Thomas Pallack that you'd slept with his mother?"

The old man laughed. "When I was being marched out of the courtroom between two guards right after the guilty verdict. Up dashed old Thomas, got right in my face. He looked wild with triumph, and I knew he wanted to gloat, and so I whispered it right in his face, and then I sang 'Maggie May' and licked my lips. He leaped on me but the guards pulled him off. I remember it so clearly, I could hear Thomas breathing hard as I laughed at him while the guards yanked me out of there.

"But hey, I've got lots of friends in here and the world is safe from me. I'm feeling tired now. I'd like to sleep so I can get back to the poker game later with Moses. He's quite a gamer, old Moses, just a bit lame on the strategy. Can't bluff worth a damn."

Savich said, "Mr. James, we appreciate your filling us in on what happened, but the real reason we came to see you—" He saw the old man's eyelids droop, and he added quickly, his voice sharp and hard, "Did you know Thomas Pallack finally married? Nearly three years ago."

Courtney's eyes popped open. He looked surprised at that. "Isn't that something. No, I didn't know. There isn't much news in here. I'm surprised, I'll admit it. It was always his mama, always. I thought he'd go to his grave mourning her, having wet dreams about her."

Now that they had him focused again, it was time to back up.

Sherlock asked, "Did you know Thomas Pallack claims to have spoken through a medium to his dead parents every Wednesday and Saturday since shortly after you killed them all those years ago?"

That perked him up. "A psychic? Nah, you're putting me on. He found someone—a medium, right?—who talks to dead people? Now, isn't that interesting? He's wigged out, has he?"

Savich said, "Whatever Thomas felt for his mother, it appears he really loved both of his parents. He claims they give him advice, that they care about what he's doing, are always there for him."

The old man snorted. "Dead people there for him. Now, what's wrong with that picture? Well, his daddy wasn't there for him. Never. And Thomas never gave a rat's ass what his daddy thought or felt. Like I told you, he loved his mama—way too much."

"So, he got married, did he? He finally found someone to replace her. Imagine that. I wonder what maggoty rotted old Maggie May thinks about that?"

Replace her?

"I wonder what Thomas's wife looks like."

"A moment, Mr. Jones." In that instant, Savich felt a rush of adrenaline. He saw Sherlock's hand shaking slightly, knew she felt it too. He opened his briefcase and handed the old man a color photo, not of Charlotte, but of Christie. But it didn't matter. He stared down at the photo along with Courtney James.

Courtney twisted his head up to look at Savich. "What the hell is this, Agent?"

"A photo of Thomas's new wife, like I told you."

"No, no, come on now, I'm not that old. I remember so well Maggie's swingy dark hair, those bright blue-green eyes of hers. And her white skin, so soft—" Courtney James fell silent, and simply stared and stared at that photo. Finally, he said, his voice bewildered, "My God, that's Maggie May, but a lot younger. And the clothes and the hair can't be right. You're telling me this is Thomas's wife, Agent Savich?"

"It is indeed, Mr. James," Savich said.

"I don't get this at all."

"We'll let you know when we figure it all out," Savich said. "I promise you that. You've been of immense help to us. Thank you."

"You gonna nail that pissant Thomas for something?"

Savich only smiled, shook the old man's hand. Sherlock squeezed his thin forearm, let him touch her hair once more, took Savich's arm and turned to leave the hospital room. They heard Courtney James say to Warden Rafferty, "I never believed in reincarnation before. What do you think?"

The warden said, "I don't know, Courtney. I haven't really thought about it. What do you think?"

"I just don't know anymore. I'll tell you, Warden, that photo—it was Maggie May, and how can that be?

"And all that psychic crap about Thomas speaking to his dead parents. That fair to creeps me out."

"It does me too, Courtney."

The old man closed his eyes a moment. "I'd sure like a glazed Krispy Kreme about now."

CHAPTER 57

SAN FRANCISCO

Thursday night

The Pallacks' building was tucked behind beautifully manicured trees and bushes on a small cul de sac just off Leavenworth Street on Russian Hill. The penthouse was dark, as were the two condos on the floor below it. A total of eleven dwellings shared the address in the hundred-year-old-plus building. Dix saw only two lights, one on the third floor, one on the fourth. The rest of the windows were dark. The occupants were either out or asleep. As for the Pallacks, they were at a political fundraiser at the Hyatt Embarcadero, which was expected to run very late.

He'd finally found a parking place on Chestnut Street, two blocks away, and too close to a fire hydrant. But he hoped the police wouldn't be handing out tickets so late on a Thursday night.

Dix looked down at his watch—it was nearly eleven o'clock. He should have plenty of time. It had taken him only about seven minutes to drive here after he'd walked quietly out of the Sherlocks' house.

He locked Judge Sherlock's Chevy Blazer and started back to the Pallacks' building, careful to keep to the shadows. He was tense, his nerves stretched tight. He was a cop, he believed in the law, yet here he was preparing to break into the Pallacks' penthouse. And he was carrying a gun while doing it. Even though he was a sheriff, he knew that could put him away for the next ten years. But he'd already had these arguments with himself a dozen times before he'd found that meager parking place. He paused a moment to calm himself. He'd made his decision, and now it was time to get the job done. He prayed Ruth wouldn't figure out what he was doing and come after him, bringing Cheney and Julia or even Savich and Sherlock after him. He'd be out of here by midnight, and if something did happen, well, he'd left an e-mail for Ruth's cell phone set to alert her at midnight—just in case he needed her to bail him out of jail.

It was past time to bring all this to an end. If he'd acted sooner, perhaps Soldan Meissen wouldn't be dead. He'd been floored by what Savich had reported Courtney James told them—that Christie and Charlotte Pallack were both the image of Margaret Pallack. The madness of it twisted in him, the plain insanity of fate that had brought Christie to Pallack's notice.

Despite Savich and Sherlock's discovery, Dix still knew it wasn't enough to get a search warrant, knew Pallack could destroy everything incriminating at any time. He'd get away with murdering Christie, and Dix would never find out what had happened to her. His plan was the best way. The only way.

If only Ruth didn't get suspicious. He'd told her he wanted to walk, clear his head, think about what he was going to tell Rafe and Rob. When she'd offered to come with him, he'd told her he wanted to be alone, and she'd given him one long look and nodded, joining in a discussion with Julia and Cheney about August Ransom's journals. Had they been destroyed in the fire at Julia's house? Maybe he'd find the damned journals in Pallack's apartment. But what he wanted most to find was Christie's bracelet. Then he'd know. Of course Pallack could have gotten rid of it. Dix couldn't bear to think what he would do if he couldn't find something solid to nail the bastard.

Dix moved around to the back of the building. He had taken care to wear dark clothes, black boots, and a dark watch cap, had even blackened his face to blend into the shadows. His arm didn't hurt much. He moved it, clenched his fist. He would manage.

He found the alarm system quickly, recognized it as top of the line, just as he'd expected, and disabled it.

He had little trouble with the lock on the back service door of the building. He slid silently out of the storage and receiving room into the small elegant foyer, with mailboxes and palm trees. He took the stairs, not the elevator, to the top floor. Six seconds only on that lock, and he gently eased open the Pallack front door. He stepped into the foyer, and the enormity of what he was doing hit him again. No, no more doubts, no more questions. It was time to act. He'd broken and now he'd entered. Dix immediately went to the windows and pulled down the shades, closed the curtains. Only then did he switch on his flashlight.

The penthouse occupied the entire sixth floor, and covered at least four thousand square feet, on two levels. Dix started on the second level. He found the master bedroom and immediately went to Charlotte Pallack's jewelry box, an antique French affair large enough to hold Liechtenstein's crown jewels. He carefully searched through the various pouches and boxes. Lots of expensive stuff, but not what he was looking for.

Either Charlotte was wearing the bracelet tonight, or, since Dix had nailed her with it, maybe Thomas Pallack hadn't let her out of the house again with the bracelet on her wrist. Maybe Pallack had destroyed it. Or maybe it was in a safe.

Dix methodically searched the large bedroom with its extravagant furnishings, the space completely dark except for his flashlight, the incredible views hidden behind the heavy closed drapes. He didn't find a safe even after lifting each of the six modern paintings off the walls, carefully searching the large walk-in closet, even tapping the walls behind Pallack's shirts. He opened the drapes before he left the bedroom and looked back. It looked the same as it had before he'd come in.

He didn't bother searching the remaining rooms on the second level, but went immediately downstairs to Pallack's office. It probably looked somber and dark even in daylight with its burgundy leather furniture and floor-to-ceiling bookshelves lining three walls. It was his last hope, his best hope, really. Dix moved behind the big mahogany desk that smelled faintly of expensive cigars, and tried the top drawer. It was locked. It took him only a few seconds to pick it.

Dix was pleased to see it was a master lock and all the other desk drawers opened with it. He searched all the drawers thoroughly. He was hoping to find bank statements, a checkbook, records of any kind that might link Pallack to Makepeace, or to

David Caldicott, or Christie, but there were only invoices in ordered piles, newspaper clippings on Pallack and his fundraising, some correspondence with various bigwigs, and the usual odds and ends in desk drawers. He said a silent prayer and powered up Pallack's computer.

It was passworded, something he'd expected, and so he'd made up a list of likely words and numbers. He typed each one in, tried variations and additions, but none of them worked. He simply wasn't good enough to hack in. He could have used Savich for that.

He found the safe behind an original Picasso line drawing featuring weird forms that resembled no human he'd ever seen. It was a tumbler safe and there was no way he could get into it without the combination, or a blowtorch. He went back to Pallack's desk, got down on his knees, and pulled out each drawer, looking at the undersides. There was no combination underneath any of them. Then he lifted the keyboard and there, taped under the *g* and *h*, was a set of three double numbers. For the first time since he'd left the Sherlock house, Dix smiled.

A moment later, he pulled the safe handle open. It was about half full—mostly papers, separated with rubber bands, a big accordion-pleated folder, a stack of one-hundred-dollar bills, probably totaling five thousand, and underneath them, several velvet pouches. His heartbeat picked up as he pulled open the drawstrings of a dark burgundy velvet pouch and upended it. A magnificent diamond necklace and earrings filled his palm. He opened a dark blue velvet pouch—more diamonds, an emerald the size of his thumbnail, and a half dozen loose blood-red rubies, maybe ten carats each. Nothing else. No bracelet. He put the jewels back in their pouches and carefully replaced them by the pile of hundred-dollar bills. He pulled out a stack of papers, remembering how they were arranged, and methodically went through them. Pallack's will, Charlotte's will, half a dozen sets of partnership agreements, deeds to homes spread throughout the world, documents in French and Greek, insurance policies, business contracts he didn't have time to read thoroughly but that had no immediate import to him.

He lifted out the single fat accordion folder, pulled away the rubber band. Inside were notebooks, maybe a dozen of them.

What was this?

There was a photo on top of them. Dix lifted out a five-by-seven color photo of David Caldicott standing next to—he became very still. Was it Christie? Charlotte? He couldn't begin to explain it, but he knew to his soul he was looking at Christie, not Charlotte Pallack. David Caldicott had said he'd known Christie, said she'd admired his playing, that she'd come up and spoken to him. But they'd obviously known each other better than that. He could make out the familiar architecture of the Stanislaus buildings in the background. It was fall, with red, gold, and brown leaves mixed thick on the ground, tree branches nearly naked. Both David and Christie were smiling into the camera. Who'd taken the photo? He turned the photo over. There was a date scrawled but nothing else. Three years and four months ago.

He slipped it into his jacket pocket. He looked at the stack of thin notebooks and realized he had indeed found August Ransom's journals. But how did they get here? Three folded sheets of stationery stuck out from under the cover of the very first notebook. He opened the first one, and stared down at a note pasted together out of words cut from a newspaper.

He read:

Mr. Pallack, I have August's journals. He told me all about you, and now I have proof. I want five hundred thousand dollars. Tomorrow noon leave the money in a carry-on bag on the foot of the statue in Washington Square.

Dix quickly read the other two notes, none dated so he didn't know how far apart they'd been sent. The demands totaled two million dollars. He stared thoughtfully at the second note, read the final line several times:

We've had such a lovely thing going here, haven't we? But August never believed I was greedy even when others said I was. You won't hear from me again.

But of course Pallack had heard from the blackmailer again. The third note was short, simply instructed Pallack to leave a million dollars in a briefcase by the first jewelry counter just inside the entrance of Neiman Marcus, again at noon. It wasn't signed, but the blackmailer had written *Hasta Luega,* whatever that was supposed to mean. More blackmail notes to come? Or had it indeed been the last demand?

Dix read them all once more, and realized that the tone, the implied intimacy of the words, bothered him. It hit him between the eyes—of course, it sounded like Julia Ransom had written them.

It all fell into place. Pallack had hired Makepeace to kill Julia because he believed she was the blackmailer.

But Dix believed her when she'd said she'd never even seen any journals, that she really didn't think they'd even existed. So Pallack had been wrong.

Who then? It took Dix only a moment to realize it must have been another of Pallack's psychics, probably none other than Soldan Meissen.

Meissen and August Ransom had known each other for a long time. Meissen must have known about the journals, even seen them. After August Ransom was murdered, he could have gotten into Julia's house, stolen the journals, and discovered he had a gold mine. He's started off with the blackmail, then lured Pallack in as a client.

Dix wondered what Pallack had thought when he finally tumbled to the fact that Meissen was not only his blackmailer but had made Pallack believe he could communicate with his parents, convincing him by using conversation notes lifted from August Ransom's journals. Dix remembered clearly on the tape recording Sherlock had made of their interview with Pallack, how he'd sensed he'd had similar conversations with his parents before, a sort of déjà vu.

Did it all become clear to you the moment you voiced that un-

derstanding, Pallack? Did you realize then that Meissen had a lovely scam going on you? All that money you paid him and it wasn't enough. He sucked you into being his client twice a week, made a fool of you.

Dix wondered if Pallack had paid the last million before he'd killed Meissen or if he'd paid the money to Makepeace instead.

The rage Pallack must have felt. He'd moved quickly, Dix thought, and Makepeace had moved quickly as well. How convenient that Pallack had his own private assassin close at hand.

Dix thumbed through the first journal, sessions with Thomas Pallack, but he didn't see anything incriminating, only reminiscences. He picked up the last journal, opened it to the last page, and read:

Thomas is frightened of me. I've tried to speak to him about it, but he refuses. I sense he deeply regrets talking about that other woman. He spoke of her only because his mother kept asking him where she was, what he'd done to her, and then his mother laughed, such a laugh that my flesh crawled. And he told her he'd met a woman who was her twin and he loved her the first instant he saw her. But she wouldn't have him. He'd had to—Thomas shook his head, shot a look at me, and didn't say any more, but of course, he'd already said too much, and he knew he had.

Here he is still taking orders from a woman thirty years dead. Though I'm not his psychiatrist, I've told him this link with his mother is unhealthy, counseled him it's time to leave the dead alone, and look to his own future. He was abusive.

It was the last entry.

Dix could barely breathe. Christie, he thought, you were that woman, and he wanted to weep with the knowledge of it. He'd known she was dead, but the proof of it was finally staring him in the face.

Dix pulled out his cell phone, turned on the camera, and took pictures of the last pages in Ransom's last journal. It wouldn't serve as legal proof, but it was the hard truth nonetheless. He wished he had time to photograph everything, but when he looked at his watch, he realized he had to leave. He closed the journal, placed it at the bottom of the dozen or so others. He placed them back in the accordion file, pulled the rubber band around it, and slid it in the safe, exactly where he'd found it, closed the safe, and put the Picasso over it, and began to set everything back in place.

Then he heard the front door open.

CHAPTER 58

Dix looked over Pallack's desk, prayed he'd gotten everything back in the right order, and locked the drawer again. Pallack would never know—but what if Pallack or Charlotte went into the living room and wondered why their gorgeous view was gone?

He heard the front door close, heard their voices and their footsteps. Dix looked at the long draperies on the far end of the study, a cliché, but there wasn't any other good hiding place he could see. He quickly moved across the study and slipped in behind the thick dark green brocade curtains that dragged to the floor. There was a chair in front of the drapes. Hopefully that would be enough. He made a small opening in the seam of the drapes and looked out onto the study. The Pallacks walked nearly to the study doorway and stopped.

Pallack said, his voice irritated, "Damned alarm system went off again, third time this month."

Charlotte's voice sounded tired, on edge. "The neighbors have probably already called."

Pallack grunted. "It just pisses me off. Could you believe the talk about Barbara being too far to the left?"

Charlotte's voice sounded indifferent. "They might be right.

I'm surprised you can actually remember anything anyone said tonight. Thank God you got us out of there. I thought I was going to scream if I had to listen to any more of that claptrap. Thomas, what are we going to do?"

Dix heard annoyance in Pallack's voice. "No need to get hysterical. It's done, there are no more loose ends. Meissen is dead and we have the journals. It's over. Once Makepeace leaves town, we can forget about everything. Give me a minute to call Berenger Security, find out why the hell the security's out."

"But they know!"

"Those ridiculous FBI agents? Julia Ransom? Who cares? Their beliefs will get them exactly nowhere."

Dix heard Pallack's heavy footsteps, watched him step into the room and walk across the carpet to his desk phone.

Charlotte followed him in, but not all the way to Pallack's desk. She said in a weary voice, "I certainly hope you're right about the FBI. But we can't stop worrying about Makepeace—he's out of control, you know that. When he brought you the journals earlier, all he could talk about was killing Julia."

Dix saw Pallack shrug. "It doesn't matter. Julia's not important. If Makepeace kills her, it's on his own dime, not ours. That's what I told him. Go to bed, Charlotte. I'll be up soon."

He heard Charlotte's heels lightly tapping the wooden hallway, then muffled by the thick Persian runner on the stairs.

Pallack sat down behind his desk and pulled the phone close. Dix listened to him report the alarm failure to Berenger Security, nasty-bitch the individual on the other end of the line, and hang up. Then he booted up the computer, began to hum as he typed.

What was he typing at midnight?

The phone rang.

Pallack said, "Yes?"

Pallack listened for some time, said finally, "I don't care if she is staying at the Sherlock house, there's no reason to go after her now. Dammit, you shouldn't be calling me here. A public phone? Still—look, now that I have August's journals, our business is at an end. You should leave San Francisco as soon as possible.

"Dammit, Julia Ransom isn't important. I don't want to have to deal with any fallout from that. No, I don't want to see you tonight."

Pallack's fingers tapped impatiently on the desktop as he listened.

"You've lost perspective, Xavier. Listen to me, go to Costa Rica, lie on the beach. Enjoy your money. It's over, do you hear me?"

Pallack jerked the phone away. Dix supposed he'd been hung up on. Pallack slowly put down the phone. Dix saw him stare at it, shaking his head.

Through the slit in the drapes, Dix saw Charlotte walk back into the study, wearing a nightshirt that read across the front *I Only Swing Left*. The shirt ended at the top of her thighs. Those weren't Christie's legs, not the same shape at all. "Thomas, was that David?"

Pallack said irritably, "No, it wasn't David."

"I do wish he'd call. It's been over two days now."

"Yes, I'm worried now as well. Maybe we should hire someone to look for him." Pallack struck his fist on his desktop. "If only I could convince that psycho to simply leave San Francisco.

But he's fixated on Julia. Makepeace just called and wanted to meet to discuss it again, but I said no."

She started wringing her hands, pacing back and forth in front of his desk. "He won't stop, you know he won't. I don't think he can."

"Look, as I told you, the police have only a whole lot of coincidences, bits and pieces, conjecture, but nothing to stick. If Makepeace kills Julia, he kills her. It won't matter, not in the long run. They still won't have anything on us."

She didn't look like she believed him, but she stopped her pacing and crossed her arms over her breasts, hugging herself.

"What about the alarm system?"

"The guy at Berenger Security said they'd get the system up again, said they'd do a thorough investigation since it was most of the building this time. They got hold of three of our neighbors, two others weren't home, but none of them had even noticed. They said they couldn't understand how it happened."

"It's going on midnight, Thomas. You're tired, come to bed. There's nothing more to be done tonight."

There was a moment of silence, and then Dix heard the computer click off.

The lights went out. Their footsteps receded. Dix waited, listening, for another ten minutes. He'd heard enough, seen enough.

Dix heard no sound at all. The Pallacks were upstairs in the bedroom. And he was alone downstairs.

Dix eased out from behind the curtain and felt his way slowly around chairs, lamps, and a sofa until he got to the door. He looked out at empty darkness. He took several more steps, paused, listened intently again. He saw the red blink of the alarm system on the hallway wall. The security company had gotten the system running again. Thank the good Lord they didn't suspect a burglar yet. Maybe they would, once they investigated. All he had to do was disarm it and leave.

He stepped down the hallway.

"Stop right there or I'll shoot you!"

Dix froze. Thomas Pallack stood not more than three feet behind him. Dix knew he couldn't see him clearly, didn't know who he was. He pictured Pallack, about four inches shorter than he was, pictured him holding the gun in his right hand, about chest high, straight out. It was either run like mad and pray he didn't get shot in the back, or—

Dix whirled around, kicked out with his right foot, and clipped the gun in Pallack's hand. He heard it land hard on the oak floor and slide, until it finally hit the baseboard with a hard thud.

Dix was on him in the next instant, one clean shot to his jaw and Pallack was out. He leaped up, and stared down at the shadowy form of the old man who'd murdered his wife, and was fiercely glad he hadn't run. He heard Charlotte yell from the upstairs landing, "Thomas, what's wrong?"

An upstairs light came on. There was no time to deal with the alarm—Dix was out the door in a couple of seconds, the alarm ringing wildly in his ears. He knew that with the alarm system blaring, the cops would be there fast. He bolted down the stairs and out the front door.

He ran, hugging the trees and shadows. He heard a cop car.

Not more than two minutes had passed. Yep, the cops were fast to a 911 from an upscale neighborhood.

He waited, listening to the doors of the cop car open and slam shut. He heard men's voices, running feet. He waited another minute. Just as he was ready to run again to his car, he heard a deep voice say close to his ear, "I don't think you want to move at all. I don't know who you are, but I'll find out soon enough, won't I?"

A cop, Dix thought, and relaxed a bit. This guy was good, moved as silent as the moon climbing up the sky. Without turning, he said, "Look, I can explain this. Call Captain Frank Paulette of the SFPD. He'll vouch for me." He started to turn, to face the cop, let him see he wasn't a threat to him, but the man said, "Move again and you'll get a bullet through your ear, you got me?"

"Okay, I'm not about to move. I'm Dixon Noble, a sheriff from Virginia. I'm working with the local police. My wallet is in my jacket pocket. If you pull it out you can see my driver's license."

"I have a feeling if I go hunting for your wallet you're going to come at me. You figure you're a big guy, strong, ready to go, ready to tune me up. With my luck lately, you just might manage it."

Dix felt the gun muzzle press harder against the back of his neck. "That surprises you, doesn't it, that I can tell what you'd do by only looking at you? I don't have a silencer on my gun and I really don't want to risk the noise, not that you'd be around to hear it, of course."

There was something in his voice, something faintly British, and Dix knew in that instant who it was.

The man behind him laughed. Dix felt the flutter of his breath in his ear.

"Imagine a cop breaking into a private citizen's house—and it's not just any house, is it? It's a penthouse owned by that distinguished gentleman Thomas Pallack. Now that doesn't look too good, does it, Sheriff?"

Dix said nothing.

"Ah, you finally figured it out, huh?" The butt of a gun came down hard behind Dix's right temple. Dix didn't hit the ground; he wasn't completely out. He felt the man lift him in a firefighter's carry, and he wanted to puke with his head dangling down. "Now, I'll take us back to Mr. Pallack's little house in the clouds."

The cops, Dix thought, his brain nearly gone, surely the cops would see him.

But they didn't.

He passed out cold when Makepeace started climbing up the stairs to the sixth floor.

CHAPTER 59

D ix heard distant voices, then a woman's voice closer—it sounded a bit like Christie, but it was Charlotte Pallack's voice. He felt bile rise in his throat and wanted to gag, but he didn't. He swallowed and kept swallowing until it eased. No way was he going to vomit. He didn't move.

He heard Thomas Pallack's angry voice, then Makepeace's, but he couldn't make out the words. Slowly, his mind cleared. But it wasn't the time to raise his head and say hi to everyone. He didn't move, he just listened.

"Why the hell did you bring him here? Are you insane?"

"The cops had already been in here, I saw them leave. They were out front, not in back anymore. So I got the sheriff in through the service entrance to the stairs. I thought it was a good way to make a point, don't you think, Pallack? I thought you might want to pay me to take him away."

"Do you have any idea who this is?"

"He said he was Dixon Noble, a sheriff from Virginia. Why did he break in here?"

"It doesn't concern you. Jesus, the damned man was carrying

an arsenal," Pallack said, and looked down at his desk, where Makepeace had piled the sheriff's weapons.

"He was ready for business. A cell phone, one big Beretta, one little derringer in an ankle holster, and a tough little five-inch Fällkniven, a fine knife."

"It's a knife, so what?"

Dix wondered if Makepeace was going to take the knife his father had given him when he'd turned sixteen.

"One should enjoy fine tools, Pallack."

Dix could hear Pallack prowling, back and forth, in front of him. "This is all we need, this fool sheriff playing vigilante. At least he didn't get into the safe."

Charlotte asked, "But why did he break in? What could he have hoped to find?"

"Don't be stupid, Charlotte. The sheriff wanted to find the bracelet. If you hadn't worn the damned thing—"

"Then why did you give me that bracelet for a wedding present? Of course I'd wear it, for God's sake."

"The sheriff broke in here to find a bracelet?" Makepeace said in a bemused voice. "What bracelet? Why should he want this bracelet so much?"

Charlotte ignored him. "Thomas, you didn't even bother to tell me it belonged to another woman until after the sheriff saw it on my wrist and recognized it. Why didn't you tell me that when you gave it to me?"

"Like you would have appreciated wearing another woman's jewelry. Look, it doesn't matter, Charlotte. I wasn't really the one who wanted you to have that bracelet, it was—never mind. What's done is done."

But Charlotte wasn't buying it. "It was your little joke on me, wasn't it? Yours or that bitch mother of yours."

"Don't call her that! She isn't—wasn't a bitch. Damnation, I should have known you'd never have my mother's heart, or her intelligence. You were supposed to find out what the damned sheriff knew, pretend you were interested in him, but did you manage it? Of course you didn't. And look what you've brought us now—the sheriff breaking into my home."

"Again, why is the sheriff so interested in this bracelet?" Makepeace asked.

Charlotte said in a flat voice, "It belonged to the sheriff's wife."

"Shut up, Charlotte."

"Why? It doesn't matter if Makepeace knows."

"Did the sheriff find the bracelet?" Makepeace asked.

"No, of course he didn't find it," Pallack said. "I threw it in the bay an hour after Charlotte told me he'd recognized it."

"So the reason this guy came to San Francisco was because of this bracelet? But how did he even know about the bracelet?"

"It was a piece of bad luck," Pallack said.

"What'd you do, Pallack? Kill his bloody wife, decide you liked her bracelet, and take it off her?"

Dix thought his heart would stop. It was the hardest thing he'd ever had to do, sit there and pretend he was still unconscious. He wanted to yell at Pallack to answer Makepeace, but Pallack ignored him.

"So this guy has nothing to do with Julia Ransom?" Make-peace asked.

"No," Charlotte said.

Pallack said, his voice low and vicious, "If only the cops had arrested Julia Ransom for murdering her husband, but you didn't leave enough evidence to point at her. If you'd done it right, found those journals in the first place, I wouldn't have had to call you again."

"And if I weren't here again, the real blackmailer, Soldan Meissen, would still be bleeding you dry."

"All right. Yes, you're right," Pallack said. "Now you've only got one more thing to do, and that's get rid of the sheriff. Then you leave town. No more questions, do you understand? Just do what I tell you."

Dix could swear he felt the air change, and it was coming from Makepeace. Was Pallack nuts? Talking down to a psychopath who'd just as soon slit his throat as breathe?

Makepeace gave a clipped laugh that wasn't a laugh at all. It made Dix's skin crawl. His head was clear now. He could focus, at last. Makepeace had pulled his arms around the back of a chair and tied his wrists. He began to work the ropes.

"So what if the sheriff did find them? Those journals?"

"He couldn't have gotten into the safe even if he'd found it. The journals are there, exactly where I put them."

"I don't know why you still have them. First you believed Julia Ransom had the journals and I burned her house down to make sure they weren't found. Then you told me it was Soldan Meissen who'd stolen them from Ransom's house all along. Why not just destroy them? Are you planning to read them like bedtime stories?"

Dix felt Pallack's fury at that dig. One sharp-edged moment passed, then another. But he said only, "If you'd found the journals when you garroted Ransom like you were supposed to, none of this would have happened."

"The journals weren't there. I told you that then. If they had been, I would have found them."

"Soldan found them, didn't he?"

Dix pictured Makepeace, a smile on his mouth that should be scaring the crap out of Pallack. Oddly, he sounded amused. "Yeah, Soldan was so good he didn't even know I was in his ridiculous sheik's room standing behind him, reading his stupid book over his shoulder. He didn't look up until I had the wire around his skinny throat. Do you know he'd wrapped the journals in a red silk cloth and just shoved them under that low table? Lots of confidence. The fool."

"Yes, yes, it's over now. Forget the rest of it, Makepeace. Take the sheriff out of here, and make sure he's never found."

There was a pause, then Makepeace said, "I'll remove him for you, bury him deep, maybe in one of the forests up in western Marin. Then I'll kill that Ransom bitch and I'll be through here, Pallack."

Pallack's fist hit his desktop. "Dammit, Julia doesn't matter now. She doesn't need to be dead—I don't care if she lives to be a hundred."

Dix heard Makepeace say very quietly, "I do. How are you going to speak to your parents now that Meissen's dead?"

"Only August spoke to them, never Meissen. He was repeating conversations with my parents from August's journal notes." His voice filled with grief. "My poor mother has to think I've forgotten about her. Six months now without a word from me. She must be distraught."

"I didn't think anything could surprise me anymore, but you do," Makepeace said. "I didn't imagine a rich guy like you could believe in that crap."

Dix heard a sneer in Pallack's voice. "You think I'm a credulous fool, do you? How many times have you tried to kill Julia Ransom, Makepeace? What makes you think you're smart enough to kill her?"

Dix wanted to yell at Pallack to shut up. Didn't he realize he was putting the spurs in so deep Makepeace wouldn't stop until Julia and Cheney were dead? And him too?

"Since you're paying me handsomely, Pallack, I'm smart enough not to kill you. For one hundred thousand dollars, I'll take care of the sheriff. Then I'm heading over to Judge Sherlock's house to take care of Julia Ransom."

Dix heard the surprise in Pallack's voice. "How'd you find out where she is?"

"I followed those FBI agents. I saw her through the window with that other agent, Stone."

Charlotte said, "So what are you going to do? Set off another bomb? Blow up Judge Sherlock's house with everyone in it?"

Dix lifted his head a fraction to take in the three of them. He saw Makepeace's dead eyes glitter. "Hey, not a bad idea, wiping out all the losers at once."

"You go murdering a bunch of FBI agents," Pallack said, "kill a federal judge, his wife, and whoever else is staying in that house, the cops will hunt you forever."

"Let them hunt, they've done it for years. No cop in the world will ever get close to me. They won't get you either, Pallack, if you're as smart as you think you are."

Charlotte said, "They're too close now. Kill Julia if you must, but leave the rest of them alone."

"Look, Makepeace, I'll pay you the hundred thousand to get rid of the sheriff but you must promise to leave Julia Ransom alone."

There was thick hot silence.

Makepeace was looking over Thomas Pallack's left shoulder. He said at last, "We have a deal. Wire the money to the same bank account you wired the other million."

Dix sensed Makepeace was looking at him now, deciding how to get him out of here, where to kill him.

Dix was wrong. Makepeace wasn't finished enjoying himself. "Do you know, after I took Ransom's journals, I found I had a little down time? So I did a bit of reading. In this one section, Charlotte, I read that you look just like Thomas's mother—like the other woman did—and I found myself wondering what it was all about. Now that I've met the sheriff, I'm thinking his wife had the misfortune of looking like Pallack's mother too. Was she the woman Ransom wrote about in his journals?"

There was stone silence until Charlotte said, "Yeah, can you believe it? Two of us who looked like that old witch. Only the sheriff's wife, Christie, wouldn't go away with him, so he killed her."

"Shut up, Charlotte!"

"I really don't care if you whacked the First Lady, Pallack. But I do have to tell you—the whole thing with your dead mother— it's sick, crazy, you know?"

"You call me crazy? You're a hired assassin, a psychopath. And I didn't kill Christie, it was an accident, it wasn't my fault. I didn't mean for it to happen."

Makepeace actually laughed. "Maybe she thought you were a little old for her, Pallack. You think?"

Dix's wrists were raw. He felt the stickiness of his own blood, smelled it. He realized that more than anything he wanted his bloody hands around Pallack's fat neck. He wanted to kill him the same way he'd killed Christie. He heard Pallack say in a sad, dreamy voice, "I promised her the earth, but she wouldn't be reasonable. She tried to get away from me. I didn't mean to kill her. It was an accident. My mother wanted to know about her, through August, and he knew. I didn't want him dead either, I needed him, but I had no choice. None of it was my fault."

Dix could see Christie arguing with Pallack, begging him, then finally, trying to escape him. Only she hadn't made it. He'd killed her—and he believed it wasn't his fault.

Charlotte said aloud what he'd been thinking. "You talk about none of it being your fault, Thomas, yet even now my brother is missing."

Pallack said, "I don't know where David is, I've already told you that."

"But why would he run, just because the FBI asked him some questions?"

Makepeace looked from one to the other, and said, a smile on his face and malice toward Pallack in his eyes, "I guess your husband didn't tell you he asked me to have David killed? Yep, I made the calls." He snapped his fingers. "And no David."

"You bastard!"

"Go ahead, Pallack, tell her. You might as well."

And Pallack yelled at Charlotte, "Let me tell you about that sleazy brother of yours! He knew I'd killed Christie, the bastard had followed me, he confronted me. And then he laughed at me, did you know that? He laughed, then he told me he had a sister who looked just like Christie, who could easily fill Christie's shoes. He said you had no ties to anyone, and all you wanted from the world was money. Your precious brother and I struck a deal—I paid that mealy-mouthed bastard what he called a finder's fee. I knew he called you—told you how Christie wore her hair, what color it was, how she walked. I knew you were setting me up, and I wasn't sure, but when I saw you, I was happy. I felt blessed. Imagine, there were two of you in the world."

There was silence, thick and angry. Dix saw Charlotte move closer to Pallack. She was still wearing only that nightshirt, and no one seemed to notice or care. She said right in his face, "You're lying. Sure, he told me about you, how you coveted me, that you'd give me everything I ever wanted. You know I loved David. You vicious old man—how could you tell Makepeace to have him killed?"

Makepeace said, "Well, now, you asked, didn't you? I'm sure

all of this was quite cathartic for both of you. But frankly I'm bored. You have exhausted me. It's getting late, time to take our boy away and make sure he's underground. As for Julia Ransom, I've decided I don't like our deal anymore, Pallack. I think I'll plan something special for her, maybe that Semtex, after all, that'd do the trick very nicely."

Dix pictured the Sherlock house blowing up—Ruth, Sean, all of them asleep, not expecting any trouble, all helpless. He heard Makepeace walking toward him.

There was only him, no one else. He readied himself. Makepeace bent over him, grabbed his chin, jerked his face up. "Still woozy, are you? What's wrong, pretty boy? I didn't hit you all that hard."

Dix gave his arms a final jerk, ignored the flash of pain through his injured arm as the ropes cut their way over his wrists and jerked loose. He jumped to his feet, leaned onto his back leg, and slammed Makepeace in the kidney with the side of his foot.

CHAPTER 60

Makepeace made no sound as he stumbled back. An instant later, he whirled and kicked out smoothly. Dix turned fast and Makepeace's foot struck his hip, not his groin. Dix felt a slap of sharp pain, feinted left, whirled on the balls of his feet, and sent his right foot high into Makepeace's chest.

Again, Makepeace made no sound. He landed on his back, rolled once, and came up, panting, his gun in his right hand. It was a .38 and he pointed it at Dix's heart. "Enough of that, Sheriff." He rubbed the heel of his hand over his chest. "You move a whisker and I'll shoot you right here. It wouldn't be my problem, you see, just Pallack's."

A shot sounded, deafening in the small space.

Makepeace flinched. He slowly turned his head to stare at Pallack, his expression bewildered. A dribble of blood snaked out of his mouth. Slowly, the .38 slipped out of his hand and fell on the carpet. He tried to turn, but couldn't. He crumpled to his knees, then slowly he fell backward, his head striking the edge of Pallack's desk.

Pallack pointed the gun at Dix.

Charlotte said, staring down at Makepeace, "Why didn't you let him kill the sheriff?"

Pallack's face was flushed, his eyes brilliant with excitement. "I figured Makepeace was the most dangerous. No, Sheriff, keep back, don't try any of your fancy kicks or I'll shoot you right now. I've got to think—okay, the way it'll go down is that Makepeace tried to kill you and you shot him first."

"It's all over, Pallack," Dix said, not moving a hair. "You kill an assassin and the law won't put the needle in your arm. Kill me and you'll go down hard. They're getting closer, you don't have much time. Can't you hear them coming?"

Pallack froze at the sound of sirens in the distance.

Rage pumped through Dix as he stared at the mad old man. "You killed my wife, killed her because she wouldn't leave me or her boys. Do you know how insane that is?" Dix lurched to the side, and drove his foot toward Pallack's right arm, but Pallack jumped back and fired. The bullet went wide, and slammed into the dark wood wainscoting.

Pallack made a strangled noise, and ran out of the study.

Dix grabbed his Beretta from the desktop and ran after him.

Pallack fired again. Dix felt a bullet fly past his head and slam into the wall, and he hit the floor. He heard Pallack run all out, pause a moment to jerk open the front door, then he was through it. He jumped to his feet, saw Charlotte, white-faced, hugging herself, and left her standing next to her husband's desk, Makepeace's body close to her foot.

The sirens were close now.

Dix ran out the Pallack front door to see a metal door slam shut at the end of the short hallway. He jerked open the heavy door and ran up the dozen concrete steps to a small square landing. He shoved open the steel-reinforced roof door, fell back when a bullet caromed off it.

Dix yelled around the door, "Pallack, the cops will shoot you for sure if you go down those fire stairs. Give it up, it's over now. You can still come out of this alive."

He heard Pallack breathing hard, and wondered if he was going to have a coronary. He eased out from behind the door onto the roof, six stories up. Pallack was standing at the edge, looking down, his knees pressed to the roof guard, his gun dangling loose in his right hand.

Dix heard voices from the street, recognized Savich and Ruth.

"Give it up, Pallack," he said again. He raised his gun and began walking toward Pallack.

Pallack slowly turned to face him. He didn't look at all worried. He still held his gun at his side. He smiled. "You had a beautiful wife, Sheriff, but in the end, she wouldn't have me." He laughed. "She told me about you, about her sons, on and on trying to convince me to let her go, until—I've got to admit it—I lost it." He shrugged. "She was blind to what I could give her."

Dix's finger was trembling on the Beretta trigger. It would be so easy, he knew, the slightest squeeze, the small buck of recoil, and it would be over.

"You insane old man—you killed my wife because she looked like your damned mother. She was just a face, nothing more to you."

"I told you, it was an accident."

Dix knew he didn't have much time before cops poured out the roof door. If he was going to kill Pallack, he would have to do it now. He leveled his Beretta at Pallack's chest. "Do you know how long I've been trying to find her? Can you even begin to imagine how much I hate you?"

"So? A sheriff is going to shoot me in cold blood?"

"If I shoot you, Pallack, it will be an execution." His finger tightened on the trigger. In that moment Dix felt something warm and soothing touch him. He knew it was something outside himself, but it didn't matter, it gave him balance and understanding, and it gave him hope. His breath slowed. He lowered his Beretta. "No, I don't want your blood on my hands. Drop the gun, Pallack, now, or I'll have to shoot you."

Pallack laughed. "I knew you wouldn't shoot me, Sheriff."

"The sheriff won't need to, Thomas."

Dix whirled around to see Charlotte standing just inside the roof door behind him, her nightshirt blowing around her legs. In her hand she held Dix's two-shot derringer. "There are two bullets in my gun, Thomas."

"Shoot him, Charlotte! It'll be self-defense. He's insane with grief, came here because he believed I killed his wife—"

"Shut up, Thomas. But you can put your gun down, Sheriff, won't you? As I said, my little gun has two bullets. They're for you, Thomas."

"No, Charlotte, don't—"

She spoke right over him—"You vile old man, you had David killed. You had my brother killed."

"I had no choice, do you hear me? He called me, hysterical, yelling that the FBI had come to see him, asking him all their questions about Christie, and he wanted money or he'd tell them everything. I had no choice, dammit, it wasn't my fault. I couldn't let him live."

Charlotte pulled the trigger.

Pallack's gun went flying as he grabbed his shoulder and staggered back. For several seconds, Dix thought he was going over the roof guard, but Pallack managed to jerk sideways and fall to his knees. Dix saw blood flowing through his fingers from the shoulder wound.

Pallack raised pain-glazed eyes to his wife. "You bitch! You're nothing without me, nothing!"

She fired again, but she missed.

Dix heard Charlotte crying as he leaped at Pallack. He slammed his fist into his jaw, felt it break. Dix hit him again, knocking him down on his back, and straddled him, grabbing his shirt collar. He brought his head up and slammed it down on the rough stone roof. "You murdered my wife! What kind of insane monster are you?"

He hit him again even though Pallack was nearly unconscious, and moaning, and then Dix lowered his own head, and started to cry.

He felt a hand on his shoulder. "He's unconscious, Dix. You can stop now."

A woman's voice. He turned to look up into Ruth's face. "He killed Christie."

"Yes, I know."

Dix looked over to see Sherlock cuffing Charlotte Pallack's hands behind her.

The roof filled with people. He heard Savich's voice, heard Cheney speaking to Frank Paulette on his cell. And Julia was there, telling a uniformed police officer that Xavier Makepeace was dead, in the study, and that he was the one who'd been trying to kill her.

Dix said to Savich, "Pallack had David Caldicott killed. Charlotte didn't know about that." He hated to say it because he knew she was an accomplice to everything else Pallack had done, but he added, "Fact is, Charlotte shot Pallack."

Charlotte said calmly, "By shooting him I saved your life, Dix. If we can make a deal, I'll tell you all about what Thomas has done. I'll tell you where Christie Noble is buried."

"You don't know," Dix said slowly.

"Oh yes, I do. My brother told me. David said he followed Thomas several times to her grave. David said Thomas spent hours there, sitting on the ground beside her, ranting and raving at her." She smiled. "I'll even testify against him."

Ruth said, "You're a regular Mother Teresa, aren't you, Charlotte?" She held out her hand to Dix and pulled him to his feet. "Come on, Dix, it's over."

SAN FRANCISCO

Cheney and Julia stood side by side on the Marin Headlands looking down at the Golden Gate Bridge, watching thick gray threads of fog weave through the suspension cables. They both had on their leather jackets and gloves. A sharp wind was whipping Julia's hair around her face.

"I'd like for you to stay in San Francisco, Julia," Cheney said. "With me. I'll bet we can find a nice house that'll suit us."

She cocked her head to one side, tapped her fingertips to her chin. "Say, is that a proposal?"

He looked surprised. "You know, I hadn't started out with that particular objective, but I guess that's how my brain wanted it to come out of my mouth. Goes to prove I should trust my brain. I'm crazy about you. What do you say, Julia? Will you marry me?"

He saw a leap of excitement in her eyes, felt his smile ready to split his face, but what she said was, "That's a huge thing you're saying, Cheney. You've never been married before. I have, two times, and neither had a good result. We haven't had what you'd call a normal dating relationship, let alone a single date, other than that one wild time in the Sherlocks' gym—well, I'm thinking maybe we should take our time, let things settle down some more—"

He laid his hands on her shoulders. "Look at me, Julia. Yes, look at me. You can see what I'm feeling for you right on my face. When something's right, it's right. I know it is. Do you?"

She chewed on her bottom lip a moment, looking away from him. Just when his anxiety level was nearly in the stratosphere, she looked up at him and gave him a big smile. "Yes, oh boy, yes, I'll marry you. You can forget what I said, that was just depressing maturity and common sense leaking out of my mouth."

"Is that a note of sarcasm?"

"Maybe. Now, Cheney, are you willing to accept my psychic friends without rolling your eyes? Can you restrain yourself?"

"Even with Bevlin?"

"Especially with Bevlin. He's still becoming who he's supposed to be, trying to fine-tune his gift."

Cheney rolled his eyes, then saw the smile she was trying to hide.

"I saw that," he said.

"I can't help it."

The wind kicked up and Julia hugged him closer. She said between kissing his neck and jaw, "You'll admit, won't you, that at least Kathryn acts pretty normal, some of the time."

"Okay, maybe."

"That's because she thinks you're hot, and doesn't want to

scare you off. Or maybe it's Savich she thinks is hot, hard to tell. But me, I'd take you any day."

He cupped her face in his hands and kissed her. "I'd take you any day too. I could offer her Savich, but I think he'd hurt me."

She kissed his ear.

Cheney said, "I called my folks, you know, told them about you."

"Oh dear, I hadn't thought of your family yet. You got a big one?"

"Oh yeah, three brothers, two sisters, a dozen nieces and nephews and my parents, of course, and none of them are very good at minding their own business. But my family will adore you, Julia, fold you right into the mix, whether you want that or not, and begin meddling immediately—career decisions, vacations, where we'll spend Christmas, where our children should go to school—won't ever stop, even if we move to Alaska. Once you're married to me, your privacy is over. Can you live with that?"

"That sounds wonderful. They don't know much about me, do they?"

"No, but when they find out, they'll cheer you for being such a heroine."

Julia saw a couple of tourists in jeans and short-sleeved T-shirts, trying to brave the cold wind, shivering violently. She should tell them the sun would come out, maybe, but instead, she threw back her head and broke into "Tomorrow." Several more shivering tourists standing some twenty feet away turned and listened. When she finished, they applauded. She gave them a small bow and waved.

She said, "The district attorney called me today. Are you ready for this, Cheney? Fact is, he apologized. He's got a truckload of proof against Thomas Pallack, and with Charlotte more than eager to testify against him, I know he meant it."

No matter how many apologies the D.A. gave Julia, Cheney would still like to smack him in the chops.

"I'm big with the paparazzi again, for a short while anyway. They photographed me at my house speaking to one of the insurance people."

"So long as they don't trail you to my condo, we're safe."

She sighed and snuggled in close. The wind died down as the fog thickened, the tops of the bridge towers nearly covered now. She was sorry, but there was no chance of sun today. They both shivered at the sight of two lone sailboats on a broad reach, heeling sharply.

"There's no more beautiful place on earth," she said, "even if you freeze half the summer."

He smiled, felt happy enough to burst with it. Not all that long ago he'd gotten himself a date on a Thursday night for the Crab House on Pier 39. He hadn't gotten his cioppino, he'd gotten Julia.

Fate was something he marveled at, but accepted. As for the local woo-woo wizards, he imagined it would always be hard not to roll his eyes. He pictured Bevlin Wagner in his slipping towel and grinned.

He said, "Let's go brew some coffee and talk about that new house we're going to find."

MAESTRO, VIRGINIA

I t was easy to dig Christie's grave. Bobby Ray Parker and Lynn Thomas hadn't used equipment, no need. In the early morning hours beneath a soft steady rain that had begun the previous evening, they'd shoveled deep and deeper still and the earth was still damp and yielding. They spoke of Christie Noble, her kindness, how she'd yelled her head off at her boys' games, and how sometimes life was just too bitter to bear, and it wasn't fair, now was it? But at least she'd finally come home.

Four hours later, Dix stared at that massive wet black mound of rich earth, at the three red roses laid carefully atop it, and felt pain like a gash to his heart.

He held his boys' hands, theirs squeezing his hard during Reverend Lindsay's brief graveside litany, his deep quiet voice somehow reaching to the last person in that crowd of at least five hundred people, all of whom had come directly from the memorial service at the First Presbyterian Church of Maestro to Penhallow Cemetery, to attend Christie Holcombe Noble's interment next to her mother.

Dix looked over at Lone Tree Hill, at the single oak, an ancient sentinel, keeping vigil over the rolling hills and the row upon row of graves. Its leaves were greening up nicely. Suddenly the sun came through the clouds, blurring through the gentle rain, and he saw raindrops sparkle fiercely on the oak leaves. He squeezed his boys' hands and slowly they raised their heads and looked to where he nodded, toward that old oak, at the sunlight coming through the rain. He heard Rob sigh, felt both boys move closer against him.

Dix felt Savich and Sherlock behind him, Savich solid as a wall, and Sherlock, her hand resting lightly on his shoulder throughout the entire graveside service. His anger toward Savich was long gone, but he remembered how he'd wanted to smash Savich in the face when he'd refused point-blank to let him see Christie's remains. *Why?* he'd asked. *You already have the image of her you want to keep in your mind and your heart for the rest of your life, Dix. Let it rest, let her rest now. It's over, finally over.*

And Sherlock had stood with Savich, united against him. Ruth hadn't said a word, he remembered, simply listened to him rave and yell. He knew she would never say anything about that remote site in southern Tennessee where the dogs had found—no, it was over, Christie's life was more than three years over.

He straightened when Reverend Lindsay called for the final prayer, a prayer of acceptance, of granting oneself a measure of peace and the chance of becoming. What did becoming mean for him? But of course he knew. It meant bringing Ruth in fully, it meant bringing his boys forward now that they'd said a final good-bye to their mother, and it meant becoming what they were meant to be. He wondered what that would be for each of them. But whatever happened, the four of them would be together now.

It was over. Reverend Lindsay finished speaking. Dix felt hands touching him, heard quiet voices speaking to him and his boys, accepted the endless stream of words he couldn't take in now, but they would be there in his memory, and perhaps he'd recall them one day.

Chappy, tears running down his face, didn't want to let him go. He held the older man, Christie's father, so many times a pain in his butt, but still Christie's father, who'd loved her more than anything, and his grandsons, her sons, at his right elbow. Behind him stood Christie's godfather, Jules Advere, who'd collapsed when he'd seen Charlotte Pallack in San Francisco. The phone call from Chappy seemed a lifetime ago, but it wasn't.

The gentle monotone of voices went on and on until he thought he might start to weep, and not stop.

At the end of it all, Reverend Lindsay came over to shake Dix's hand. The reverend had a strong hand, dry and firm. "Dix—"

Reverend Lindsay said nothing more until Dix raised his face and looked at him directly. He said very quietly, his voice as firm and steady as his hand still holding Dix's, "Christie's home now. And she knows you and the boys will always hold her in your hearts, in rich memories that will never leave you." Like Savich's words, Dix thought. Reverend Lindsay laid his hands on both boys' shoulders. "Rob, Rafe, I want you to remember your mother as a woman of joy, laughter, and endless goodness. She loved you both with all that was in her." He drew both boys against him. "She had such great pride in both of you, enjoyed both of you so very much."

When he turned to Chappy, he enfolded him in his arms as he had the boys, and held him, not saying a word. The sun went behind the clouds again, and the rain began to fall more heavily.

Ruth raised her face to the rain and felt how warm it was, and how it seemed to soothe away some of the deadening pain. Dix looked at her over his boys' heads.

She smiled, and nodded, and took his hand. The four of them made their way through the lingering crowds of townspeople, some who'd known Christie only by sight, some dear friends, their eyes still red with tears, and they walked slowly through them, trying to make eye contact with them, shake hands, so many hands, all of them wanting to say the right thing. Rob sobbed and Ruth leaned down and kissed his cheek, nothing more. He plowed ahead, doing what his father was doing, speaking and nodding, grateful there were so many people who'd wanted to say good-bye to his mother.

Savich and Sherlock stood beside Tony and Cynthia Holcombe. Tony's cheeks were stained with his tears, but he smiled as he shook Savich's hand.

"Thank you for helping Dix. Thank you for bringing my sister home."

"Dix managed that all by himself," Sherlock said. "He wouldn't let it go. It was Dix who brought it to an end."

Hours later, when everyone had left Dix's house, and it was quiet, and the four of them were finally alone with themselves and with each other, Dix suddenly stilled. He could swear he felt Christie close, felt her warmth, the memory of the light sweep of her fingers against his cheek. He felt her there, in front of him, smiling and nodding, and then, slowly, she backed away, farther and farther, until there was only the still warm air, and his family.

WASHINGTON, D.C.

Savich walked out of Reagan Airport into bright late-morning sunlight that nearly blinded him. He slipped on his sunglasses, hefted his carry-on clothes bag and MAX, and looked toward the line of taxis.

He couldn't remember feeling this ground under or burned out, like he wanted to chuck it all and catch the next plane to—somewhere, didn't matter. He was filled with frustration, his own and the cops' in the Cleveland PD, and anger at failure. He'd helped them locate their suspect, but the guy had gotten through their net despite everyone's best efforts.

He sighed as he walked across the median. Nobody's fault, just a really lucky murderer now in the wind, out of their reach, at least for a while. Joseph Pinkerton Painter had killed four people and could now be in Rio, basking in the sun. Savich thought he wouldn't mind being with him he was so tired.

He wasn't more than a forty-five-minute taxi ride from Georgetown and home. Maybe he could nap a bit on the way so when he stepped through his front door, he could catch both Sherlock and Sean up against him, laugh and kiss them, and mean it.

He stepped forward to claim the next taxi when a loud horn brought his head around.

It was Sherlock in her steel-gray Volvo, waving wildly at him. Seeing her happy, welcoming smile, her wild red hair curling around her face, lifted at least ten pounds of weight off his shoulders. She screeched up beside him, much to the fury of two taxi drivers, both of whom yelled at her, one in Russian, one in Arabic, but doubtless yelling the same things.

He threw his clothes bag in the backseat, carefully laid MAX on top, and climbed into the passenger seat.

Amid all the shouting, the gimlet eye of an airport security guard coming toward them, he kissed her. She stroked his face, smoothed his hair behind his ear, and let her hand slip beneath his belt buckle, all while whispering into his mouth how much she'd missed him.

"We'd best get ourselves out of here before the guard hauls our butts to the slammer. As for your hand, sweetheart, I'm so tired, I'm numb from the neck down."

Sherlock laughed as she refastened her seat belt. "We'll see about that, but later. You don't want to drive my baby?"

"Pul-ease" was all he said.

"I can't believe how you despise my wheels, good solid wheels—"

He rolled his eyes.

She laughed. "All right. You look ready for an eight-hour nap—so why don't you lower your flag to half-mast and close down until we get home?"

Savich was asleep before Sherlock turned out of the airport exit.

He felt something on his cheek, heard soft breathing, no wait, there was a slight hitch, then—it was kisses all over his face, warm, wet, smelling of honey. Honey? He opened his eyes, stared into his wife's brilliant summer-blue eyes.

He cupped her face in his hand. "We're home? Already?"

"Well, not exactly." She kissed him again, this time a kiss with her tongue that brought him awake like nothing else could have.

He paused a moment. "Not exactly what? We're not home yet?"

She shook her head, patted his cheek, and slithered away from him to open the driver's-side door. "Come on, Dillon, time to get yourself together and face the world."

He didn't want to face the world. Not for a long time. It was Saturday morning. He didn't have to face any world at all until Monday. He wanted to sleep, to make love to Sherlock, play basketball with his boy. He yawned, finally taking in his surroundings.

"What? This isn't Georgetown?"

"It sure enough isn't, you're right about that. Come on, Dillon, we've got some things to do."

He got out of the Volvo, started to get his gear out of the backseat, but she grabbed his arm. "No, you don't need your stuff, just come with me. I've got a surprise for you."

A surprise? He stood up and looked around him. He was in the driveway of a big shingled house with a huge yard, trees creeping in on both sides, and it was familiar—

"Why are we at the Maitlands' house?"

"You'll see. Come on."

She took his hand and more or less pulled him up the flagstone walk, both sides bursting with more flowers than Savich had ever seen. They were Mrs. Maitland's pride and joy.

"But—"

Suddenly the front door burst open and Sherlock tugged him inside. At least a zillion people mobbed him, yelling "Surprise," all laughing and talking at once, telling him he looked like warmed-over toast. Everyone was on him, shaking his hands, both of them, slapping him on the back, the women kissing his cheeks, and finally there was Mr. Maitland, built like a bull, his small wife grinning up at him from beside her husband, flanked by the four Maitland boys, bruisers all of them. He hugged Mrs. Maitland, high-fived the rest of them.

"Papa!"

Sean ran full tilt at him and Savich scooped him up and held him high over his head, Sean yelling, "You're not going to believe what Mama—"

"Sean, no!"

"Okay." And Sean started telling him about his new goldfish and how his terrier Astro kept trying to put his head in the fish tank.

Finally Savich managed to get a word in. "Sherlock, are you going to tell me what all this is about? What's—"

Mr. Maitland grabbed his arm. "Come this way, my friend. I'm going to give you a huge glass of iced tea and a disgusting cold pepper and olive sandwich Sherlock told my wife is your very favorite lunch."

"Well, I—"

He was pushed and prodded toward the back of the house to a long line of French doors that gave onto the back patio and a long expanse of lawn and oak trees.

The doors opened, and Ollie Hamish said in his ear, "Take a step outside, just one step, yes, that's right. Sean, my man, come to your uncle Ollie."

Once his son was safe in Ollie's arms and swung up onto his shoulders, Savich went down the three steps leading to the patio.

"Dillon, look to your right!"

That came from Ruth, and he grinned toward her, saw Dix and the boys, and slowly, not knowing what was going on, he turned and saw a truly beautiful thing—a brand-new shiny red Porsche 911 Carrera Cabriolet, sitting splendidly alone in the driveway, a huge red ribbon wrapped around it, a large red bow on the steering wheel.

"Happy birthday, Dillon!"

"It isn't my birthday," he said, not taking his eyes off the incredible machine.

"No matter, it is now," Mr. Maitland said, his hand on Savich's shoulder. "Sherlock decided you'd been stoic long enough driving that Fort Knox Volvo of hers. She's tired of all that crying in the dark hours of the night over your burned-out Porsche. Ain't it a beauty, Savich?"

But Savich wasn't capable of talking. He stood staring, taking in the incredible fire-engine red convertible with its black leather interior. He heard Agent Ford MacDougal shout out, "I hear it goes from zero to sixty in under five seconds."

"Four point eight seconds actually," Savich said, not looking up as he ran his hand lightly over the top of the driver's-side door and then around to the back. Classic, clean lines. He rubbed his hand down the smooth sweep of the trunk.

He heard laughter, mostly from the women, and one of them said, "So this is what guys need for transcendence?" Then he heard Mrs. Maitland say, "Four point eight seconds? What in heaven's name is that sort of blastoff good for? Are you going to race to the grocery store?"

Mr. Maitland said, "It's the fact you can do it that counts."

"Dillon?"

He turned slowly to his wife, who said, "As you can see, Mr. Savich, it sits on eighteen-inch alloy wheels. Not to mention the interior glows like a spaceship with everything lighted up—the dashboard, the communication system, the navigation system. It even displays entertainment info. Oh my, this baby's goodies just don't end—it's got a fabric top, carbon-fiber interior trim, and a Bose surround-sound stereo."

"I know," he said, grabbed her up, hugged her hard, and kissed her.

"Papa, can I drive it?"

Not for another twenty years or so, but he said, "Sure. Your legs have to grow a bit more so you can reach the brakes, though."

"I can sit on your lap!"

Like that'll ever happen, Savich thought, reached out and ruffled his son's black hair. Sean looked as excited as his father, his eyes back on the Porsche.

"Here are your keys. No, Sean, you can ride with your father next time. This first time, well, he has some bonding to do, it's a man and his machine sort of thing."

Savich took the keys from Sherlock's outstretched hand, and without another word, grabbed the end of the huge red bow—

exactly the same blast-off red as the Porsche—and pulled it loose. He threw it back over his shoulder, like a bride with her garter, and everyone laughed. It was Dane Carver who shouted, "I got it! What do you think, Nick? How about a new Porsche in hissy-fit yellow?"

Savich opened the door and eased down into the driver's seat. He closed his eyes and inhaled the rich-as-sin leather smell, let the seat enfold him. He put the key in the ignition, and felt the Porsche all but hum around him as the powerful engine roared to life. Ah, sweet music for the universe.

He threw back his head, marveling at the perfection of the world and his place in it, eased the gear shift into first, and pressed lightly on the accelerator. Well, lightly at first.

Everyone heard him laughing as the Porsche roared out of the Maitland driveway and attacked the road.